FROM LIMBERLOST PRESS

Always Something
A New Chapbook of Poems by Jim Dodge

Limberlost Press announces publication of a new letterpress-printed, limited edition chapbook of poems by northern California poet, novelist, and pioneer bioregional advocate Jim Dodge. The poems are laced with a good dose of self-deprecating humor, poignant insight into a good long life, and a wry focus on getting older, living off the grid, and knowing one's family, community, and place.

On Destroying My Third Refrigerator in Seven
Years by Defrosting It with a Filét Knife
  True accidents are never senseless.
  If nothing else, the slaughter of large appliances discourages cupidity,
  And the brain-mushing pamper of convenience is surely deterred.
  The gods appreciate a smile when you accept your fate:
  Not every blossom becomes a peach;
  So few of us reach the pure state of relentless stupidity.

Jim Dodge is a self-described "Taoist dirt pagan and practicing pantheist who may have been born enlightened but pissed it away through thousands of sweet attachments and too many random acts of sheer folly. Dwindling into decrepitude, he splits his time between an isolated ranch in the coastal wilds of the Gualala watershed and the semi-settled Eureka peninsula." He is also is a Humboldt State University Professor Emeritus and the author of three works of fiction: the hilariously brilliant tale *Fup* (City Miner Books, 1983; Simon & Schuster, 1984), the novels *Not Fade Away* (Atlantic Monthly Press, 1987) and *Stone Junction* (Grove Press, 1998), an earlier collection of poems and prose, *Rain on the River* (Grove/Canongate Books, 2002), and a number of other broadsides, chapbooks, and screeds.

Always Something was letterpress printed by Rick Ardinger in a limited edition of 400 copies in the summer of 2023, each sheet fed into the jaws of a century-old platen press, and then collated, folded, and sewn by hand into beautiful paper covers. $20.00 (Plus $5 postage) Idaho orders please add 6% state sales tax. Purchase this and other books at: www.limberlostpress.com

FROM LIMBERLOST PRESS

Burning Time

A Chapbook of Poems
By Annie Lampman

If, as poet Jerry Martien says, "the poem arises from the ground of its making," then Annie Lampman's poems rise from the intimate touch of a tree's growth rings, the harsh passage through a desert canyon, the uncertain challenges of raising sons, quiet stories of time burning away, the ways we make a living, the ways we make a life.

> Centuries, decades,
> last week. Today.
> Each one burned away—
> these stories we tell, lit and smoking,
> waiting as one after another we all ignite.

—from the title poem

ANNIE LAMPMAN is the author of the novel *Sins of the Bees* (Pegasus/Simon & Schuster, 2020). Born in a 19th century log home without running water in north central Idaho, Lampman later moved with her family to Headquarters, Idaho, a logging company town surrounded by mountains. From a young age she explored the North Fork of the Clearwater River, hiked into high mountain lakes and into Hells Canyon. She earned her MFA in writing at the University of Idaho and now teaches in Washington State University's Honors Creative Writing Program. Recipient of several major awards, her poetry, stories, and essays have appeared or are forthcoming in over 70 literary journals and anthologies. She lives in Moscow, Idaho.

Burning Time was letterpress printed by Rick Ardinger in a limited edition of 350 copies in the summer of 2021, each sheet fed into the jaws of a century-old platen press and collated, folded, and sewn by hand into hardy paper covers. $20.00 (Plus $5 postage) Idaho orders please add 6% state sales tax. Purchase this and other books at: www.limberlostpress.com

LIMBERLOST LETTERPRESS

www.limberlostpress.com

THE LIMBERLOST REVIEW

No. 1, 1976

No. 2, 1977

No. 3, 1977

No. 4, 1977

No. 5, 1978

No. 6, 1979

No. 9, 1981

No. 13, 1984

2019

2020

2021

2022

The Limberlost Review

A Literary Journal of the Mountain West

Edited by
Rick & Rosemary Ardinger

A publication of Limberlost Press
Boise, Idaho
2024

A LITERARY JOURNAL OF THE MOUNTAIN WEST

2024: The Black & White Edition

Editors
Rick & Rosemary Ardinger

Contributing Editors
Chuck Guilford
Bob Bushnell

Sports and Social Media Editor
Jennifer Holley

Layout and Design
Meggan Laxalt Mackey, Studio M Publications & Design

Website Design
Erin Jensen, Golden Ratio Northwest

Cover Images
Front Cover: "Frosted Leaves," photograph by Jan Boles
Back Cover: "Untitled," ink on paper by Jinny DeFoggi

Limberlost Press
Boise, Idaho 83716
www.limberlostpress.com

THE LIMBERLOST REVIEW is published annually by Limberlost Press. This issue Copyright © 2024 by Limberlost Press, with all rights to the individual contributions returned to the authors and artists.

ISBN 979-8-869-14096-8

This journal features some of the best writing from the Mountain West and beyond, including poetry, fiction, memoir, essay, translation, commentary about books we come back to again, interviews, artwork, and more. We welcome the submission of manuscripts, but can not accept responsibility for lost items or electronic correspondence problems. For copies of THE LIMBERLOST REVIEW, please email editors@limberlostpress.com or visit our website: www.limberlostpress.com.
Printed in the United States of America.

LIMBERLOST LETTERPRESS

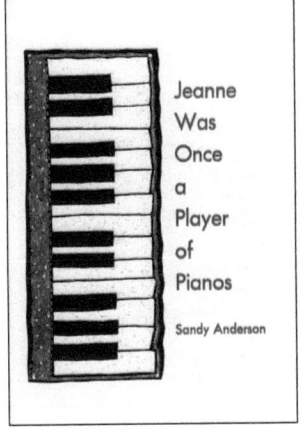

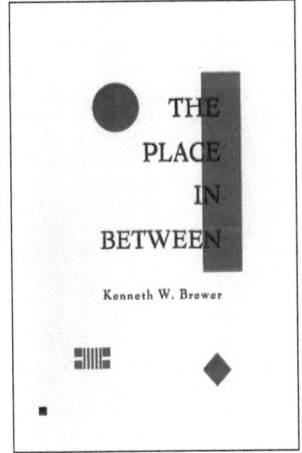
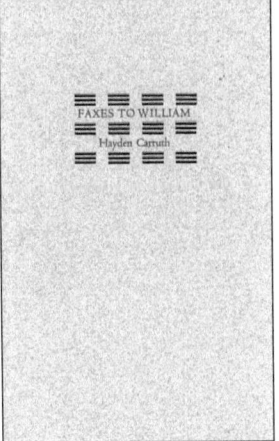

www.limberlostpress.com

LIMBERLOST LETTERPRESS

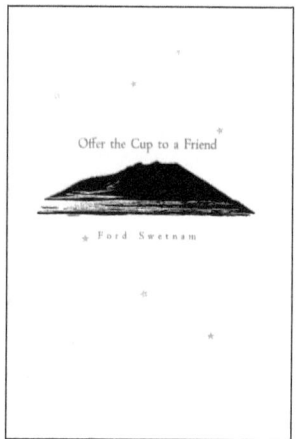

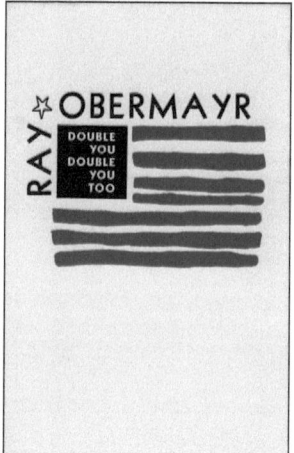
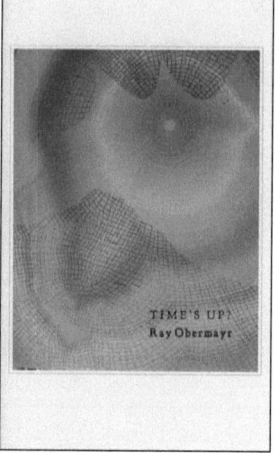

www.limberlostpress.com

TABLE OF CONTENTS

EDITORS' NOTE
Rick and Rosemary Ardinger 15

POEMS & STORIES
Bonnie Jo Campbell, *Five Poems* 21
Daryl Jones, *Two Poems* 27
Jan Minich, *Two Poems* 29
Gino Sky, *All Hunter's Eve* 31
Sherman Alexie, *Three Poems* 47
Krista Lukas, *What if I Left You* 55
David Lee, *Two Poems* 57
Chris DeVore, *Mondays with James* 61
Will Peterson, *Three Poems* 67
Greg Keeler, *Five Sonnets* 71
Ken Rodgers, *Two Poems* 75
Maureen McCoy, *Martin in Gigscape* 77
Baron Wormser, *Two Poems* 95
Jim Heynen, *Three Poems* 97
O. Alan Weltzien, *Tobacco* 99
Margaret Pettis, *Forget this Body* 101
Geof Hewitt, *Two Poems* 103
Jay Johnson, *Tough* 105
Jim Hepworth, *Two Poems* 127
Rebecca Evans, *The Confessional of Two or More* 133
Shaun T. Griffin, *Letter to Joe from Big Hole National Battlefield* 135
Gary Gildner, *Father Honor's Spa* 137
Mark Clemens, *Two Poems* 149
Bob Bushnell, *Four Poems* 153
Anne Bledsoe, *Quaking* 155
Mary Clearman Blew, *Miles City, Montana, November 1882* 157
William Johnson, *Two Poems* 165
Nancy Takacs, *Two Poems* 167
Samuel Green, *Two Poems* 171
Charlotte Mears, *Two Poems* 177
Don Zancanella, *A Woman on Horseback* 179
Paul Zarzyski, *Going It Alone* 193
Kim Stafford, *Two Poems* 195
Jim Dodge, *Two Poems* 199

INTERVIEW
Dan Armstrong, *Further Flashbacks of a Long Strange Trip:
    An Interview with Writer, Editor, and Merry Prankster Ken Babbs* 202

ESSAYS, MEMOIRS, NONFICTION

Kent Anderson, *Praying in Jail* 225
Paul Beebe, *A Killing Gone Wrong* 235
John Rember, *Why I Don't Write for* Travel + Leisure *Anymore* 239
Ron McFarland, *Educated on the Henry's Fork* 247
Lois Welch, *Meeting Jim Welch: Opening Day of Fishing Season, May 20, 1967* 259
Paul Zarzyski, *Five Wild Reminiscences of Rick DeMarinis* 271
Gary Gildner, *A Late Omelet* 281

RE-READINGS

Rick Johnson, *Stumbling toward Antelope Butte:*
   Reflections on Jim Harrison 287
Kurt Caswell, *Much that Was Noble, Nothing that Was Gracious:*
   Re-reading Wilfred Thesiger's Arabian Sands 297
Paul T. LaPrise, *Making the Apple Fall: Re-reading Edward Abbey's*
   The Monkey Wrench Gang 305
Barbara Olic-Hamilton, *Only on Earth:*
   Old Questions Explored in Three New Novels 311
Ted Dyer, *The Greater Hugh: Homage to the Works of Hugh Kenner* 317
Grove Koger, *Paul Bowles' Later Years in Tangiers* 333
Alan Minskoff, *Time Traveler: A Re-reading of E.L. Doctorow* 339
Susan H. Swetnam, *On Re-reading Dylan Thomas's*
   "Do Not Go Gentle into that Good Night" 347
Brant Short and Nile Spears, *Searching for Forrester Blake:*
   Re-reading a Forgotten Novelist of the American West 353

GALLERY

Graham Blair 246
Jan Boles 134, 164
Rod Burks 76
Tom Callos 126, 132, 194, 374, 380
Jinny DeFoggi 148, 156, 364
Virgil DiBiase 54
Jackie Elo 152, 398
Greg Keeler 70, 73, 368
Alberta Mayo 56, 100, 102
Riley Sophia Penaluna 14, 198, 224, 234
Betty Rodgers 66, 74
Sarah Trudeau 192
Janet Wormser 20, 26, 46, 94

FROM THE ARCHIVE

Greg Keeler, *Waltzing with the Captain: Remembering Richard Brautigan* ... 367

LAST WORD

Clay Morgan, *Considerations* 375

CONTRIBUTORS 383

LIMBERLOST LETTERPRESS

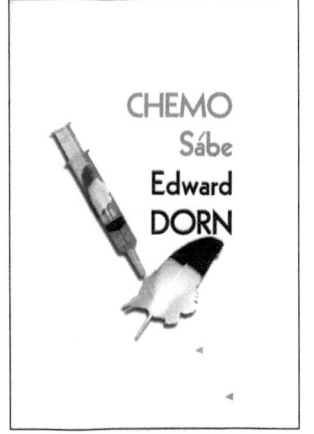

www.limberlostpress.com

"Howl" by Riley Sophia Penaluna. Linocut, 6 x 4 inches.

EDITORS' NOTE
A Literary Bus of Another Kind

At long last, *The Limberlost Review 2024*. This black & white edition of *The Limberlost Review* is about six months later than we had hoped to deliver. Too many excuses to lay out here, the intrusion this fall of septuagenarian geezerhood not the least of them. Thanks especially for the patience of our many contributors who've been waiting to see their work in print among all these other voices and images. We know it is worth the wait.

Since the release of *Limberlost Review 2022*, we gathered the contents for this edition, had our Limberlost Press website completely redesigned by a most capable individual and a company we're happy to recommend. And we letterpress printed a chapbook of poems in the summer of 2023 by northern California novelist, poet, and bioregional advocate Jim Dodge, titled *Almost Happy*. An ad for Jim's new chapbook appears at the beginning of this edition and two poems from the book appear in these pages as well as in previous editions.

This all-black & white edition is something we've wanted to do for a while, featuring photography, drawings, paintings, linoleum prints, wood cuts, ink to paper. Although printing this edition saves a little money from a full-color edition, this black & white take offers an opportunity to explore some new perspectives worth exhibiting.

But of all editions for an interview with Ken Babbs to appear. If any writer deserves full tie-dyed-color treatment it is Ken Babbs, author of *Cronies: Adventures with Ken Kesey, Neal Cassady, the Merry Pranksters, and the Grateful Dead*, a burlesque of LSD-colored remembrances of the 60s, Neal Cassady, Allen Ginsberg, Jack Kerouac, Timothy Leary, Baba Ram Dass, the bus Further's cross-country exploits, and a truly renewing take on a time, a place, an America in need of enlightenment—a book with true resonance for our time. Babbs's story is not just a look back on the counter-cultural old days, but a wake-up call to us all to step up and bring more empathy into the world again.

A group of us brought Ken Kesey, Babbs, and the Merry Pranksters to Boise in June of 1994 to perform a play to do just that—but that's a story for a future edition.

To have Ken Babbs included in this edition of *The Limberlost Review*—which we've always kind of imagined as a literary "bus" of another kind—is a special event worth celebrating.

Meanwhile . . .
Across the country, as more librarians and teachers become targets of vilification by the political rightwing, it is hard for an editor of a literary journal not to comment on the need for the country to come to its senses. And the issues hit close to home. Recently a large school district west of Boise announced it is banning books and among the first 10 banned are a graphic-novel version of Margaret Atwood's *The Handmaid's Tale* and Allen Ginsberg's *Collected Poems*.

As appalling as this action is, if the school district thinks they've curbed the number of under-18 readers of Ginsberg's poems, they've done just the opposite. The best publicity for a book is to ban it, as Ginsberg well knew. It reminds me of a story.

Back in 1993, when Boise was still relatively undiscovered—compared to today—a group of us got together to bring more noteworthy writers for readings to our part of the world. Not much in terms of readings was happening back then and we managed to bring a number of writers to Boise, including a visit from Allen Ginsberg.

Allen said he had never read in Idaho and was happy to accept for the cost of a flight and—by today's standards—a very modest fee. I helped raise some money for a short tour of readings in Twin Falls, Hailey, and Boise, driving him around in the spring of that year in my 1974 Toyota Landcruiser.

Three decades after the publication of his *Howl* (1956), enough folks in Boise had read or heard about the National Book Award-winning poet to show up for his reading which was free and open to the public in a Boise State University Student Union ballroom.

The stage was a simple riser to elevate Ginsberg enough for all to see. I was getting my notes together to introduce him to an audience of about 600 when I witnessed something I will never forget.

EDITORS' NOTE

With most seats in the ballroom taken, as if on cue, about a hundred middle school and high school students streamed up the main aisle and past all the taken seats to sit on the floor cross-legged around the stage at Ginsberg's feet—the best seats in the room.

Ginsberg read with a break for intermission, the first half reading early work, the second half newer work. He read *Howl* in its entirety. When he was finished, the young students surrounded him like a rock star. This was four years before he died.

The students obviously knew about Ginsberg not because they'd been studying him in their textbooks. They found his work on their own at some point just as I did when I was their age. We must remember how important such personal discovery is to young minds. Attempting to stifle that in any school district, in any high school student, is the real crime.

We hope we are approaching an Edward R. Murrow moment in this country when we'll look back on this time in history the way we look back at the fraud, lies, hypocrisy, and injustice of the Senator Joe McCarthy era of the 1950s. We hope the nation will snap out of its walk to the Kool-Aid line to shrug off Democracy like an old wet coat.

Such fear of poetry is hard to imagine even thirty-one years ago. Yet here we are.

Allen Ginsberg in our kitchen door, 1993.

* * * * *

Some readers say they read *The Review* from cover to cover, while most probably pick and choose. While our impulse is to bring attention to some personal favorites in this edition, the list is too long.

THE LIMBERLOST REVIEW

We open this edition of *Limberlost* with poems by Michigan writer and National Book Award finalist Bonnie Jo Campbell, whose new novel, *The Waters* (Norton, 2024) was released just days prior to this writing. This *Limberlost* is an anthology to get you through the winter, with poems by Nancy Takacs, David Lee, Shaun Griffin, Greg Keeler, and Daryl Jones, new stories by Mary Clearman Blew, Gino Sky, Maureen McCoy, Gary Gildner, Jay Johnson, Don Zancanella, an essay section this time we could have called "Montana" with remembrances of writers James Welch, Rick DeMarinis and Richard Hugo, and re-readings of works by Dylan Thomas, Jim Harrison, Hugh Kenner, Paul Bowles, E. L. Doctorow, Wilfred Thesiger, Barbara Kingsolver, Edward Abbey, Forrester Blake, and more.

Meanwhile . . .
Let's put the fear of poetry in them and do our part to ensure this isn't the last edition of *Limberlost*—or the last election—under a Democracy. ■

—Rick and Rosemary Ardinger

POEMS & STORIES

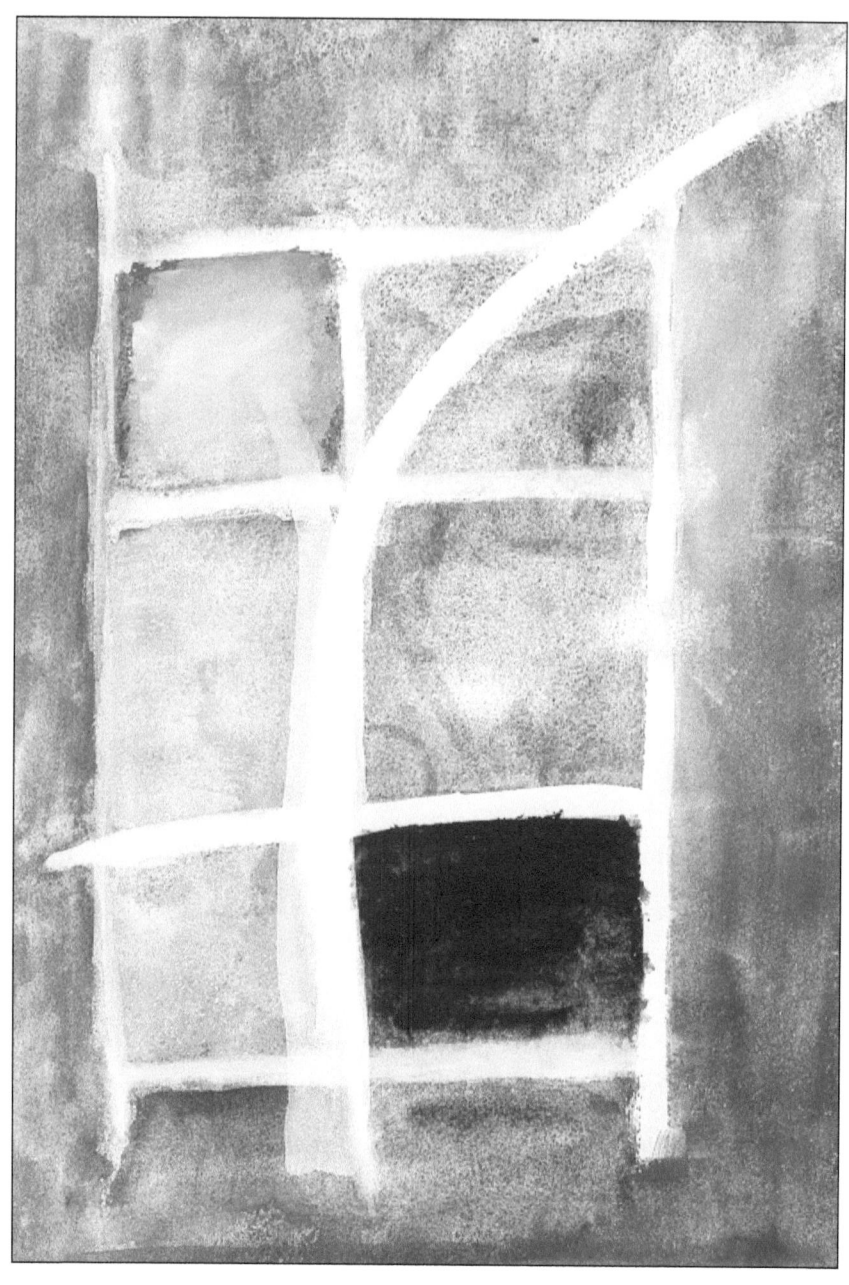

"Passages" by Janet Wormser. Watercolor and gouache on paper, 10 x 12 inches.

BONNIE JO CAMPBELL

At the River Shack on a Winter Morning

I didn't ask for ecstasy, just planned to sit
quietly. But a yellow jacket slipped inside

with her yellow jacket untied. I put her outside
to die. On the silver plated river I spy

golden eyes. Those wise guys dive
under the ice for silver plated fish.

The crooked hackberry tree looks just like me.
An icicle upside down is a unicorn's

horn! The river won't stop running off
at the mouth. I hold back for propriety,

but you know how when you dam
a river, that's how you get electricity.

After 35 Years of Marriage

The Webb telescope brings us moony Jupiter,
wind-striped swirling psychedelic brilliant
beyond our expectations—with rings, too! The
great red spot is a hurricane that's raged for
350 years, ten of our marriages! The gas giant
spins so fast a day is done in ten hours, but it's
twelve earth-years to circle the sun—we'd be
approaching only our third anniversary.
There's no surface, nowhere to land, the God
Jupiter could toss down all his thunderbolts
and get no flash. We don't have kids but offer
to watch Io, Europa, Ganymede, Calisto. The
other 63 little ones wear us out.

Locomotion

I don't fly, not even in dreams. My wings are heavy,
and I respect gravity and heed my family's advice. No

place to make a life they say, at the end of the two-track.
Wherever there's trash and brambles, though, you find

berry bushes, fruit trees, a stone wall, an old foundation
where there was a house that only jonquils remember.

I've never left my body, never floated outside myself,
never even left a party early, out of fear of being

rude. I stay, put away chairs and cover food with foil.
When I finally climb a tree on a hill and look down,

I see people in their outfits, some driving cars—so small!
As I said, I don't fly, but a few times while high

up, out on a limb, out of sight and earshot of the folks
below, I've stepped off into the air and did not fall.

What Only I Know

I've wrapped myself in an old family blanket—
scratchy wool—stolen from the home place

before it collapsed. They wanted to tear down
this leaky shack, too, but I'll burn it myself.
This is my body where mad spirits took refuge.

With each creak of spine and hip as I rise
from the mattress, before I heave the ghost
off myself, I hear the old voices, *If you keep*

quiet, you'll survive the storm, save us all.
Rumination is not salvation, and in my family
looking back turns a woman to salt, but when

the lights went out, I should've thrown open
the cellar doors, kicked aside wooden crates
of Ball jars and run into the rain and lightning,

instead of just lying still, counting seconds
between gasping thunder and kaleidoscopic
lightning. Then I wouldn't have to know

the wind moaning, wouldn't still feel branches
scraping the window glass like fingernails.

A Kiss

Eating berries is bewildering
their sweetness so close
to being nothing, so close

to being what sweetness was
before it was berries and kissing
Christopher makes me cry

A kiss rises up from
where kisses rise up from
and blossoms. An ordinary kiss

like an ordinary flower, unfolds
to become the universe, reveals
a way in, a need for a bee

before falling apart, like
when a friend lives and then dies
and briefly you know her.

"Finale" by Janet Wormser. Gouache on paper, 10 x 12 inches.

DARYL JONES

Vicks

As though I'd walked through a spiderweb. Or brushed
a ghost. One minute I'm walking alone,

tramping through drifts of leaves violent with color,
the brilliant turmoil of another year,

when out of the scuff and rustle it comes to me,
a faint whisper, that voice I'd know anywhere,

saying *Shh, there there,* and suddenly
I'm six, in bed, wheezing and feverish,

stuffed-up in my stuffy room, her fingertips
moving in slow circles, smearing cold fire

over my chest, my collarbones, my throat,
spreading that homely, soothing unguent

I'd long forgotten but remember now
so vividly its vapors fill the air,

mentholated, sharp, as she rubs it in,
firmly but tenderly, giving me

again, as she did the first time, breath.

And so, a Dilemma

One of those instances when the door
of the hurtling armored truck

swings open and a swirl of flittering bills
spins out into the slipstream, whirling

up and out along the interstate, fives
and tens, twenties and hundreds,

suspended in the updraft, twirling,
then slowly fluttering down across

the eastbound lanes, the westbound,
onto the median and down storm drains,

onto cars swerved to the shoulder
or stopped in the fast lane, doors

flung open, and the motorists
scrambling, fanning out, stooping

and running, stooping and running,
or squatting, duckwalking along

the pavement and brandishing fistfuls
of cash like bright bouquets as bills

float down all around them, snow
in summer, manna from heaven,

and everyone, everyone
for a moment, believes.

JAN MINICH

The Recluse

Folding napkins at midnight,
he wonders where the sun
has gone and why napkins
have to be folded
when no one has stopped by
for years, this desire
for self-doubt and solitude
on a calm night he knows
will yield a storm by morning
when he'll rise
to the wind and cold
like a fish caught in a trap net
weaving to the end with nowhere
to go except into the boat.

Ruins

We step over foundations
as if walking through walls,
our lives open to inspection
and our arms not used to
this much emptiness reaching out
to what was promised once
by parents and grandparents,
the crickets and fall beetles
on a still dark night.

GINO SKY

All Hunter's Eve

Idaho-Montana Border, 1955

Lo, yonder, the Holy Place
Yea, swift and far I journey.
—Navajo Mountain Song

ONE

It was the morning before J. Golden Moon's private elk hunt near Henry's Lake just south of the Beaverhead Mountains. A heavy mist was hanging low around the pines, firs and quakes, as the first light of morning moved across the sky. With the light, the cold bowed lower into the forest. Two young men, Buddy Sunday and Joe Coyote, were folded like children into mothers around their campfire as they waited for their coffee to boil. The fire was radiant—created from a large gathering of coals left over from the night before—re-kindled with dry wood for their morning ceremony. The heat melted into their bodies as the fire told them new stories and interpreted their dreams from the night before, a fire that changed the coffee into a dark fluid of warmth, like cocoon to butterfly.

They had already located the elk herds, and now they were waiting for Buddy's father to arrive with three hunters from Texas. Three days before, they had left Golden in West Yellowstone so they could ready the camp.

"Jus git up there, and make yerselves a honeymoon camp," the old man ordered his son and long-time friend, Joe Coyote, as they were saddling their horses. "I'll be there as soon as that *aeroplane* flies in from Texas."

Buddy Sunday and Joe Coyote built shelters, rigged a makeshift corral for the horses and mules, and gathered enough grass to keep them fed for a month. The big snows had just started, but where they set up camp the ground was spotted like the rumps of Appaloosa ponies. The sky that morning was a bright white closing into the soft winter harmonies of the earth. A flat surface with multiple tones of white, grey, brown, and green held in a deep silence of wilderness. Joe Coyote poured coffee into enamel cups and handed one to Sunday. He graciously accepted the cup and retreated into the only spot of sun that had broken through the mist. Joe Coyote placed a few pieces of wood onto the fire and backed himself into his cherished buffalo robe. Their silence wasn't ready to be broken.

Joe Coyote was somewhere between 40 and ancient. A chameleon spirit of all ancestors who moved completely without passport, he had removed himself from cities, towns, tribes, and nationalities until he was all of everything that existed. He lived life as it gave itself back to him and he passively loved it. He was a silence who moved without tracks. He had left his adopted family when he was a teenager to live with Golden and his family, and, after he had graduated from high school with honors, he left to see the world, and many years later he was back. It was time for him to become a teacher.

Buddy Sunday, 18 years old, was like a deer of male and female disguised as a young man. He was gentle in spirit, and beautiful in body. He could have been a dancer, or an athlete—or perhaps just a dreamer—but his life at this rites-of-passage had him working for his father as a hunting guide. In the mountains, where manhood is defined in such roles as masculinity, to be a professional hunter was considered a high honor among men. Buddy only wanted to be loved and needed by his family.

He saw the miracles of life as most people see only snow and rain. He would walk out his front door and see visions and rainbows inside deer and birds as they were running and flying through prisms of light. He would see rivers running through women, and soft spring rain melting birth into seeds. He tried to explain his visions, and the men would laugh and tell him all he needed to do was split twelve cords of wood and go out and get laid. But the women regarded him as a special child, carrying the wisdom from all of the earth's miracles. Still, because he could move as if floating, he became an excellent hunter. He would always bring back what was expected of him. It was like putting on some other person's skin, as he moved into the mountains to hunt for the animals who lived inside his body. He learned how to be tough, but he never stopped dreaming about his sacred flying. He did not know what it was to disobey, but only to be within the order of his family. He was happy, even when he had to ignore the voices from his inner vision.

"Here they come," Joe Coyote said, before anyone was visible. Buddy had also heard the noises from the hunting party, but he knew that Joe Coyote knew, and it was the older man's dibs to announce their arrival. He looked up just as they were coming over a rise which dropped them down into their camp's cradle.

When the three men saw the camp, they nudged their horses into a trot. And further back, Jedediah Golden Moon rode carefully, holding onto a pack line of two mules. He didn't wave or make any signs of excitement. He just grunted and farted like an old buffalo when he smelled the fire, especially the coffee.

Buddy took the pack line from his father and walked the mules to the corral that he and Joe Coyote had built from lodgepole pines and deadfall. He removed their packs, and rubbed them down until they were dry, and then gave each of them a special treat of nuggets of grain-mix and molasses that he had packed in for them. When he finished, he stuck a shaft of crested wheat grass into his mouth, and leaned against a Doug fir so he could watch his father. J. Golden was moving around the fire, poking and snorting and telling his customers how they were going to find the record elk that could shoot fire from his nostrils and rockets from his asshole. He was full of fun-loving bullshit which sometimes captured an occasional truth. And once in awhile all of these fantasies and questionable truths would dovetail into one strange creature which would be carried back as great mountain wisdom. It was J. Golden Moon's theater in the round.

He was a man of great size, shoulder-length white hair, who always had on some kind of deer- or elk-skin leather jacket, summer or winter. He had left home when he was twelve years old so he could live in the mountains, which were to him the only religion he needed. When he was 29, he married identical twins because he couldn't make up his mind which one he loved the most. Although polygamy was illegal, there were places high in the mountains where any kind of social severance from the law could be maintained if you were wise enough. It just took dedication. When the law would be sent up to J. Golden's mountain retreat to investigate this wild ass'd mountain man with two wives, there was always a secret place to stash one of them, in the still or in a cabin higher in the mountains that he had built for anyone who needed a sanctuary from city life, or the largess of himself. He also used it as a base camp for hunting in the higher mountains, which was a mystery as to who owned that land. Joe Coyote claimed it had belonged to his people, and that he had full jurisdiction of his ancestors' land and all of the forest spirits. J. Golden believed it belonged to his wives' family and that's why he married them. The Forest Service was happy just to leave it alone for the time being.

"Hey Sunday," the old man yelled. "We're headin' up to the South Fork and have a looksee. I want these dudes to git used to the altitude. We'll jus' sneak around and do some window shopping."

Buddy Sunday was wondering about which hunters his father was talking about, and their names.

"Oh yea, I forgot," J. Golden added, and he made some half-ass'd attempt for an introduction, but all he did was call everyone a cowpoke, or buckaroo. The three hunters were accepting to their introduction, and they showed the refinement of money and education. Joe Coyote checked out their rifles and guessed at least $1,500 apiece. He poured the coffee and passed it around. Golden moved in closer to the circle to make certain he didn't miss anything that was being said. He stuck a pine needle into his mouth and kicked at the fire waiting until he had everyone's attention. And, as grizzly and gravelly as he could, he explained his plan.

"My old sidekick, Joe Coyote, and my son Buddy Sunday has got three herds spotted about four miles from here. And we'll find those ol' trophy bulls hanging around the outskirts protecting their harems. It's the end of the rut and we're gonna find some angry, old, snaggle-toothed bulls pissed off as hell jus' like we'd be if we didn't have any poontang for the entire winter. Let's be careful, one of those old bastards could throw you 30 yards into the air faster than you could get a boner in a nudist colony. All we want to do is take a looksee and find out what's happening. If you see an eight- or nine-pointer, that's what we're here for. Trophies. The meat won't be much good because of all the testosterone running through them, but that's not what we want, right?"

He turned away from the fire and faced the canyon . . . placing his arm around one of the hunters.

"This Texas buckaroo and I'll go up the west ridge. Joe Coyote and his brother will go up the east. Buddy 'ol boy, you take this young buckaroo and follow the crick up to the lake . . . jus' in case we spook anything down. Follow 'em, and find out where they go. We don't want to lose any of 'em."

He took out a large, gold pocket watch, and opened the case. He studied its hands, and then looked up to locate the sun.

"Well," he said, "looks like my watch is off a few seconds. Let's meet at the lake around three or four. If you see an old Wapiti that drops you to the ground in total amazement and makes you a true believer in that so-called magic of life, that's what we're lookin' for. Nothing else is gonna

do. And for you fine gennelmen from the city, let me add that an elk has a big white spot on its rump, jus' in case you're not sure. We don't want anyone shooting a griz, deer, or stray mavericks. We'll take our guns jus' to get the feel of packin' 'em around, and . . . " J. Golden paused.
"Jus' in case we run into an old bull or maybe even ol' Eph."

He knew that his guest wouldn't know what Eph meant, but he just wanted to put on a show.

"That's what we call a grizzly bear up in these sacred mountains." He locked on to each guest, and gave them each a knowing nod. "But no fireworks if we can help it. One shot and we'd scare 'em so far away they wouldn't return until the Second Comin'."

He moved closer to Joe Coyote, talking out the side of his mouth. "Pass out the jerky and pine nuts. We'll gnaw on them until supper. And go easy, these dudes ain't used to these mountains. And don't forget to tell them some of your Indian stories." He nudged Joe Coyote. "That's what they're paying those big bucks for."

He started to leave but came back and leaned in closer to Joe Coyote's face. "How's the kid?"

Joe Coyote smiled. "Just like always. He floats and sails, but he's always right on time." He nudged J. Golden back. "That's Indian Time to you, hoss, just in case you needed to know."

Smiling, J. Golden accepted the dig.

"Strange kid but I love him. He can shoot the balls off a horse fly at two miles. Knows everything about this part of the world, but don't let him know I told you."

He looked over at his son.

"We'll shit-oh-dear, let's get movin'."

He walked over to the corral and checked out the remuda of horses and mules.

"Hey Buddy Boy, douse the fire before you take off, give these animals a good-bye kiss. You're good at that. We'll see you at the lake." Golden picked up his rifle and nodded to his partners. They moved off in a slow, even-smile pace—a steady tug into the mountains.
A minute later, J. Golden Moon looked like the landscape—full of life, but always camouflaged.

Joe Coyote motioned to his companion, and they began their climb up to the East Fork, and soon vanished immediately into the dense forest.

After the fire had been extinguished, and each horse and mule had been consoled, hugged, and treated with bunches of grass,

Buddy Sunday slipped back into the lean-to, and returned with his scopeless rifle and day pack. He had on a reversible hunting cap with the brown showing, and an owl feather stuck into the head band. He slipped on a down vest over a faded Pendleton shirt, and nodded to the young man he was guiding. Buddy looked right at home, someone who had been in the mountains since the beginning, as if he were the natural son of the sun and moon.

    They started up the canyon side-by-side, Buddy giving space and ease to the young man. Inside the forest the snow had not reached the floor, and the Aspen trees had laid down a soft blanket of yellows and orange in the dream puzzle of Fall.

TWO

Buddy and his young client carried themselves silently up the trail, completely captured by the silence of the still early morning. It could have been a hundred years ago, or a thousand. The trees were giants and looked as if they were waiting for those big snows—the healers of what was their civilization. At the third waterfall they stopped to rest. Buddy checked out the plants that surrounded them, and pointed out the chokecherry, serviceberry, needle grass, blue grass, current bushes, wild rose, and quaking aspens.

"With this much food, the elk will be hanging around for another month."

At the bottom of the falls, a Water Ouzel was standing on the bank, balanced for its dive for food into the icy water. Buddy was thinking about how the bird, when back on her observation rock, would sing like a canary. He quickly turned around when the kid interrupted him.

"You know what I'd like to do?" he said to Buddy.

These were the first words he had spoken to each other. Buddy looked up hoping the conversation would be easy. All he could say was, "What's that, hoss?"

"I'd like to take this $2,000 rifle and shove it right up my father's ass, and then spend the rest of the time studying the animals, trees and plants like you do," he said. "Forget about the hunt and all of this he-man bullshit. The last thing I ever want to do is kill an elk. Goddamnit! Such a great animal. And they've got a spot all picked out where the head will go. Right above my desk. They've got everything planned. A triple-threat law firm, and it feels like I never had a choice. I'm going to kill an elk because there's an empty wall behind my desk. Jesus, I'd rather dig up a big worm, have it stuffed, and ceremoniously place it above my desk. Big game hunter opens up law practice. Oh, by the way, my name is Jayson, and yours is Buddy." He put out his hand. "Or, is it Sunday? I'm confused."

Buddy took his hand and held it for a second without shaking it, and then let it go. It was hard for him to tell strangers about his family. He always felt so different from everyone else, and his own family was strange enough.

"Well, ah, my first name is Sunday, and my last name is Moon. I was born on Sunday. After that, my grandfather started calling me Buddy. Go figure."

Buddy moved closer to Jayson.

"You know, you don't have to shoot anything. Aim high, and let it sail away."

They started up the trail. Jayson turned around to let Buddy know that he'd do his job when the time came.

"I guess I've got to start sometime," Jayson said. "They're already talking about a lion hunt in Africa."

Buddy watched his companion move up the trail. He was graceful, and walked with an easy confidence.

"It would be nice," he thought, "to have the answers given to you."

Buddy sniffed the air searching for the deep fall scents, the ripeness, and the pungent smells of mating. They might run into a young bull elk who didn't have his own harem. He would be hanging around trying to sneak a lady or two for himself. Or, they would find him polishing up his antlers, and dreaming about the next rut season.

"This is a strange time to have a hunt," he continued his thinking, but vocally. "Right in the middle of their bedroom, but it's his land, or my mother's family, or, before that, I guess it was Joe Coyote's people's. But, I know, it will never be mine."

Once out in the open, the snow started coming down harder—flakes like paper cutouts. Leaving his rifle on his shoulder, Buddy flipped it so the barrel was pointed downward, and motioned Jayson to do the same. "Keeps the snow out."

It was his grandfather's Winchester with an extra-long barrel so it would hang heavy in the wind. He had it sighted in so that he was hitting the center bulls-eye nine out of ten times. "That's close enough," J. Golden had told him, "Let's leave something to chance."

Buddy was drinking at the stream when he smelled the smoke. He ran over to Jayson and slapped the cigarette out of his mouth.

"If the elk get a sniff of that smoke," he whispered, "they'll be off for Canada before we could figure out which direction we're headed. Here, let's cover our smell."

He went over to the stream bank.

"Take some of these bushes and rub them over your clothes," Buddy said and took some Rabbit Brush, sage, and chokecherry leaves and handed half to Jayson. "And keep track of the wind so it's always in your face. I'm sorry I scared you, but we might as well do it right. If we're lucky, we can sneak up on a herd and watch them do their elk thing."

He looked over at Jayson for a nod of acceptance. "Deal?"

They ate some jerky that had been marinated in chokecherry juice, wine and fired-peppers. Buddy took out a bag of shelled pine nuts from his pack and offered the sack to Jayson.

"These came from the north rim of the Grand Canyon," Buddy said. The nuts were the size of pinto beans and roasted in salt.

"We were there last fall and gathered up some 30 gunny sacks. You can still smell the pitch," he said. "When I was younger, I preferred to sleep in the store house on top of the bags. What a great place to sleep. When Joe Coyote came with us, he wouldn't allow us to shake the trees to get the pine cones down. We had to wait until the wind did it for us. The Indian way, was all he said. It took us five times as long, but . . ."

"He's the one with my dad?" Jayson asked.

"Yeah, that's the one. When he left the Res, he came to live with us because our land had once belonged to his people. Perhaps, he's planning a coup." He paused, to allow a new direction into the conversation. "This is like a reservation for the elk, and we've got them up against the wall. The only way it would be fair is to hunt them on pogo sticks using sling shots."

"So why do you do it?" Jayson asked.

"I really don't know. It feels so good to be here." Buddy Sunday had a soft smile on his face as he checked out the terrain. "I love my father, love to hang with him, but I have to wear a tougher hide than I was ever given. Someday it will fall away."

He put his head down as if he were trying to pick up some inaudible sounds. He raised one hand as a signal for Jayson to hold up. "It's got to be snowing a lot harder up there, and the elk should be moving down."

THREE

Where the canyon ends, a waterfall cascades from granite cliffs 50 feet into a deep lake, full of trout and endless stories. From the beginning, it's been used for healings, visions, and spiritual ceremonies. Since before the turn of the century, the natives were barred from using their sacred place. Their survival depended on other sacrifices. J. Golden Moon was shown the lake when he was 14 years old by Joe Coyote's grandfather. An ironic twist of the knife since, later on, the land was bought by J. Golden's wives' family, and given to them as a wedding present.

Buddy was surprised that his father had decided to hunt in this area. It was the first time he had ever gone to the lake with anyone except his family. But his father needed the money, and there would be a large bonus if the hunters got their trophies. The week before Joe Coyote and Buddy had seen five very large bulls, each one was carrying a magnificent set of antlers. Seven to eight points on each side. Two years before, Buddy had come upon a magnificent elk which probably weighed fourteen hundred pounds with an antler spread of five feet. The brow tines were at least a foot long. That one must have been the lord of the whole range, moving like the warrior king with a harem in every meadow.

Buddy was nervous about meeting at the lake.

"Perhaps," he thought, "they might move over to another drainage. "This is a place where we should be at peace with the mountains." He adjusted the rifle strap, and pulled harder into the trail. "Especially for Jayson."

FOUR

They came to the last granite headwall that separated the canyon from the top lake and a waterfall way over 50 feet. Buddy was in front, as he cleared the last part of the outcropping. He stepped aside so Jayson could see the lake as he topped the ridge. It was like the opening of the universe to a person who had never been there before. An explosion of water that showered the senses.

"Oh my God," Jayson said softly as he drew out the word God into a hymn. He took off his rifle and pack and walked quietly to the edge of the clearing. "I've only seen photographs . . ."

Buddy put his finger to his lips and pointed to the right of the lake. On the far side an elk herd was grazing in the morning sun-lit foliage.

"Over thirty cows," Buddy whispered. "The bulls must be up higher. Let's sneak around to the other side."

They stayed inside the trees until they were directly across from the herd. As quietly as the snow falling on the earth, they silently built a blind from deadfall. It was big enough for them to kneel and be comfortable, but low enough so that it wouldn't look any different to the elk than the surrounding deadfall. Buddy removed his down parka from the day pack.

"We should stay right here for awhile and let the air clear itself," he whispered. "Our vibrations will soon be gone, and then we can go out there and watch them." He pointed to an outcropping of granite near the edge of the water. "See that, as soon as the wind feels right, you can sneak over here. It's high enough so you check them out. I'll stay here."

Jayson looked over at Buddy with a grin that didn't fit with his previous enthusiasm.

"Guess what?"

Buddy Sunday suspiciously turned toward Jayson.

"What . . . ?"

"I've got to take a crap."

Where do I go? Was that what he was being asked. Buddy looked around for the best place for Jayson to go so he wouldn't disturb the herd. He pointed over to a stream bed that had been frozen over.

"Over there," he whispered. "That log over the gully. Sit over that, and you can watch the elk at the same time. But, be quiet. If some old bull comes wandering by, we might as well take off for the Yellowstone."

Buddy Sunday knelt on his parka and covered his rifle with a poncho. He looked up to see what Jayson was doing.

"Over the log, over the log," he mouthed the words to Jayson, as he rolled his index finger.

The great hammer of enlightenment struck, and Jayson got the idea. He was laughing inside himself, as he rolled his bare backside over the log.

"What a great place," Jayson was thinking, as he lifted himself just a little to watch the elk. They were kicking at the new snow trying to reach the grass below.

Suspended in time, as the earth and the sky moved into each other as one color, even Jayson was beginning to be a white hump in the middle of a ravine. Buddy waited and Jayson watched, and time became a study of the serenity of balance. The oneness came into Jayson the way opium sails slowly through the blood penetrating the brain.

Then came the startling report of a rifle, somewhere he thought his father or Joe Coyote would be. And then came the thumping that began to vibrate though the trees.

Buddy stood up and looked around to see what had changed the atmosphere. He heard voices up on the west ridge. From out of the forest came the largest elk he had ever seen.

"Holy beast of God," he thought, "that baby is huge."

The elk had his head tilted back, and his antlers were touching the back of his rump. He was mad, and he was moving like a runaway locomotive. His wives were in danger, and he was their army to defend. Buddy looked over at Jayson who was frozen on the log looking like just another slab of snow-covered granite. Buddy moved to the edge of the clearing, hoping that the elk would see him and not Jayson. At that same moment, Jayson stood up to see what was going on. The bull saw Jayson, and changed his direction as his huge head began to lower closer to the snow.

Jayson turned to point out something to Buddy, and that's when he saw the bull.

"Jesus Christ all-mighty," he shouted into the silence. He tried to pull up his pants, but remembered that he hadn't wiped himself. He collapsed back onto the log, and whatever it was that took over his body he was frozen in place. Everything became a white, unfocused jell of collapsed muscles, as if he had been caught in the king's bedroom with his pants down.

Buddy knew that it was up to him. To do what, but he was sure what that was. All of the answers began racing through his head. He could try and turn the elk, or he could kill it, but it was the largest trophy he had ever seen. Perhaps, the elk would just make a pass at Jayson and take off with his harem. He already had his rifle ready, as the answers were being previewed.

"Maybe, I could just graze the skull," he thought. "But then I could miss so easily, and that would make the bull crazy with anger?" His father's words came running through his head: "When you must kill for survival, make goddamn certain you know how to do it. But, whatever you do, first bless the spirit that is life, and that spirit that belongs to the animal, you, and the universe."

Buddy slowly shifted the rifle into its shoulder cradle. And like a mother holding a child during a storm, he held it without smothering its life. He felt the soft touch of the walnut stock. It smelled of the wood oil that he and his grandfather had rubbed into it so many times. The long blue steel barrel held flat and steady in the wind, as he moved it down onto the animal. He found the back sight, and looked down the barrel until he located the gold bead on the tip. He listened and felt for his heart beat. It was a little fast, but he knew that it too would relax. He had one shot. And there was only one place that would stop a 1400-pound elk. A shot that would drop the bull a tenth of a second after impact. He had seen it so many times before: the rifle barrel jumps a foot into the air, and before the elk has heard the hollow booming of the explosion, his heart has been blown into unimaginable pieces. The front legs would buckle from its weight and propelled by the collapsing life. First the knees, and then the plowing through the snow until the back legs and enormous rump would hit the ground which would then throw the head high into the air, and the antlers would swing all the way back to its tail. And then the long skid through the snow as the elk would disappear into an enormous spray of snow powder . . . dead.

Buddy was concentrating on the lead he had given to the elk. He moved one spider web hair to the front locked onto the elk's heart. From the 300 grains of powder, the hollow point bullet would travel at 2500 feet per second. At 50 yards from trigger finger to elk there was only the mind of a greater power that could change the direction.

Jayson was still frozen into another reality of white curtains covering his senses. Buddy gently pulled his rifle in closer, and took a long, deep breath, and then slowly expelling it. He began the ritual of squeezing the trigger. The release—the poem from the poet—the infinitesimal pull of wet leather drying in the sun. The contraction was timeless, but exactly perfect. Twenty-five feet away, and the finger was moving as all sexual bodies move in contraction in the act of love. Two bodies lost in oneness as the forces of life flowing together to create the beginning of life, slowly moving into the one beginning and end of everything. Twenty feet, and Buddy knew he was at the micra point of pressure which would release the firing pin into explosion. Fifteen feet, the elk raised his glorious head, and beautifully shifted his front shoulder weight slightly onto his back legs—preparing for the confrontation that would be a direct thrust into the body of the interloper.

The elk, the grand bull of 15 winters and 30 cows, opened up all of his sensory receptors to determine his next move. The enemy in front of him was a motionless body of frozen life that seemed harmless and incapable of any challenge to his authority. At that same moment, Buddy released the pressure on the trigger. The elk pulled way back into its story of a million lives and took off into a 30-foot leap that carried him high and far away from the creature cocooned in his pre-life womb.

The elk found his harem, and took them running through the newly fallen snow, into another canyon where their lives would continue until they were discovered once again by the hunters and their angry tongue of a million bullets. That moment they were alive, and their spirits were alive, and Buddy had lost his protection from the world. He had discovered that what is deeply believed, and felt, can also be lived. And his life into the universe, far from the earthbound, began its true journey.

Fortunately for Jayson, his pants were down when he lost everything. He was still sitting on the log when Joe Coyote came up behind him, "I thought for a second you were going to be singing with the angels. Clean yourself up in the creek, and I'll get a fire going and we can have some coffee. I think we all need some." He started to turn away, but then stopped. "Your father is still up on the ridge. He doesn't need to know."

Whatever corrections Jayson would have to make, whatever man-to-man, surrendering he needed for his ego, he would have to figure it out by himself. Perhaps later, when he would shoot his first trophy, or back in his office, or home in Dallas with his family. But it would take a long time for him to discover what had actually happened, what saved his life from being skewered by a record set of antlers. All he needed right now was to get cleaned up, and find his own understanding.

Buddy knew inside his body, way down deep where the truth gets buried most of the time, that accidently he had done something important. One more step into his own skin. He sat down next to the fire, slipped back the rifle's bolt and carefully removed the cartridge. Buddy stared at it as if it were an icon of great mystery. Harmless as it was in his bare hand, it possessed so much more than he could ever imagine. He could see it charging into the elk's heart and then he couldn't go any further.

Everything disappeared into the thickening snow, and he knew that his life had changed forever. He kissed the shell and slipped it into his breast pocket.

Joe Coyote came over and sat down. He pulled out two frazzled cigs from his top pocket, and lit them with a kitchen match. He looked into Buddy's eyes, and saw what he wanted to see.

"Here you go ol' buddy . . . a little tobaccy to sooth and calm the elk's nerves."

Buddy took the cigarette, and held it between his thumb and index finger. After two puffs, he put it out into the snow.

"I knew that you were around here someplace," Buddy said. "I could feel you. Just as I had the elk locked into my breath, I started to think whose life was more important, and the elk won. But I knew what you were doing, and the elk knew, just before he jumped over Jayson, the elk knew."

Joe Coyote was smiling with the cigarette stuck in his mouth. "I'll get this fire stoked up," and then turned back to Buddy Sunday. "It's a strong feeling of power to be able to kill something. But its like being a junkie. I like the power of being able to stop, better. Besides," he added, as he picked up two pieces of firewood, "you could have missed."

"Oh, go piss up a rope. You know that I could never miss. If Jayson had been killed, I would have had to face the music. I didn't want to see Jayson stuck like a hunk of beef on that bull's antlers, but I would rather have had that happen than kill that beautiful elk. I guess it's just a matter of nobility. At one point I could see a river of rainbow colors running through the elk's body, and I felt a stronger power than the one that was trying to save Jayson. The strength of that elk's life was much too strong for any ideas I had about trying to save Jayson. I was folded into another mind, and it was beautiful and scary at the same time."

Cautiously, Jayson came walking into camp. Buddy stood up to welcome him to the fire. He knew that he should say something, but he didn't know what. Jayson knew that some kind of a decision had been made between Buddy and the elk. But he didn't know how, or why. Perhaps this was just one of Joe Coyote's tricks, and they had all played their parts for him in his own ancestral grounds. They looked at each other and said nothing. The fire would help them, tell them stories, and keep them warm. The words would come later. Joe Coyote knew that he could supply the easy conversation to ease the silence, but he liked the quiet, with people isolated deeply into their own bodies. They had another week to spend together. There was enough time for talking.

The daylight was slowly being devoured by the falling sun into snow. As soon as J. Golden and the two hunters returned, they would either stay at the high camp, or if their guests wanted more comfort, it wouldn't be too difficult to return to their hide-out cabin five miles below. Perhaps the clouds would clear and the moon should be almost full. The hike down would do them good.

The night came into the meadow, and it was the eve before the hunt. The elk had moved into another canyon far away from the eyes of the exploding bullets. Joe Coyote knew that there was not an elk around for miles. They moved closer into the fire to find the heat, and watch the flames laugh at the snow. The fire challenged the darkness for a pocket of warmth as the sun dropped and gave the night back into winter. ■

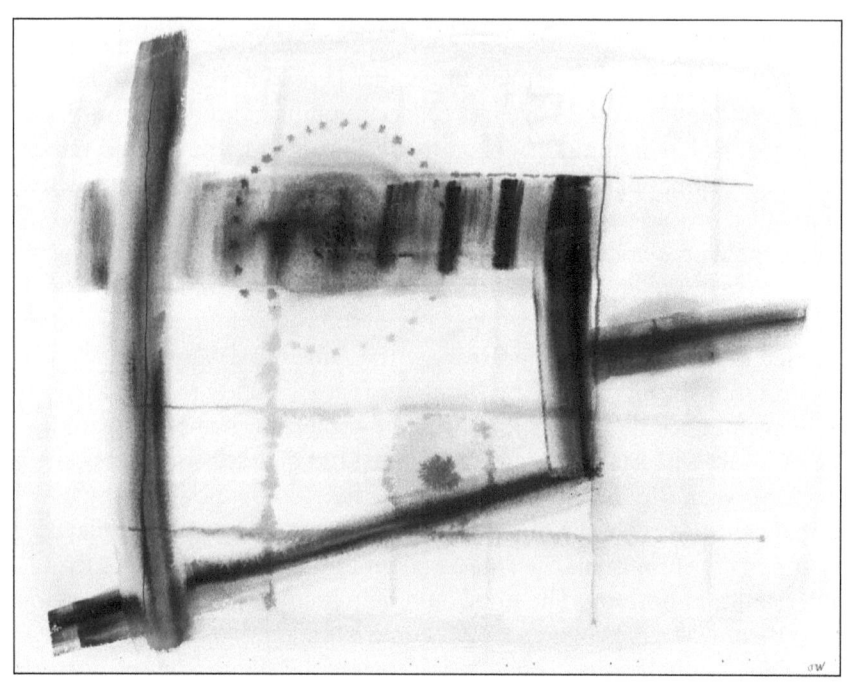

"Static" by Janet Wormser. Watercolor and gouache on paper, 10 x 12 inches.

SHERMAN ALEXIE

Highway Lazarus

I understand why white
people want to be Indian.

They think we wield
spiritual powers

that don't exist
anywhere else.

That's not true,
of course.

Our preachers
and priests

aren't more gifted
than any others.

But if I did carry
special powers

then I'd pull my car
over to the side

of this highway,
kneel next

to that deer dead
in the ditch,

and pray until
all of its shattered

THE LIMBERLOST REVIEW

and separate
pieces knit

themselves back
together. Yes,

I'd use my newly
acquired power

to save that deer.
I don't know why

this particular
deer

has caused me
to wish

that I could make
magic from

my empathy.
But, look,

this poem
just made

that deer rise
from the dirt.

It trembles
and trembles,

stunned
by its rebirth.

SHERMAN ALEXIE

I lean close
to its ear

and whisper,
"Go tell

other deer
that I'm here.

Tell them
not to fear me.

Tell them
to bring me

their dead.
But not

too many.
Every poet

has limits.
Every poet

is arrogant
but I know

this poem
can't resurrect

every deer.
It can only heal

three or four
at the most.

But please
carry your dead

to me
and I'll write

today
and tonight

and bring a few
broken

things back
to life."

SHERMAN ALEXIE

Two Rivers Calling Me

I think of those reservation-
raised Indians who move
to the city and live there
for years—sometimes

decades—but then move
back to the rez. I think
of them returning
to their tribe, returning

to their clan and cousins,
returning to the ancient
landscape, returning to rivers,
trees, and elk; or desert, cacti,

and lizard; or saltwater,
driftwood, and seal.
I think of them returning
to their mothers and fathers

or the ghosts of their mothers
and fathers. And, as I age,
I wonder more and more if
I'll someday move back

to the rez. Probably not.
But I more often wonder
where I want to be buried
when I die. Will my grave

be in Seattle, my beloved
city, or will my coffin rest
on the rez among the graves
of my mother, father,

siblings, and dozens
of cousins? I don't yet know
the answer to that question.
I suppose at some point

that I'll write it into my will.
All I know for sure is
that I'm lonely for the rez
when I'm in the city

and I'm lonely for Seattle
when I'm on the rez.
This is how it goes
for Indians. We grieve—

we constantly grieve
for who we've become,
who we were, and who
we were never allowed to be.

SHERMAN ALEXIE

Beadwork

My mother and aunt, both wearing
purple head bandannas, took me along
to the bead shop in Spokane.
The shop was owned by white women
but that didn't matter. Beads are sacred
in every culture. My mother and aunt
were choosing the beads they would use
to build the regalia of a dozen powwow

dancers. I was never a dancer. Not once.
But I was always a dreamer,
so I dipped my little hands
into the loose bead barrel
and pretended that I was sifting through
all the molecules in the universe.

"Forest," photograph by Virgil DiBiase.

KRISTA LUKAS

What if I Left You

What if I left you
with one redeeming memory?
The beach—seaweed
tangled in my hair, skin
saturated, wrinkled, pale.
You'd take my hand
to look for a scar, a ring.
Rinse your conscience of failings.

I'd wait, calm
as a storm's eye
passing through, a false promise.
A forecast of screaming
gusts around my shoulders.

Named for a woman
unknown to you,
I'd be waiting, still
a pool untroubled by tides.

If I left you—if we closed
our mouths, hushed
to utter silence, we might begin
the circling slash of winds.

Untitled by Alberta Mayo. Mixed media, 4 x 6 inches.

DAVID LEE

On the Domes on the Rock Porch: A 5 p.m. Community Kodak Memory Moment 55-Plus Years in the Past

Cloud lumps
like nursing piglets
wallowing against themselves
and the horizon,
and a Mason jar

of purloined excellent clear
whiskey from R. B. McCravey's
somewhere up the branch
hidden still—
bottled conviviality

two drinks and one sip
with the power
of bringing even the taciturn
to speech and
the thick-tongued to song

singfulness and loquacity
being the bestowed gift
of tongues
worthy of Luke's Apostles
at Pentecost in the Book of Acts

and gleeful conjoined memory,
footprints left like a walk
through dewgrass
with moisture welling up
in each step

Autumn Memoir: Outside the Church House after the Sunday Sermon

> *Out of the mouths of babes*
> Psalms 8: 2

Larry Joe Williams said to an audience of himself
with the obvious intention of being overheard
I thought today's sermon was pretentionus and
shortsightedly in its avoidance of the immediate need
for an additional qualified Elder in the quorum
and Darrell Glenn who had been standing by
Clovis Ledbitter and Jerry Kuykendall talking
about nookie and the Antelopes losing another football game
who anyone of right mind would have thought
too young to be actually eavesdropping
on matters of impending and desirous irruption said
Oh my lard it aint nothing you ever have anything to say
except yourself good about, is there?
and Larry Joe Williams said Son the Good Lord
will condemn you to Hell Everlasting
for taking His name in vain and Darrell Glenn said
I aint your son and I never done it this time
and Larry Joe Williams said I quote, you said
Oh my Lord and Darrell Glenn said
I was staring at your belly
I said Oh my lard like hog fat in a bucket
for refried red beans for supper and I never
used nobody's goddam name in vain
just your Dunlop all over your belt top disease
and that for Hell's sakes is all there are to it
you need to find something else to talk about
standing outside the dammed church house
on a Sunday. Period. We all are tored of it.
Sick as Hell tored of it, ask anybody.
He'll tell you.

DAVID LEE

And Mrs. Kitchen who had taught 2 of us in 3rd grade
all those years ago before Darrell Glenn's family moved here
and we became organized bosom buddies of the low order
came right over and said to us
Now now boys.

Mountain Home, mural capital of Idaho.

CHRIS DeVORE

Mondays with James

Six inches of wet, heavy snow falls overnight and children all over town are hoping for the day off. It seems like they're missing something essential, checking their email rather than huddling around the radio, wrapped in afghans, waiting to hear if their school has canceled. Outside the window there're a thousand sparrows puffed up, chattering, with the sound of plastic raking against concrete even further back in the subconscious. Snow continues.

We sit for coffee.

"I will tell you one thing," says James. "I will always have story in my life. It's the real secret ingredient in the stew. It's the poet saying baseball is maybe more beautiful than a sonnet. It's why your dad is so damn grumpy in the morning. And it's why Mary remains a virgin after 2,000 years."

These are the homilies James is prone to deliver over the steam of Monday's coffee—drip, a skosh of half & half. James and I have been friends for the better part of a quarter century, and he has been my therapist for the past seven. He's helped me through marriage, kids, suicidal thoughts, and my mom's cancer.

We laugh.

"I'm getting tested for an STI after coffee, so we might have to keep to our time this week," he says.

I just look at him. Only he would try to make an STD sound more sophisticated.

"What?" he says. "I do."

I sip, burn my tongue, cough, and then cough several more times into my arm. It's this year.

"Do I even want to know?"

"Of course . . . I mean. Well. It's quite a story."

I stretch my neck.

"You know. I provide the house, the coffee, lot of times some breakfast. You come here every week and it just doesn't feel all that professional …"

"Professional?"

"I mean, appropriate."
"You mean start with a prayer?"
"It wouldn't be the worst—"
"What's your go-to karaoke?"

I stretch my neck. Take a short draw of coffee with almond milk, something new I'm trying.

"Probably Bon Jovi."

"Bon Jovi? What? Nah, I guess I could see that."

* * * * *

The thing about talking with James is he is sketching the whole time as if the conversation just isn't enough to keep his attention. He also sometimes plays chess on his phone. His sketch is of a cartoonish man with huge ears and an asinine smile that brings the heat to my cheeks. He does have some touch and an almost encyclopedic knowledge of the chess middle game.

He brushes back his hair and I notice a new tattoo. I'm worried this too is *quite a story*. The frustrating thing is that I love stories. Any and all, but I just can't. Not right now. It's my turn. We have a deal. I need this ritual. I need to hear myself speak.

Mountain Home is the mural capital of Idaho. Downtown holds nearly 200 murals by more than 100 local artists. Each one a story, a tattoo, a chess piece, and a karaoke song.

"You know all these trials and tribulations will make you a better person," he says.

"I don't know that."

He smiles and leans back in the chair like a teenager.

"Why do I even try?"

"I don't know, why do you?"

James pours more coffee even though he is only down to about two-thirds of a cup. This time he puts in a little of my wife's flavored creamer. I think it's vanilla, but it could be hazelnut. He adds it like it's whisky, with tradition and a little twist at the end. James looks out our back window and watches a few squirrels fight over the last seeds in the entire world. He sips and pulls the cup away quickly. He utilizes the professional pause.

"What's wrong with you?"

"Nothing. Everything just pisses me off."

"You need to eat something stat," James says, trying to hide his smile behind his cup. He fails.

The thing about living in a small, Air Force town in Idaho is not everyone wants to be here. The stories are often quite similar. It's an assignment or they can't afford to sell the house or they're too young or old. In the land of tumbleweeds, however, people grow strong roots, and for so many reasons, decide they love it after all.

"Okay. I'll tell you the truth," I say. "I don't want to be here."

"Who does?" James says. "You've got to stop worrying your prayers."

"No. I mean in this room with you. Right now, I don't want to be here."

"Then why?"

"Where else would I go?"

We both drink our coffee and look somewhere between the other and the window.

"You know," says James, "the snow isn't going to last forever. The sun will come out and melt everything we haven't made into a pile or a snowman."

I nod, look down, wish it was whisky, wish this was going somewhere. It becomes more difficult to justify when there is no forward progress. *Worrying my prayers*, what the hell does that even mean? It's almost biblical like someone pretending to speak Spanish utilizing their ten-word vocabulary. Dammit, but isn't that life?

You can't walk down the alleyways of Mountain Home without awe and wonder. Each mural healing the mental, physical, and moral injuries of life.

"I used to speak with confidence before the pandemic," I say, maybe out loud. "This not being around people wasn't the joy I thought it might be. Turns out all that time in your own head isn't all that healthy. I found it so surprising that I had to learn that we actually do need other people. I mean I knew that like I know kids grow up fast because everyone knows that. But. You don't really know it until your daughter is 14 going on 40 and she's doing things that let you know you don't know your kid at all. Yeah, I'm struggling.

Yeah, but what does it really matter? I'm not sure the point. I mean it's nice to have someone to talk to but when are we going to figure some shit out? How long until we reveal that this is all my dad's fault? I mean, isn't that the hero's tale?"

"I like you like this," James says. "All sass and soliloquy."

James stops sketching for a moment.

"What makes the best story? Truth, emotional truth, the highest truth, is always the best story, right? The best story with an award-winning soundtrack. So, what's the best story, what's playing on Side 1, Track 1?"

The homilies. Sometimes the enthusiasm just eats you up.
God is really testing me now! I'd like to shout, but it doesn't seem right. In Mountain Home, there are so many scenarios where people start wondering about conflicts of interest like when you're running the local brewery and are a real estate agent, volunteer fireman, president of Rotary, on the school, chamber, and library board, chair of Air Force Appreciation Day, deacon at church, and head football coach. A small town is a conflict of interest with roads and a post office. And a lack of air. In such times and predicaments, maybe we should just stop for a moment and say thanks.

* * * * *

There're things about Mountain Home I can't tell you. Not because there are things, and not because I have secrets, but because I just don't know. I didn't grow up here. I'm not a very good listener; a nice way, of course, of saying I talk way too much. I do want to tell a great story. But. I don't know how. I'm just a pair of glasses among a million. I own that. But. The story is out there. I'm sure of it. It's in the libraries and it's maybe in the libraries of my mind. I hope it starts with a baseball because that's where I've hidden my treasure, bitcoin, books, vinyls. I don't care who you are—I don't want to watch you die. Don't watch me either, I think during a pause. The funny thing about this is that I swore off the first-person narrative. Never again, I said. Too self-indulgent. And yet here we are. This story is on life-support. I'm not sure where we're going. We're writing the great novel of our lives—and everyone keeps telling me to go home.

That's where I thought I was.

James says, "We'll pray for it to rain. Pray hard. And then when it rains, we will pray for it not to rain. We'll have faith. We'll live with dignity."

"What?" I say, rubbing my eyes.

It's amazing how much this helps.

James just sits there with a smug look.

"Time's up," he says and reaches behind him for his coat.

* * * * *

Right now, I would trade my computer for a clarinet or a stand-up base—New Orleans for an afternoon. But, in Idaho, you only hear about potatoes and politics. But. There is air between the generalizations. "Be not afraid of greatness. Some are born great, some achieve greatness, and others have greatness thrust upon them," was surely written by Shakespeare with Idaho in mind. This may surprise you, but some of us didn't choose Idaho. We're not even sure why we are here rather than say Montana, Oregon, Washington, or Louisiana. We do know we keep exploring the past for one line, one metaphor, that runs the race. Help and thanks, we pray, and we ask that we don't die many deaths, or, if we must, James is there to tell all about it. ∎

"Ephemera," photograph by Betty Rodgers.

WILL PETERSON

Fireman

You'd watch a steam engine train
Make the grade up a Rocky Mountain canyon
Knew its progression was provided
By the shoulders and hips of a fireman firing coal.
      It turned
A lot of hard-drinking railroad men to religion
Those July afternoons: the sun burning the cliffs
A deeper red, the grasses a paler gold.
Heat waves on the track the way snakes like it.
      Retrieve not that crowbar barehanded
You left a moment ago on the track
Nor use the grab bar to enter the cab on the sun side:
Burns take time to heal.
Nor forget the leather apron as you kiss the wife. That pivot
Between furnace and firebox will crisp the coveralls
She laid out new that morning.
      Stick a fork in him. He's done.
But those U.P. wheels got to keep rolling.
      It turned
      A lot of hard-drinking railroad men to religion:
The idea they got how: hot it could get.

Driftwood

He was one of those guys that had to get to the bottom of everything:
There wasn't a bottle made he'd leave unfinished.
Knew his limits: Just seemed to pass out before he got there.
She was a nice gal—thirty-five and easy on the eyes—
Just had a few bad habits. Knew what she wanted
Though still too young to know—when they finished with each other—
They'd not share another day though shared in that night
Devotion of eyelid, nipple, and thigh.
      It was cold that spring. The woods cold like November.
In the night sky Orion made a pass at the crescent moon.
The comet—on her way to the Pleiades—gave them not a backward glance.
Nor would for four hundred lifetimes.
      Sometimes you have love for a night and it's worth the lifetime.
She remembered the driftwood on the beach
The breakers coming in, the twisted seaweed.

WILL PETERSON

Postcard, Fairfield, Idaho

This red rock offers its resistance to the wind, to the sun
Above the plain where the camas lilies are pretty
Until the wind comes knocking at forty below.
The abandoned farmstead that leans
Above fields that winnow like the sea
Betrays the builder's final comprehension
Of the terms of his exposure: outbuildings near enough
A rope could be tied between so friends and family members
Having intended only a trip to the outhouse
Might not end up in Camas Creek Canyon.
        The window that remains proves to you glass bends:
The slow twist—and fall of timbers framed on glacial till
Has torqued it to convexity. After dark—
Amid the scuttling of creatures you trust are mammalian—
The mountains of the moon are clearly visible.
The only landscape in sight nobody's tried with an FHA loan.
        It's a non-linear equation in which
Depth of time, heat of sun, and weight of loss—
Though measurable—remain inconstant.
        But it's an easy country to figure
If you've enough acreage to make it on two cuttings
And your wife has a job with the county.
Sun and wind come from the same direction
And though Main is boarded up there's a saloon on Highway 20
Where you can watch the Sunday games.
None of the redneck farmers need act like they know each other.
        And leaving the Prairie a look back at that escarpment—
That lone juniper that has evaded wildfire for three hundred years—
Will remind you: anything that stands long in this country
Is going to get a little twisted.

"Hyalite Tigers" by Greg Keeler. Acrylic on canvas.

GREG KEELER

The Naming of Birds

Throttle-necked bottle-whomper,
Nadar's chuckler, drab-sided donkey
honker, chestnut hunk, tufted
truffle-pecker, two-toned tweeter,
common prat, iridescent prat,
Horton's spackler, diamond-crested
spackler, stubby-billed bog trotter,
puffy chubber, black-throated pog,
Georgia squealer, Michigan sprawler,
Alabama bug-sucker, creeping cheeper,
cheeping creeper, Jill's stench, waffle-
nosed nut-whacker, bag-tailed hack,
mud bubbler, lesser mud bubbler,
pocketed pucker-pock, emerald gobbet.

Disturbed Poodles

People use the word epiphany loosely
these days, as they do existential and unique.
They think that something can be very unique,
that they can have epiphanies about shampoo,
that their poodles can experience an existential
threat. I would start talking about the decline
of the language here but that I find disturbed
poodles and miraculous hair conditioners
to be quite unique. So let's drill down here and
put our hopes and fears in these here buckets.
After all, it's only optics. Let's hold our pinkies
out when we drink champagne. Let's
pronounce the *t* in often so people
will think we're smarter than we are.

As They Say

Those who don't know history flunk
it and have to repeat it. Misery loves
fudge. Give a man a fish, you feed
him for a day. Teach a man to fish,
he will deplete the ocean. Every cloud
has been formed by condensation. If
the shoe fits, wear a size smaller. Give
a man enough rope and he will start
a rope franchise. His crosshairs are on
the sparrow. If you can't lick them
suck them. A bird in the hand might
have lice. If life gives you lemons,
squeeze them in the eyes of your enemies.
It is better to give than to be robbed.

Whacking

I am very proud of my new weed whacker.
It is rechargeable so that I might whack
weeds at a considerable distance from
my house. It doesn't make much noise.
It is easy to reload the nylon line with
which it whacks the weeds. It is like
a gangster in a torpedo suit whacking
snitches right and left. I like the feeling
so much that I run out of weeds and
start whacking my garden. The peonies
don't last long anyway, so why not
whack them? You haven't lived until
you've whacked a patch of lettuce. I went
after the onions just for the smell of it.

At Home

A swallow probes the wind for its soft spots,
the pockets where mayflies reside in
the moment it takes to catch them.
There sure are a lot of them, swallows
I mean, coming in low, looping up high.
They don't see me here, flat on my back
by the river. One comes so close I feel
the wind from its wings on my face.
The mayfly it missed lands on my nose
and stays put for a while. I close my
eyes and imagine myself at home,
writing by the green lamp on my desk
and realize I really am at home. I don't
have to imagine myself here at all.

"Swallows" by Greg Keeler. Acrylic on canvas.

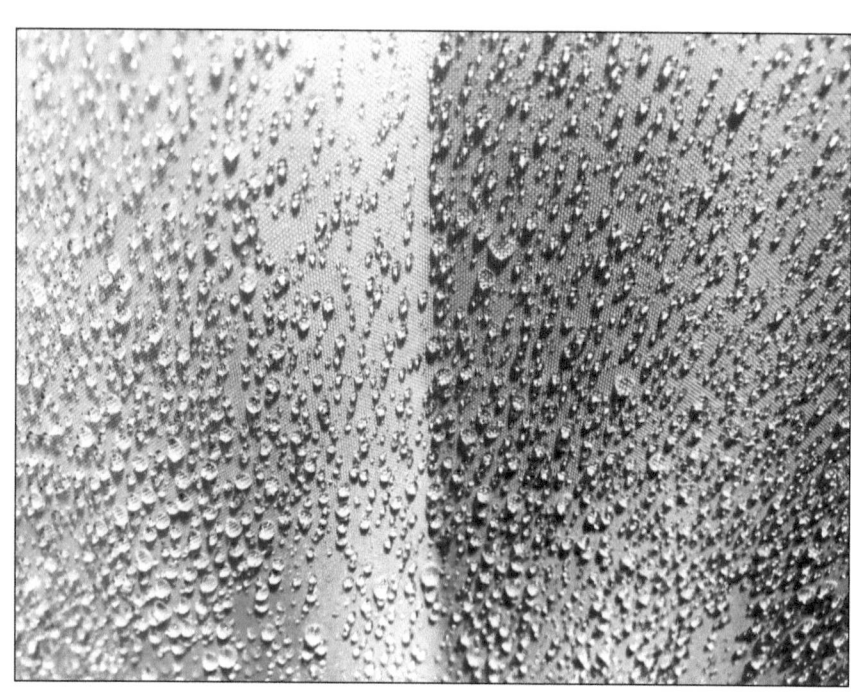

"Duet," photograph by Betty Rodgers.

KEN RODGERS

Verdin

Someone flames a number.
Psycho-odor floats in the gloaming.
The scent scrapes the evening's light.
Long-armed cactus.
Trees with thorny means.
In the night breeze, remnants of the day's tail wind.
Hints of visitations: Anna's hummer, yellow-cheeked verdin.
A dog struggles down the walk.
The cracked concrete an obstacle.
Mosquitoes sing.
Lights on old porches.
Cars stop in the street, hip hop voices.
A lone jogger. Lamplight shines off sweat.
Old chimneys crumble from gravity's embrace.

I wait for a song. A coyote. An owl.
Words of comfort swift and sure.
But nothing.
I have searched for these phrases.
Decades of work.
Maybe later. Tomorrow.
Or the morning after.
Old stories haunt.
Scriptures on sin.
A bullet's whisper.
The last words from the warrior who loved to dance.
My father, now dead, his angry warning.

Song

Long and low,
evening spreads its wings.
The Canada geese in the gaggle,
haggling.
The red tail hawk's
scree.
Slight breeze
in the teasel.
The feathers of light.

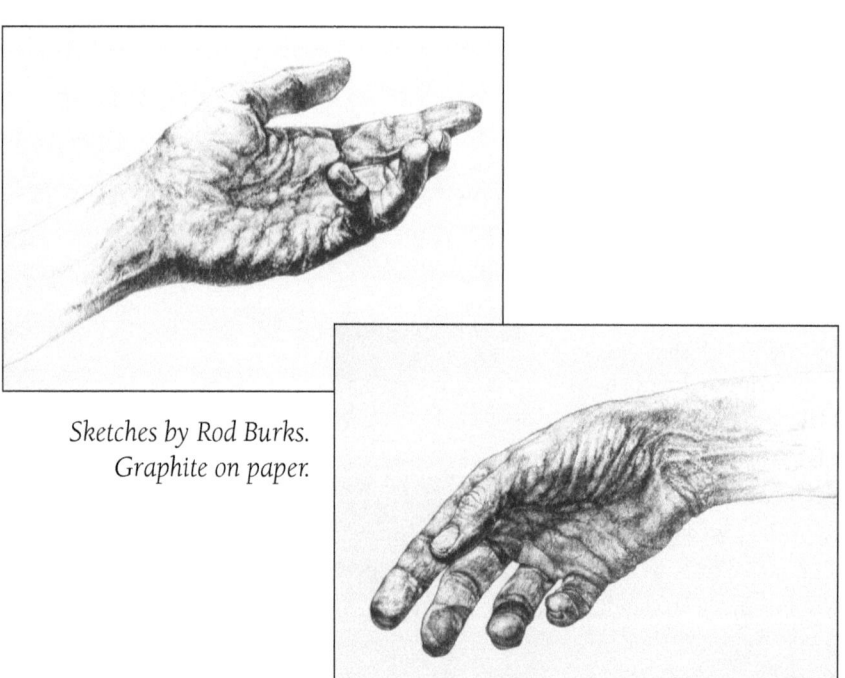

*Sketches by Rod Burks.
Graphite on paper.*

MAUREEN McCOY

Martin in Gigscape

By now, six months into working at the NuUze charity shop, Martin had acclimated to the role of genial penitent. Self-effacement was not so difficult when mordant gratitude figured. Further job devolution would mean facing the abyss, the fryolater. He feared the fryolater abyss. There, under bright lights and visor, olden guy gangly and damned, he'd be buffeted among stoics of the realm, the world's unremarked sages whose frontline grit had no doubt prepared them to shame loonies down from the ledge, boot cheaters out the door, and with a merry grunt jab Narcan into failing flesh. Dark arts had them rebuilding wrecked cars into ageless beauty. He'd seen the parades. Such was Martin's low sense of self, he feared if he fell into the fast-food demimonde, they'd conspire to finish him off: sure, gut him and salt him, why not? Unmoored from years of contemplative clock-watching and actual project successes in city planning, Martin had allowed the fryolater horror to shock imagination and enhance his regard for working at NuUze.

Now he faced wrath. Into the dusty peace of morning had burst a big boss from NuUze state headquarters fuming and castigating. Her entrance was a memorable severity of intention matched to showtime optics. Her hair, it might be a wig. The brassy mop-top curls lent an outdated porn look that briefly drew Martin into serious obeisance. Her whipping voice flayed the skunked air that collects around ditched furnishings and their apologists, as she hoisted the NuUze sign she'd wrenched out of its weedy berth down the road. The fretful manager Holly froze at the sight. "Can I get you something? Water?"

"I'm doing outreach visits, driving on this bumfuck back lane that GPS refuses to place and I see this sign. You want to tell me that not a single one of you employees noticed the defacing of the store sign? *LeUzi!* in ugly black lettering, no less? Does someone here think that's just the laugh riot of all times? A Christian charity shop re-named for a vicious gun? An Israeli gun. And French sickens me to the core."

As she spoke, she looked especially scathingly at Martin who, as a man, would be in cahoots with aggression. He bent slightly forward, imagined the drollery of "King" Charles's life, and nearly laughed.

He'd been fired from an office where artful amnesia marked people's responses to any ripple of concern.

"I'm sorry," he said. "I'm Martin. This is Holly, our manager." The intruder begrudged: "Candace Dowd." Perfect. For mental merriment Martin dubbed this woman with the porn hair Candy. *Candy* was the first salacious book he'd read on entering popeyed adolescence.

"Who would do this?" she demanded.

"A prankster. Kids, I suppose," he said.

The young temp Jude, who'd been dusting jelly jars down the way, shrugged adorably and turned off a sale radio. "Weirdsmobile," she said and retreated to a far corner, instantly clattering things around. Fiestaware. It had arrived in bulk from a restaurant gone down. Jude was on leave from school and claimed Beatnik Studies—"the upside Fifties"—as her major. She'd explained to Martin that working for peanuts in a do-good place counted bigtime for the resumé. "Hey, the Beats did scruff work too." Martin, a fifty-five-year-old professional clerking at NuUze was, she explained, now in temp-time, in gigscape. Great owling eyes of pity searched for his reaction, then went bright with revelation. "Think hep cat status."

Holly, the lapsed Mennonite manager of NuUze, now a generic Christian, burned with shame as Candy bannered the sign before her. Dolefully advanced into her thirties, she admitted that she'd never heard of an Uzi. "We're so open, so welcoming to all," she offered as generalized appeasement and personal absolution. Martin recognized the agitation in Holly that meant she itched to call a prayer circle.

"No other NuUze store has suffered this insult," Candy snapped. So saying, she dropped the sign, its plywood damnation thin enough to curl up at the edges and stiffen into a crustaceous death pose while emitting a squeak. Candy lifted a three-legged stool, priced at six-fifty, over to the door and sat heavily on it. Her feet gripped the rungs, but her body slumped. The misery of imperfection blanked her face. Fiefdoms were the pits up close.

"I'll get you water, if you like," Holly repeated. "It's bottled."

Curls shook. Mortal comfort could not address the situation. As Jude had wisely done, now Holly and Martin turned from the outsider and found busyness. Humor dared not be invoked, but someone had had fun re-doing the sign that was located in scrub, after all, not even on the premises, where the shiny lettering above the door remained pristine. Fun was in short supply here, and maybe everywhere in the new universe of pick-up work. Customers assumed, insinuated, and even joked that Martin, of an age past mattering, had retired into comfortable benevolence, that his role at NuUze was that of a counselor, a mediator, a tall priestly presence, meaning a dupe, stooge, patsy of sexless persuasion consigned to khakis and green polo. Candy was treating him thus and Martin bore the mantle as workaday rite. Put an ankle lock on him and people would realize he was helplessly beholden. Let go in the downed economy, as a job seeker Martin was sucker punched with rejections ranging in kind from robo text to blunt scoffers and one too many glad calls that detailed matters such as his clothing (stiff) and even suggested that his face, also, was simply wrong. At first, he'd gone for comparable positions, even ranged out to art direction, layout, management work at the Pennysaver, no less. Stunned by rebuff and wiped out by his divorcing wife, he'd reasoned himself down a ways, applying for insurance sales, house inspection, minor mall exec, even night sorter at the post office and doing fingerprinting for the state, but it was all no-go. Indeed, Jude was right: the NuUze job, listed only in the paper's print edition, mattered greatly.

The resident young hanger-on Donny now showed up in the doorway calling "Martin? I'm ready to work."

Jude whispered the kid back outside as Candy, taking on the role of bouncer seated on that stool, gave him a sharp once-over. No need to point the kid out as an accidental criminal benignly engaged by NuUze and paid out-of-pocket by Martin. He hovered, eager to do chores. Young Donny's confusion over lost meds had caused him just the once to drop his pants in public. And there stood girls. This happened at an aspirational beach, at the man-made pond of a lake slightly south of the Bottoms neighborhood that dribbled out in brush to the river. The pond was dredged of carp every year in time for summer swimming. Donny went half-mast there and froze. Shrieking mothers contrived all-out calamity. He'd been arrested and released conditionally. He was, someone remarked cruelly, "now on the no-fly list." NuUze was Donny's safe zone. Would that his trainee lawyer show up now and praise them all to Candy. Send this shrew the hell away.

On this sluggish morning, mid-August, customers shuffled in and out, Candy eyeing them without sympathy. Martin and Holly began working together on pricing as if not under surveillance, using the top of a plywood dresser tagged at ten bucks. Martin agreed with Holly: reduce the set of Hopalong Cassidy cocoa mugs. They'd gathered dust for ages and were even passed over by the ironist of history, Jude.

Of all times, though, now fiddling down the aisles was one of the occasionally appearing immigrant couples shy of English comprehension except when switching price tags on items. The sentry Candy came off her stool gasping.

"What did I just see? Call them out," she demanded in a steam pipe's hiss.

The couple already stood smiling at the counter. Holly quickly rang them up and they floated away.

"Why further stress them?" Martin argued and Holly's head bobbed agreement. "These people aren't lifting a lamp for the price of a butter dish just for fun. Let's not sweat the small stuff."

Martin sounded Christian, though conflict avoidance was where he banked faith. He endured on-the-job prayer circles only to support the anxious Holly. She had confided that she was trying Zumba for weight loss and imagined death at the looming age of forty, "when it's over, no offense." Whenever prayer circles commenced Martin tried to stand with his back to the security camera. In high summer, the backroom fan added a breathy spirit presence, but at least Holly's praying was freeform, no memorization required. Everyone endured Donny's fierce grip and swinging arms.

Candy reclaimed the stool perch and insisted, "Next time, for God's sake, do your duty. Nip that habit in the bud. They try that stunt at a supermarket, they're gone, their kids are orphaned." The passionate shaking of the wiggish hair declared might. Glazed lips looked fantastically plumped. Okay, say she'd had cancer: this was Martin's thought in service to keeping calm. She'd roared back from the death march all pitbull, bite, bite.

"I'm sure they buy groceries on the up and up," he said.

Jude had appeared. "Yeah, dig. Supermarket bar codes, what else are they for?"

Holly chimed in. "They've come with nothing. They count on us for furnishings."

The sunken plaid couches, flimsy dressers, the glass vases shaped to look old-timey. Martin helped haul, dust, and arrange the goods on shelves, in piles, stack the big stuff and building materials out back. He calmed Holly's pricing anxieties on a daily basis. She let him park his Airstream in the brush out back and hook up electric.

Candy shook her head as she tapped something into her phone. "Takers take," she said.

She wouldn't know how many ostensibly honest shoppers, even those enamored of recycling, approached the NuUze counter with an injured air, some more extravagantly than others. Martin would put on a moon face for listening. Hey, man, see this china pig bank for my kid, that ice cream maker, your set of cheap-shit sockets? This stuff should go for half the (pitiful) price tagged, didn't he know? Didn't Holly and the others know the deal? You pulling a fast one here?

Patience. The freedom to hold the floor, exercise the lungs, show cagey verve—where else in the lives of hopeful scroungers did such opportunity avail itself? Nowhere, Martin understood in his concierge role, exactly nowhere. Plus, he didn't give a fat fig about price. After twenty-six years his company canned him; a wife of punishing duration sucked off the severance after a wicked goodbye—bury her last words, bury them deep again, as they were threatening resurrection, today (why?)—now let the day hold steady, wing it. Sale fans were blasting, but Martin was sweating, the usual. Holly, as victim of allergies, began to sneeze.

Good old Candy reverted to history for extra shaming. "You know that Headquarters switched us from the name Grandma's Attic to NuUze as update. To broaden the base, bring in younger customers. Refresh the brand with witty spelling." A thread of welcome wistfulness played along in breathy undertones until Candy checked herself. "I can't emphasize enough how lucky we are that this signage debacle didn't fall into the wrong hands and go viral. Our competitors would've had a field day." She did not reclaim her perch on the stool.

Tamping down scenes of Goodwill girls beating victory rhythms on charred camping pots, Martin offered, "Our young employee Jude relates well to all ages." Of course most customers, like the world's population, were younger than Martin. They were people still boxing their way into the thick of life. All moments still mattered to them, he understood; every display of self exalted and exhilarated that self. Roostering counted as coin of the realm.

That went for the neighborhood actual sex offender too. Let back into the world, he showed up now and then, afternoons only. With lunchtime coming right up, Candy should, in Judespeak, be blessedly "splitsville" before his possible arrival. If Candy got wind of the rotten apple element she'd blow for sure. But even a certified lowlife needs the odd discount fork, wastebasket, or sometimes a hammer—the last rung up by Holly with pursed, possibly prayerful lips, because what if? But no, the hammer buyer went on that day (loudly) about building his kid a playhouse and soon enough Martin was offering tips and scouring out back for wood scraps. Pride, no stage is too small for it. Plus, Jude, so keen and young and cunning, became a joyful minx if the sex offender said, "Hey, baby," walking by her. And you could count on that, a regular refrain, and Jude's genially retro response: "Cool your jets . . . bub." She'd been binge-watching *Dobie Gillis*, a TV show even before Martin's time, to hone period lingo. Light badgering gave the guy a moment of notice, then he moved right on, no problem for Jude. Count on Holly to track him to the door with her Rushmore look while whispering, "Jesus saves."

"You have the worst sales record in the state." With that, Candy strapped a great handbag to her shoulder, the Soviet prison matron's satchel.

"Our customers need us," Martin said. "Our Bottoms neighborhood really needs us." He turned to Holly and asked if she'd like something brought back from the taco truck. Jude brown-bagged, no need to call out.

"I'll skip lunch," Holly said. Let Candy note the sacrifice said her gaze lowered to the floor. Her limp hair parted itself in the helpless way of showing virgin scalp expecting the guillotines of both heaven and earth.

Porn curls shook. "A taco truck's around here? You're kidding. I didn't see it coming in."

"Over the field if you're walking, or on down the lane," Martin said.

"Dirt lanes in a city. How can this place expect anything aboveboard when it's called the Bottoms? It's vulgar."

"New York City's got us beat with their Hell's Kitchen neighborhood."

Candy shuddered at that last. She'd have none of it. "You're on probationary status here. Poor sales and that sign defacement? It's no joke. And, well, I'm sorry."

She carried the sign of whapping plywood outside, paused, and then tossed it to the ground. It might have been the staff in *The Ten Commandments* movie turned to a writhing snake the way it fired her anew. Her gasp of wonder touched Martin oddly. He threw a little kiss goodbye as Candy charged over to her white SUV, a rental regrettably fitted with Florida plates. Holly, already gone to prayer, was left blinking back tears. Jude called from ancient tvland, "Kookie, Kookie, lend me your comb."

* * * * *

Martin hiked over patchy uneven ground toward his eventual lunch, lime Jarritos soda and a three-taco special. He followed tracks that, laughably, had been suggested as a bike trail (to nowhere)— harmless evidence of human frailty he now saw sympathetically, from the axed professional's view. He disturbed two musical crows out of a corn patch hacked from scrub. Beyond, the Red Oak River flecked along, the usual, largely out of sight, indifferent to voicing its schemes. Martin had none, save gobbling street tacos. Why do grasshoppers hop was the third-grader question of the day. They rose up in elvish drama as the lug giant human blundered on.

From the field Martin came out into the neighborhood of homes, onto the asphalt that would lead to an unnamed lane and, beyond, to Taco Time. The fading frame houses along here had been fighting the new century, as well as the old. Fruitless confederates, they stood in proud defeat. If only they had arms and lungs with which to grab back lost loves and beat out repeating dooms. But even mute, the houses retained loud attitude, and the huckster gene thrived. Yakking old-hippie grandmas; questionably legal garden growth; clotheslines showing everything; scooters thrown down; radios turned up; yard and window signs told you to move on or not, like the one before him. *Starry Eyes Will Reveal Your Mysterious Future.* Here, Jeanie, a woman with a sheet of chemically flossed hair down her back worked her card game. Anything for a buck, sure.

Jeanie came onto her porch. "Hello, Martin." She spoke in the cautionary rhythms of a translator. "Half price single-card reading today, Martin."

"Not right now, but thanks," he said as heat slammed his face. Mockery or flirtation, he couldn't read the feathery jab and kept walking.

* * * * *

Taco Time was a customized Airstream, longer than Martin's and hopping at lunchtime. The Martinez clan and truck were like some freak brightness blossomed in weeds and beaten grass near Apex Recycling, YY Salvage, the Tire Kings, the packing plant and more. A food truck blasting salsa music, edging a field, why not? "Bienvenidos," said the sign. And "Hola!" Guys streamed over for lunch, stood around eating and telling tales, and you wondered what they'd done before the truck planted itself here. Maybe wives had sent them out with pickle loaf on rye and five-pak Oreos. Or, maybe wives had said, "Feed your face at Qwik Trip." These guys had wives was the thing. They knew that Martin did not.

A breeze kicked up as Martin approached, a weather anomaly in high itchy summer. A ring of high oaks threw shade down exactly around the truck. Out front, small Martinez girls were whirling hula-hoops at their hips. Fluttering in their pink and yellow and green short sets, the girls were like a tropical migration coolly at home in their secret wilds. The head man Mr. Martinez and a couple of tall boys were all action and muscle and, Martin had observed, big on smiling at each other, as if this was not work at all. The women and older girls flew from truck to their mobile home and back with the synchronic flair of trapeze artists who soar and shrug at death. He meant never to stare at their zest and beauty because Jude had warned him against public enthusiasms:

"You're still in prime perv age group," she'd announced one day. "Solid perv zone. You're heading toward harmless geezer time, but you're not there. You don't want a mistaken perv vibe attaching to you, so watch it, bub."

A new aqua sign was taped near the service window: Fresh Fish Taco. That would be carp up from the river, a money-saving brilliance. As proof, Grandma Martinez stood grilling fillets to the side of the truck. Her full-length apron had chickens running mad, all upside down. She called to Martin, "Fresco, no lie."

"That fish taco's the real deal." Guy from around, the Jesus Church pastor, had sidled up alongside Martin. "It's fresh all right, really good. I'm reminded of fisher of souls."

Martin nodded. "Rev. Good to know."

The guy, a natural outsider, irritatingly had tried to align with Martin from the start, stating upfront their superior bond: neither counted on filthy lucre in this life. At times Rev was heard delivering sermons in his shack church near the Tire Kings, without a worshiper in sight.

"Say, how's Holly?" he asked. "She's probably wondering about me. I've been so busy with religious forays, but tell her I'll come by soon for bible study."

A while back this Rev had wheedled from NuUze some freebie crap for a dime-toss game in front of his Jesus Church, meanwhile pressing Holly to join him in bible study walks and even check out the local rough bar Mullet Town, for pastoral purposes of course. Martin had heard him ask Holly after dogging her around NuUze for the umpteenth time, "Do I repulse you?" She'd replied, "I don't use that word."

Rev hung around the taco truck as if to claim dude status, which riled Martin as he did the same and liked tossing out comments such as "anyone need pallets, we've got a shit load at the shop, free" sort of thing. Okay, he wished to belong, which made him feel insane.

Martin stepped up to the window and the young man there called, "Mar*teen*, hello. Your three-taco special, no?"

It kicked good every time, hearing Mar*teen*, the casual renaming, the affection of doing so and, sure, the sky blued up.

"Thanks." Martin felt a watchful silence from the guys mopping chins, finishing off drinks. He nodded around, said, "Hey." He'd hoped the kickier version of his name would catch on among the guys, but they rarely used greetings other than "bro." And like the customers at NuUze, they kept barbs at the ready to jack the small talk when it suited them. He waited for his order, beef, not the carp, and imagined a Mar*teen* Martinez walking easy in the world.

"Fellows," Rev said, "listen to those nasty bulldozers starting up. The siege of the Bottoms is on."

Across a farther field, land destruction was underway. Rumbling machinery was digging and hauling for the new waste treatment center, some new gouge-the-earth plan denuding acres, killing off a black walnut forest in this area, this neighborhood of backroom scrappers where, it was understood, the city figured the voiceless would remain so. Detours and road closings around the project didn't even merit announcement. Stink and relocations-—Martin didn't add the inevitabilities that, drawing from the old world of planning work, he saw coming.

"No worries about gentrification," he said to all. "No high-rises will go in next to sewage. No new tax worries, guys."

"Bro" and "cool" and "friggin A" went around, that last in deference to the little girls present. The beauty of the lunch break was this: here men said nothing to ruffle Martin or the world, all the while talking non-stop. It was an art, and Martin soaked it up.

"What do you think it foretells?" the Jesus Church pastor asked the general population of male taco eaters. He cupped his ear as if seeking word from above.

"End times?" Martin's sustained jocularity got some laughs.

The Apex Recycling boss, Pat, winked at Martin, said, "Amen."

This Pat was a guy bright with fun facts about the chaos of life, and the group always listened up. Now he repeated something about the new forklift hire up from the South, this kid with the doomed middle name of Robert E. Lee. "He carries his birth certificate in a Ziplock. Darrell Robert E. Lee Moore."

An old Tire King who favored the ZZ Top look egged him on. "What trouble you figure he'll face for that again? I mean, who'd be coming at him, Feds or what?"

"With no actual singular middle name, and so no *one* initial to use? You can't write that whole mess on any official form. What were the parents thinking? Nothing. Nothing at all."

Again: "Bro" and "friggin A," and, added on: "hillbillies." Feet scuffed and an exclamatory belch added pop.

Rev needed to claim the stage again, keep to his script. "People are saying expect sinkholes, the swallowing of house and home with this operation. And our *Native brethren* are saying their ancestral bones will rise and curse the land."

"You're listening now to pagans?" the Apex boss goaded.

"We've got to stick together, people," Rev said as the group of guys edged away from him, the usual.

He abruptly switched to a low tone, catching Martin at the trash can. "Say, is Holly seeing anyone? Come clean. I need to know. I'll block her out, if so. I'll do so with grace. I'll turn my attention toward another gal. Just tell me, man. I'm laying my heart out here. I have recourse to the cross but damn."

The guy was gripping his orange soda bottle and dreaming of sin. Yearning, there was nothing more exquisite, the thing, not a god, that motored and united the human race, Martin might say, if they ever got into it.

"Why'd Holly go megachurch when she had me right here?"

"More people?" Martin offered. Rev, too, fell into the perv age classification—and possibly active perv status. After his butting into a prayer circle mid-lament, Holly had moved quickly away and then, by letter, ousted him from NuUze. Alone with Martin she'd cried, "Is this *it*? This is all I attract?"

"I'm praying for a clean fork in the road, a sign to go to A or B. Let me show you something." Rev nudged Martin's elbow and motioned him around to the far side of the taco truck. Here a tall pink fiberglass fence blocked off card tables where no bro would be caught sitting on folding chairs to eat tacos. Martin had helped the Martinez men haul this stuff from NuUze months ago. A huge batch of wavy fiberglass sheets used for some "art installation" had been unloaded on NuUze. Only a wuss would go back there behind a pink fence to eat tacos. For all anyone knew, the occasional baby enjoyed a change of diaper on said tables. Crayons were scattered like pick-up sticks on the nearest one.

But there, knowing nothing at all, sat the stunningly non-bro, with back hunched to humanity: boss lady Candy. She'd made her huffy way out of NuUze and down the road just this puny short way? Her lunch of sorts glistened in the sun, chips and salsa. Due to superstition, fear of the fryolater, Martin never touched chips or fries. Candy sitting at the card table, with chips before her, looked adversarial—and compelling. Her neck showed shockingly naked to the eye, to the elements, and pink beyond sense. The fiberglass, Martin realized, was glowing up the area with pink light. The frowsy sway of the canopied oaks above confirmed the freakishness of Candy's pinked-up presence below. She was a lost trekker. She sat tapping at her phone.

Rev's voice lowered into the panting range. "Is she approachable? I'm suffering, brother, but could this be the light of the Lord on my case? I must wipe out Holly's dissing me."

Martin shushed the guy. "I know her. Go back out front. Get another soda. Pray, whatever, and I'll deal." He spoke with cool authority because it had come clear in the bath of pink light: "She's waiting for me."

Here's the universe as Martin saw it: a woman's hunched shoulders signaled need; a man's the readiness to fight. With contrived confidence Martin came from behind calling out, "Hello, there."

Candy jerked her head up. "It's you," she said.

"I see you stopped for lunch," Martin said. Unbidden, he pulled out a chair to sit facing her. Candy. "Candace," he said.

Her head began a moppish sweep of the air, back and forth. Candy might clear her mind of this whole business with extravagant gesture, denial, but here before her was the evidence of engagement: a cardboard boat overflowing with tortilla chips so thin as to look translucent, no doubt fried at the highest heat possible. Martin looked away from them. Three saucers of salsa were lined up as cheerily as traffic signals: red, green and something brownish yellow. Idleness not being her forte, Candy began tucking in.

"GPS failure," she said through the shield of chomping.

According to his increasingly enraged ex-wife, Martin's talking while chewing had revealed a form of low-class disregard of her. *Anything that comes out through such disgusting mash is worthless. I am not listening to you.* By then the initial attraction and early comfort of her fussy-bossiness and Martin's complementary calm, and even his compliant patience in dress shops meant nothing. She had listened to his office tales, and he had fondly absorbed her gossipy dramas. She worked backstage for a theatre company, after all, *"never a dull moment!"* From the start she'd inexplicably gone hot whenever he wore his black jeans. The sweet mysteries! But the years had soured his wife to hostility expressed in murmurs that increasingly spiked on up the scale to hollering accusations. Only a brief palimpsest of sympathy rose from the old days to soften her face when Martin explained he had what the doctor called "deformed sperm." What was he to make of her theatrical yet deadly calm response: *I see. Yes, it's like the sad understudy who doesn't have a chance.* Martin being Martin had evidently ruined her life with dullness. It was not in his nature to fight. He retreated to work, to silence, while bringing home bakery treats that they'd both loved and even a stash of old *Weekly World News* covers with their mad accounts like "Sugar-coated baby born to chocoholic mother," what they'd hooted over together; all this seeming to increase the wife's rage. And by the way, Martin should note that he had nothing in common with Daniel Craig, nothing, not even with an ancient Tony Bennett. If holding his wife and laughing could banish such nonsense, fine, please, but no, not allowed. He became yet more turbulently mute, and the wife finally left.

Candy admitted, "I couldn't find my way out of these lanes. So, yes, I stopped."

"Nice to see you again," Martin said, and this was tinged with truthfulness. Even as a fish out of water here, so to speak, away from NuUze Candy looked, well, more a part of the world somehow. She'd taken off something, a suit jacket or blazer, whatever it might be called for women. The shockingly humble white t-shirt, enhanced with a little necklace of purple stones, betrayed an antic speck of heart.

"Those men—I wasn't sure—they just hang around this taco truck or what? No one said a word as I came to the window and I wondered about criminal activity. Had I interrupted some kind of transaction? Was I a witness? No one said hello."

"They're shy," Martin decided to tell her. "Small-business guys. Surprised."

"It was too late to turn back. The old woman, the kids, I thought, well, I guess I'm safe. The old woman seated me. Am I? Safe?"

"Oh, yes," said Martin. "I told guys I know you. And when you're done eating I'm happy to escort you out, give you clear directions."

"From the Bottoms." Porn curls shook again. "I've missed my next appointment anyway." Chomp, chomp.

"Can I get you a drink, something?" Spoken as if this were a date, as if Martin reposed in a fine restaurant suavely ready to signal a waiter, something he'd never been good at. The wife again: *Servant stock showing*, she'd interpreted his diffidence. *Basic manners, basic.* Her withering scorn he'd *practiced* blotting out in the after times. He hoped she was happier now, so nix these intrusions. But chips and salsa without water or Coke for Candy? "Mexican soda comes in four flavors here. You might go for the tamarind."

"I'm fine," Candy said, pulling back into boss-lady mode a moment, then softening again. "Really, but thanks. I don't know Mexican food and I'm not actually hungry." Still, she stuffed in more chips, fast, noisily.

Sitting across from a woman for any reason at all kicked in the spirit of long-lost ordinariness. Martin: might he have an amusing tale to tell, same as the other guys? He scrambled, he searched around the pleasing idea of Mar*teen* Martinez and stumbled onto the doughy old Midwestern chant from childhood: My name is *Yon Yonson, I come from Wisconson.* Not right, not right at all. He seized on the Apex Recycling story. He plunged into it, repeated ". . . and a middle name Robert E. Lee? You can't put that on any form. What were the parents thinking? Nothing, nothing at all."

Candy was staring at him, a chip held midway from dipping to her mouth. Okay, the Robert E. Lee middle name story didn't translate out of the Bottoms crowd. Fine, okay, then maybe she deserved Yon Yonson. "You have a variety of salsas there," he said in the practiced tone of his NuUze life. "The darkish one I'm sure is chipotle."

Candy worked her jaws in a winningly hesitant attempt at pronunciation: "Chi-i-i-p . . ."

Martin repeated slowly, "Chipotle. Like the restaurants? Chipotle. The pepper is smoky compared with just——" Her eyes had hardened on him, and he hurried, "compared to that tomato salsa or the green, the tomatillo you have there."

"Chi . . ."

That hiss again. It was the old steam pipe hiss she'd laid on them in NuUze when the immigrants, yes Spanish-speaking immigrants, were switching prices. She was remembering this? Where did she think she was eating, anyway? This is a Mexican food truck, cut the disdain, lady.

"Chi . . ."

"Never mind," Martin said, "let's drop it. I understand. Not everyone can get the Spanish. I like it. I wonder, do you remember my name? I go by Mar*teen* here."

"Chi . . ." hissed Candy and now her eyes were popping with a dark flare, and her hands were busy, one fiddling at her chest, the purple stones aquiver, the other flagging the air with that chip—oh, what women managed: the wife toyed with hair before the bombshell adieu—but wait, no, Candy's voice had gone to a low gurgling. Martin leaped out of his chair.

"Candy!" He came around her from behind and hauled her up, chair clattering to the side, and yanked at her chest—this was the way, he knew this—yanked again. Paused, started again.

A dim cry of "he's mauling the lady!" came at him, fists at his back following, as just then in a great moaning strangulation of sound a wet blob of chip coughed free of Candy's mouth. She was gasping, slumping forward onto the table and Martin, unthinkingly, continued to hold on, bending with her, cocooning her over the table, stunned at the entire world and the shock of quick-breathing life under his hands, the heart throbbing all down her front with bird breaths, and it wasn't until she'd struggled free and staggered to sitting and Rev stopped pounding on his back that Martin realized too: breasts. He'd been touching them. Holding them. He looked at Candy, couldn't look. He'd lifted beneath, felt soft breasts heaving. The lost world had once held such tenderness. He stood hunched still. He said, "My God, I'm sorry. I'm so sorry." And Martin began to cry.

"That's right," said hoppy Rev. "Feel the sin. Repent. That's the way."

Candy continued to pant. "No" seemed to be all she could say, a gravelly "no." Then, "No, really."

"I'm a pastor," Rev explained. "I will minister to you. I apologize for this incident."

"No," Candy said. "No, really. Mar*teen*?"

She knew him. He'd swallowed down the blubbering tears fast and now anger and thrill were harshing out of his throat. "I panicked. I overdid."

"I couldn't breathe. I just couldn't breathe."

Martin heard a suck of breath behind him. Rev had backed off but wouldn't leave the scene.

"I was trying to tell you *chip*, a chip was stuck, and then it got worse," she said.

"I thought you were dismissing me, and I was caught up. I was small-minded, defensive, awful—and I hate chipotle. I'm so sorry."

By now the gang of male taco eaters, Grandma Martinez, Mr. Martinez and the whole clan had crowded into the sheltered eating area and the sun was high and hard, determined in its throw down of mad pink light. What it might foretell, Martin thought, was nothing, or nothing anyone would know. But they had a common look of being receded, stamped in a memory of pink.

"Will you ride with me out of here?" The look Candy gave Martin enfolded in it the knowledge that he'd touched her hard and intimately. "I'm going to stop back at the store."

"Yes, you'll drop me at the store," Martin said briskly.

On the short drive Candy said, "I'm taking that sign with me. It's a souvenir of another big day I didn't die. Sorry, I sound crass. I mean, look, I was scared."

Martin had held breasts, some ancient old-world ritual forgotten, dreamed up in him again, and Candy had seen him cry. Wonder kept them mute, driving on. And neither expressed surprise when they saw, on approaching the store, that the sign stood, uncurled, by the door, freshly painted an urgent red: *NuNuUze!* Holly, Jude, and hoppy Donny quit hand-holding with a whoop, evidently finishing off an outdoor prayer circle. They stood gesturing at the sign. His people, they were. You had to laugh, a little. Maybe a faint one soughed from Candy too.

She'd stopped on the road with the engine idling. "I mean it, thanks. I'm kind of wrecked. Thanks, really."

"I'll get the sign," Martin said and charged off, but he came back empty-handed. "I'm sorry. They—I didn't tell them everything, but they want the sign, Jude does, for a while anyway, for school. Crazy, but there it is." But rushing on were more words, as he climbed back into the SUV. "You know, we've been shaken up and kind of shaken loose together. Why not just cruise around a little?" He might have been the cow to slaughter, hit by a hammer, staggered in the trance of hope right before the end.

Candy was looking straight ahead and squeezing the wheel with both hands. Martin had spoken loudly, a good feeling, it had been so long since he'd been loud. The wife leaving had taken her hands from her ears and shut him down with her poisonous last words that meant to burn through him forever, right now, before this, or any other woman: *I didn't mind your thick peasant dick, you know—but really.*

But really, yearning ignited now knew only its need: courage. Forget the hammer, yearning was the unbeatable ace drawn and flung down. Heated up to hope, it could burn scorn to ash, and here it was.

"Candy," Martin said, likewise looking straight ahead as one of Jude's expressions seized him, "let's blow this pop stand." He bungled a little laugh, as his left hand went the distance and touched her, lightly now, what, skin, surely the crook of her arm, just that—don't panic, don't look—the gesture of a gentleman, please, really, one just reaching. ■

"Balance" by Janet Wormser. Gouache on paper, 10 x 12 inches.

BARON WORMSER

Moving Pictures

"Hollywood," my mother, who grew up with black
And white, would sigh at the movie's end, which meant
Rank melodrama, implausible happiness, actresses
Adjusting their stardom to dialogue and dresses

("Katherine Hepburn played Katherine Hepburn")
And rueful dismissal of glamour, the tinsel-town
Effect that searched out obscure emotional corners
And threw my mother's longings into a limpid,

Remorseless light that led to more sitting
In the socially permitted darkness, everyone quiet—
Anxious bodies at rest—as the basic tale
Unraveled its breathless self, the one of love

Overcoming unlove, of a woman clutching
Whatever she could clutch—a man, a child,
A rolling pin, a steering wheel—and looking straight
Ahead at what did not, could not await her.

Graveyard, Virginia City, Nevada

(for SG)

Beneath the sun-bleached sky
Shipwrecked sailors from the seven seas,
Unnamed and named, once filled with ardor for all
That glittered in the silver gloaming.

Any visitor can feel it:
An almost alkali echo of grief,
The final chorale of these seekers
Who came to try their fortunes—as if fortune
Cared.

   "You'll never amount to anything."
Or "A mansion awaits you."
Somewhere. Nowhere. Some way. No way.
The adages never lacking for a clumsy word.

You bore up and bore down and foundered
And now and then succeeded at games of chance
In saloons and mines, though winning could be
More bitter than losing—all the easy pickings
There for the sleight-of-hand taking.

       And then?
The vast unmoored nation, vast stunned landscape,
Perhaps a death-bed confession. Or not.
The ends of the earth are someone's home.
Desolation has its perfections.

JIM HEYNEN

Coronavirus in Hiding

It wasn't my idea in the first place.
It's not as if I created myself, you know.
It's not as if I ever had malicious intent.
Like everything and everyone else,
I just want to be myself.
I want to be left alone.
It's you who came after me,
Not me after you.
Keep that straight.

Unspoken Words

There is so much not to be said.
The heft of the unspoken word
Resonates louder than the spoken.
It probes and invades the unknown.

Even now, my mind scurries
To think of what not to say.
I can't say it! I can't say it!
Though it has something to do with love.

Crescent Moon

The sharp toenail
Scratches the evening sky.

I invite it down
And attach it to my left big toe.

Such a simple way
To put my world back together.

O. ALAN WELTZIEN

Tobacco

At the shingle beach
we watch a Filipino teenager
raise a pack of cigarettes
with his right arm
as he side strokes
through small chop
a hundred meters
out to an anchored bangka.*

Like a hooked periscope
his crooked arm
carries the pack above waves,
a pennant or chalice.
His high arm
shrinks and I picture
eager hands grasping his offering
then him
and they tear off the plastic
and pass, shake out a cigarette
and light up.

Later on our bangka
the steersman fires up
sucks deeply
and as I watch
I damp down our family's history
of lung cancer deaths,
the gap between these slight, short men
and my wife's campaigns
banning tobacco products
from the campus where we worked.

I can't swim across this gap,
blink away that tiny arm aloft.

* *"Bangka" refers to Filipino double-outrigger boats without sails, an exoskeleton constructed from lashed bamboo poles*

"Untitled" by Alberta Mayo. Mixed media, 4 x 6 inches.

MARGARET PETTIS

Forget this Body

Unfurled on
needles pebbled
with pine nuts, a
pink orchid tattoos
the wild shoulder
of Wheeler Peak.
Star shine unmasks
at my tiny campfire
on sultry Snake
Creek.

At the girth of
Nowhere, moonlit
clouds chug over the
Confusion Range.
I slip into the sweet
arms of the Great
Basin breeze and
forget this body.

I am a spider buffeted
on a windy web. I am a
lion caterwauling in the
canyon. I am a
bristlecone sensing
another century.
I am nothing.
I am everything.

"Untitled" by Alberta Mayo. Mixed media, 4 x 6 inches.

GEOF HEWITT

People These Parts

People these parts talk like this,
at least some of them, Vermonters.
Seems we "flatlanders" found refuge, comfort
in their values, plus the landscape.
Why, we could grow our own food!

Not sure we were welcome at first,
fast-talking-from-somewhere or drive-too-fast,
but we were the ones whose cars they rescued
from snowbanks, refusing compensation,
maybe telling the story later with a laugh.

Vermont can be tough when your pipes freeze
that first winter here, and a fool crawls under the sink
with a hand-held propane torch and manages
not to start a fire and not to thaw the pipes,
and thus a lesson is learned: "Hell, it worked last time!"

If not from mistakes, maybe we learn
from the "what ifs?" of memory,
knowledge-too-late that one was a joke on a ladder
leaned against the house all three stories,
hoisted cinderblocks and mortar for a chimney.

Oh, and forgot to mix sand with the mortar,
so the thing kinda weaved.
Wendell Savage was born in that house,
squinted up at the chimney, touched his chin:
"I never saw smoke that wouldn't bend."

Haiku

Red-breasted nuthatch
Flies to trunk of old maple
Head down, moons the sky.

                                    Smart-ass butterfly!
                                    Pretends the wind is blowing
                                    Where he wants to go.

Missing two front teeth
I find folks much kinder now.
They speak more slowly.

JAY JOHNSON

Tough

They were smoking in the boys' room at Mesa Springs High School, October of 1962. The odor of burning tobacco barely overrode the institutional cleanser, and the sunlight had sharp autumn clarity, except where the smoke disturbed it. There the smoke was blue and bright as it rose to the high ceiling. Water ran in one of the sinks. Second period bell had just rung, nine-ten.

Amos Brown kept his eye on the door and his right hand near the open window, ready to throw his cigarette out. It was a matter of form, not wanting to be caught with the goods, even if it made no difference in the punishment. Dick Murrel also stood by the window. Brett Veblan asked for a smoke. "I'm short this week," he said. The others understood. Brett's father could barely afford the fuel for his tractor. Amos wished Brett would keep his embarrassment to himself.

"Amos is short every day. Every day of every week," Dick said. "He can't help it any more than you can." Amos glared at Dick and inhaled from his cupped hand. He was by far the littlest of the three, with a strawberry bruise on his cheekbone and a swelling eyelid and bruised knuckles, and his delicate-looking hair was disheveled. He shook out a cigarette from his pack of Winstons and offered it to Brett. The door opened and a voice called in, "All clear out here."

"Then keep the damn door closed, and shut up," Dick said. He sucked on his cigarette and said to Amos, "You know, Mouse, I think Mr. Birk knows every time you get thrown in the girls' bathroom and come out fighting. You know why? He never comes in here to root us out. I think he knows we come in here to cool it. What do you think?"

Amos thought for a moment. "Might be right. I don't know."

"Might make it worthwhile throwing you in the girls' room," suggested Dick.

Amos gave him a hard look, as the others glanced back and forth between the two. Dick laughed it off. "Hey, I was just saying . . ."

"How would you like it, you jerk?"

"Some guys might like it, Mouse."

"Don't call him Mouse," said Brett.

105

"Aw, ease up. We've called him Mouse forever. I can't change how I think, at least that easily."

"So he's gotta just get used to what happens, and what he gets called?"

"Like I said, ease up. And if he didn't go so wild, he wouldn't get punched out all the time."

"I get in my licks," countered Amos.

"Not as many as you get."

Amos didn't reply. He straightened up and glanced in the mirror.

"Lookit, Murrel, you don't just let people shove you around. At least, I don't," said Amos. Brett nodded, and Amos grinned. "Besides, you just said it gives you a free chance to smoke in here. Isn't that what you just said?" Dick nodded in response.

A yellowjacket flew in the window. It buzzed around as if burdened, and Amos swatted it out of the air with his *Street Rodder* magazine, and smacked it again as it lay in the sink. He took a pencil from Dick's shirt pocket and used it with his own pen to pick up the wasp and put it in a urinal. He flushed it, but the torrent missed the insect and it continued to struggle.

"Look at that son of a bitch," he said. "Still fighting."

"Great," said Dick. "Watching dead bugs in the pisser."

"Look at this." Amos poked at the wasp and flinched at the angry response, the twitching of the probing thorax. But the insect was crippled and captive.

Mouse, that's your pencil now," Dick said. Amos looked at it.

"Thanks," he said.

"Welcome. Now I got an excuse not to do my homework."

"First time you needed an excuse." Amos flushed the urinal again. "Amazing. Still swimming."

Brett moved over to watch. "They told us about this in biology class," he said. Dick burst out laughing, and Amos grinned.

"I must have missed that class, Veblan," said Amos. "Sometimes I forget where I'm supposed to be. So, you learned about dying bugs in the toilet? Swimming bees? Flushing bees?" Dick laughed again and coughed on his smoke.

"The yellowjacket crawl," he wheezed, and laughed more, and Amos laughed. Even Brett laughed.

"Forget it," he said.

"No! No, don't forget it, Veblan," Dick insisted. "C'mon. They wouldn't let me into biology class. Said I wasn't smart enough. But you! C'mon, tell us." He beckoned with his hands. "C'mon," he coaxed.

Brett weighed his options. Finally, he announced, "Bees are going to inherit the Earth."

Dick and Amos looked at each other and rolled their eyes as if on cue. There was a knock on the door, and they threw their cigarettes out the window. Dick's little brother Craig came in.

"Mr. Birk just went by," he reported.

"Good," said Dick. "Did he say anything?"

"No. Didn't even look at me."

"Great. Go keep looking."

"I left Elizabeth out there."

"Yeah, great. Looks totally normal hanging around the boys' bathroom. Idiot." He shoved Craig. "Getting your own sister in trouble. Get out of here." The little brother gave him the finger and ran out as Dick half-lunged for him. Craig's shoes scuffed on the tile, and then they heard his heel taps on the linoleum outside. Dick turned to Brett.

"Yeah, so, Veblan. The bees are going to all kill us off and have this great big beautiful world to themselves."

"They aren't going to kill us off. We're probably going to kill ourselves off, or there will be a big weather change we can't survive. There are periodic glacial periods, and . . . well, all species have life-spans. The advanced species. But there are so many of them, and so many kinds, some of them are sure to survive, no matter what happens. Evolution."

"Yeah? No kidding? We're advanced, so we'll be the ones to die off? Sounds backwards to me. But I wasn't smart enough to get in that class. Gonna come in handy on your ranch?"

Brett's face clouded. "I pay attention in class," he said.

"You know enough about biology, you'd think you'd know enough to quit ranching."

"My dad's a rancher, I'm not."

"Yeah, you're just a cowboy. But you're so broke you might as well be a rancher."

"Ranchers raise your food, you jerk."

"And get mighty well paid for it," Dick answered. "I appreciate you feeding me, Brett. And now how come your daddy owes us so much money?"

"That's business, not ranching."

"They're supposed to be the same. Ranching is a business, for smart ranchers."

"You don't throw our beef away because we're poor. I can't help it if a tractor costs more than I'll ever earn in my life."

Amos lit a match and threw it at Dick's feet. "You're being a jerk, Dick, you know that? You don't know jack, and you just keep on talking."

"Yeah, I do keep talking. Keep the pencil, Mouse." He walked out the door, held it open and yelled back in, "You like it more in the *boys'* room, Mouse?" He slammed the door. Amos and Brett stared briefly at the door, and returned their attention to the dying wasp in the urinal. It barely moved.

"Looks like this one ain't going to inherit nothing," Brett said, smiling.

"Nope," Amos said. He sighed and looked in the mirror. "Well, I guess I feel better now." He touched his cheek with a damp paper towel. "I suppose that jerk is right about me scrapping with those other jerks."

"He might be right about Birk not chasing us out of here. Beside that, what's his point? He watches the fight just like everyone else. And he's never had anybody push him around."

"That's for sure. He does his share of pushing. Obnoxious prick." He looked at Brett in the mirror and shrugged. "He doesn't throw me in the girls' bathroom, anyway."

"He might, if he thought it wouldn't cost him," said Brett. "Let's go."

"Yeah. Want another cigarette?"

"Sure, buddy. Thanks." He put it in his shirt pocket, underneath his worn sweater.

* * * * *

Brett got permission from Scott Moseley, the shop teacher, to bring the ranch pickup into the high school shop to repair the brakes. The pedal got mushy, and Brett figured it out quickly enough and added fluid and bled the system at home. But the source of the leak was the master cylinder—fluid was leaking out through the back. He would rebuild the cylinder, but he needed a clean place to work. Brett had taken most of Moseley's classes.

Amos saw the old Ford pulling into the shop, which was usually off-limits for family rigs after school hours. He walked inside and saw Brett pushing a floor jack into place under the rig, selecting a good lift spot.

"Hey, Veblen, breaking the rules. Again. What's going on here?" he asked.

"Mr. Moseley gave me permission, since the brakes were going out."

Amos grabbed a shop creeper and scooted under the old pickup. "Want some help?" he offered. The shop floor was terrific, good smooth concrete, undamaged.

"Yeah, that'd be great. I'll need a hand bleeding them when I'm done, anyway."

Amos grabbed the front of the jack to guide it into place under the front crossmember. A drip of brake fluid hit him in his neck, and he swatted at it in surprise. The master cylinder was right above him, bolted to the frame, but directly underneath the driver position.

"Whoa! Damn! Thought that was a bug. Found your leak, man."

"Yeah, that's the leak all right. Coming out pretty good. Better wipe that fluid off."

Brett raised the front of the pickup and put jackstands in place. Amos avoided another drip, scooting back. "That is the weirdest spot for master cylinder ever. What moron would put a master cylinder there? How are you supposed to get to it?"

Brett laughed. "Well, it's right above you now, pretty easy to get out."

"And you put fluid in it . . . how?"

"Access through a panel in the floor board."

"Sheer genius. Like that's going to be accessible. Clean." He grabbed the frame above him and scooted easily about. "And here's the battery, also hidden from anyone who wants to find it. What is this thing again? You haven't had it that long."

"1954 F-100. Government surplus, was Forest Service."

"Run off a steam engine or what?"

"223, like you didn't know. Good little motor."

"This thing ought to be in a museum. Look at it." He slid back to look at the master cylinder. "This thing is a single piston master cylinder! Crap! Ought to be illegal!" He emerged from underneath the truck, and popped up from the creeper. "Tell you what. We can convert that thing into a tandem master cylinder set-up, and it'll be way safer. We'll check out some from the wrecking yard, and something will fit."

"I already got the overhaul kit. It'll be fine. I appreciate your concern. Now shut up."

"Still want some help?"

"Only if you shut up."

Amos went to the shop's tool pegboard and selected two wrenches for the brake fittings. "Seriously, we could convert this into something safer."

"I looked into it. Moseley made me look into it, since he had the same reaction. Nothing more modern will bolt in there. I checked the parts house and the wrecking yard. Nothing. I bought an overhaul kit. Eleven bucks. Dad squawked."

"What else was he going to do, drive with no brakes? That's what you get with an antique."

"That truck's half your age, dummy."

"Belongs in a museum. Single master cylinder. Probably manual adjusters"

"Good little truck."

"It's kinda used up. And a technical dinosaur."

"You were going to shut up."

Amos had freed the line fittings, unclipped the linkage and unbolted the cylinder, and he handed it up to Brett. Bret made fast work of cleaning the exterior, air-dried it and disassembled the piston and seals within a few minutes. He shone light down the bore, ran a finger in that same bore, and then grabbed an electric drill and a honing tool, breaking the glaze in the old bore. He cleaned up the residue scrupulously, spread out the contents of his overhaul kit, and reassembled it. He handed it silently to Amos, who handed it back. "Why don't you bench-bleed it first?"

"I was going to. Just had to get your approval," Brett said. Amos snorted.

Brett located the shop brake fluid and bench-bled the cylinder. Amos installed it in the frame of the truck, and they bled the system. Brett adjusted each wheel, just as he'd been taught in Moseley's class.

"Thanks to the Mesa Spring Board of Education for the brake fluid," said Amos.

"Mr. Moseley said I need to replace it," Brett said.

"He had to say that. He didn't mean it."

"He said it, he meant it, and I'm going to do it. Test drive this thing, will you? I'll sweep up."

Amos test drove it in the school parking lot. The sun was low, lighting up the clouds in the early autumn sky. Amos revved the truck, jerked it to stop, drove it with the brakes dragging slightly, and finally parked it. Brett finished the shop, flipped off the lights, and locked the overhead doors. He drove Amos home.

* * * * *

Amos and Dick were seniors, but Brett had been held back a year. He would start school days later than the others, then would miss days stretching into weeks sometimes, depending on the demands of his father's ranch. In the spring of his freshman year his schedule became really erratic. He didn't arrange to take his final exams at the end of the year, and he never made up that lost time. He did not make that mistake again; he just had not known that exams were as important as they turned out to be.

His father had been hurt four years before. Ben Veblan had tried to free up a drum on his hay swather by kicking it with his heel. The engine was running and the drum freed, but his pant leg got caught on a tine of the drum. The foot never worked quite right after that. He could run equipment, but he couldn't repair fence alone or chase strays or the other real cattle work, at least by himself. There was always plenty to do, and plenty for a couple of extra hands to do, but some work never got done because he couldn't pay an extra man. Ben Veblan had inherited a ranch in debt, and he wasn't going to break the pattern in this generation. He wasn't going to leave the land, either. He'd get his two cuttings of hay each summer, sell a little alfalfa, keep enough hay to feed his stock through the winter, and if he had a good year he might make up a little ground against the debt. When he was younger he had raised potatoes as a cash crop, but that was no longer worth the effort, and he had never liked farming anyway. He had little arable land, and his water rights, although tolerable, required extensive ditch work each year. It took time. Most of his land was too rocky and the vegetation too sparse and tough to graze his cattle on through the summer.

By far the best deal he had was the summer grazing rights on some U.S. Forest Service land. Before it got hot in mid-June, he and the boy and a Mexican day-laborer would take the herd on an old-fashioned cattle drive into the high country, where there were hundreds of acres and a couple of outbuildings and miles of fence. That federal lease was one obligation he paid on time. Murrel's Co-op Feed and Ag Supply, where he bought diesel and salt blocks and fence wire, they would have to wait, often until after the October cattle sale in Delta.

Brett would rise early and work on the ranch before school, then sometimes drove the ranch pick-up to school late, and most often he checked the cattle and irrigation ditches after classes. In the spring when the calves would drop, he sometimes was absent from school for days. After his freshman year problem, he called and got his assignments. Weekends, he worked.

Amos "Mouse" Brown was uncommonly small, five foot three inches as a senior, and still growing, wiry and thin. As a freshman, the wrestling coach had asked him to try out for the team the next year, and said he would probably have to gain some weight to be competitive even in the lightest weight class. The coach liked the fight in the dog. Hallway and schoolyard battles, for some reason the boy figured he had to fight "fair," despite weighing half that of some of his tormentors. They could throw him several feet when they got a handle on him. Amos never joined the team, but joined the hot-rod club instead. A different arena, but he never stepped out of the combat zone. He certainly didn't back down.

Maybe his scrappiness contributed to the problem. Underclassmen wanted to test the senior, and he often got thrown through the door into the girls' room. He learned to extract an increasing toll, but as Dick Murrell said, he got banged up in the process.

His dad was small, too, short and light, but he told Amos he would eventually get some growth, just as he and his father before him had kept growing late. George Brown owned an Army surplus store, very small-time, and he made some money gambling. More small-time.

* * * * *

Eight weeks after Brett Veblan's bathroom lecture on evolution, he and Amos were looking forward to the after-Christmas Blizzard Ball, the annual shindig sponsored by the Cattlemen's Association. It was open to all the kids in the county, but the Association had special significance to Brett. The Association represented successful ranchers; his father was a shirttail cousin to them.

The Blizzard was three weeks after Amos got cited for excessive speed and for street-racing, headed west toward Rifle. George Brown collapsed his newspaper in his lap.

"No, you can't take the Olds to the dance. I'm sorry I bought that car. I was sorry right after I bought it. No sense in having a motor that big."

"We could put another motor in it."

"What, so you could have the one it's got? Fat chance, son."

"Just a thought. If it would make you more comfortable about letting me borrow it. We could put in a motor out of some old dog."

George shook his head in disbelief. "I guess you don't get it. You don't understand. Otherwise you wouldn't argue. This is a punishment."

"They haven't taken my license away."

"No, so I have to take the car away. Besides, they *will* take the license, soon enough. If not this time, the next."

"You know I can drive as safe as anybody," Amos said.

"Do I?"

"I'll let Brett drive."

"Brett is less hot-headed than you? Hmmm. Well, maybe he is." He paused. "Nope. Sorry. You might have to let me drive."

"C'mon, Dad. I'm seventeen."

"That ought to be enough to end the argument right there. Perhaps you should join the debate club instead of the hot-rodders." Amos pinched his nose in response. "You certainly have the attitude, you just haven't developed your delivery."

"So I ought to do what I'm good at."

"Well, you're good at arguing. But race cars? Argue instead, son. You can make just as big a fool of yourself, without killing anyone.

You think it's a safe bet for me to let you take that Olds, with that big-block engine you've already shown a taste for racing, have it full of kids on a winter night, and get egged on into a race. Not a good bet," George said.

"Good bet? Safe bet? Is this some sort of high stakes long shot? If you're so worried about a safe bet why in the hell do you give credit to old man Veblan?" Amos asked.

George cocked his head, eyebrows raised. "What in the hell does that have to do with this? What I do with my business has nothing to do with how I raise my family. Except for making a living. But yes, incidentally, these are high stakes. They don't get any higher."

"Yeah, well, you're a gambler, and you're a businessman, and you're my old man. You're willing to gamble in your business, you gamble at cards and dice, and you won't gamble on me driving safely? Shoot, I could chauffeur President Kennedy. Believe me, I'm a safe bet."

George drummed his fingers on his formica-topped end table, and slid an old Cinzano ashtray at his son. "I don't gamble in my business. Let me tell you something about Ben Veblan. I know Ben Veblan." He offered his son a cigarette.

"Yeah, you know him. You gamble on him paying all the time."

"Listen. That's the way the economy works here. Credit. Besides, what do you have against Ben Veblan? Aren't you buddies with his kid?"

Amos lit the cigarette. "Yeah. But I'd rather take your car than Veblan's truck."

George inhaled and exhaled slowly. "Ben Veblan works his butt off. He's a completely honorable man. Broke, though. There's nothing we can do but keep him going when he's broke, and we know he'll pay, eventually."

"You see what he drives? I bet we end up going to the dance in his beat-up old truck that won't even get out of its own way. We have *dates*, Dad. Four people in the cab of that old thing? C'mon."

"Yeah, hopefully you'll go to the dance in somebody else's car, because you're not going in mine. Sorry. But I'll tell you something—Ben is one proud man. He hates owing people, and he's had to swallow that since he was a kid. He covers it up. He came into the store about three years ago, needed a shovel and length of chain with a couple of grab-hooks, as I recall. Seems like an old ranch would have shovels and plenty of chain around. He said he needed 'em.

"He comes in and gets this stuff, and he says, 'I see this totals eighteen fifty-five.' Three years ago, mind you. And I'd already cut the chain for him.

"I say, 'Yep.'

"He says, 'I can't afford eighteen dollars.'

"I said, 'Nope? Hmm,' and I go to put the chain back by the barrel.

"He said, 'I'll give you fourteen.' So I looked at him and said, 'The price is eighteen dollars and fifty-five cents.' He says, 'I ain't got eighteen dollars, and I need a shovel and chain.' I did some quick figuring and I said, 'Okay, I'll sell it to you. I'll sell it to you for fourteen dollars and fifty cents. That's what it cost me.' And that was pretty close—he took about, let's see, fifteen foot of chain. Chain was costing me—three-eighths chain, it was—cost me about forty cents a foot, plus the hooks, plus the shovel at over four bucks, my cost. Six bucks, two bucks per hook and clevis, shovel. Fourteen.

"He says, 'Can I put it on my tab?'"

George acted out an expression of disbelief and then smiled at Amos. He spun the triangular ashtray, watched it wobble on an imperfect circle.

"I just about blew my stack. I figured he had fifteen bucks *in his jeans*, for Christsakes, if he's *dickerin'* with me! I was steaming for over a minute. He looked at me steady all this time. I turned to him and said, 'Look, I'll put it on your tab. I'll put it on your tab for eighteen dollars and fifty-five cents.'

"He looks at me and says, 'I ain't got eighteen dollars.'

"I yelled right out loud in the store, 'You ain't got five dollars! You need a shovel and chain, *take* the damn shovel and chain. You owe me eighteen bucks! And some change!' I had already cut the chain, for crying out loud!

"'Goddamn it,' he says. 'I didn't think this was a bank.'

"I says, 'It's not a bank. I'm not in the banking business. I'm in the retail surplus business. Buy low, sell high, make a profit. All that good stuff.'

"He says, 'Yeah, I'm in the ranching business,' like I didn't know, or something.

"So I say, 'Yeah, you're in the ranching business. You want a loan, go to the bank.'

"'All right,' he says, 'I'll go to the bank.' He goes away, comes back to the store, gives me fourteen dollars and fifty-five cents, and takes off with the chain and shovel. The bank probably loaned him a C-note, he banked eighty-some of it, and probably celebrated with a six-pack of pop. They'll get that hundred, but it'll take them a while. But they're banking eighty of it, like I said, and he's losing interest on that deal. If they ever decide to take that ranch, it'll be a slow process, and they won't get much out of it." His cigarette had burned to a long ash now, and he picked it up and inhaled a last time. "We got it straightened out, Ben and me." He paused again. "And he'd rather die than let it go, that ranch. Understand? It's all he can do. He won't let it go. It would kill him."

Amos said, "Dad, all I wanted to do was borrow the car."

"I thought you said you could go in Veblan's wreck. Isn't Brett going too?"

"Yeah. I told you. We . . . Brett lined us up a couple of dates."

"Good. Don't race his truck."

"Okay. Don't worry. There will be four of us in the cab. Like I said. And it's an old thing with a 223."

"Good. Have a good time." The father grinned. "It'll be cozy." He idly spun the ashtray on the formica top.

* * * * *

It was snowing lightly and starting to blow hard when they took the girls home. Over two inches of snow muffled the tire noise, and little was said. Snow tires all around on the Ford. A little rubber-bladed fan was mounted on the dash to help defrost the windshield, and the heater fan hummed, and the old-truck body rattles were quieted by the snow and ice. Brett was focused on driving, and Martha sat next to him in a satiny long dress and a military-style parka her mother had forced on her. Amanda was next to her, in a long wool coat her mother had worn earlier that day, and Amos was on the outside. No plastic on the dash or doors, straight-up utility truck, one visor only and no radio at all. Amos anxiously sat between the frigid door and Amanda, not wanting to press against her.

"Mind if I smoke?" asked Amos.

The girls, both sophomores, looked at each other. Martha smiled, and Amanda frowned, and as if cued, Martha said, "No. Well, yes, I . . . I can't stand it. So, could you wait?"

Amos sheepishly said, "Okay, sure. Can't exactly open a window." Amanda shot Martha a look that said, *thank you*. Martha smothered a giggle.

"I mean, I get a little sick from it, it seems like."

"Okay, okay, Martha. I get it. No problem." He looked at Amanda, and she caught his look, and he shrugged his shoulders slightly and raised his eyebrows, perplexed by the response. "I get it," he repeated. Amanda dug her elbow into him slightly and crinkled her nose, and mouthed, *It's okay.* Brett focused on the road, cramped by his passengers.

"Lucky it's not a floor shifter," offered Amos.

Martha laughed, and said, "Yeah, that's real lucky. Like, I don't know where I'd be sitting." Brett reddened.

"Glad we got a ride, I'll say, without my dad driving," Amos said. The girls nodded in unison.

"Yeah, thanks for driving, Brett," Amanda said.

The temperature outside was only slightly above twenty degrees. Ben Veblan had made sure there was a wool blanket in the cab, but the occupants sat on it. The drafty pickup had a huge radiator, a small half-plugged heater, and a cold thermostat that Brett had salvaged out of some blown-up baler engine. That worked well when they were harvesting hay and pulling a hay trailer in hundred-degree heat and was no help in the winter. Amos fidgeted and then leaned into the cold door, looking out into the snow past the bolt-on framed mirror.

The boys had agreed that Amanda would go home first, since it was Brett's truck and Martha was his date. Neither girl commented when they recognized the route Brett took. Amanda lived in the east part of town, on a cul-de-sac in a new development. It could have been transplanted from a Chicago suburb, but this subdivision contained empty lots and a few unsold houses and had left a developer broke.

"You know they call these houses 'ranch homes'?" Amanda said. "Isn't that weird?" Brett clenched the steering wheel.

"How quaint," Martha replied, smiling. Amos leaned forward and looked at Brett, and Martha did too, on the sly. When at last Brett stopped the truck at the broom-swept concrete path to Amanda's house, the ranch kid sighed and grinned at the girls.

"Good night, Amanda," he said.

Martha said clearly, "Call me later, Mandy," and Amos slid off the blanketed seat and hopped off the running board to the sidewalk. He took a quick step and slid on a long-frozen puddle, plowing up snow with his shoes, his body crouching like a surfer. Brett cringed and waved him back. Amos waved back and made a foolish face and hopped back to the truck. He mis-stepped on the ice and recovered his balance. As she scooted over and stepped out, Amanda said, "No doubt, Martha, I'll call." She cupped a hand and waved genteelly to Brett. Amos offered her his arm, and they walked carefully to her door. Martha had to slide over on the seat to close the door. She then came back to her spot, exactly.

At the door to her home, Amanda took Amos's right hand in both of hers and smiled. "Thanks, Amos," she said. He looked at her blankly, unsure.

"You're welcome, Amanda. I think it was my pleasure," he said, and he swallowed. He withdrew his hand, and he took her forearms and leaned forward; she leaned forward and almost closed her eyes but kept them open a slit. She pursed her lips, but her front door opened from within, and the teens stood there with light basking over them. The light illuminated the falling snow, gaining substance.

Brett and Martha sat close but motionless. She had a suggestive grin, and she wouldn't look right at Brett, but she took stock of him carefully. His odor reminded her of her grandfather, an earthy strong smell even in the cold, even all cleansed. She liked that. Brett was afraid his shivering would betray his nervousness. He glanced at the couple on the front porch, noticed their awkwardness, then saw the door open and the light envelop them.

"Hey, look," he said. Martha saw them and giggled, and he snickered. She looked back at him, and he shyly examined the instrument panel through the steering wheel; he idly stepped on the accelerator, then faced her teasing grin. Her lips were pressed shut and her eyebrows were raised in question and coyness. He shifted in the seat and bent toward her, and she moved to accommodate his posture, begging the kiss. It was little more than a dry pressing of lips, barely more than a brush. Neither of them closed an eye. They heard Amos's scuffling footsteps approach the truck, and he climbed in. He stared out his window, back at the house, afraid to look in their direction. Brett grimaced in apology. He slipped the column shifter into first and gently nursed the truck into motion.

In a few minutes, they kissed again at her doorstep. Brett murmured, "Good night" and gently held her shoulders in his strong hands. They kissed again. He felt his pulse pound and a quiver in his chest. They heard a feminine voice from within the house call out, "Is that you, Martha?" and Brett drew back.

Martha touched a finger to his lips and withdrew it and wagged it at him. She suppressed a laugh and leaned forward and kissed him again. Then she answered loudly, "Yeah, Mom, it's me. Expecting anyone else?" She squeezed his hand as she turned the doorknob, then she released him and stepped inside, trailing her hand behind to wave good-bye. He too was then flooded in light as she switched on the porch light. Martha poked her head outside the door and added, "Thanks!" and looked out at the idling truck and yelled, "Good night, Amos! Thanks!"

Brett stood as if stunned, then waved awkwardly and turned and jogged carefully to the truck. "Helluva night," he said. "Let's go get a coffee." He snugged up his overcoat tight around his suit coat, as if to stop shivering.

"Fine by me," Amos said. "The A to Z?"

"Unless you know some other place open this hour," Brett replied.

The A to Z was the only place like it for miles, a highway fixture with big neon and plastic, and diesel smoke clouding the sign. The food wasn't good; the scent was a mix of diesel, deep-fry oil, and seared hamburger. It was open twenty-four hours, and the back room had a liquor license.

There was a half-moon somewhere above the snow clouds. The rate of snowfall was unsteady now, and occasionally the sky would brighten. They could see the outline of clouds moving fast.

The highway west of town ran through mostly ranch land, and on a rise there was an apple orchard. Patches of cottonwood stood where the irrigation ditches ran close to the highway. Just past a billboard, a deer crossing was marked with a yellow diamond road sign, then a speed limit sign, and a billboard for the A to Z. Amos lit a cigarette. Brett looked down at the speedometer—forty-five miles per hour, needle bouncing and the mechanism chattering at that speed because the drive cable was old and dry. From the right side of the highway a doe mule deer sprang up from a ditch and stopped on the road. She stared in panic.

"Watch it!" Amos shouted, and Brett cursed. He swerved left and hit the deer in its shoulder and foreleg, smashing it with his right fender. The rear of the truck started to spin, Brett overcorrected, and it spun out left across the highway. A rear tire bashed into a solid frozen snowbank, bounced, and the front end hit a soft spot in the snowbank and stopped hard. Amos crashed forward into the windshield, and the steering wheel bent a couple inches from the force of Brett's weight, his strong grip averting more damage. The animal had gotten caught briefly on the framed mirror before falling off the truck. The right headlight pointed crazily into the sky.

"Stupid muley," Brett said. "Damn it." He looked over at Amos. "You all right, Mouse?"

Amos had taken much of the impact with his right arm, instinctively raised, but his head had cracked the windshield.

"There's a deer crossing marked back there, you know," he said.

"Yeah, I know," Brett said. He fumbled in the glove box for a flashlight, and shined it on Amos's head, which was beginning to color at the temple.

"Sucker hurts," he said. He reached down and picked up his cigarette and tried to inhale, but the paper was cracked. He snuffed it. "Got any more cigarettes, Brett?"

"Yeah. There in the glove box." Amos reached in the open lid and pulled out a new pack and groaned. "Geez, Brett! These are Salems! And they're menthol! What the hell?"

Brett said apologetically, "I got them in case the girls wanted to smoke. I figured they would want something like that if they did."

"Well, you might be right about that, I guess," Amos conceded. "I suppose that's it?"

"Yeah. That's it. Unless you brought some."

"Nope. I'm out. Okay." He opened the pack.

"I better get after that deer." He reached into the glove box and pulled out a hunting knife, sheathed, and set it down at his feet.

"What the hell are you doing?"

"There is a deer behind us in the road. And I'm gonna get killed if I show up with a smashed truck and some lame story about a deer. Besides, we need the meat. That's a big doe."

"Aren't you going to get a coffee first, at least?"

"In a minute. You're all right. You get thrown into the girls' bathroom at higher speeds than that."

"Yeah, but I know what's coming."

"You haven't known what's coming since I met you, and that's been twelve years." He smiled.

"Yeah. Very funny. *You* haven't got a fractured skull. Good luck with the deer, you loony cowboy."

"All of us cowboys are crazy. Let's go." He stepped out into the wind and checked the front wheels in the snowbank, and yelled at Amos, "Drive, will you? I'll push." The motor hadn't stopped. Amos slid over on the seat and adjusted it forward, and the truck rolled out of the snowbank on the third rocking motion, and Amos backed down the left shoulder of the highway. A passing semi sounded its air horn and whistled by in a blast of snow and cold wind. Brett trotted behind the pickup for a few steps. Amos stopped at the deer and got out of the cab. Brett seized the animal by an ear and a handful of neck-hide and wrestled it to the road edge. Her rear legs were stilled but she frantically looked about and tried to move. There were spasms in her neck and back.

Brett reached back into the cab and grabbed the knife, unsheathed it and checked the edge. Not perfect, but it would have to do. He stepped on the deer's snout and leaned over and slit her throat, cutting deep, making sure the windpipe and esophagus and big arteries were severed. He stepped back; in several seconds the spasms ended. He stepped up again, pulled the tail, and gingerly cut around the anus. Blood stained the snow as the boys stood in the red cast of the truck's single taillight. "Wish we'd had a gun," said Brett. He looked at the blood on his right hand and wiped it in the snow to clean it. He pulled off his overcoat and suit jacket and put them both on the truck seat. Looking at the deer, he unbuttoned his white shirt.

"What the hell has come over *you*?" demanded Amos.

"Hot or something?"

Brett glared at him and removed his tie. "Maybe you don't know, Amos," he said sarcastically, "that these are my best clothes. And some of them aren't even mine." He peeled off the shirt and set it in the cab.

"So they're your dad's, so what? I'm wearing an old jacket of my dad's from when he was a kid," Amos said. Brett looked at him hard again.

I mean, I better not screw them up," he explained. Amos shrugged. Brett took out some boots from behind the seat, and replaced his shoes, and returned to the deer.

"Want me to get the blanket? The one we were sitting on?"
Brett nodded.

"Maybe the exhaust is warmer to stand in. If you can stand the smell," Amos suggested.

"No, the exhaust is pretty wet. Not a good idea." Brett turned and leaned over the deer. "I think there's a rope and some tools behind the seat, too. Would you bring them?" He dragged the lifeless deer to the driver's door. "Wish we'd had a gun," he repeated. Amos handed him a rope and Brett tied a loop between the rear legs, above the second joint; he motioned to Amos and they hoisted the animal to hang in the mirror bracket. The carcass bent grotesquely because it didn't clear the ground.

Amos stood with the blanket unfolded, ready to help but not wanting to interfere. The cold pimpled Brett's back and shoulders. He wore a tank-top undershirt. For seventeen, he was well-muscled. His shoulders and neck had worked against heavy stubborn objects since he was little. Hatless, largely shirtless, feet spread wide, he secured the steaming animal to the mirror frame. "Grab me a file, will you?" he asked of Amos, then Brett quickly sharpened the knife on the file. He wiped the blade on a rag and opened the belly at the base of the ribs, then inserted two fingers of his left hand into the abdomen, and guided the knife blade upward between his fingers, as he pulled skin up and away from the stomach, careful of nicking it and spilling rumen. He finished the slice and removed some lower organs, flopping as they spilled from their cavity, and Brett narrowly missed getting splattered in the mess. He extracted the large intestine, standing awkwardly for a moment with a handful of entrails.

Snow continued to fall, and the headlights picked up the slanted path of the snow, and the taillight dimly illuminated the scene from the rear. The boy worked fast in the shadow of the cab and carcass. Amos was mildly amazed, standing and freezing in his dress clothes, watching Brett work on the deer, cold and half-frenzied. Brett's hands were warmed by the organs and flesh, but Amos noticed tremors across his back and shoulder muscles, no fat on his torso at all. Vapor rose from the carcass.

Brett bent and picked up the entrails and threw them over the snowbank, "Magpie food," he said, but he kept the liver. The smell of butchery competed with the smell of exhaust. He stood and exaggerated shivering, and Amos quickly moved in with the cab blanket to rub his shoulders with. He accepted the gesture, then shook it off. "Thanks," he said. "A little more to go." He cut the diaphragm and removed the lungs and heart, saving the heart also.

"Won't that meat be tough? I always heard road-kill meat wasn't worth eating," Amos said. Brett glared at him again. "No offense," Amos added. Brett skinned the animal and then they lowered the carcass and Brett examined the shoulder, the point of the impact.

"Sometimes it's tough, and sometimes it tastes funny. That's right. Stew meat. Hamburger," answered Brett. "But that's true of deer that's been shot, too, sometimes." He wiped the knife in the snow and threw it in the toolbox. They lifted the deer carcass into the back of the truck. "You think it's better to bury it, or feed it to the dogs at the pound? Everybody needs to eat." He wiped his hands in the snow again, and Amos rubbed the blanket on his shoulders again, and Brett dried his hands on the blanket.

"I guess so," said Amos. "But you ain't supposed to eat road-kill."

"Says who?" said Brett. "Where the hell are those clothes?"

"Here." Amos retrieved them from the cab. "Let's go get some coffee."

"Yeah, let's go." He hurried into his clothes and stashed the toolbox behind the seat, and they drove the remaining mile to the cafe, one headlight askew and Brett driving too fast. The snow had just about stopped. Amos had almost forgotten about his head injury, and now it started throbbing.

It was quiet in the cafe, and the odor of diesel was subtle with so little traffic. A middle-aged woman waited on customers and cooked the orders. A young couple sat in a back booth, huddled over their plates. Travelers, unfamiliar with the territory.

The waitress-cook recognized Brett and he nodded to her, but neither knew the other's name. He had been there on errands, getting fuel and odds and ends at late hours. Smiling slightly, she studied him: the poor young man dressed in an overcoat and dress slacks, entirely rumpled, with what appeared to be traces of blood on the backs of his hands. Flecks of blood on his ear, and neck, and a little in his hair. He and Amos sat at the counter. The cook grinned and said, "Must have been one hell of a dance, boys. Anybody left alive?"

Amos first really noticed Brett's appearance then, and he laughed out loud. The couple in the back looked up, startled and annoyed, awakened from their murmuring.

"You ain't looking so sharp yourself, buddy," the cook said to Amos. He reddened.

"One less deer marauding and pillaging on Highway Six," he answered.

"'Marauding and pillaging?' Where in the Dickens would you come up with this stuff like that? Reading too many Marvel comics?" Brett asked.

She brought them water. "Coffee, kids? Or some hot chocolate?"

"Coffee. Black, please," Brett said. She looked at Amos, who nodded.

"Quick-like, too. This crazy sucker stripped down to practically his shorts to dress out a road-kill deer," Amos said.

She brought them the coffee. "That's pretty crazy, all right. You kill the deer with your head? Must have really impressed your dates."

Amos smiled. "Yeah, we wowed them, didn't we, Brett?"

Brett still shivered. "Yeah, we really showed 'em a time." He asked the cook, "You got any aspirin here? My partner might need some."

"Sure, we're a regular pharmacy," she said. She peered at Amos's temple. "Looks to me like he might need his head examined."

"He's needed that a long time. This was my last attempt to knock some sense into him," Brett said.

"Listen to Einstein here," Amos said. "Ask him for his talk on the birds and the bees, ma'am." He smirked as he touched his head again.

The cook looked from one to the other as she pushed a bottle of aspirin to Amos. She arched her back, coldly.

"Anything else, *boys*?" she asked. She looked hard at Amos. He flushed and sipped his coffee. "Ought to go wash up, now, son. You, first." She nodded at Amos. "Then you probably better call home. It's getting late." He stayed at the seat a minute, just to show her. Then he went to the restroom, to inspect the injury.

There was a crease of blood on the bump. He figured his face would get pretty bruised and ugly before it healed. The knot was already hard, and the puffiness seemed to stretch his skin tight. He knew the flesh around it would color up blue and purple and then some yellow, and the bruising would shift places while it healed. He dabbed at it tenderly with a damp paper towel, testing the puffiness and trying to clean the wound. He grinned. The Olds had good snow tires, and they wouldn't have been there when the deer was. He looked forward to going home. ■

"Eudora Welty" by Tom Callos. Linocut with hand-coloring, 11 x 14 inches

JIM HEPWORTH

Some Keep the Sabbath

—for Wendell

Mass begins, more or less, at sunrise with that
song the river played all night long. Geese
somewhere up there test organs for sound.
A doe and yearling graze along the far
bank then disappear. Maybe Jesus, soft
and tenderly, called them. I didn't hear.

But time is not fleeting though moments are
fleeing and shadows are gathering now as first
light breaks gold glory Hallelujahs on the tops of the firs
high on the mountain. Squirrels call near, chattering,
chirping. I wade then walk to the second pool,
watch and wait, wait and watch. Not much happens.

I like it this way: the sky blue above
me, a few thin clouds, the pool a mirror
of green glass reflecting it all. Beauty
before me, beauty behind me, beauty above
me, beauty below me, as the Navajo say.
And, for a moment, at least, I, too, disappear,
am no one—everywhere—no thing—nothing.

Report to Friends from Last Chance, Idaho

1.
Open spaces
open minds.

2.
In the angler's mind are many fish
and some of them
are real.

3.
I do not tell any more lies
than the river does.

4.
I don't want breakfast
just these last few stars
to help me remember my father.

5.
Who can stop the sun
from rising like blood and ashes
through the young lodge pole pines?
Who would try?

6.
The rich all live like pigs—
very clean.

7.
When I was a young man, I touched a girl
on this river in a boat under a crescent moon
she kissed me first. Her name was Karen Lockyer.
It was her father's boat, I think
we were very tender with each other.

8.
It hurts me to remember things
that happened thirty and forty years ago.
This morning the smell of pines
reminds me that I was once
a reservation white boy walking
into a room on the first day of school
all those Indian eyes.

9.
The most beautiful women in America
all have deep brown eyes
and skin like chocolate

or red hair and freckles
the color of cherries

or . . .

10.
My brother cooked me eggs
and bacon for breakfast.
The food was hot and delicious.
I gave nothing to the dogs.

11.
The odometer says I am 547 miles from home.
Outside the window: the river.
I love my wife.

12.
My only son won't fish with me anymore
says I know nothing.
He's right.

13.
Before I left home, my youngest daughter
kissed me on the forehead
as she went out the door
to meet her "artist" boyfriend.
I closed the door.

14.
The wind blew then quit. Up came
the bugs then one big trout head
began to surface
hiding among
the splashing ducks.

15.
Going into debt is like wading.
Sure, I catch trout in the shallows
even big ones but sometimes the fish
are out farther, deeper.

16.
Standing on my brother's railing at sunrise
over there Montana over there Wyoming
here in Idaho the sound of one hammer
pounding! pounding! pounding! pounding!

17.
All my fine new pencils have become tiny pencil stubs.
Too much soul chasing too many erasures.

18.
I wouldn't mind being a well-placed rock
in a river—all that water, all that time—
whereas the wind is everywhere
and nowhere
all at once.

19.
If I could just shut my mouth
and keep it shut.

20.
The river today nothing but sky and trees
moving moving moving moving
always in place.

21.
All through the meeting
the men talk, the women
listen.

22.
What? You don't love me?
Fine then, my bag is already packed.
I keep it packed.
It's a very small bag.

23.
After a static hour the osprey
springs off the snag
and drops/falls
down
and down
then opens wide her wings.

24.
Two fly fishermen wade out of the river in starlight
lose the trail but not the thread of the argument
keep arguing, find the trail.

25.
My friend, one thing is almost certain
one of us will bury the other.

"Toni Morrison" by Tom Callos. Linocut reduction print, 24 x 18 inches.

REBECCA EVANS

The Confessional of Two or More

You never minded, but you mind and though
you hurt, you rarely hurt. You were used,
and, despite mindfulness, you use.

> Never minded, you mind.
> Hurt, you hurt rarely.
> Used, you use.

Admit this. Your admission frees
the mind, offers permission, though
you won't permit more using.

> Free admission
> offers permission.
> Admit: Using frees you.

They'll arrive—hurt you with your own
admission—until you realize you always
minded and all that mattered was their minding.

> Admission hurts. They'll realize
> you've arrived. All that mattered
> is they admitted using you.
> This. Admit.

"Frosted Leaves," photograph by Jan Boles.

SHAUN T. GRIFFIN

Letter to Joe from Big Hole National Battlefield

I

In Big Hole Valley we rode
the summering grass, no voice
in the wilderness of ghost tents.
At the museum the curators assured
Chief Joseph was not alone
and we blew in on mosquito rain.
My friend Joe, tall on two wheels,
didn't understand—and I didn't either:
the mask of indifference battened down
for the formalities of tourism.

We had dinner a few nights later
and he asked why I didn't write about
Big Hole Valley? I couldn't I said,
fingering a map of Lewis and Clark's
footsteps. A voyage before—
how do we understand it now?
The vigilance that is, that smokes
the kingdom down.
And we rode away, two clouds on the ridge,
like boys who should have known.

II

I'm trying to listen,
the wheels bite the mosquito wind,
heavy rain in Wilson. The rise
of the Bitterroots. How many
on its flanks—cattle, conifer,
man? The scree of civilization—
we follow dust to its tributary.

At river's edge, the drift boats
bloat to shore, heavy with Coors
and relief from tawdry jobs in the city.
I ask a guide: "We did fine. Fished
our share." I worry it may not be enough
for the killing to end,
and the ghost tents blow like sails.
Someone was here before.
We try to let them go,
burnish the collar with lime
in this blue-green valley.

III

At dinner Joe tells me about the film
on Chief Joseph—shooting the ghost tents
like cans—and the chief walked
in the mosquito mist. A monument
to ease the driving by
and the valley blurs to who
carries this upheaval,
the strange soliloquy of dying
before land could speak. And memory
at river's edge. Like a trout in the cutbank
we move to shadows—
nowhere to go without us.

GARY GILDNER

Father Honor's Spa

A full house, as befits the territory, is waiting in the Outer Room. Mainly newcomers. They join those who have been here before in looking down, looking around, looking despondent. They see very little—their shoes, a tree beyond the window. Smiling, I pass among them offering best wishes for a healthy tomorrow. I also bear the basket from which they are free to choose a Mystery Chip—a chance to sit down one-on-one with Father Honor himself.

"And you are?" a distracted and grumpy newcomer demands.

"Yes," I return, bowing, "the great question: Who am I? Well, for me, personally, I am nobody much, Your Worship, which brings me modest but real comfort. Moreover," I whisper near his outsized, hairy ear, "as a descendant of wood pussies I am one for whom a careful step is not to be sneezed at." This kind of response in my confidential, side-of-mouth manner usually confuses that kind of questioner, and I am able to move smoothly on.

I approach a suffering beauty of note who raises needy eyes at me. I take her hand and place my lips upon the wrist. "He will see you, Your Loveliness, at the perfect time. Prepare your most comely thoughts. Please, try the earth-colored chip, it has brought noticeable satisfaction lately."

At my exit, I turn and count twelve heads, the maximum I let the casino send over. Everyone will pick a lucky Mystery Chip to see Father Honor; but there are those who, upon reaching the deepest part of their sadness and cannot believe in much if anything anymore, who have lost their self-esteem, balance, standing, their good name, or what is left of it, and even all gaming verve for a spell, will toss away their chip. They are nonetheless entitled to graze the catered buffet and cure in the mineral waters as long as they wish, perhaps find their weary way to a comfortable chaise looking out over the Chippewa River, where, as a boy, I pursued the now extinct grayling, a pretty trout.

Thus Father Honor's Spa acts as a way station providing relief and, to some, perhaps, real help. It is definitely not what the superior citizen might dismiss as a sideshow for weak characters in a world calling for cold calculation, flops who will fall for anything, including another crooked deal, a sham show of friendship to keep the flop from staying away forever—in other words, a scam to help the poor gambler forget his losses and, in due time, rush back full of fresh hope to the wheels and dice. Oh yes, I have heard the grumbles. Which include the suspicion that it is I who am Father Honor, a faux native son in confusing camouflage. That when our daily dozen have been welcomed and I slip away from my, as it were, maître d' duties, I repair to the Inner Room and there trade my crimson tuxedo jacket, fake hump, and wig of tight curls for the white pajamas, mustache, and dark glasses which blind and gleaming-bald Father Honor dons to receive his supplicants.

Personally, I don't care for the word *supplicant*, in the singular or plural, but I can't think of a better one. It came seductively into use one day and stayed, thanks to the sweet widow Bloom, Wendy Bloom, who, in rather lyrical gear, offered, softly, "I am but a mild supplicant unmindful of the hurtful winds."

Presiding over these *communions*, let us call them, is not easy, for even though they are nothing if not secular they carry petitions, indeed pleadings, for an understanding that our religious experts might well label spiritual. If you were a fly on the wall, however, here is what you would most likely observe: Silences of a rich hunger sometimes lasting beyond the allotted but not strictly adhered to half-hour, the supplicant on her divan quietly trying to compose herself, Father Honor patient in his recliner; subtle melodies wrought by violins and oboes, perhaps a French horn speaking up in the distance for occasional accent purposes, issuing *ensemble* into the serenely lighted room from a recorded location that we can imagine is leafy, tenderly breezy, and rhythmically fixed, it seems, to a beating heart but in reality to a shyness of water caressing sand at the end of a long, satisfying journey. To some of course—the infrequent blustery male comes to mind—this setting can be maddening and will sooner rather than later drive even the most dedicated of such types away from Father Honor's Spa, never to return. Why they come in the first place is something of a surprise, although a fierce curiosity fired by jealousy can be fairly suspected—a former girlfriend or wife having mentioned seeing Father Honor to good purpose and, well, some men get worked up about that. No, we here at the Spa attract, almost exclusively, those who, having been dropped low by a heartless god, seek the simplest and yet the most profound of human touches, let us say: to be seen—*recognized*—in the fallible flesh.

Frankly, at the end of a workday I am exhausted. I will take my own mineral soak and afterwards a piece of baked cod brought over from the casino. Before bed I jog my mile on the treadmill, lift a few light weights, lubricate myself—skull to feet—with an excellent almond oil, and quite likely, as an antidote to life's difficult adventure, I will play a selection from my old movies collection. Tonight I know it will be Fellini's La Strada, a favorite from my sojourn at Harvard. The suffering beauty, whose earth-colored chip brought her to Father Honor rather quickly, seemed to him from the first moment to require the kind of gentleness that poor Gelsomina in that film does not receive from the brutish strongman gypsy, Zampanò. At least I think of him as a gypsy. The suffering beauty's name is Vespa. We ask for no last names at the Spa. Tender, wooable Wendy Bloom stars, by choice, as the exception.

"Are you a fan of classic films?" I asked Vespa.

"I am so dull. Yes, sometimes."

"Would you care for tea?"

"I don't know." She sat on the edge of the divan as if thoroughly defeated and looked at her loafers positioned one on top the other's toes.

"We have herbal, green—all kinds."

"Doesn't matter."

I brought her a cup of Sleepytime.

"You were saying, earlier?"

"I don't know why I came here. I am not a gambler."

"Why did you come?"

"It's so pointless."

"Go on."

"Everything. My life. Relationships—"

She stood up then and without another word departed.

That night, during my mineral soak, her lean eyes and sharply constructed face rose in the steam. When my cod arrived I was unable to enjoy it. Jogging, I wondered where on earth I thought I was going. I poured almond oil in my palm and rubbed it over my dome and aching neck but could go no farther. Watching *La Strada* I saw in Gelsomina only the unloved Vespa.

A week later she was back, waiting, as previously, to see Father Honor. Again I took her hand in welcome and suggested a certain Mystery Chip to choose from the basket I carried. She glanced at me before taking the chip and, as if we were in this together, winked. Later, in the Inner Room, once more on the divan with a cup of Sleepytime, she regarded me.

"Ready?" I said.

"Are you the man in the red tuxedo jacket?"

"Crimson. Why do you ask?"

"I need to learn *some*thing. I can't keep screwing up."

After I admitted I was that man, she finished her tea, removed her loafers, lay back on the divan, and began, in a fetching whisper, to speak. She was in theatre, familiar with guises, and I was quite careless last week, and again today, she said, about my wig. Being in theatre— less rather than more—was a large part of her problem and why she had fled New York, for the summer anyway, and returned home to Mount Pleasant and its cool northern Michigan nights. She had not been getting called back after auditioning for parts she really wanted, and was depressed by those she could get on daytime TV: the frightened face on the operating table, the hated homewrecker, the forgettable loser.

"I want to be exhilarated," she said. "On top."

Her monologue ceased. I almost confessed that theatre, in an approximate but pertinent sense, was a part of my own life. But perhaps she already had her suspicions. Via the remote control at my side, I brought softly into the room those violins and oboes I mentioned. Their music sometimes encourages my visitors, and, lo, Vespa soon said, "Do you know Puccini's *Turandot*? That icy princess?"

I confessed that my education in opera, unfortunately, had not been as developed as I wished. I knew of course *of* Puccini, his great success both artistically and financially, and his avocation—driving fast cars. "But aside from the basic plots of two or three of his works," I apologized,

"I am not able to discuss with you, intelligently, his musical gifts."

"Yes, that's too bad," she sighed. "He was so fine and so modest."

"High qualities, Vespa."

"Do you like saying my name?"
"I do."
"I almost chose Turandot."
"When was that?"
"High school."
"But you chose Vespa?"
"For the irony."
"The irony."
"It's an Italian scooter."
"Yes, I know."
"Imagine a skinny school girl named Vespa zipping here, zipping there in her saddle shoes, and singing in cold, high-flying phrases why no man can ever possess her."
"I can't."
"Of course you can't, not knowing opera. But if you had ever heard Joan Sutherland, as Turandot, and Luciano Pavarotti, as Calaf, going back and forth so powerfully 'In questa reggia,' you would *begin* to know. And I would invite you to this divan to hold me."
I was speechless, and reduced in breath.
"By the way, someone said Father Honor was blind."
"Aren't we all, in our own weaknesses?" I managed.
"Why do you talk the way you do?"
"I don't understand."
"Well, funny for these parts. Bookish, maybe. Although in the red tux you sound closer to normal."
"I lived for awhile in Cambridge."
"England?"
"Where Harvard University is."
"Oh." She was clearly puzzled.
"My father was an Irish pub singer and knew Tony Cronin, Seamus Heaney, the Clancy brothers. My mother, Honor Gayfeather, who had significant Saginaw Chippewa blood, was a poet. I grew up appreciating the art of song. I could also express passion with a pen, run fast, and catch a football."
"Oh, wow."
"My pedigree and natural gifts appealed to Harvard's devotion to range."

"No wonder you talk like you do."

"I'm sorry if my speech offends you, Vespa."

"So at Harvard they got you to not talk normal?"

I could only shrug.

"Anyway," she said, consoling me, "you're still an Indian."

"Half-Irish. Hugh Honor Duffy's the name on my birth certificate. The Native American portion allows me to occupy this parcel of land I live on."

A short walk, through a little buffer of birch trees, from the bright lights of the casino."

"Why did you run away so abruptly last week?"

"I have issues with approach-avoidance. Or so says my therapist."

"You're not afraid of me?"

"Maybe I'll come back. If I can skip the casino. And if I do we can talk more."

I gave her my card, which revealed my private number. She put on her loafers and left.

After I saw my next supplicant, a sad woman in masochistic love with blackjack, I could not muster energy to hear more confused suffering. Not strung out one at a time, anyway. So I called all those remaining to come in together for the AA-style gathering I am tethered to. Shyly, six mature women and one middle-aged man entered the Inner Room and found tentative purchase on the edges of various furnishings. The previous night the man had gambled away a nest egg that, over many years, he and his wife managed to build for their wheelchair-bound daughter's college tuition. He was sagging with addled eyes, fear, and self-hatred. One of the women, who said her name was Suzy Stupid, wagged a finger at him.

"Whatever you do, Chuck, do *not* kill yourself."

"My name is Eugene," he said, his head hanging down.

"To me it's Chuck," she said. "Chuck away this, Chuck away that. Even killing yourself could give you trouble, you're so useless. But if you did manage such an act, it wouldn't help anybody and just leave a mess for others to clean up. Go home, confess what you did, then work your tail off to fix things. Amen."

The others applauded this speech with anemic clapping. Indeed, a wan coloration lay on all their faces. Guilt thick as the axel grease I used to put my hands in at Ralph Trueblood's Auto Repair, earning summer money, larded the room. Completely abandoning my groomed character, I blurted, "Look. If you must visit the casino, bring only the money you can afford to lose. When it's gone, leave. Just leave. Believe me, I know how you feel hearing such simplistic advice, but I don't care. It's either leave, when it's time to leave, or haul around the bag of emptiness you apparently want to be, like Eugene."

Almost a total waste of breath, of course, but I'd had more than enough for the day.

"Please, good people, go in peace."

I called the casino and informed Stanley Sweetwater that I would be closed for a while.

"Until when?"

"Further notice."

"Are you drinking?"

"No."

"Sure?"

"Go to hell."

"Maybe you're just sick."

"Maybe."

"Sweat it out."

Toward dusk, Wendy Bloom phoned.

"How are you, Honor?"

"Time will tell. And you?"

"I feel a need to risk everything. May I come over?"

She lived farther north, on the way to Traverse City, in cherry orchard country. I said I would come to her; I didn't want her to make the journey to me in the dark, or to stay all night. Also, I wanted to get away from my own litter box. The sturdy house she lived in, constructed largely with fieldstone, had been in her family for three generations. Her son and his wife, who tended her cherries, in addition to their own, lived just down the road in a modern house. They had a son who was sickly. Wendy feared he would be her only grandchild.

When I arrived she brought bowls of beef barley soup, my favorite, to the table. She held my free hand. "Tonight we must snuggle together like children," she said. But after we had found comforting positions in her grandparents' brass bed, we could not resist helping ourselves to more.

"Dear Moon," she whispered. "My dear Moon."
It was what my parents called me.

II.

How absurd my life seems today as I sit beside the Chippewa River and toss pebbles toward those deep holes I mused over in my youth. Am I trying to tempt the grayling's ghost to rise? In my pocket I carry a cell phone that off and on has been trembling against my leg. Vespa? Is that you? Who saw so quickly through my foolish wig and crimson coat? How easily I can call up the inspiration for all that crap. How clever I was to keep the hump! The complexity, the symbolism! Suddenly there he was, that old man I saw my first year in Cambridge. On a beautiful autumn Sunday. I thought he was lost, perhaps a panhandler. I had some change in my pocket. I wanted to give him all of it, plus the few dollars in my wallet. I had the whole world on that day, a full scholarship, recognition, a place—what did he have? An old rumpled tweed coat from some charity, baggy pants, and that growth on his back. I caught up with him and said, "Sir! Please! Here!" and thrust my money at him. He looked me over, appalled. Then an expression of complete disgust informed his face, and he turned away. A few days later I saw him on campus. He was a distinguished professor.

A mockery, my hump. In line with my basket of Mystery Chips, the tuxedo, dark glasses, and everything else. Which, yes, yes, I have always known.

There's my cell phone again.

What difference does it make if I take my feelings to someone, my real feelings, and in return try to absorb theirs? No, no, I am not in the trading business, I do not believe. I am in the listening business. And yet, little by little, when you tell me this and I tell you that, boom.

I take out my trembling phone. "Hello?"

"It's me, Vespa."

"How are you?"

"Same as you, probably."

"What is our purpose?"

"Our purpose? Oh, wow."

"At Harvard I studied the history of religion—in addition to some theatre."

"Okay . . ."

"Not just running fast downfield to catch a football."

"Okay . . ."

"In many, many ways, they are all similar. Indeed, triplets."

"What are you trying to say, Honor? May I call you Honor?"

"I am trying to say what Fellini is trying to say. Yes, Honor is my name."

"It's also a girl's name. I like it, Honor."

"I think we both came back to Mount Pleasant for reasons that may be indistinguishable."

"Could be," she says.

"Yes, could be."

"I have a lot of Irish in me, but no Indian that I know of. Should I come see you?"

"Father Honor's Spa is not open today. Maybe never again. Yes, if you wish. I am sitting outside by the sluggish Chippewa."

The days passed and she did not come. I remained closed. The casino sent over my baked cod but no buffet, and only Ralph Trueblood's nephew to clean my mineral pool once. Then Stanley Sweetwater showed his face. He sat with me beside the river.

"How goes it, Honor?"

"The same."

"You have been closed up now three weeks and four days. I can smell the beginnings of fall."

I said nothing.

"Have you had enough of this counseling?"

"Is the casino cashing in its chips?"

"Make sense, man."

"You bulldozed my mother's ancestral home."

"We gave her a better one. We also cleaned you up, gave you a job."
"Yes, proctoring the mineral baths."
"We agreed to the counseling idea you proposed."
"You strut in your silk suits."
"It has turned into a nice little service. We appreciate it, brother."
"Go away, Stanley."

When Vespa finally came to see me, I gave her a sweater to wear so we could sit outside by the Chippewa and watch the sky. I pushed two chaise lounges together. She said she might be going back to New York soon. Her parents were driving her crazy and her old high school boyfriend only wanted to get drunk and fuck and badmouth his ex-wife.

"Could we just hold hands and look at the stars?" she said.

I took her hand.

"Maybe I need a big cardboard box to hide in, like I did as a kid. You ever do that, Honor? Find a big cardboard box and make it your cave?"

"I went fishing."

"When I come back I'll be your assistant and help you find the light."

"Maybe you should stay away from men like your old high school boyfriend," I said.

"Would you like that, Honor?"

"Which?"

"All the above."

Then she came and curled in my lap.

Sundays I drive to Wendy Bloom's and we enjoy a baked chicken. Her son, daughter-in-law, and the sickly grandson, Charlie, join us. Charlie is very bright, a high school junior, who is considering MIT, Stanford, and Michigan.

"Were you happy at Harvard?" he asked me just last Sunday.

"I had my ups and downs," I said. "Like anyone."

"Were there many Native American students?"

"Not enough. And the small group I met gave up on me."

"Why?"

"Maybe I was distant and they assumed I felt superior."

"How did you feel about that?"

"Oh, hurt a little. Then mad a little. Then I suspected they were envious because I was successful and I forgave them."

Charlie wanted to hear about my successes, but they were most visibly on the football field and he had difficulty walking a short distance, so I changed the subject. I said, "I would rather hear about your plans for college, Charlie." He was glad to explain, in detail, how he thought his future should go, which brought a glow into the faces of his parents and grandmother.

When Wendy and I were alone, she said, "You made all of us very happy tonight, urging Charlie to speak. Taking his dreams so seriously. What a wonderful father you would be, Honor."

"I no longer think about that," I said.

"I know something either beautiful or painful is on your mind, though."

"A great poet once said, 'My mind is a monastery, and I am its monk.'"

"I never want to be a heavy stone around your neck."

"You are a feather, Wendy Bloom."

"From which bird?"

"The surprise bird. The one of many melodies."

"And if I sang to ask what you are thinking—I mean right now—you would tell me?"

I told her that soon the leaves would fall and we would see our breath. The cornfields would be brittle with stubble, but they would sparkle in the icy ruts when the sun came up and we would have pheasant for our Sunday dinners. ∎

"Untitled" by Jinny DeFoggi. Ink on paper.

MARK CLEMENS

Crossing Nisqually

Taking a chance to glance away from three lanes of hurtling freeway,
looking out the rider's window at the landscape for a moment,
two moments: the soaked browns and brooding grays of a Northwest dusk,
winter here, the end of a long day, long year.

Driving home this holiday evening is moving through moody illuminations,
like gliding through one of the muted, blurred paintings by Russell Chatham,
land and sky ominous and sodden, sliding by in the falling rain and fading light,
almost too dark to discern.

Meanwhile, who knows what holiday hoodoo might strike on this,
the last commute before Christmas, high-speed gamblers passing left and right
and early revelers jerking back into their lanes amidst a host of working schmoes,
just trying to make it home.

Darkening woods left and right as traffic growls along three abreast,
motored wave in motion, a horde clearing the western boundary of Fort Lewis
and dropping lockstep into the swell and sweep of the Nisqually Delta,
a panorama it would be a privilege to paint—

Gray wall of trees along the river running left-to-right beneath the freeway
on its way to the Sound, woods solid and impenetrable, taupe and dun,
on the upstream side of the freeway, pastures moldering ochre downstream,
standing water black down in the roots,

Trees and houses lining the crest of the bluff on the far side of the Delta,
stretching across the horizon above the scrim of river trees—too risky
to take in now, eyes stuck to the task at hand, even as a familiar sensation
that lies dormant in the routine rhythms

Of work and living resurfaces anew, an ocular awe that is a clear recognition
of this landscape's cornucopia for the eyes, its infinitely subtle palette,
this dusk turning indigo, the ebony edge of night that will fall chill and stealthy
on the fecund understory, unseen duff and rotting leaves, and the pearlescent mist
that will rise undulating in the white-wreathed dawn.

Eight geese lift from the water-logged field to the right and climbing
to cross the freeway, head south, tilting down the flyway to Mexico,
while rearing up ahead to span the river—

THE LIMBERLOST REVIEW

Two old bridges, steel girders bearing three lanes each, shudder invisibly
as cars and trucks barrel across west and east, bumper-to-bumper,
seventy, eighty miles-an-hour in opposite directions, all at cross purposes
with the Nisqually flowing underneath,

Brown eddies whirling in a dance with themselves, current born
from the many slopes of an ancient volcano, now pulling that water home
to the blue-black Sound, a world seemingly besotted and depressing,
now all aflow with color, a gift.

MARK CLEMENS

Heaven in the St. Joe

Several summers running Vaughn and Burl
used to take Byrd on all-night fishing expeditions
in the old flatbed Ford. They would fish the banks
of the Grand River until sometime after midnight
then jump up on the back of the truck
and throw blankets over themselves and go to sleep.

And the river was alive. On the bank those nights,
bank lines set and a fire burning, their hands dirty
and stinking from rolling big putrid balls of catfish bait,
even as they washed their hands, leaning over the bank
and splashing in the river, arms bare and brown,
rinsing in the mud-brown water, sluicing the muck
away in the dark water moving through in the night
unseen beyond the jumping firelight, away from the low
trees around them, weeping willows making a drooping
canopy of yellow-green, rustling, rattling, dry.

And the sound of the spillway faraway, water flowing
dark in their minds, breaking smooth in their minds,
slipping down the long concrete chute, rapid white and
rushing down to the deep pool below where the moss
so green and cool grew slippery and so wet on the cement
works along the river, the slick warmth alive beneath
their feet as they stood, toes squirming, slowly sinking
in the green cushion, a bed of flesh in the darkness.

And at last, when the fishing was done, climbing aboard
the broad-beamed flatbed among the willows
and lying back with the old dusty, khaki-dyed
G.I. blankets drawn up to their armpits and
the star fields sown above them all across the night,
glimmering in one quivered glory that seemed
fueled from below by the city lights that lay
downriver, the lights hovering above
the line of trees across the river,
a distant heaven haunting the horizon,
the lights they knew to be St. Joe.

"Tin o' Fish" by Jackie Elo. Clay sculpture.

BOB BUSHNELL

Summer Solstice

The sun takes
its own
sweet
time
climbing up
the eastern sky,
then lollygags
its way
down
for
the sunset,
on this longest day,
when even clocks have
more time on their hands.

F Words

I find fewer
familiar faces
where I once found
fond friends.

But I feel
fortunate
to have found
yours first.

Just Tell Me

I wish you wouldn't
look at me that way.

You know what I mean,
the way you glance
from the corner of your eye,
or over the glasses
that hang on your nose,
then push them up again
and look away.

If you have
something to say,
just tell me,
as long as you don't
raise your voice.

Parts

I'm proud
of the part of me
that speaks from
the heart of me.

But other parts
have a say
and often they
get their way.

ANNE BLEDSOE

Quaking

The hulls of burned trees still stand
stark on the ridge, one here, another
there. Up close, the charred surface,
weathered to a gloss, reflects the June sky.

Young aspen have risen along the course
the fire took, around a pine burned black
a grove of slender white trunks, letting through
the light and wind and flickering shadow.

In the lightest drift of air, the leaves spin,
tapping on thin stems, a quiet easy speaking
chorus, reckoning in murmurs through
twenty summers. Beside them I wonder

how is it to be so easily stirred, in ready
sympathy. How do they bear it? They seem to
endure together, leaning in the breeze as
the roots, shared, go ever deeper.

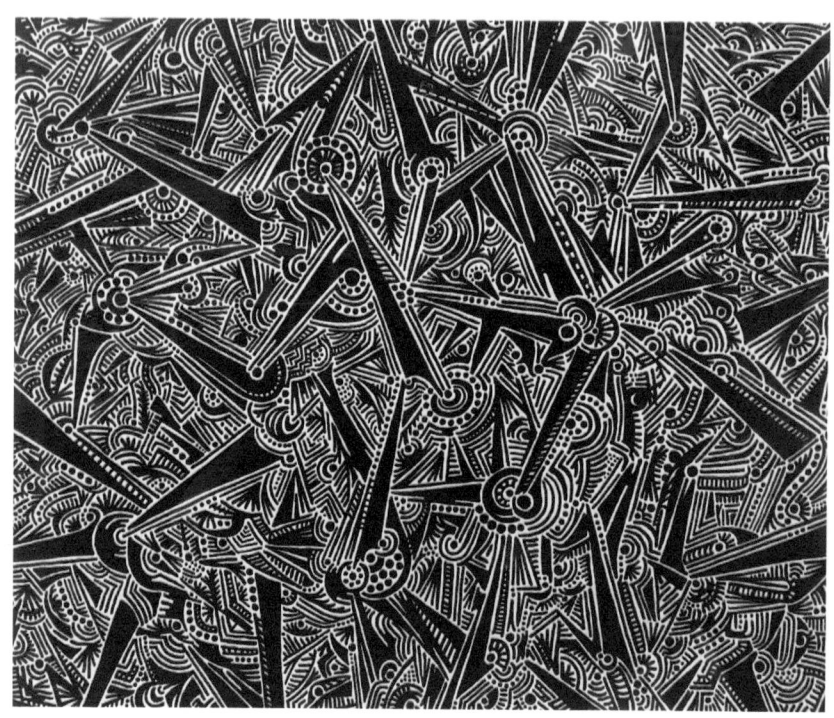

"Untitled" by Jinny DeFoggi. Ink on paper, 2006.

MARY CLEARMAN BLEW

Miles City, Montana, November 1882

Light from the kerosene lamp makes a mirror of the single window of what once was a bedroom in a jerry-built, thrown-together frontier hotel and now is a—well, a cell—at least it is a cell until the woman walks out of it. The light also would present a startling picture for any man who might be passing below the window on the dark and mud-rutted street, but the woman who stands naked, gazing at the reflection that gazes back at her, is oblivious of any potential audience.

Her body. She studies it closely for the first time since—the image of herself as a toddler comes to mind, her small sturdy self being set in a galvanized tub of warm water, her mother's hands soaping the little girl's back and arms, lifting one leg after the other to soap in turn, taking special pains to soap the little bare feet, between the little toes. She can't see her feet now in the window turned mirror. What she can see is the outline of her skull, the shape of her face under the stubble of hair that has begun to grow back. Her shoulders, which droop. Her breasts, which also droop. Waist, hips beginning to widen. Then, blessedly shrouded by shadows, the vee of coarse dark hair that conceals the forbidden place.

I can't do this.

Well. She turns from the window. Reaches for the clothes she has sorted out of the donation box. Pulls on the pair of bloomers, the ribbed undershirt. Then the unfamiliarity of a cotton shirt with buttons up the back that she fumbles to fasten.

Drawing on the stockings and fastening the garters. Stepping into the only shoes that had come close to fitting. Lacing and tying. Then the coarse wool skirt, smelling of cooking—fried grease, onions—and the yeasty odor of an old woman. Almost certainly it's a dead woman's skirt. A dead woman's clothing. She considers the irony.

I can't do this. She turns to the garments on the bed. Coif and wimple, white in the lamplight. The unrevealing black shadows of veil and tunic. The belt. The rattle of rosary beads as she folds and gathers up the garments, hooks her satchel over her shoulder, takes up the lamp in her free hand, and turns to leave the room.

No. One last thing.

Setting the lamp on the plank that has served as her desk for five years, she reaches for paper and pen. Dips the pen into the ink bottle and writes in the beautiful cursive she had been taught as a child:

I can no longer endure my present condition. I have decided to sever myself from all connections with the past. I am fully aware of the baseness and selfishness of my act, but I ask one favor: leave my name unconnected with any other.

Shutting the door behind her, she pauses on the landing and raises the lamp to light her way to the stairs, a shaft of raw boards without risers that vanishes into the darkness below. No handrail. So. One step at a time, folded garments under one arm, the lamp in her other hand, the drag of the satchel from her shoulder. One step, two, three. Another step, two, three. Feels her knees weaken under her. *Falling headfirst down the rest of the stairs, the lamp flung ahead of her and shattering into a flaming puddle of kerosene*—no. She straightens her knees and walks stiff-legged down the remaining stairs.

No. She will not give herself permission to sit on the stairs for a moment to rest. With rest may come irresolution. Instead she takes a breath and juggles garments and lamp while she opens the door into the church itself.

One of the first things the Ursuline sisters had done was to take out most of the partitions from the original first floor of the hotel, leaving only the walls that Miles had yelled were weight-bearing—*be careful! Watch what you're doing, Sisters!* They let Miles do the heavy carpentry to convert the hotel into a church and convent, but the nuns had done their share with hammers and crowbars. Then they swept up and mopped away the filtering dust and filth. Planks from the walls had been refashioned into benches to seat a future congregation on both sides of an aisle leading to the altar that even now waits in shadows beyond the reaches of her lamp.

I can't do this.

But this I can. In her stained shirt and skirt, in her clunky shoes that already rub against her heels and gnaw at her toes, she makes her slow way down the aisle as the altar emerges from shadows into lamplight and reveals the heavy wooden cross hanging above it.

A chain of nuns heaving on the rope that raises the cross until Miles, on his stepladder, can guide it to the hook in the ceiling and secure it in place.

Miles's hands. His long straight fingers, scarred by the tools of his trade. How long ago? Five years? A lifetime, after all that has happened? She sets down the lamp to use both hands to lay her garments on the altar. Takes a minute to stroke the wool and the linen, smooth its folds. Hears the click of rosary beads and pauses. No, although her fingers yearn to caress and count the wooden beads, just as her knees long to genuflect before the altar.

Body, you've betrayed me in too many ways.

She turns from the altar, remembers to lay her note on the piano. Touches an off-key B flat. Takes up her lamp and hears more than sees the opening door.

"Sister?"

She takes a step or two until the rays from her lamp reach the tall dark figure, made bulky by his sheepskin coat. His eyes shaded by his Stetson, his mouth a straight line.

"Are you ready, Sister?"

"Don't call me that."

A pause. She cannot see his eyes, but she knows he is assessing her. Quiet Miles, who always considers the scope of the task before him before he acts. Measuring rafters with his eyes, counting tools. Now this errant nun.

"What should I call you?"

What indeed. Immaculata de la Croix, which has been her name for nearly fifteen years? And before that, a name that wasn't exactly taken from her, but which she relinquished?

"Juliet."

He's thinking it over, she can tell. Not just her name, but the task, and she feels a stab of guilt at how much she is asking of him, even though she had no one else to ask. But now—*load-bearing walls between them*—must she walk alone as far as the railway depot on the edge of town and face the curious eyes of the stationmaster as she checks the train schedule and purchases a ticket with cash she has stolen from the donation box? The moment stretches. But then Miles nods, doffs his Stetson to enter the church, and walks up the aisle to her. Takes her satchel and slings it over his own shoulder.

"Where's your coat?"

She shrugs. There hadn't been a coat in the donation box. Who would donate a coat with cold weather coming on?

"You'll freeze," Miles says. He shakes his head, turns, and walks back up the aisle. She hears the door open and shut behind him. A minute or two passes, long enough for her to wonder what she must do—the walk to the railway depot— if he doesn't return for her. But no, he's back, carrying something bulky, a horse blanket, which he folds into a triangle and wraps around her shoulders. The warm smell of horseflesh somehow is reassuring. Then his arm is around her waist, bulky skirt and bulky blanket and all, and he is guiding her to the door, out the door and closing it behind them. She looks back once, sees the closed door silent and unrevealing as the stars beginning to break through the cloud cover of early nightfall.

Miles's team of Percherons waiting, comfortably hipshot, at the hitching rail in front of the church. The cloud of their breath rising in the chill. Stir of movement in the wagon box, Miles's dog. His light wagon with its high seat and its box loaded with indistinct shapes— his carpentry tools, she realizes. So this is happening. He is taking her away, and he is taking his tools with him.

A whistle from a mile away. She turns to the sound of the approaching train, still a novelty in Miles City, Montana, a cow town with a few blocks of hastily thrown-up wooden buildings with false fronts and board sidewalks that line the main street. But Miles is helping her to the high wagon seat, climbing up himself, and clucking to his horses to move, not toward the depot, but down the dark street that leads to empty prairie.

She turns to look back toward the depot, feeling the cold settle through the horse blanket, and shivers. "Why aren't we —"

He shakes his head. "First place they'll look for you."

And yet she can't help but look back, at the ugly little town superimposed over the dream of streetlights and a paved main street where once had been nothing but prairie grass. A dream that went much further, of a church with a congregation, a hospital, and a school for the newly converted dark-skinned children, while she, Sister Immaculata, had been left behind to bring the dream to fruition while Mother Amadeus and the other nuns forged deeper into the Montana Territory, lately become the State of Montana, to establish more schools and more churches for more and more converts.

I can't do this.

As the silhouettes of the flimsy false fronts blur into deepening nightfall, it seems to Sister Immaculata—*Juliet,* she has to remind herself—that the town is dissolving, the prairie grass returning to a primal time where the night sky was disturbed only by starlight falling on the tepee poles of the Crow village. All as it once was, before Sister Immaculata had been left behind to fail at realizing the dream of brown-faced children in her school.

The wagon road has taken a turn down a slope to follow a coulee. The lights of Miles City have disappeared. Juliet shivers.

"Cold?"

Trying to keep her teeth from chattering, she can only nod.

"Only thing colder than riding horseback in November is riding in a wagon."

He has stopped the team, hitched the lines, seems to be fumbling with his coat. When he leans toward her, she realizes that he has slipped his right arm out of his coat sleeve to pull her toward him. Startled, she stiffens, then allows herself to lean into his warmth while he wraps his coat around both of them, supplemented by the horse blanket.

He glances back—"Ring?"

The dog stirs in the wagon box. Rises and slips under the wagon seat to rest its muzzle on Miles's leg.

"Get down here, Ring," he says, and to Juliet, "Kick off those damned shoes and put your feet under the dog."

She is too befuddled to do anything but obey. Then realizes what the dog's warmth is doing to the frozen blocks her feet have become as the dog—Ring—curls around them and makes himself comfortable.

"How much farther?" she whispers.

"Couple hours."

She opens her eyes to darkness. Where—what is happening—disoriented, she casts about her and realizes she is alone on the wagon seat, still wrapped in Miles's coat, his dog still at her feet. She must have been, yes, lulled to sleep by the rhythm of the wagon wheels and wakened when the wagon stopped. But Miles—without his coat—

Her eyes have adjusted enough to the dark to make out the outline of a low sheltering hill, and a flat stretch of prairie ahead that rustles with a breath of night wind through the grass. A few yards from the wagon, a flame suddenly rises from a pyre of branches and reveals the outline of the man bending over his fire.

"Miles!" she calls, struggling with his coat and the horse blanket. The dog raises his head, looks around, and jumps down from the wagon to join Miles, who looks up, lays another dried sage branch on his fire, and tramps over to the wagon.

"You got some rest, then? I'll have the tent up in a minute and get you over in front of that fire. And I'll heat us up some stew as soon as I unhitch and grain those horses."

"Where are we?"

"Ranch pasture of a buddy of mine. He lives over—" Miles gestures with his head, and she notices the outline of a cabin's roof with a light in a window and a farther, dimmer roof over what must be a shed.

"He won't warn anyone—?"

"Nah. He's good."

She sits quietly for a few moments, watching by firelight as Miles digs a can from his satchel, opens it, pours the contents into a pan. Recognizes all over again the economy of his movements as he takes the little tent from the wagon box, unfolds it, and sets it up facing the fire. Unrolls a bundle of soogans, spreads them on the floor of the tent.

She—her name is Juliet, she has to remind herself—watches as though from a distance. The wagon, the hobbled horses. The silhouette of the man who now turns to stir his pan of food. Whiff of the food, faint rustle of night wind through invisible prairie grass and sagebrush. Stars overhead. The Big Dipper, the one constellation she can pick out, that points to the North Star over the lighted cabin window.

Cabin window. "Miles," she calls. "Why are we sleeping in a tent when you have a friend who lives here?"

He brings her a bowl of hot stew, pours her coffee from a pot on the fire. "I want him to be able to say he hasn't seen us."

"Oh."

The improbability of her situation is sinking in. Alone here by firelight with Miles Bennett, his horses indistinct as they graze on what they can paw through snow, his dog at his heels—how has she reached this point?

Remembering the cup in her hand, she sips coffee, finds herself hungry and spoons stew from the bowl. Watches as Miles finishes his own stew and cleans out his bowl with a wad of dry grass. Watches him walk around the fire, watches him kneel. The familiar rattle of his beads, the thought of her own lost rosary—Loss consumes her. All she has lost through her own failure. *I can't do this.* How true, how true. The darkness opens around her, the dying flame from Miles's fire a mirage, and only the indifferent stars to watch. She sets down her empty bowl on the wagon seat beside her, thinks to step down and clean it as Miles has cleaned his, knows it is not right to let Miles wait on her, take care of her, she who has abandoned hope. Still, she sits, picking out the one point she can locate, the North Star. ■

Excerpt from a novel in progress.

"Near Lick Creek Summit," 1964, photograph by Jan Boles.

WILLIAM JOHNSON

Gathering Berries Near Paradise

In the dry woods of July, clambering over
deadfall to the squabble of a jay
and the blitz of an irascible deer-fly,
we wade through brush the color of brandy,
baskets dangling from our necks gifts
of your native mother woven before
dementia locked her in the bathroom
waving at her fourth husband
who gets out of a cab from the bar
and tumbles into wind-swept leaves
to be blown angrily to death, waving back.
Today, wind blows the other way,
a coniferous hush far enough from the highway
it bids us welcome. On a slope ratcheted
with dozer-tracks softened under grass
we're ambushed by berries dark
as the eyes of our youngest in his infancy
which seem almost to leap into our baskets
with a sound like rain tattling split shakes.
One or a few find themselves at our lips,
the manna of the northern woods
whose phenols, anthocyanins and sugars
are bearable only in scant increments,
a pleasure so intense it makes death taste,
our teeth gritted black with seeds.

Beautiful Things

Over the bones of a crumbling
brick foundation, the house sloughs
its history of dry-rot, black mold
and rain-sagged plaster. With a shrug
rooms let the outside in, cupboards
furbished with moss, the smut
of rotted laundry and a mattress
claw-ripped, its stuffing strewn
like whitecaps. Punctured by ribs of lath,
walls sag heavily inward.
When you peel back the paper
in search of the original daisy print,
the past blossoms under my skin.
We skirt the shrapnel of a stove exploded
on whose iron hood heat kissed
socks of hired hands wool-sweated dry.
In snake-deep grass, under slumped concrete
the root cellar sleeps.
The year we married you led me down
steps groaning with the weight of years
your grandmother sent you
for a jar—peaches, onions or pears
like foggy winter suns. From gunnysacks
on the earthen floor, pale tentacular eyes
probed the grave of your childhood.

NANCY TAKACS

When I Read a Certain Poet

I'm reminded of how
he uses words I haven't thought of
like *banshee* and *chi-chi*
in his poem about the waning moon.

And how I don't have a woman
in my poems waving
a spray of pink azaleas
as her ex-lover walks home
eating the last enchilada.

When I wear the long silk skirt
of my poems, I'm an old woman
in the wind, rushing into
the ballroom of Walmart
for a prescription that will,
hopefully, preserve my heart.

Lately I only write down
what happens in my day,
like being surprised by
a fox, her black feet
and smoky tail, disappearing
quickly into the ochre brush.

I like colors in my poems
because I wore them on my fingers,
painting scenes for my mother,
copying postcards of German
castles and Jersey beaches
sent from her distant friend.

THE LIMBERLOST REVIEW

But this poet doesn't write in color.
I like his humor, self-deprecation,
boldness, and social consciousness.
I like how his voice floats
like cranberries in a secret bog.

He knows something.

I keep reading his poems
this afternoon, while it snows
between the hemlocks,
my heart almost stopping,
while my chihuahua's legs
move and tremble, maybe
chasing that brilliant red fox.

Wanting to be Irish

I could be like that Celtic fiddler,
clicking my heels,
calming her violin
to violet, tuning in the elves
who are tricky yet kind,
as the audience claps to horses
who speak in emeralds.

I could always be green
rolling down hills
like an Irish friend did
in her high school essay
Sister Mary Brigh read
aloud to our class.

I could be from those
who came after the Ice Age,
have a name beginning with O'
or a Mc, or a Fitz. I could be
the daughter of a Patrick
who used his carp-tongue sword
or end-winged axe,
or be named Kathleen
whose y-chromosome
could be traced all the way to Norway.

I was ashamed my Polish mother
wouldn't let me dye my hair
food-coloring green even
on Saint Patty's Day.

I wanted to be Irish
like our neighbors, the Coughlins,
who slipped me quarters
and begged for a jig.

THE LIMBERLOST REVIEW

And Mrs. Denver,
my 4th grade teacher,
concerned about my father
deadly sick that year,
and brought my mother
soda bread, corned beef,
and whiskey fudge.

I loved their merriness,
those green-eyed beer drinkers
thumping their mugs to the beat
of the bodhrán, unlike my
Baltic ancestors, who listened
to the same old rhapsodies
with a glass of red wine, teary-eyed.
I never felt part of them.

Instead, I knew that my torso
was built for strength, digging
potatoes, climbing Iverna's
rocky hills, that my head was stubborn,
to be poised over a flute or a pennywhistle,
over feet that would never die.

I loved their ancient deities:
Morrigan, poet and musician,
a raven who could transform herself
to an eel or a wolf; Dagda, lampoon
and a jokester at his own expense.

And there are so many others to love:
Yeats, Joyce, Fitzgerald,
Boland, O' Brien,
Lady Gregory, Murdoch,
Hepburn, Enya,
George Clooney.

SAMUEL GREEN

Casualties

> —i.m. Willis Toomes, Born April 9, 1947, KIA Vietnam, 1968

It's been a wet spring again, Willie. Last year
the bees didn't get into the orchard, so there
was almost no fruit set. We got a few Gravensteins
& Johnagolds, a child's basket of Sweet Sixteens,
nothing on the Orange Pippin or Pink Pearl.

Some early plums made it all
the way to ripeness. The year before we put
aside a cellar's portion large enough to last till
March, gave boxes to neighbors, & still left a mess
of apples & plums for rats, birds, & wasps on the grass.

Today's your birthday, Cousin. You would
have been seventy. Last time I saw you we
were kids, playing war with BB guns
in our back yard. You shot me right between
the shoulder blades with my brother's Daisy

pump. Kansas was so far away we seldom saw
you. My mother wrote to yours, who
gave us news. I sent you gifts sometimes
at Christmas. We both put on a uniform
after high school. You were drafted,

while I chose the safety of the sea. There was no
question of you saying no. Your mother said
you were a good boy who loved your car,
your girl, your home town, a church-going kid
who did what our fathers did in the war

we grew up hearing about. By the time I got
to Vietnam you'd been there nine long
months, already earned a Purple Heart,
Bronze Star, but felt something was wrong
with it all. My ship was somewhere

off the Mekong the day the mortars caught
you, as best I could work out
later. The letter from my mother didn't come
until I was back in the bars of our home
port near Manilla. By then your folks

had your folded grave flag on their wall. I did three
more tours from Cua Viet to An Thoi
before a drunk in a jitney sent me back to the life
you'd never have: school, a wife
& son, the work of making books, ten thousand

students & more than fifty years
of reading poetry every day to keep me
sane. At sixty I drove across three
states to see your folks in Kansas. Yours
was the first photo I saw inside the door,

dress uniform, surrounded by medals, & twenty-one
forever. Your mother's hair was still
the color of fire; your stone mason father's spine
was arched in a permanent curve. It was painful
to watch him walk. They fed us barbecue

at a place they said my grandpa liked, & made
me promise to put my hand beside your name
on the Wall, when they heard I'd spend some time
in the Capitol. I told them yes. There was hard
rain the night we hiked from our hotel. It was fall,

& after dark. We started down the ramp, the number
of names increasing, & there was yours, on panel
43W, Line 58: *Willis Albert Toomes*, rain channeling
through the letters as Thomas Hardy's somber
line described: *Down their carved names the rain-drop*

ploughs. I stopped a ranger with a question, began
to cry, & could not stop. She didn't look
surprised. Back home the nightmares took
me up, whips of tracer fire lashing the coast,
the racket of medevacs shattering past,

bound for the bouncing decks of hospital ships,
the *splash splash splash* of bullets skipping
across the Bassac River toward us, rifle kicking
against my shoulder as I fired at shapes
in the high shore grass, the stink of mud below

the Cat Lo privies out on stilts, too close to the shacks
of refugees. And the eyes of locals—empty, or turned
away, frightened, angry, hungry. I started dreaming
I couldn't get a grenade to leave my hand
after I'd pulled the pin & let the lever fly, or aiming

my sidearm at a sapper in the water, & the trigger
wouldn't pull. I caught myself tapping out Morse
on the kitchen table with two fingers. It's all chance,
isn't it, Cousin? The shore rounds passed
me by; the Filipina who took me home with her once

chased away three men with knives; the jitney driver hit
me at a slant. I've had a life of luck, while you stepped
into your random death & simply stopped.
I fend away my demons writing poems. When it
works, chance shimmers into tangible

grace. I imagine you stepping aside just one
mere inch, so the shrapnel missed.
We could have shipped you birthday jam
from figs & plums, sweet canned cherries, applesauce,
if only we had more sun, less rain,
if only the bees got into the blooms on time.

SAMUEL GREEN

Listening to Leonard Cohen off the Coast of South Vietnam, USGC Blackhaw, 1969

—for QM3 Hans Burkhardt (1949-2011)

Because the shit kickers outnumber
the rockers, it's Willie & Waylon
& Merle on the ship's mess deck
sound system, so the eight-track
that came with the California newbie
goes into the chartroom just behind
the bridge. The only tape he owns
is by some Canadian we've never
heard of, ten tunes we learn mile
by nautical mile, from Phan Rang
to Chu Lai, Qui Nhon to Da Nang,
Cam Ranh Bay to the Mekong
Delta & up the Bassac River. I can croon
the whole album six times standing
the mid-watch alone at Cat Lo
on the quarterdeck, 45 cocked & locked
on my hip, tracking tracer fire to the south,
more than a hundred rounds stitching
the night sky in the time it takes
to say *Sisters of Mercy*. Each concussion
grenade I toss over the side into the river
to scare away enemy divers is five seconds
of lyrics before the geyser of water. Stunned fish
& dead snakes rise, twitch & float toward the sea
in the current. We are listening to Leonard
intone about love though our girlfriends back home
have stopped writing. It is sing or go crazy,
sing or go dumb, as the lyrics he gives us mark time,
& we borrow his tunes to dampen the pain

as it comes. We are listening to Leonard while green
blips on the radar could be smugglers
with a hold full of weapons, or the buoys
we service could be rigged with a mine. We are
singing with Leonard who beckons us homeward,
one promising word at a time:

Oh, her name is Bian, & she lives near the sea in a hut
And she smells like the fire where she heats up the food that you've brought
Someone hammered out cans so her roof will not let in the rain
When you lie in her bed you can almost forget about blame
If the girl who once loved you has found someone closer to home
Then you both have a secret that keeps you from feeling alone
Yes you both have a secret that keeps you from feeling alone

CHARLOTTE MEARS

From the Circulation Desk

As the air dips nearer to freezing
an elderly couple carries bags of books
through the door to donate.

The man sits blankly on the couch
while his wife picks out
swap paperbacks to take home.

What is it he's thinking, when ready to go
she calls his name and he doesn't respond?
Could it be white nothingness?

Is it he simply doesn't share
his wife's thirst for what she finds
inside the pages of worn books?

Perhaps a nagging irritation
he's kept to himself all his years of marriage
rises hot and quick.

He sees himself as a young man
axe sharpened, oiled, ready to split wood
for the cold that will come and

feed the woodstove to fend off the chill
that will wrap them.

Left to Our Own Devices During the Pandemic

While walking around Liberty Park
with its ghostly vacant soccer fields
I spot a heap of shape in the distance.
Closer, it's a tangle of teenagers
all dressed in black
lounging on and over a picnic table
draped like fainted figures
just hanging out in The Now
loose in their solidarity
with endless time ahead
like roots reaching out to a somewhere
by pure wonder
full-throated yearning
heads brimming with existential questions
expecting a future
to coalesce.
But who am I to say?
Just an aging baby boomer with wavering
hope the younger generations will be left
with the earth intact and thriving
while in passing I outwardly nod
a tentative acknowledgement to the teens
instead of my teacher-impulse to stop and ask
something unsolicited like
What do you think about the mess the world's in?
How would you change it?
But I don't and walk on
knowing I would intrude
on whatever brought them together
this isolated day with others to come.

DON ZANCANELLA

A Woman on Horseback

I
Wyoming 1889

elena Bothwell is walking along the Sweetwater when out of the stone-gray dusk a woman on horseback appears. Helena fears she'll be trampled but then the rider catches sight of her and draws back on the reins.

Goddamn it and watch your step, the rider shouts.

Gracious me! Helena cries.

The rider is soaked from the waist down. The horse is soaked from the withers down. Helena stares up at them in astonishment. Who are you? she asks.

Your neighbor. Assuming you're the Bothwell girl.

Neighbor? I didn't know we had one. She's thinking of the kind she's read about in novels, who live within shouting distance. There's not another house within miles of the Bothwell ranch.

I'm from over by Horse Creek, the rider continues. Near Jim Averell's place.

Now that Helena can see her more clearly, she says, Your hair is down. She knows it's bad manners to remark on someone's appearance but she can't resist. The woman looks wild. Beautiful and wild. Like a goddess who lives in a cave.

So it is. You disapprove?

No ma'am, she replies, regretting her comment. It's none of my concern.

The woman smiles and tosses her hair—a great auburn cascade that most would choose to pin up. Well, I'm Ella Watson and if ever you find yourself on the other side of Horse Creek, do stop in. Then she stands up in the stirrups, rearranges her water-logged outfit, and says, I'm getting shivery now so I'll be on my way.

Helena jumps back to give them room, the horse springs forward, and they disappear into the willows. When they come into view again, they're on the ridge that parallels the Sweetwater, a fast-moving silhouette in the fading light.

Helena is pleased to have had the encounter. When you're seventeen and live far from the nearest town, strangers are more precious than wild animals (which she sees on a regular basis). For one thing, animals are seldom willing to converse.

No doubt she will someday find herself near Ella Watson's place. When that happens, she'll definitely stop for a visit. Once, upon hearing her mother use the phrase *my social circle*, it occurred to Helena that she herself lacked a social circle and would find it difficult to assemble one there on the Wyoming plains. But apparently Ella Watson is her neighbor, which suggests opportunities she's been unaware of before. Imagine, for example, an impromptu tea party. It's an almost inconceivable idea if your only previous experience with tea parties involved a month of planning, a full day of travel, and so many fluttering mothers and giddy girls you couldn't wait for it to end.

When she gets home she doesn't tell her parents who she crossed paths with; they wouldn't approve. Besides, she likes having a secret. Ella Watson is quite possibly the only person she's ever met who her parents haven't known in advance. She's intrigued by the idea of a mysterious acquaintance and by the figure Ella cut as she galloped off into the night.

II

Months later, when Helena is away at school, some men come looking for Ella Watson. On a sultry morning in July.

Ella hasn't been able to sleep so she gets up early and goes outside. She checks the gate, feeds the horses, and brings in the wash she left hanging on the line. A little after eight John DeCorey arrives. A kid who occasionally works for her, DeCorey ought to bathe more often but when it comes to chores, he's a reliable hand.

He says, That Arapaho woman who does beadwork is down by the river again. I wager she still has the moccasins you like.

Well let's go then, she replies and hurries off to saddle a horse.

When she's ready, they ride west, across the valley floor. But at a certain point she glances back and sees five riders and a buckboard wagon approaching from the south. One of them looks like Albert Bothwell. No doubt he's coming to complain again about her new fence and how it obstructs his access to Horse Creek. She can't tell who the others are but maybe they'll go away upon finding she's not home. Clouds are piling up in the north and she wonders: Will the heat be tempered by rain?

DeCorey leads her to the Indians and she buys the moccasins, deerskin, the right size, and beautifully decorated with beads of red and white. Her first offer is three dollars. In the end she pays three and a half. There aren't many Indians left in these parts and those that remain are having a hard time, so why not pay a fair price?

She says, What do you think, Johnny, don't they look fine? and holds out a foot for him to inspect. She likes them so much she wears them home, tucking her old boots into a saddle bag and admiring the beadwork as she rides.

Unfortunately, the men they saw earlier are waiting at the house. In addition to Bothwell, she recognizes two more: Tom Sun, owner of the Hub and Spoke ranch further up the Sweetwater, and John Durbin, who is already ripping out her fence. Gene Crowder, another boy who works for her, comes riding up and tries to make Durbin stop. But some other fellow, one she doesn't know, grabs Gene's horse by the bridle and holds boy and horse in place.

What the hell are you doing? Ella says as she approaches.

Bothwell affects detachment but can't disguise his contempt: We're taking you to Rawlins. Get in the wagon. I warned you it would come to this if you didn't stop.

She reins her horse left intending to help Gene, but Bothwell cuts her off. Don't test me, Ella, he says. Then he draws his gun.

Johnny, go tell Jim, she says, trying to remain calm. But Tom Sun has DeCorey hemmed in as well.

If we're going to town I need to change my clothes. Give me a few minutes. Maybe she can think of a way out of this mess if she has a little time.

Bothwell shakes his head. Wear what you got on. I'll rope you and drag you if it comes to that. Put yourself in the wagon now. She's afraid he'll hurt Gene or Johnny so she dismounts and does as he says. The driver of the wagon is a big bearded fellow named Ernest McClain, one of Bothwell's hands.

Let's go, says Tom Sun and the wagon lurches forward. DeCorey tries to follow but Sun orders him to stop: Get in that goddamned house and don't come out 'til noon. The boy looks to Ella for guidance. Do it, Johnny, she says.

To get to Rawlins they have to pass Jim Averell's place. She doesn't want him to get involved and hopes he's not at home. But there he is, jouncing up the road in his little one-horse trap. As if he intends to welcome them to his establishment, to the general store and roadhouse where she sometimes works as a cook.

When Jim is close enough, he says, What have we here? His tone is genial, but she can see he's alarmed. And has reason to be because they all draw their guns. Apparently they've decided Jim Averell is some kind of vicious desperado—when in fact he's merely a college-educated shopkeeper whose only sin is writing letters to the newspaper. Letters in which he points out how the owners of large ranches are making false accusations against homesteaders in an effort to seize their land.

Helena first met Averell in Rawlins where she was working in a hotel. He told her he was opening a business near Independence Rock and asked if she'd like to help. She said, I ain't gonna marry you if that's what you're saying. I tried it once in Kansas and it didn't work out. In response, Averell looked hurt. I meant nothing of the sort, he said. After a period of negotiation, she moved here and built a cabin. Now some nights he spends at her place and others she spends at his.

But today she wishes they'd never met. Bothwell makes Jim get in the wagon and sit beside her. Then Tom Sun leads them north. Rawlins is in the opposite direction so Bothwell lied. Ella nudges Averell with her elbow. Look at my new moccasins, she says.

Before they've gone very far, they turn off the main road and proceed toward the Sweetwater, stopping when they reach the water's edge. By then Averell has recovered and is talking in his usual manner, without caution or constraint. Bothwell and Durbin are riding behind them and Jim keeps telling them why, in his view, they're land grabbers and cheats: If a man gets in your way, you simply declare him a *rustler*.

You think the word itself gives you permission to do as you please. And Bothwell, what about that house you live in? Sitting out there like a Norman castle. No one needs a house that big.

Eventually Durbin gets fed up. Shut your goddamn mouth or I'm gonna drown you, he barks. In response, Ella, who's been looking at all the sand bars and exposed gravel in the river says, That's not enough water to drown a cat. Feel free to throw me in.

Her remark unsettles them and they begin arguing amongst themselves. McClain says, You ought not to do this, and Durbin, Let's get on with it. Amidst their bickering, Bothwell takes out his pocket watch, studies it as though he's allotted a particular amount of time for this task, and says, Ernest, they're maverickers. You don't think she *bought* those cattle, do you? Only Tom Sun remains silent. Terrifyingly so.

When they're done arguing, they turn the wagon and backtrack for a while, and Ella's outlook improves. Maybe they're taking them home. But no, they turn into Spring Creek canyon. The road narrows, the rocks on one side and the trees on the other leaving scarcely enough room for the wagon to pass. She considers leaping off and making a run for it, but either the canyon walls or Tom Sun would stop her before she got away. Jim continues berating their captors but now the ground is so rough it's difficult to hear him over the rumble of the wheels.

The trail ends in a mass of boulders and stunted pines. Bothwell says, Let's get this done, and someone strikes her from behind. As she's dragged from the wagon by her hair, her vision blurs and a spasm courses through her, beginning in her chest and spiraling out. They stand her up beneath a tree at the edge of a cliff, and suddenly she feels empty, as though all that's left between her skin and skeleton is desiccated air.

She glances at Jim. He's entirely still. Not talking, not resisting, the rope already around his neck. She tries to prevent the same thing from happening to her but she hasn't the strength. She thinks: I am being murdered but perhaps an angel will come down from the great blue sky and carry my soul away.

III

A week later, all six men have been arrested but none of them has difficulty posting bail. They hire the best lawyers and the judge is one of Bothwell's oldest friends.

Ella leaves behind only the meager possessions of a struggling homesteader:

2 horses
9 chickens
1 cook stove
1 bed w/bedding
1 grindstone
1 shovel
1 clock
1 pine table
1 starred quilt
3 chairs
2 good dresses
1 breast pin with matching earbobs

and the four-by-six-inch mirror she looked at herself in every morning, even if she was only going out to feed the stock. Not out of vanity but out of self-respect. As for the thirty-six cattle in her herd, they are sold off to the very men who lynched her, for one dollar a head.

Bothwell had the foresight to wire his version of events to the newspapers in Cheyenne the day before the hanging took place. He has a convenient ally in the editor of the *Daily Leader*, an easily-influenced man who loves death and degradation in all their forms—because they help him sell copies of his own paper and because he can make extra money peddling stories about such matters to the papers back east. The more sensational the account, the more he can charge. Using Bothwell's notes, the editor composes this dispatch:

DON ZANCANELLA

Cheyenne Daily Leader
Tuesday, July 23, 1889
A Double Lynching

> *Postmaster Averell and his female accomplice hung for Cattle Stealing. The man weakened but the woman cursed to the last. Two rustlers were lynched near historic Independence Rock on the Sweetwater River in Carbon County Sunday night. They were Postmaster James Averell and a whore who had been living with him for several months. Their offense was cattle stealing, and they operated on a large scale, recruiting local youngsters to help.*
>
> *Averell and the woman were fearless maverickers. The female was the equal of any man on the range. Where she came from no one seems to know, but that she was a hellion everyone agrees. Although her given name was Ella Watson, she answered to nothing but Cattle Kate.*
>
> *Early on Sunday from ten to fifteen men, made desperate by the steady loss of their cattle, quietly galloped to the Averell ranch. A few hundred yards from the cabin they dismounted and approached. The leader of the regulators stationed a man with a Winchester at each window and led a rush to the door. A shout of "Hands up!" sounded above the crash of glass as the rifles were leveled at the astonished pair of thieves.*
>
> *Averell begged and whined and protested innocence, saying the woman did all the stealing. The female was made of sterner stuff. She cursed and called upon the Deity to strike her enemies dead.*
>
> *They were hung from the limb of a big cottonwood tree on the south bank of the Sweetwater. Averell died quickly but the woman fought with unholy strength until she at last she succumbed.*
>
> *Yesterday morning the bodies swayed to and fro in the prairie breeze. The faces were discolored and magpies had taken their eyes. An inquest may be held but it is doubtful if any attempt will be made to punish the lynchers. They acted in self-protection, as all honest citizens should.*

IV

When the lynching takes place Helena is at school in Philadelphia. Her father sent her there because of her many transgressions: lying, stealing, profanity, blasphemy, playing hooky from school, and participating in horseback races with hired hands. But especially because when he went to backhand her over some small impertinence, she realized what was coming and hit him first. For a few seconds, they stood looking at one another, his fist still raised and the imprint of her hand fully visible on his face. Then he hit her so hard she was lifted off her feet. But later, as she staunched her bloody nose, she concluded that defending herself had been deeply satisfying. Of course, that wasn't the end of it. The next day he told her to pack her things.

The school is known as Mrs. Crawford's and at first it seems rather nice. The teachers are tolerable, the food better than expected, and the grounds so green and park-like, she wonders why on earth people from such places would choose to pack up and go west, to the desolation of the high plains (which is precisely what her own parents did). Yet before long she begins to feel claustrophobic, as though she's been thrown in jail. Students aren't allowed to leave the campus, classes take on a boring sameness, the food takes on a boring sameness, and Mrs. Crawford and her staff begin to show their true oppressive colors. Take, for instance, the weekly room inspections. Any sweets are confiscated, as are scented items such as sachets or perfumed handkerchiefs. But what Ella really resents is the absence of horses. There are none for student use, not even a pony or a tired nag. She was promised horses, so either Mrs. Crawford or her parents lied.

When she can take it no longer, she starts misbehaving. Promptness is an obsession at the school, so she begins showing up late, first for morning convocation and then for every meal. And she dresses not according to their genteel standards but however she pleases. They punish her with extra chores and study sessions on Saturday afternoons, the only time students are supposed to have for themselves.

Miss Bothwell, to the laundry.

Yes ma'am.

And after dinner you'll work with Miss Plummer. She says you're stubborn, that you don't take instruction well.

But when the meal is over, instead of going to Miss Plummer's quarters, she slips out and goes exploring on her own. She ends up getting lost in a neighborhood of ramshackle boarding houses and tiny shops, where children play in the alleys and rough-looking men in shirtsleeves stand on corners laughing and smoking and making obscene gestures as she passes. Eventually, a tall man with yellow whiskers crosses the street and comes up behind her.

Pardon me, Miss, but I wouldn't be ramblin' around here at night. Allow me to escort you home.

No thank you, she replies, but he fails to go away.

You look like a spirited gal. Suppose I give you a kiss.

No thank you. She speeds up.

Slow down or—

Take your hand off me.

Well ain't you the randy little bitch, he says and Helena begins to run. She doesn't stop until she's on a busy street. When she turns he's disappeared and she feels a rush of relief.

By the time she gets back it's after dark and the entire school is in an uproar. As an excuse, she mentions the man with yellow whiskers. I expect you invited it, Mrs. Crawford says, You'll sleep in the cell tonight.

But if they think they can break her, they're mistaken. For one thing their idea of punishment is rather mild. Extra chores. No dessert. Nights in a room with only a cot. She grew up with a father who knows what real punishment consists of. Once, he came after her with his belt but grabbed the wrong end (at least that's what he claimed) and the buckle opened a deep gash beneath her eye. She bled so much that when her mother saw her, she shrieked and fell to the ground. Helena was left with a permanent scar. If Mrs. Crawford's goal is to cause her to submit, she'd best have a look at that scar.

A few days later she sneaks out again, walking until she comes to an open field where dairy cows are grazing and a fine-looking young sorrel is standing in the shade of a maple tree. She climbs the fence and coaxes the horse over with a fistful of grass. When it no longer fears her, she grabs its mane and pulls herself onto its back. For a while she rides back and forth across the field, with no bridle or saddle but still at a gallop, like only a girl who has spent her life on horseback could. Then she heads down the road toward the school. She stops in front of Mrs. Crawford's house. Her skirts are hiked up, her hair is undone, and soon girls are coming from everywhere to see what Mrs. Crawford will do. When at last she emerges from her house, she's trembling with anger. You're finished here, she says.

You'll have to convince my father of that, Helena replies.

Over the next ten days there's a furious exchange of telegrams between Pennsylvania and Wyoming but Mrs. Crawford prevails. By the end of the month Helena is on the train home, her stay in Philadelphia having lasted only twelve weeks. Before she leaves Miss Plummer gives her a book. *Wuthering Heights*. You remind me of someone in here, Miss Plummer says. Helena reads it from Philadelphia to Chicago and then a second time across the Great Plains. The book dazzles her. It stuns her. It disturbs her dreams. She's not sure which character Miss Plummer meant but the landscape in the book is the landscape where she grew up. Bleak and terrible and sublime and crushingly lonely all at once.

The day she arrives her father takes her out behind the house, says What in God's name were you thinking? and raises his hand to strike her. This time, instead of fighting back, she dodges the blow, but in so doing stumbles backward into the wood pile. He takes a step forward and glares at her. She fears he'll grab a piece of wood. Instead he shakes his head and goes back inside. Why did he stop? Maybe there's some scruple, some principle he prefers not to violate. You can beat a girl but not with cord wood. Not when she's flat on her back. Or maybe he's decided she's not worth the trouble—which would be a low position to have ended up in, a low position indeed.

When she was twelve years old, he took her hunting. A mountain lion had been stealing livestock and he wanted it dead. They left the lush prairie and rode out into the Red Desert. The earth was cracked and the buttes rust-colored and way off in the distance the mountains seemed to float above the ground. As they traveled, her father showed her how to live off the land and how to track. He took her to see a herd of wild horses and then some wind-carved cliffs that looked like an abandoned city. He took her to see an alkali flat that was as smooth and white as a field of fresh snow. One afternoon, as they stopped to examine the sun-bleached bones of a bison he said, There are two things that matter: water and family. However, you can live without family. Such were the lessons he taught.

At night they gazed up at the great river of stars and he told her stories about his youth: And then that grizzly came at me. We drove three thousand head across three rivers. She could see he was trying to be a good father but it was obvious he'd have been happier if she was a boy. In the end they failed to find the mountain lion and he never took her hunting again.

Now, as she restacks the wood, she decides the best thing is to avoid him. She'll go riding during the day and spend the evening in her room. She reads the book a third time. It's a fiend of a book. Maybe her father was once a Heathcliff, handsome and vengeful and arrogant. Striding across the plains. But her mother is no Catherine, at least not anymore. Whatever wildness was in her has been ground to dust. She does only what he says. Her mother should tell him to go to hell but she never will. Helena doesn't want to be like her. She can pity her but still refuse to follow her path.

Then one day Ernie, a man who works for her father, says, Something bad happened while you was gone. You know that woman who lived over by Horse Creek? Well your daddy and some others kilt her. And the postmaster Jim Averell too.

He tells her this when they're in the stable, away from everyone else. She stops what she's doing and stares at him, unable to utter a word.

They lynched 'em up above the river, he adds. Because they was rustlin' cattle.

When she can finally speak, she asks for the rest of the story, exactly what happened, exactly who was involved.

Miss, you don't want to hear it, he murmurs.

You better tell me, she says.

When he's done, she doesn't know what to think. If Ella Watson was a cattle thief, then she should have known better. You reap what you sow. The girls at Mrs. Crawford's would have been thrilled to find out her father is a vigilante. She remembers hearing that Ella Watson was Jim Averell's paramour, what cowboys call a Saturday wife, so maybe she deserved it. As much as Helena hates her father she's not sure she has the right to question his judgement about matters like these. About cattle thieves and the punishment they deserve.

 Her father would be pleased to know she's experiencing such uncertainty. She wishes she could see herself through his eyes. Despite all that's happened does he think she still respects him? Perhaps. He believes fear is evidence of respect.

 Were you there when it happened? Helena asks.

 Ernie, a big shambling fellow, lowers his eyes. I drove the wagon.

 At least you didn't do the bad part. The stringing up itself. Or did you?

 No. But I watched. I didn't shut my eyes.

V

A month later she's looking for a lost calf in a canyon when her eye catches a flash of color between two slabs of rock. It's a moccasin, all covered in red and white beadwork and so clean it might never have been worn. Where there's one, there ought to be two, so she peers into the crevice again. Finding nothing, she climbs atop a large boulder and scans the area. There it is, in a tangle of sagebrush, not ten feet away. This one is in worse condition, having suffered more exposure to the elements than the first. Still, the beadwork is undamaged and the application of a little saddle oil will make it good as new.

 She pulls off her boots and tries them on, curling her toes against the deerskin. They're beautiful and, better yet, they fit. After spending a moment admiring them, she puts her boots back on, slides one moccasin into each of her jacket pockets, and resumes her search for the stray. But then it occurs to her where she is. Looking up, she can see the cliff and the trees at the top, and the blue sky overhead, across which careens a hawk. There, attached to one stout limb, are the remnants of the rope.

 In that moment she feels a thickening in her throat, a twisting in her gut, an overwhelming sensation of revulsion and disgust. She wishes she was brave enough to get a gun and use it on him. She pictures Ella

Watson. Wet from the river. Water is what matters. Her hair. The skillful way she handled her horse. I'm getting shivery, she said.

God knows there are plenty of guns lying about the house. She's been taught how to use them. He used to beat her, until she hit him back. Now it appears he's stopped. Has he? She's not certain. The next time he might simply beat her to death. What are her choices? Her poor mother. No matter what happens things won't go well for her.

That evening she reads the book until she finds this line: *The murdered do haunt their murderers.* Outside the sky is purple with a ribbon of orange at the horizon—a dusty purple, and beneath the orange, a wall of jagged bluffs. A pair of coyotes have begun to howl. On Ella's behalf, she puts on the moccasins and goes looking for him. He's in the library, reading the newspaper behind his massive desk. He hears her enter, lowers the paper, gives her an impatient look. She directs his gaze to the floor.

I found something, she says.

He looks and looks. Then comes the recognition. Goddamn you, he says, goddamn you. The gun is concealed, there if she needs it. But he doesn't rise up. In fact the opposite. He slumps.

She turns and walks down the hall. Out the door and through the gate and across the prairie until she overtops a ridge and can see the house no more. ■

"Night Hunt" by Sarah Trudeau. Linoleum block print, 11 x 14 inches.

PAUL ZARZYSKI

Going It Alone

> *The secret of a good old age is simply*
> *an honorable pact with solitude.*
> —Gabriel Garcia Marquez

Not just for the metaphorical hell of it
but instead, here and now, for good reason,
while peering into this macro-lens
windshield, I think of Amelia's
Lockheed Electra, of Dick Hugo's Buick
Skylark, of everything falling
inevitably through the surrealistic
filter of cumulonimbus—heavy
weather swirling into focus
as first my father, then my mother,
slipped into their final silences. I,
with no sane way out of this
mortal storm, this viscid
mythological maze of biblical
ebb and flow, have come to see
why I never again will thrive
as once I thrived in the same
exact triangular time
with Mom and Dad. Thus, alone,
I embrace the wild
disorder, the metamorphosis, this life
sentence amidst the faithful. No longer
just one more fading pin-tip
blip upon the radar screens
of the gods, I, in solo flight,
am swallowed into the welcoming black-
garmented arms of the dark, far
beyond the blurred
purgatorial borders between
heaven and earth—my cargo of light
grown brighter, pulsing with all
the hope, all the fear,
one disappearing soul can hold.

"Maya Angelou" by Tom Callos. Linocut, 11 x 14 inches.

KIM STAFFORD

Wind Brings Word

As I tumble from the sky, as I bully
through the pines, as I whisk across
the playa, as I savor sage's scent, as I
whisper through the grass, as I touched
the leaves in Eden to be spirit breath
for Eve, as I traveled from the garden to be
sutras of the Buddha, to be quatrains of
Muhammad, to be wisdom of the Talmud
as chanted by the cantor, to be parables
of Jesus, I was lullaby of mother, I will be
your true confession as I waver at your ear,
as I flicker past your face, I was once the breath
of Caesar, I will be your words of anger, I will
blur the leaves of willow as I rise to carry
rain, as I sweep away the storm, I was
whimper of the youngest, I was final word
of friend, I will be your chance for witness,
I will be your song of blessing as I slide
below the stars, I will riffle through
your hair as I roll along the road, as I
rumble past the house as I whirl
across the field, I will question your
resistance, I will answer from your
heart with stories of your father, I was
carrier of pollen, I was humming of the bees,
I was calling of the wren, I was rustle
in the reeds, I was waves across the water,
I was ripples on the river as I stumbled
down the valley, as I climbed across the hills,
I will be the clap of thunder, I will sift your
mother's ashes as you sing her song again,
I will honor your duration, I was all you ever
needed, I was treasure beyond other, I was lover's

cry of pleasure, I will be your gasp of sorrow
as you choose your words of honor, will you
use me well in parley, will you tell your truth
in story, will you speak your piece for kinship,
will you strengthen all relations, will you use
your breath to gather all who breathe together,
the infant and the elder, all the cousins
and the creatures, all the little lives
in danger, I will give you breath again
if you promise to return it, if you use it
well in council as you testify for earth,
as you listen deep in stillness before your
breath is over, if I touch your face in passing
as I whisper through the grass.

Back Then, His Words Were Not Enough . . . Now They Are Precious

We stopped on a road in Montana.
My father sat on the passenger side.
I turned off the car and poured out
my sorrows, my life falling apart,
all my landmarks gone.

He was silent. We listened to the river.
Two crows flew over. They could go
anywhere. The river flowed silver.
My father put his hand on my sleeve:
"Be of good heart, my friend."

"Best Friends Forever" by Riley Sophia Penaluna. Linocut, 4 x 6 inches.

JIM DODGE

Poem Ending with a Line from Black Bart, PO8

The helicopter landed
right out behind our barn
and this young slim guy in jogging shorts
holding his hair in place
ran over through the prop-wash and engine roar
told me he worked for some advertising outfit in the city
represented Wells Fargo Bank
and they were looking to shoot
some of those stagecoach commercials
and our ranch looked likely—
there were two big flats, a vague dirt road,
old hand-split picket fences

and you couldn't see a thing
that wasn't there in 1870
(except the five cars
which he said could be moved
though I couldn't remember a day
when more than two were running at once).

So I said sure, look around,
and if you like it you can use it for free—
the kids will love the stagecoach—
but I do have one condition:
I get to play Black Bart.

He laughed and said he was sorry
but there was no way in hell
Wells Fargo would ever go for that,
and as I watched the chopper roar up
flattening the pasture grass
I had to wonder what this damn country
is coming to. I would have made
a great Black Bart,
you fair-haired sons-of-bitches.

Always Something

My bank account is belly up
and my truck would need new tires
if the engine wasn't seized.
I'm down to couch-change, my library card,
and a rocky garden of limp mustard greens.
All my creditable friends are in the doldrums too,
near penniless or already short,
we're long out of interesting drugs,
and summer has bloated our hearts
with a merciless torpor
you've got to fight to survive.
It's always something,
and when it's not, it's something else.

Let it all fly to shit.

I wander down to where the woods level out,
singing to keep myself company,

Someone's in the kitchen with Di-nah,
Someone's in the kitchen I know-ho-ho . . .

I hit the *know-ho-ho* real hard.
That's my favorite part.

INTERVIEW

Cronies: Adventures with Ken Kesey, Neal Cassady, the Merry Pranksters and the Grateful Dead, *published by Tsunami Press, 2022.*

Further Flashbacks of a Long Strange Trip:
An Interview with Writer, Editor, and Merry Prankster

KEN BABBS

Dan Armstrong

Editor's Note:

e was Ken Kesey's closest friend, known among the Merry Pranksters as the Intrepid Traveler, one half of the "toothsome twosome," riding high on one of the most famous bus trips in countercultural history. He was a Wallace Stegner Fellow at Stanford University, a Vietnam helicopter pilot, an LSD adventurer, a participant in coast-to-coast "happenings," a novelist, editor, co-author, thespian, chronicler, filmmaker, and visionary peacemaker. Ken Babbs rubbed shoulders with some of the best minds of his generation and survived to tell the tale. As Hunter S. Thompson once wrote, reflecting on Kesey, Babbs, and "the Acid Tests" of the 1960s: "There were no rules, fear was unknown, and sleep was out of the question."

In a new book, Ken Babbs presents "a burlesque" in *Cronies: Adventures with Ken Kesey, Neal Cassady, the Merry Pranksters and the Grateful Dead* (Tsunami Press, 2022), an embellished chronicle of adventures in the mind, in the world, exploring the depths of long and lasting friendships, and offering witness to eruptive history and enlightening times.

A Case Institute of Technology engineering student-turned-*Magna cum laude* English major from Ohio's Miami University, Babbs, a member of two NCAA basketball tournament teams, landed a Woodrow Wilson National Scholarship to Stanford and acceptance into novelist Wallace Stegner's famous creative writing seminar and soon after arriving in the fall of 1958 met a young Ken Kesey at a party for program fellows on the deck of Stegner's home in Palo Alto. Kesey and Babbs, two athlete writers, hit it off instantly and the rest is a story of one of the greatest friendships in the countercultural canon.

After Stanford, a Navy ROTC scholarship obligation took Babbs to train in the U.S. Marine Corps as a Lieutenant and helicopter pilot and then from 1962-1963 to serve among the "advisory forces" in Vietnam, realizing just weeks after his arrival that American intervention was a mistake. While there, however, he wrote in his downtime a novel titled *Who Shot the Water Buffalo?* inspired by his experiences in southeast Asia. On his return to the states to circulate it to possible publishers, the manuscript was lost until an old friend found a carbon copy 40 years later and returned it to Babbs in 2010. After some rewriting and editing, the novel was published a year later by New York's Overlook Press to some serious acclaim.

Over the years, he collaborated on many different projects about times with his fellow Merry Pranksters. With Kesey he helped write the novel *The Last Go Round* (Viking, 1994) about the 1911 Pendleton Rodeo. And he was an editor of the literary journal *Spit in the Ocean* in the early-1980s, compiling the most popular edition of the journal about a friend he knew well, Neal Cassady, Jack Kerouac's hero of *On the Road* and the driver of "Further," the famous 1939 International Harvester school bus that carried the Pranksters to cross-country adventures chronicled in such books as Tom Wolfe's *Electric Kool-Aid Acid Test*, Kesey's *The Further Inquiry* and now in Babbs' own new book.

At 87, Ken Babbs still attends to various film and literary projects related to the era of the bus at his home on a six-acre farm near Eugene, Oregon, with his wife Eileen, a retired high school English teacher.

Eugene novelist Dan Armstrong recorded the following interview with Ken Babbs shortly after *Cronies* first appeared, and Limberlost is privileged to transcribe and publish an edited version of that exchange for the first time.

—*Rick Ardinger*

Ken Kesey's 1939 school bus, "Further," carried the Merry Band of Pranksters across the country.

AN INTERVIEW WITH KEN BABBS

Armstrong: *Ken, you call your new book* Cronies: Adventures with Ken Kesey, Neal Cassady, the Merry Pranksters, and the Grateful Dead *a "burlesque." Why do you call it a burlesque?*

Babbs: Well, as I was writing the book, I knew it wasn't a memoir, nor was it fiction. And I came across the literary form called a burlesque, a legitimate literary form. One of the most famous ones, written in the early 1800s, was called *Knickerbocker's History of New York*, and it caused a sensation because of the things that were in it. Like 'why is the mayor of New York City meeting all the boats as they come in from other places and hiring all the beautiful young women to work in city hall?' At that time there were advertisements in the newspapers, asking, "Who is this guy, Knickerbocker?" And it turned out that the author was Washington Irving, and he was the one writing all those things about Knickerbocker in the papers to enhance the sale of his book. It was quite a sensation. The neat thing about Washington Irving is not only that he was a writer of great stories, but he's the first author in America to make a living off his writing.

Ken Babbs. Photo by Jay Blakesberg.

Armstrong: *So, it was a way you could tell your stories as memoir with the freedom to exaggerate and no one would come back and say, 'Hey, Ken, that's not true,' Kind of an escape hatch for you?*

Babbs: Totally true. In fact, the definition of burlesque is an historical occurrence embellished with inventions and exaggerations. There are 70 stories in *Cronies*, each one a standalone story. The stories don't move along like a regular memoir. Each stands alone. But they do move through time, starting with when I met Ken Kesey in 1958 at Stanford University in Wallace Stegner's writing seminar to when Ken died in 2001. That encompasses a lot of adventure.

Armstrong: *I have a chapbook that you published a few years ago that is called* We Were Arrested, *and it's one of the stories you tell in* Cronies. *It's about a bust at La Honda, California, where Ken Kesey and you were living. The second part of the story tells what I think is the precursor to the Acid Test and the early days of the Grateful Dead.*

Babbs: Yes. That is a chapter in *Cronies*. When we took the bus on the famous trip to New York City back in 1964, we audio-taped and filmed it all. And we came back to La Honda, California, and Kesey and I began editing the movie. We would work on it during the week, and on Saturday nights we'd show what we did. Word got around the Bay Area we were doing this, and people started pouring in on Saturday nights. Anyway, one night the cops raided the place. A DEA agent in San Francisco thought that Kesey was running a big pot operation out of there because Neal Cassady was driving in and out and he thought Cassady was the driver. And one day he was down in San Francisco's North Beach, and he heard these people say, "Let's go over to Kesey's, it's Saturday night, get loaded."

    A judge granted a search warrant, and they came in, 17 cops and a dog, and busted 14 of us, and we all went to jail and spent the night. And then we had to go to court. Our lawyer, Brian Rohan, argued for us and the judge let everybody off but Kesey because it was his place. They did find a little bit of pot there.

    They also got this other guy, a friend of ours, Page Browning, who they'd been after for a long time because he had been running pot from Mexico up to the Bay Area. So, Page and Kesey eventually both did six months together at the San Mateo County Farm. The neat little thing about that was that the Honor Camp butted right up against Kesey's property at La Honda.

Armstrong: *So how did you get to know Jerry Garcia and The Grateful Dead members? Were they just living in the neighborhood?*

Babbs: Well, when we were going to Stanford, Kesey lived at this place called Perry Lane, a bunch of cottages in the woods across the street from the Stanford Golf Course, and it was kind of on a hill. And down at the bottom of the hill was this house called The Chateau where Alan Trist and other musicians lived. Alan Trist brought Jerry Garcia and the band

AN INTERVIEW WITH KEN BABBS

The American rock band The Grateful Dead was formed in 1965 in Palo Alto, California.

up to Perry Lane to meet Kesey. And when they left, someone asked, "Who were those guys?" And Kesey says, "Oh, I don't know, just some hairy musicians."

I lived down in Santa Cruz then at a place called The Spread. And one Halloween we were having a party. The Merry Pranksters were actually a band then. We all played instruments—guitar, electric guitar. I played bass and the piano and drums, the whole thing. And we were all getting high, and we went out and communed with the moon and elevated two to three feet off the ground. Then all of a sudden, we heard these strange noises coming from the house and—oh my God—it actually sounded like music! And we went inside, and all those hairy musicians were in there playing our instruments.

Armstrong: *Your book begins when you meet Ken Kesey. Just before that you went to Case Institute of Technology in Cleveland, Ohio, for a couple of years. You were a basketball player at Case.*

Babbs: Yeah, I got a basketball scholarship to Case School of Engineering but I couldn't hack it, so I transferred to Miami University in Oxford, Ohio, and I picked up a scholarship there too.

Armstrong: *You were also in Navy ROTC.*

Babbs: Yeah. I was wondering how I was going to pay for school, and I read that you could get an NROTC Scholarship, so I applied for one and got it. And that paid my tuition, and books, and an extra $50 a month.

Armstrong: *So, when you went to Stanford, Navy ROTC paid for your time there as well?*

Babbs: Well, I paid for part of it. When I transferred, I had three years of eligibility in basketball. I stayed at Miami University for three years, but I had one more year on my NROTC Scholarship and I was going to Stanford, but actually I applied for a Woodrow Wilson Fellowship and got that. Both of those scholarships paid my way through Stanford that year. Kesey also was there on a Woodrow Wilson Fellowship that was designed for people who wanted to be college teachers. That'd been a laugh, both of us teaching in college instead of being on the bus driving around America.

Armstrong: *Tell me about meeting Kesey. You were in ROTC, probably pretty clean cut. And the Wallace Stegner writing seminar was loaded with talented writers: Wendell Berry? Peter S. Beagle? Larry McMurtry? Robert Stone?*

Babbs: McMurtry got in the program the year after me. The other big-time writer in there was Ernest Gaines, who wrote *The Autobiography of Miss Jane Pittman*. It was a high-quality class. Before the class even started, Wallace Stegner had a cocktail party at his house. And on his deck out there, I saw this guy standing at the other side of the deck and I went up and started talking to Kesey. We sized each other up and shook hands, and we didn't try to squeeze each other to death or any of that bullshit. We hit it off right away. And I'd go over to his house at Perry Lane all the time, and we just became good friends right from the very beginning.

Armstrong: *What was your interest in writing?*

Babbs: When I was at Miami University in Ohio, I had a great writing instructor there named Walter Havighurst, an Ohio writer who wrote stories and novels. I took his class, and he encouraged me to keep at it. I knew I was going to graduate school, and at that time Columbia, Iowa, and Stanford were the three best schools for writing. I didn't want to go to New York City. It's too close to Ohio. And Iowa? Who wants to go to Iowa? The West Coast—oh boy. When I hit the Pacific Ocean, I knew I was never going to live in Ohio again.

AN INTERVIEW WITH KEN BABBS

Armstrong: *Wallace Stegner's seminar was loaded with great writers. What was it like for someone who was just beginning to write, to walk into a seminar of such talent. None of you had proven yourselves yet. Could you feel that when you walked in?*

Babbs: Well, there was a little bit of competition going on there. But the neat thing about that class was that everybody was very positive about each other, and we encouraged each other, no back-biting or anything. Wendell Berry has been a good friend of mine for years and years and years. I still call him and talk to him all the time. And the same with Ernest Gaines before he died. And Kesey, of course. We also had a real character in the class named Mitch Strucinski. He was this Polish guy from Chicago. And it turned out he had just gotten out of prison for stealing rare books from libraries. He wrote stories and sent them to Stegner. And Stegner thought he'd take a chance on this guy and do his part rehabilitating a criminal into a life as a writer.

Armstrong: *How did that work out?*

Babbs: He wrote a story that everybody still talks about. It was about a farmer who had this hog that died, and he didn't know what to do with it, so he chopped it up into pieces and stuffed it down this hole, or this dry well. And everybody in the seminar was like, "Whoa, whoa, whoa, whoa!" He was an interesting guy. He had a pregnant girlfriend, and after I left the program the following year, she got caught in Stanford's Hoover Library hiding rare books under her tummy. Mitch was having her steal rare books. So, Mitch went off to prison again in California. Kesey and I went and visited him. But the funny thing that happened was years later this car that I drove across the country from Ohio, a 1948 Pontiac that I had sold to Mitch, was parked in Wallace Stegner's son's driveway after Mitch went to prison. And one day they decided to move the car, and they opened up the trunk and it was full of rare books stolen from the library.

Armstrong: *So, at some point, during that time at Stanford, Ken Kesey stumbled onto LSD. Did that bleed into the seminar? Kesey must have introduced you to LSD at that time.*

Babbs: Well, I was at Stanford only one year before I had to go into the Marine Corps. Kesey was there another year. And one of his neighbors at Perry Lane, Vic Lovell, told him about this thing that he was doing at the VA hospital near Menlo Park. Which required you to go in every day and researchers would give you some kind of a pill and watch you to see what the effects were-—and pay you $25 each time.
It was an experiment the government was running at the VA Hospital.

Vic asked Kesey if he'd wanted to get in on it. And Kesey said yes. And so, they'd give him the pill, and sometimes he'd feel something, and he'd have to answer questions and they'd take his blood pressure the whole time. And other times they'd give him a placebo. But every once in a while, they'd give him the pill that was really good.

And so, Vic and Kesey and a couple others got together after a session and said, "Listen, when they give us the good stuff, let's act like nothing's happening." Because if they give you the placebo and nothing's happening, they'd cut you loose. Then they could be out on the streets high.

Meanwhile, Kesey also got a job as a night aide at that same VA Hospital, and he sat up watching the mental patients down in the day room. And he happened to notice the office of the doctor who ran those experiments. And so, he got the keys down off the ring, unlocked the door, and went in and looked around. He opened the middle drawer of the desk, and in there was a bottle of 500 tabs of pure Sandoz Laboratory LSD from Switzerland. Oh my! So, he just slipped those in his pocket and took them home. And that's how we all got introduced to LSD.

Armstrong: *Did Kesey just say one day, "Hey, Ken, this is something I found. You want to try it?"*

Babbs: This happened before I went to Vietnam. When I was in the Marine Corps, first I had to go to Officers Basic School for a year, and then I had to go to flight school for a year, stationed in Southern California, flying helicopters. On weekends sometimes I'd take a flight in the helicopter up to the Bay Area and spend weekends with Kesey. And that's when the LSD would happen. We wrote letters back and forth and he talked about it. And when I went up there for a visit, we all got high together. It was a lot of fun. But then I went to Vietnam

AN INTERVIEW WITH KEN BABBS

and was gone for a year. When I came back, I got off the helicopter and onto the bus in 1964. That's when we took the bus across-country, filming and taping everything—and with a big gallon jar of orange juice laced with LSD.

Armstrong: *From the helicopter to the bus . . .*

Neal Cassady.

Babbs: Everywhere we stopped with the bus all painted up and everything we would attract crowds. And we'd get out and play our instruments, and we had our costumes on and everything. And then a party would start. And then we'd jump back in the bus—and we'd record it all on film and audiotape. Long hours on the bus filming and taping, and everything was complete improv. We didn't know any songs except what we made up, and played on the spot, and the dramas we'd get into, we just played parts we made up. And people out there would take on parts and play them too.

And like I say, when we got back home, our plan was to turn it all into a movie, but we got busted. The Saturday crowds were getting so big that Kesey decided we had to get a hall somewhere to show the movie. So, we started renting a hall to show our movie. And we called it the *Acid Test*—"Can you pass the Acid Test?" And the musicians showed up. They were called the Warlocks then. By about the second or third Acid Test, they changed their name to the Grateful Dead.

Around this time, Kesey went on the lam. They were after him. They were going to send him to jail. So, he faked his suicide and went to Mexico.

Armstrong: *Great idea...*

Babbs: He sent me and the rest of the Pranksters in the bus down to LA to do the Acid Test with the Grateful Dead. And at this one show, at midnight, LSD was going to become illegal in California. Up to that time LSD was not illegal anywhere. And so, during this Acid Test, while the band was playing, I got all the Pranksters together and I said, "Let's get out of here now, because pretty soon the heat's going to be on this." And we all drove down to Mexico and hooked up with Kesey and spent six months in this little town called Manzanilla on the beach, a tiny fishing village. And we had two places there, right on the beach. A wonderful time.

    Neal Cassady came down there with us and was with us all the time. We had a neat studio set up in this building next door, an old Purina warehouse. We had gone into studios and made some really good audio tapes. And we were getting good now with our instruments as background, and with Kesey and me recording stories just off the tops of our heads, and then overdubbing them. My big project right now is to try and find those Mexico tapes.

Armstrong: *When you got to Stanford, Jack Kerouac's* On the Road *had only been out maybe a year.*

Babbs: Yes, On the Road came out in 1957.

Armstrong: *Kerouac's original draft of* On the Road *was a long scroll, didn't have chapters, didn't even really have paragraphs. His method was quite experimental for its time. Is it fair to say you were trying to do something even more radical than what Kerouac was doing—essentially, live, dynamic, improvisational interactions with people along the way?*

Babbs: On the Road was a huge influence on us. It was the same thing when we were doing all the stuff with the camera and music and all that. The same way—let it flow, let it go. This was a whole new movement that came from the Beats. And the Pranksters came along right between the Beats and the hippies. And now it's part of life everywhere where spontaneity rules.

Armstrong: *Kesey's novel* Sometimes a Great Notion *came out around the same time as your 1964 cross-country bus trip.*

Babbs: Yeah, he wrote it in 1963, and that was our reason for going to New York in 1964.

AN INTERVIEW WITH KEN BABBS

Armstrong: *That was an experimental novel in its own right.*

Babbs: Absolutely.

Armstrong: *And yet it seemed like Kesey wanted to go further. He wanted to take literature even further than the written word.*

Babbs: Of our travels and performances and spontaneous interactions with people and among each other, Kesey said, "This is my art form now." It wasn't something on the page but something happening right now in live time. When we went to New York City, we were a traveling troupe. We were performing on the bus and the people on the sidewalks were reacting and performing back at us. It was all a "happening."

Armstrong: *So, what was it like when you got to New York? Was that where you met Allen Ginsberg and Jack Kerouac?*

Babbs: We were staying at an apartment of a friend of ours and Neal Cassady went out one night and got Ginsberg and then Jack Kerouac and brought them over to the apartment. Jack was tired and you could see he was tired. He sat on the couch, and they gave him a beer and he sipped it a little bit. And we went into all our crazy shenanigans, playing our instruments, and filming, and taping.

Armstrong: *Another part of that bus trip that I always found fascinating was you ended up going to Millbrook, New York, and visiting Baba Ram Dass and Timothy Leary, another LSD guru on the East Coast.*

Babbs: Well, the myth is that visiting Leary was not a happy time or that his Millbrook tribe didn't like us and all that, but that's not really true. Allen Ginsburg took us up to visit Leary. And we came in at dawn with the bus, with the music playing, and we threw a smoke grenade off. A green smoke grenade was blowing over the porch.

Armstrong: *That's always a good introduction.*

Babbs: They were all out there just taking it easy and everything after a night of LSD. And so, it was like our wild, crazy scene coming in on a mellow scene because the way they did acid, they'd take it at night, and they'd commune however they do it. And then the next day they'd sit around and analyze what went down. Leary being a Harvard professor—it was more scholastic, maybe that kind of scene.

But we all got along fine. And we had a good time there eating and swimming in their pond. And then the next day, when we were leaving, we hadn't even seen Leary up to that point. It was Baba Ram Dass who was running the show. And he says, "Hey, come on back here." He took us behind the house and Leary was there. And Leary said, "You West Coast guys are out in the streets with your bus and being that way about it. We're more internal and doing it our way, but essentially, we're doing the same thing." And he said, "I want you to know that we want to get together and do stuff together all the time from now on." And it came true. I have a whole chapter in *Cronies* about going to Millbrook.

Armstrong: *Cronies isn't the only book you've done, Ken. After Stanford, you went to Vietnam as a helicopter pilot. You wrote a novel based on that experience called* Who Shot the Water Buffalo? *Can you tell me a little bit about the writing of that book?*

Babbs: When I was in Vietnam, every night I'd go into the tent where they had all the guys working, clerks and all that. And I'd get on the typewriter and I'd type up stuff and send it home. And I did that every night. And then when I got back home, I had a whole pile of pages. I took 30 days' leave and I worked it into a novel. I made up all the characters. I didn't want anybody in my squadron thinking I was writing about them. But I was able to use the actual settings.

I sent it to Sterling Lord, Kesey's New York literary agent, in 1963. And when we were there with the bus in 1964, Sterling showed up and took me in the kitchen of the apartment we were staying at, and he went over it with me and showed me things he thought I should do and all that. And he gave me the whole manuscript back to take back home with me.

So, I put it in a box and put it on the bus. But somehow the whole manuscript got lost. So, I said, well, that's that. But I'd forgotten I had sent a carbon copy to a friend of mine in the Marine Corps to read. And many, many years later, he heard the story that I had lost the manuscript and he sent those carboned pages back to me in about 2010.

Armstrong: *Wow! So, you had lost the novel for decades?*

Babbs: Yeah, it was lost 40 years. Anyway, then another guy I happened to know who worked at Hewlett Packard in Salem, Oregon, heard I had these typewritten pages. He says, "I've got just the thing for you." And he sent me down this huge scanner, and the typewritten pages came out as Word Docs I could edit. I went through the whole thing, sent a new edit to Sterling Lord, and he sent it over to Overlook Press, because the owner of Overlook Press was once with Viking, which is Kesey's publisher. I had met him once at a book fair in Las Vegas. So, this was all like a family thing, and he snatched it right up and published the book in 2011.

Armstrong: *I've read it more than once, and I really think it's a pretty great book. Some of the dialogue exchanges between the officers and so forth are excellent. You wrote it in 1962 or 1963, and I wonder if that book had come out at the time it was written with the angle that you put on the Vietnam War, it might have been a bestseller.*

Babbs: That's true, but it wouldn't have been as good a book.

Armstrong: *Because you had the opportunity to rewrite and edit once you found it after 40 years?*

Babbs: Yeah, I spent a lot of time revising it. And my editor at Overlook Press was terrific going through that book page-by-page-by-page.

Armstrong: *So, after all the bus trips, you moved back to Oregon, lived there near Kesey in Pleasant Hill, Oregon. You and Ken, and probably some* *others, were still really following a literary line. And you decided to publish the literary magazine called* Spit in the Ocean. *What was going on then?*

Babbs: *Spit in the Ocean* started back in the '70s. One of the things we learned when we were in the Bay Area was how so many people were taking writing back from the traditional publishers. There was this huge movement all around small literary magazines and small presses getting started then. So, we decided to do one called *Spit in the Ocean* from the poker game where the dealer throws a card out on the table, a spit, and that card becomes wild in everybody's hand. It's a seven-card game, so we thought we'd do seven issues and each issue would have a wild card editor.

Armstrong: *And a card on each cover, I believe.*

Babbs: Oh yeah. One card on the cover of the magazine shows Neal Cassady as the Joker. The covers were all done by the same artist, a guy in Kentucky named Paul Simon. Terrific artist. He was a friend of Ed McClanahan, another great writer we knew through Wallace Stegner's seminar at Stanford. I was the editor of *Spit in the Ocean #6*, "The Cassady Issue," all about Neal Cassady. It's become the most popular number.

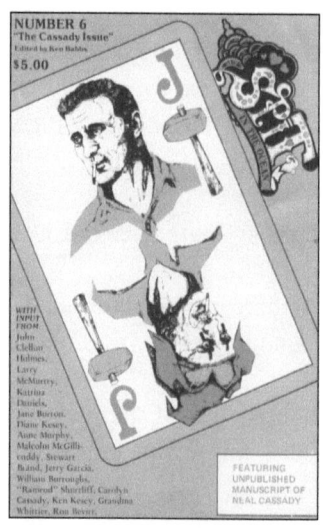

Armstrong: *Not only does "The Cassady Issue" offer a great portrait of who Neal Cassady was, it features your own stories. And a great essay about Cassady by Kesey.*

Babbs: "The Day After Superman Died."

Armstrong: *Yes, "The Day After Superman Died" is the story that Kesey wrote after hearing of Neal Cassady's death in 1968. The "Cassady Issue" also has a letter from William Burroughs. It has a letter from Larry McMurtry, which I found interesting because he says Neal Cassady just seemed like an ordinary wild man from Texas. You have a piece written by Cassady's*

Spit in the Ocean #6, "The Cassady Issue."

AN INTERVIEW WITH KEN BABBS

wife Carolyn, and one by John Clellon Holmes. You have a piece written by Neal Cassady's friend Anne Murphy.

Babbs: Anne Murphy was his girlfriend.

Armstrong: *The "Cassady Issue" is an excellent edition from the* Spit in the Ocean *series, and I hope you reprint more of them because I think this is a unique piece of literature.*

Babbs: It's very entertaining. Cassady was talking all the time when he was driving the bus. We were audio taping and filming everything then. And I was able to use those tapes to get his actual dialogue. In both *Spit in the Ocean* and in *Cronies*, when you read Cassady's dialogue, those are his real words.

Armstrong: *Cassady was a real expert at rap. I believe you mentioned he often went on sometimes for several days straight without stopping.*

Babbs: He was a real speed freak. He liked those little cross tops, those little five-milligram bennies. He'd take one or two, and then a little while later he'd take three or four. And then a little while later, he'd take six or eight, work his way up to 10 or 20. And then he'd be really high. Some people thought he was a motor mouth who didn't make any sense. But if you listened to him, every time it was a story. He used race car driving as his metaphor for life. He was teaching a lesson in every one of his stories. It took a while to get to it, but that's what he did. And if you stuck with him long enough, you'd really dig it. Yeah, Cassady was a good guy. He wrote some neat stuff too. He wrote this thing called "The Joan Anderson Letter" around 1950, which also got lost for decades, but it resurfaced recently. It's a letter, written before Kerouac wrote *On the Road*.

Cassady wrote this 40-page, single-spaced letter all about a woman he had met named Joan Anderson and the things that they did together. And it was after Kerouac read that letter that he wrote *On the Road* in that same spontaneous prose style.

Armstrong: *In* Spit in the Ocean #6, *you have a really cool story about* The First Third, *Neal Cassady's partial autobiography that was posthumously* *published by City Lights in 1974. But the "Prologue" to the book was lost— until you published it in "The Cassady Issue."*

Babbs: Yeah. "The Prologue" was lost for many years. It's the "Prologue" to *The First Third*. I don't remember who found it. I think Kerouac originally typed it up from Cassady's longhand. And Neal in the typescript and along the margins and in between lines in pencil for I don't know how many pages embellished it or corrected it. And Ed McClanahan sent that to us when he heard we were doing the *Spit in the Ocean* "Cassady issue." So, I had to take that thing and figure it all out and type it all up. And we put it in the "Cassady Issue" in 1981. And when it was done, I sent it to Lawrence Ferlinghetti at City Lights Bookstore, who had published *The First Third* in 1974 and I suggested he might want to add "The Prologue" to the next edition of *The First Third*. And so, it is part of the book now.

Armstrong: *Where could someone get a copy of* Spit in the Ocean?

Babbs: You can get them from Ken's son Zane at Key-Z.com. Issue number six, "The Cassady Issue," has always been the most popular one.

Armstrong: *You also did a novel with Kesey,* The Last Go Round. *It tells the story of the 1911 Pendleton Round Up and the story of three cowboys, a Native American, a black man, and a white guy from the South. It says it is by Ken Kesey "with Ken Babbs." What part did you play in that book? Did you help him write or e dit it? Were you a researcher with him? What part did you play?*

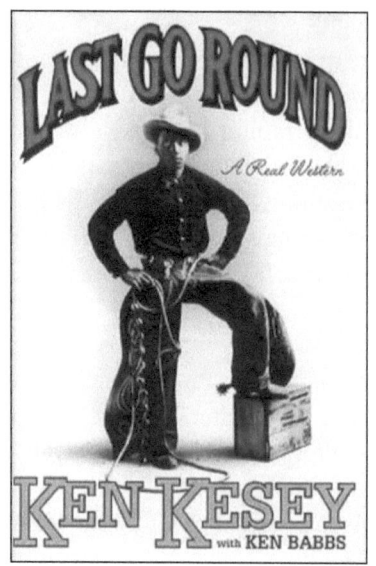

Babbs: Well, we started going to the Pendleton Round Up back in the 1970s. And the arena there in Pendleton is exactly the same as it was in 1911, with everything kept up to date. Nothing has changed. And Kesey was saying, this would make a great setting for a movie. The story of those three guys is a story that everybody in Pendleton knows. And so we made that the basis of the story.

We thought of it as a screenplay originally. And Kesey got to work on it with our friend Irby Smith, who's a writer from LA originally. Worked there for years. The two of them whipped up the screenplay and then tried to get it sold in Hollywood, but nothing ever happened with it. And so, I said to Kesey, "Well, let's take that screenplay and turn it into a novel." And now people who read that novel say, hey, this would make a great movie.

Armstrong: *It would make a great movie.*

Babbs: Absolutely. Because it's written to be a movie. Kesey wrote all his stuff in longhand, gave it to me, and I'd type it up. And as I typed I would change things, add things, and add my thing to it. And I'd give him the pages back, and then he'd go over that again, all with his corrections. And then he'd give it to me, and I'd type that back in again, and do that. And we did that back and forth until we both liked it. And then we'd set that aside and saved it on one of those six-inch floppies at the time. Did that on every chapter all the way through the book until we were both happy with it. And then we sent it off to the publisher.

So 'with Ken Babbs' was done because that cut me in. Kesey cut me in on the advance but not the royalties. Which was fine with me. It's his book really.

Armstrong: *You were a big part in that process.*

Babbs: Big part of it.

Armstrong: *When I read it—I'd already read your work and I'd read Ken Kesey's work separately—I could recognize some of your phraseology, and some of Kesey's.*

Babbs: We both liked it a lot.

Armstrong: *And it's a western. And there's a love story and the whole thing.*

Babbs: And all those other characters coming in there.

Armstrong: *Absolutely . . . Buffalo Bill.*

Babbs: Buffalo Bill's in there. Yeah.

Armstrong: *Recently Michael Pollan wrote a book called* How to Change Your Mind *in which he kind of gives a history of LSD and of certain labs, clinics at John Hopkins, UCLA, and NYU, where researchers had used it before it was illegal for fighting alcohol addiction, cigarette addiction, heroin addiction, and also to help terminal cancer patients come to terms with dying. LSD has a very mixed history. How do you feel about it being legalized for research again?*

Babbs: I think it's a good idea. When we were doing the Acid Test in LA, we stayed at this guy's house, a big house. And he would go out at night, and he'd go to skid row or whatever it is in LA, and he'd bring two or three drunk guys back to the house and he'd give them LSD as a way of helping cure their alcoholic addiction.

Armstrong: *It seems that the Merry Pranksters as a group learned how to work with it. Did you feel like you had, through your experiences, learned how to work with a very slippery kind of psychological state?*

Babbs: When we did the Acid Tests in LA——we were at Watts—a woman there became known as the "Who Cares" lady because she kept screaming, "who cares?" She was really out there, and Wavy Gravy and the Hog Farmers calmed her down by giving her a lot of attention. One time in a house I lived in, there was a nest of bees in the wall, and I cut a square out of the wall so I could look at the bees in there as they were coming in and making honey and doing all that. Every once in a while, one of those worker bees would freak out. It'd just flop over and go crazy like that and everything. And all these other bees would come over to it and with their little feelers, they'd be pulsating, palpitating, and everything until they got the crazy one all cooled down and, and then he'd go back to work again. Wavy Gravy did that with this Who Cares woman at the Acid Test and cooled her out.

Armstrong: *I do believe there are lots of positives to LSD research, but it's not a simple thing and it's not a casual drug.*

Babbs: True. True. But at my age now I'm kind of out of all that anyway. But I'm very positive about hoping it'll all go well. And the same with studying psilocybin. In fact, they're saying micro-dosing psilocybin's really good for you when you get old.

Armstrong: *Getting back to* Cronies, *Ken, is there anything you'd like to add to our discussion?*

Babbs: Well, I can give a little philosophy or a little sermon. We became really good at reaching out to people. We'd be in scenes where there'd maybe be a scuffle or an argument among people, and we got to be really good about defusing it with our antics.

One of the best examples was when we were at a big Vietnam War rally in Berkeley. And there were provocateurs there from the government trying to incite a fight so the cops could come in and beat up on the protesters. And so, we were walking through the crowd as a group, and the provocateurs were going at it. And you could tell these guys by their shoes. They all had shiny shoes and they were provoking the protestors and about to really go at it. And Neal Cassady gets right in the middle of them: "Dentyne gum, anybody?" He steps right in the middle of them, "Dentyne gum, cleans your palate, cleans your mind, cleans all the ills that are in you. Do you good. Here, have a Dentyne. Have a Dentyne." And they all went, What? What? Who? Whoa… Cassady diffused the whole thing. And we walked away and the whole tense scene just collapsed.

Armstrong: *You had a knack for putting yourselves into edgy situations like the Acid Trip in Watts. You invited Hell's Angels out to La Honda for a party. What was the thinking behind that?*

Babbs: Well, we were pretty open about all that, and pretty confident about being able to deal with everybody. We were lucky too. We never really got into any violent confrontations where people attacked us with guns or knives or any of that kind of stuff. We got to know the Hell's Angels. And when you get to know them, they're regular guys who also happen to be Hell's Angels. And LSD was a real kind of leveling thing through it all.

Armstrong: *You have a chapter about the Hell's Angels in* Cronies.

Babbs: Yeah, *Cronies* has 70 stories, covering just about everything. The great thing about Kesey was when he'd walk down the street, he'd look everybody in the eye. I don't care if he was a bum lying in the gutter, or some guy asking for a handout, or some crazy guy screaming obscenities. Kesey treated each one like a real person. And I've learned that too. I always give money and stop to talk to people in wheelchairs who have a sign and want money. And you realize the money's nice, but what they really like is you treating them like a human being, a fellow traveler.

Armstrong: *Well, that doesn't surprise me. Ken, and thank you, I've really enjoyed this opportunity to talk to you.*

Babbs: Well, you're quite welcome. It's really grand to talk to you, Dan. ∎

Ken Kesey and Neal Cassady in the school bus "Further."

ESSAYS, MEMOIRS, NONFICTION

"Spirit Quest" by Riley Sophia Penaluna. Linocut, 6 x 4 inches.

KENT ANDERSON

Praying in Jail

I'd been vomiting blood from an ulcerated esophagus for months, and passing black blood from a bleeding stomach ulcer for much longer. In the mornings I'd wake up and start my day with beer, move on to vodka from the bottle, and pass out early every evening, the only way I could get to sleep now. I was 54 years old and done for, finished, a dead man walking. If the alcohol didn't kill me soon, somebody on the street would. I made hard eye contact with anyone I caught looking at me—on sidewalks and parking lots, waiting in line at the grocery store, pumping gas, crossing the street—locked eyes with them until they looked away, which they always did. So far. Whenever I left the house I was armed with a chromed Browning High-Power pistol and extra clips of 9mm half-jacketed hollow points.

Early that Monday morning, more than twenty years ago, in our split-level house in the Boise Foothills, I was lying on the carpet downstairs, waiting for the 7-11 to open so I could buy a quart of beer. I'd run out of liquor on Sunday and the burning ulcer had kept me awake all night. Alcohol dulled the pain, but not like it used to, and it made the ulcer worse. My wife Judith wanted to take me to the emergency room but I said no, they'd only make me sit in a chair and wait. She called the VA and talked to someone who told her that if I went to the VA hospital ER I wouldn't have to wait at all. I agreed to try it and she drove me out to the big VA hospital there, massive 19th century red stone buildings with towers and turrets and barred windows. We found the emergency room where I was told to have a seat. "No thanks," I said, and walked out.

I bought a quart of beer and drank it on the way home, but beer didn't help so much anymore, nothing did. The ulcer was making me crazy. I had to get out of town before I did something that would get me arrested. Judith tried to stop me from leaving, following me outside to the truck, but I told her I had to go and drove away. The liquor stores were open by then. I bought two fifths of vodka, opened one in the parking lot and slugged some down, then locked both bottles in the back of the truck. On the way out of town I passed the university where I'd been denied tenure after eight years as an assistant professor of English—no surprise to anyone. Judith and I had been living on a generous advance I'd gotten for my second novel, but it wouldn't last much longer.

I was on my way to Midvale, a tiny farm town in central Idaho, where I'd follow Farm-to-Market Road to where it ended, and from there take a series of unmarked gravel roads to Robert Painter's bleak 640 acres. He was an eccentric old man, a Christian creationist and horse breeder who lived up there alone in a tar-paper shack. His kitchen table was a sheet of plywood on sawhorses, cluttered with bibles of different versions, editions, and translations, with concordances, dictionaries and religious tracts. He had a herd of almost a hundred and fifty all-but-wild Spanish Barb horses, stock that he had been breeding for thirty years, having gotten his first feral Barb from a ragged band of Ute Indians back in the Book Cliffs of Utah. He said that the Barb was "the original horse," the horse God put on earth when He created the world in seven days. All other horse breeds had descended from Barbs. He couldn't afford to feed them, didn't have time to train them, and wouldn't sell them anyway. In good weather I camped out on a hillside where I could watch the horses below. At night I heard them running in my sleep. In the winter I slept in a tool shed on a cot, zipped into a minus-30-degree sleeping bag, safe out there from the rest of the world and, I thought, from myself. It wasn't a place many people would be able to find if they'd never been there before. I helped Robert move and stack hay, clean out the creek, and anything else he needed. In return he let me hide out there and walk among wild horses.

The Interstate took me as far as Weiser, about halfway, a farm town known for its annual fiddle convention, where I always stopped for a beer at the Weiser tavern. It was barely noon, but they opened early, serving draft beer in frozen mugs. On the way into town two police cars —an Idaho state trooper and a Washington County deputy sheriff— fell in behind me for a block or two, then turned on their lights and sirens. The Sheriff swung out alongside the truck, the state cop right on my rear bumper, forcing me off the road by the Beehive restaurant. It was a serious felony stop, something that I recognized right away from the years I'd spent as a cop. With my truck blocked in, they got out of their patrol cars, guns in their hands, positioned so that they could both shoot me if it came to that, without getting in each other's way. I found out later that they'd been given a description of my truck, been told who I was—my history in Special Forces and the police—where I was going, that I was drunk and probably armed. The VA had called Judith back, gotten that information, and put it out to the state police.

I turned off the ignition, put both my hands on the top of the steering wheel and looked straight ahead as the state cop came up from behind to my window. He asked me to step out of the vehicle Sir, which I did, keeping both my empty hands away from my body. He asked me if I was armed and I told him no sir just a pocketknife in my right front pocket. The deputy stepped in closer as the state cop holstered his pistol, patted me down from behind, and took the knife out of my pocket. I failed his field sobriety test and he told me that I was under arrest. I nodded ok, thinking, "Just let him handcuff you. *Let* him handcuff you," talking myself down. I'd handcuffed a lot of people, but had never been handcuffed myself, and was worried that I might break away from him when I felt the cuffs and get shot—or take his gun, shoot him, and kill the deputy. He was reasonable though, polite, a good cop, so I put my hands behind me, turned my back to him and offered my wrists. He cuffed me and put me in the molded hard-plastic back seat of his patrol car without shoving my head down the way a lot of cops do, then nodded to the deputy who got into his car and drove off. He closed the door on me—didn't slam it—and, speaking through the cage between the front and back seats, said he'd ask the manager of the Beehive if he could lock the truck up and leave it parked there by the restaurant, rather than towing and inventorying it. I thanked him and he went to the restaurant, keeping an eye on me from the doorway. I was glad he'd arrested me instead of the deputy. I had a pistol under the seat of the truck, a shotgun and God knows what else in the back.

On the way to the Weiser courthouse and jail he looked at me in the rearview mirror, "Well, it's a beautiful day anyway, eh?"

"Yes, Sir," I said.

"Spring always seems like a miracle after the winters we get up here," he said.

At the jail I declined—No sir, thank you—to blow into the Breathalyzer machine, planning to plead "not guilty."

"Up to you," he said, checking off a couple of boxes on the arrest report before turning me over to a jail deputy, swapping cuffs with him.

As he was leaving the interview room I said, "Thank you, officer."

"Good luck, Anderson," he said.

"What size jail clothes do you wear," the jail deputy asked me.

I shrugged and shook my head, "Medium?"

"Close enough," he said, handing me the folded set of orange jail scrubs marked "Extra Large" already tucked under his arm, and took me to a little locker room where there was a bench, a single open shower, and two more deputies. I just looked at him.

"You allergic to water?"

"No Sir," I said.

That's good," he said, twirling his finger for me to turn around. "Every new intake in my jail takes a shower," he said, taking off the cuffs. "Put your street clothes in the paper bag on the bench there," he said, "and swap those cowboy boots for the shower shoes. We get a lot of cowboy boots in here, but not many cowboys. You a cowboy?"

"No sir," I said, taking off and folding my jeans and T-shirt, thinking that, sick as I was, could kick his ass. He probably knew what I was thinking but didn't care as long as I shut up and followed instructions. He was just doing his job. The ulcer had burned through the vodka and was back bad as ever, worse than ever, but naked under the shower, in front of the three uniformed deputies, I did my best not to show how bad I felt. Soaping up, I asked politely when I'd be able to see a judge, hoping that maybe I could recog out that afternoon, get back to my truck and the vodka, and be home by dark.

"Judge'll be here in the morning."

I nodded as if that was the answer I expected, which it was. After I'd rinsed off, the water still running, I looked at the deputy, and he nodded, "Close enough. Put on your jail clothes then and follow Deputy Hicks there." Still wet, I cinched on the oversize orange pants, rolling the cuffs up, slipped into the rubber shower sandals and pulled the shirt over my head. The scrubs hung on me like a big brother's hand-me-downs. They were, I realized, just part of the humiliation and control routine they must use on every new prisoner, along with having to be naked in front of the uniformed deputies.

"Could I get a phone call, deputy?" I asked him. He looked at me, sizing me up, looked at the other deputies. "Yeah, give him his phone call." I had to call collect, but no one was home to answer the phone and accept the charges, so I wasn't able to leave a message. Judith would assume that I was up in Nowhere Central Idaho with the horses.

* * * * *

It was a small concrete-block cell, alone at the end of a long hallway, painted light green, a stainless-steel toilet on one wall, a fold-down chain-hung bunk on the opposite wall. A narrow slit window in the steel door lit the room from a skylight out in the hall.

You've been in worse places than this, I told myself, lying on the bunk, the plastic-sheathed mattress crackling beneath me when I shifted my weight. I looked at the ceiling while the ulcer cooked my stomach, up in the V of my ribs. It already hurt worse than the ankle I'd broken one night in a parachute jump, worse than any of the concussions I'd had, a lot worse than broken ribs or a broken nose. I'd always been proud of my ability to deal with pain. I could ignore it and keep marching, dismiss it, hurt it, add more plates to the weight bar, slam it into a wall, run it off, sprint uphill until I overwhelmed the pain with muscle cramps, burning lungs, and tunnel vision. But I was trapped with it now and it wouldn't leave me alone. The scrubs stunk of other prisoners baked-in sweat, none of it ever completely washed out, then thrown into an industrial dryer.

I sat up suddenly, sprang to my feet, crouched and poised to fight or run, but there was nowhere to go. I sat back down, lay back down, told myself to breathe. Calm down and breathe. Be cool. Deal with it. I felt spiders walking aimlessly across my chest and face while the tinnitus I'd brought back from the war chittered and chirped and whined in the silence. Recycled air moaned down the hallway outside the locked steel door. A thermostat clicked on somewhere.

If there was a clock in the cell, I thought, I could watch the second hand sweep around, minute-by-minute, and *see* the time pass, but there wasn't a clock. It was getting dark and after a while the light went on down the hallway outside the cell.

I tried watching myself from the other side of the cell, and got over there, out of my body, a trick I'd learned and used in other situations, but the ulcer fried and hissed and pulled me back. I closed my eyes and imagined myself on another planet, the real Kent, light years away, observing the false Kent in the cell who was *not me*. *I'm not me. I'm not me*, I silently recited, trying to distance myself from the pain, *I'm not me*. But I was me, locked up alone with myself.

I decided to pray. I didn't know what else to do. The ulcerated esophagus, pulsing and bleeding in my throat, felt a lot like fear. It was going to be a very long night, and I was afraid.

"God," I thought, directing my thoughts to whatever and wherever God might be, if there actually was one. "I need some help. I don't think I can do this by myself. If you could help me out Sir I'd be very grateful."

The last time I'd tried praying had been almost 25 years before, in Vietnam. I was new in-country, on my first combat operation without another American, a five-day recon with five Bru Montagnard tribesmen. I was spread-eagled and pushing my face into the dirt, green tracer rounds snapping past just overhead, looking for me, flailing the dead Elephant Grass into brown dust that collected in my hair and on my sunburned neck, sweating it down into my ears and eyes. Just a little bit lower, I thought, and those bullets would punch into my shoulders and through the top of my head. It wasn't much of a prayer, didn't take long at all, and I remembered it very well: "If you're really up there and get me out of this—I don't know what I'll do, but it will be *appropriate*." That's the word I used. I waited for something to change, some kind of miracle, but the firing didn't even slow down. "Yeah, that's what I thought," feeling foolish, suddenly more angry than afraid, rolling into a bomb crater, trying to figure out what to do next. Praying wasn't working in the Weiser, Idaho, jail either. The ulcer was eating me alive.

But maybe praying while lying down didn't count. Maybe I had to get down on my knees and say a real prayer. I slid off the bunk, made it to the door, and looked through the narrow little wire-reinforced window to be sure no one was out in the hall watching me. Back at the bunk I got on my knees, wedged my elbows into the plastic mattress, and clasped my hands. I didn't know any real prayers.

Breathe, I told myself, think, expect the best for a change, and from somewhere I remembered a real prayer, the best I could do:

> *Now I lay me down to sleep*
> *I pray the Lord my soul to keep*
> *If I should die before I wake*
> *I pray the Lord my soul to take.*
> *Amen.*

I waited. I hadn't really expected anything, but I had hoped for something. I climbed up on the bunk, lay down in the dark, and crossed my hands just above where the ulcer was burning its way out of my chest. I could see it glowing just under the skin. It was whispering to me now, and I closed my eyes. It was stronger than I was, smarter, tougher, and meaner. It was killing me.

When I opened my eyes a band of smoke hovered in the dark above my chest, a smoke ring, rising and slowly turning till I could see from below that it was actually three rings, the smaller two nested within the outer ring, a bulls-eye directly over the hissing ulcer. They wobbled off-center and into one another, collapsing on the way to the ceiling where they flattened out, dissipated, and the next three seeped out of my chest. They were interesting.

I discovered that if I controlled my breathing, in and out, I was able to keep the rings centered, concentric, one after another, all the way to the ceiling where they broke apart and disappeared. As long as I didn't try too hard, *allowing* them to stay centered rather than forcing them. If I kept them concentric all the way up, the pain faded, carried away by the smoke, and in a while the pain was gone. I wasn't angry or afraid and I felt absolutely safe for the first time in my life. I finally understood everything—who I was, and why, clear and simple and exactly as it was supposed to be. It was all ok and I didn't want the night to ever end. I was happy.

When dawn lightened the hallway outside my cell door I was back on my bunk, feeling fine. Light-snakes were rolling beneath the door into the cell, half an inch thick and as long as the door was wide, transparent as glass and striped like candy canes but in all the colors of the visible spectrum. They rolled in by the dozens under the gap beneath the cell door as the sun rose, piling up at first just inside the door before untangling themselves and swimming to my bunk where they covered me like twisting little rainbows. Made of light, they weighed nothing,

"Good morning my little snake brothers," I said to them, delighted. After the years of liquor and drugs I had learned that hallucinations are as real as anything else, but they can't hurt you as long as you refuse to show fear, and anyway, the snakes were friendly, like pets. On the ceiling above me a black wire cage that had covered an air vent was walking about upside-down, like a tarantula.

When someone unlocked the door at the far end of the hall outside my cell, the snakes faded away, back into the light, the tarantula crabbed back to the air vent, and I got off the bunk so that I could meet whatever was coming on my feet. A food cart squeaked and rattled down the hallway to my cell, at least three guys, laughing and shouting.

"Rise and shine, monkey!"

"Drop your cock and grab your socks!"

When they unlocked and opened the door though—a deputy and two trustees—they fell silent.

"Good morning," I said.

They just looked at me.

"Could I have please just a couple of those little cartons of milk?" I asked them.

The trustees looked at the deputy, who was poised on the balls of his feet, studying me. Finally he nodded, his eyes still on me, and one of the trustees fished two cartons of milk out of the ice bucket and handed them to me.

"I guess that's all I need," I said. "Thank you."

They left the cell without a word and were silent all the way down the hall, just the squeaking wheels of the food cart, then out the other door and gone. I drank the two milks and immediately threw them up into the stainless-steel toilet, but I didn't feel sick and there still wasn't any pain, my stomach just didn't want the milk.

Sometime later another deputy unlocked the door and swung it open, but didn't step inside the cell, looking at me as if he'd been told what to expect, whatever that was. "Let's go over to the courthouse," he said, and I followed him out of the cell, down the hall and through the other door. We had to pass by a holding cell where there were six or eight prisoners who started hooting when they first saw me, then they too fell silent as I passed by.

In one of the courtrooms, empty except for the deputy and two women clerks, I spoke to the judge on a speaker-phone and he released me on my own recognizance. Back in the jail I was given my boots and the grocery bag with my clothes in it, my wallet, pocketknife, and keys to my truck. I nodded, smiled and thanked them, changed back into my own clothes, folded the orange scrubs and set them down on the bench. I walked out of the jail and down to the Beehive, where I got in my truck and drove home.

The next day I called the courthouse and changed my plea to "Guilty." I took my last drink sometime in August 1999, and the ulcer never bothered me again. I had no idea what a long haul was ahead of me. ■

"Mama Possum" by Riley Sophia Penaluna. Linocut, 4 x 6 inches.

PAUL BEEBE

A Killing Gone Wrong

> *All the past we leave behind;*
> *We debouch upon a newer, mightier world, varied world;*
> *Fresh and strong the world we seize, world of labor and the march,*
> *Pioneers! O pioneers!*
>
> —Walt Whitman

Thirty years old, and after several misadventures and false starts, I was finally rolling in the right direction. I had a good job. My wife was happy in hers. We had quit the East and now were migrants in a new land without precedence in our lives. We were beyond the Hundredth Meridian, in the Old West, where in 1980, the country's wilder past still felt alive.

Here we were in southeast Idaho, where the landforms were magnificent: arid, alien, imposing, enormous. There was no adjustment period. I was where I was meant to be. For me, a useful way to know I am on home ground is when the natural features of the place summon unprompted emotion from my subconscious. This place, rich with desert, mountains and rivers, Indians, railroad workers, and college professors did that. There was much to see and ponder and absorb. A lifetime of uncommon experience surely lay ahead.

So on a cold and overcast winter day, when Rose suggested a soak in the mineral pools of Lava Hot Springs, I was aching to go. The sights I knew I would see on the drive would be excellent. A gap between two mountains through which a four-hundred-foot wave of floodwater once roared. A thick tongue of black lava filling a valley floor. Graceful aprons of alluvium flanking the slopes of steep mountains beneath a moody sky.

Down the interstate, through this dreamscape, we drove, bathing suits and bath towels on the back seat, my eyes, as usual, wandering left and right, up and down, and my mind sinking deep into reverie at the sights. At the town of McCammon, we turned onto U.S. Route 30, which I knew was the third-longest highway in America and stretched eastward all the way to Pennsylvania, where Rose and I met and married seven years earlier.

Beyond McCammon, the road runs beside the sluggish Portneuf River. No more than a few yards wide, the river curls back and forth as it trickles through a number of unlovely sagebrush hills. It was here that we noticed a car creeping towards the road from what seemed to be an impromptu garbage dump between two hills. Running alongside and circling in front of the car was a large white dog. It appeared to be wearing a red kerchief.

The car was probably a hundred feet in front of us when it reached the road. It turned and moved slowly in our direction. The dog was in the road, trying to stay with the car. Without conscious thought, I slowed down, and as our car passed the other vehicle, I looked out my window to see what was happening.

The car was a mid-1960s Ford Fairlaine. On the front bumper was a Montana license plate. I caught a glimpse of the driver as I drove by his car. His window was down. He was a heavyset man, with a scraggly beard covering the lower half of his face, looking at the dog which was looking back at him. As long as I live, I will never forget that man's face. It was in shock.

We drove a few yards past his car, then stopped. Something came over us in that moment, and we weren't going to leave. More than likely, we thought that going on as if nothing was amiss would be immoral. Maybe our subconscious selves were saying that against logic or reason we owed it to the man and dog to offer help. I don't know. Whatever the cause, I swung our car around and pulled alongside the Fairlaine, as it coasted forward on the shoulder of the road. We looked at the man. We stared at the dog, an old female, with enlarged nipples, a mother dog, still on its feet, heaving and swaying, her eyes fixed on the man, imploring him to not leave her behind. Blood spilled from a wound in her neck onto the pavement.

Rose rolled down her window.

"What happened?" she said.

The man's face sagged. His mouth opened and closed. He gripped his steering wheel and stared into the distance. Seconds ticked by. Unable to think or respond properly, he sat mute in his seat.

"You shot her, didn't you?" Rose said.

I turned our car into a pull-out beside the river and shut off the engine. Rose got out and walked back to the man's car, which had come to a stop.

"You have to finish what you started," I heard her say. "You have to do it now."

She spun around and marched back to where I was waiting, dumfounded, in our car. Rose opened her door and got in. A few seconds went by in eerie silence before we heard a single gunshot.

I still think of that disturbing day more than forty years ago. What did any of it mean? Of course it was necessary to understand why the man had committed such a horrific act. That meant putting ourselves in his place. We decided he was not a bad person. In those days, the taking of the life of an old or sick animal wasn't altogether unheard of in places like Idaho, Montana or Wyoming, where attitudes about land and livestock were usually practical instead of sentimental. The man's actions seemed in keeping with that utilitarian mindset. He had made a calculation, what economists call a cost-benefit study, and concluded the dog was no longer useful. So he made up his mind to put her down.

All that was true but was only part of the truth. I believe Rose and I also witnessed the destruction of certitude about how the world operates and how the unforeseen consequence of truly botched decision-making could turn a man's world upside down. Nothing for him would ever be the same again. We could only hope that a lesson was learned: When someone ends another life, great care must be taken to ensure the animal experiences love and little, if any, discomfort—especially when a dog's unconditional loyalty is involved—for I have come to believe that if there truly is a Divinity operating in our world, it is life itself. One should not tamper with life heedlessly.

I know now that I had learned something about Rose. I had always thought of her as a strong person. Most people would not have confronted the man. They would have hurried on and would quickly dismiss the incident as unpleasant but having nothing to do with them. Not Rose. What she did was in keeping with the resolute person I knew. But this was resolution of an entirely different kind. I realized that I had never seen a finer display of character in my life until then.

Eventually I came to understand something about myself, too. A child of the 1960s. I had cheered the civil rights movement, grieved the deaths of John F. Kennedy, Martin Luther King and Bobby Kennedy, opposed the Vietnam War and admired the courage of Muhammad Ali, who was stripped of his heavyweight boxing title because he refused induction into the Army.

But none of that had touched me directly. In hindsight, what did I know about racial prejudice and war? I had never seen racial discrimination. I had never smelled death. All I ever did was listen to people talking on television. None of the turmoil of the decade of the Sixties had intervened in my life. Now, horror had found me, involved me in its unpredictability. The actions of the man and the sad death of his dog forced me to face what my privilege had sheltered me from. Nature is terrifying. The universe is indifferent to mankind. It operates by laws and patterns that have nothing to do with us. The best we can do is take what we have learned from our experiences and shoulder on into the future as best we can. ■

JOHN REMBER

Why I Don't Write for Travel + Leisure Anymore

I don't normally eat dinner with federal judges, but one evening fifteen years ago, I did, with a half-dozen of them. The occasion was a Federal Judicial Retreat at a local guest ranch near our home here in Sawtooth Valley. A dozen judges had gathered there for a working vacation, and I had been invited to read to them from my memoir, *Traplines*, and after that, have dinner with them and answer questions about my childhood.

Our family had moved to the valley when I was three. I had grown up in a place where the roads were unpaved, the power lines unbuilt, the air clear, the climate the closest thing the Lower 48 had to the Pleistocene. Enough of that past world remained, out the windows of the ranch lodge, that it could serve as a rustic retreat for people whose usual world ended at the walls of a courtroom.

One of the chapters in *Traplines* was about fishing in the Salmon River when salmon were still thick in the river, and it had gone over well with other guests at the guest ranch. I read it to the judges, who listened politely.

At dinner, the judges didn't want to know anything more about my childhood or fishing. They talked shop, mostly. With relish, judges told of criminals they had sentenced, sentences they had decided on before the jury delivered a verdict, and people whose guilt had been fixed before they even entered a courtroom. They took much of their judicial identity from their former identities as prosecutors.

The idea of justice was less abstract than I had been led to believe. At this level of the law, it tended toward a gleeful pragmatism.

The judges were accompanied by two U.S. Marshals. When I finished my main course, I took my dessert and after-dinner coffee to their table and sat down, in the hope that the conversation would be better.

"How'd you get to join the party?" I asked.

"We're protection," said one of them. "Some people don't like judges. Some people have relatives in jail, or have been in jail themselves. I had to read your book to make sure you weren't one of those."

"Did you like reading it?" I asked.

"Not really. You've got a chapter on making bombs and shooting rock chucks for fun. It's a good thing you were doing that when you were seventeen and not thirty-seven. Otherwise, you wouldn't be here."

"I have nothing against judges," I said.

"If you did, we'd have to shoot you," said the other marshal.

"We also shoot bad writers," said the first marshal. "You barely made the cut."

* * * * *

The judges were all males. A female judge was supposed to attend, but after she had flown into Sun Valley, she had driven her rental car to the overlook on Galena Summit and had stopped and looked down into Sawtooth Valley. The 30 or 40 miles of air between the overlook and the Sawtooth and Salmon River mountain ranges had caused an acute attack of agoraphobia. She had turned around and flown home.

In the ensuing 15 years, I've become more interested in the judge I didn't have dinner with than the ones I did. I've wondered about controllable space, and how, if you're a judge, your courtroom is a place where you can make reality behave the way you want it to. I've thought that being agoraphobic, if you're a judge, means that you haven't mastered the trick of taking your courtroom with you everywhere you go, hermit crab-like.

For the duration of my dinner at the guest ranch, the lodge was a court in session. The stories that were told there had nothing to do with a retreat in the mountains of the American West. Instead, they evoked the invisible structures of law and custom that dictate what is real, at least within the legal profession.

In a similar process, the marshals drew their reality in the shape of a gun. For them, control had nothing to do with the law. It lay in identifying a threat and eliminating it, and they lived in a world where that transaction was as natural as breathing.

But the judge who didn't make the cut—the one who got back on her plane and went home because of the great authority-obliterating abyss that confronted her on the Galena overlook—must have seen, in our valley, a flash of the world's vast chaos, and for a moment, must have lost her faith in her ability to defend against it.

I don't think it was a matter of gender, unless women are better than men at seeing the world underneath its cultural overlay, and better at appreciating its power in the face of human intention. I won't attempt to map that dangerous territory, but I do think that in various ways, the judges and marshals who made it to the retreat succeeded in turning the guest ranch into a courtroom, at the expense of entering the unfamiliar, seeing what there was to see, and listening to what there was to hear.

* * * * *

A couple of weeks ago, my wife Julie and I left the snow and ice of Sawtooth Valley for the American Southwest. Two years of informal pandemic quarantine had made the valley too small instead of too large. Still, my remembered agoraphobia victim was accompanying us as we headed for spaces that dwarfed our home. Distant dark mountains, barely visible through haze and dust, marked horizons we would never reach. Rattlesnakes and prickly pear, lurking just beyond the barrow pits, waited to kill you if they could. Gas stations were far enough apart that being safe meant filling the tank whenever it ticked below the full mark.

If there was a place where space could provoke panic, this was it. Even though we had been there before, the invisible structures of American culture had weakened in the interim, becoming less predictable, less able to reduce the world to a friendly dimension. It wasn't scary, exactly. It just threatened to show again and again how small you were, even if you'd graduated from law school.

We made it to Ely, Nevada, the first night, and Cedar City the next, moving through vast sagebrush basins and between mirage-like ranges, past dry lake beds and the empty parking lots of closed roadhouses. The third night we made it to Page, Arizona, and were astonished when we visited the marina on the north side of Lake Powell. The lake was a hundred and eighty feet below the full mark. Where water had once been was a vast, tire-tracked stretch of gray dirt, dotted by a hundred dusty motorhomes—parked where they could see downhill to the water—and tiny, growing dunes on the lee sides of rocks and mummified driftwood.

A sign warned against going off the pavement, because you could get stuck in loose sand and gravel. Some of the motorhomes looked stuck, and we wondered if the people sitting beside them in camp chairs would still be there, motionless and desiccated, when the hot weather began to ease in October.

By the fourth night we were in Sedona, Arizona, staying with our friends Tom and Ellen, who had left their home in Sawtooth Valley for six weeks to rent a condo in a warmer place. Sedona is a tourist and retirement city now, in contrast to the hippie village it had been when I first saw it in the 1970s. It's gone far upscale and has spread out into its surrounding canyons.

Sedona's traffic roundabouts resemble circular games of chicken as more and more drivers have gotten less and less patient with the city's deliberate lack of traffic lights. Still, a good many of its two- and three-million-dollar houses are empty. I wondered if the owners of second homes in Sun Valley had third homes in Sedona.

Sedona has been plopped down in an area of great geologic beauty. Parks and wilderness separate its suburban pseudopods. Strict zoning has given even its strip malls a tasteful pueblo look. Restaurants are plentiful and good, and from what we saw when we went out to dinner, packed.

Julie and I took a high trail in one of the wilderness areas that looked down on thousands of houses. The forces of tourism and financial planning have created a most improbable Shangri-La in a drought-stricken desert, and I found myself wondering how it all could last in a world running short of non-pragmatic justice. Housing for the help is becoming a problem in Sedona and every city like Sedona, and gasoline is set to become exponentially more expensive as energy supplies go from surplus to deficit. Water is already priceless.

Once, as a ski journalist, I visited British Columbia's ski city, Whistler-Blackcomb, and was housed in a glittering slope-side hotel that contained a starred restaurant, a spa, and library, among other amenities. Every luxury an expense account could buy was available and I was wondering what it would be like to stay there for life when a local paper reported the arrest of a Whistler homeowner who had been caught with forty-nine service industry employees sleeping, in shifts, in his crawl space.

Outside Sedona, Arizona.

You wonder how many architects in Sedona and Whistler-Blackcomb and Sun Valley are incorporating the contemporary equivalents of slave quarters into their designs.

I'm making this trip sound awful, but remember we were traveling with an imaginary agoraphobic justice, fearfully glancing at geographic space that could suck her soul into a near-infinite void. The void that Julie and I experienced was ethical, centering on the sustainability of a civilization consuming too much water, too much fossil fuel, too much scenery.

That was a spiritual problem, one fortunately susceptible to workarounds.

* * * * *

We had a wonderful time. In Sedona, we relaxed and hiked for a week, visiting national monuments and old mining towns converted into shops, galleries, and ethnic restaurants. Once we got used to the idea of sharing every space with hundreds of fellow humans, life became an exercise in creative anthropology, a human Serengeti, where herds of migrating animals slept, danced in the sunlight, congregated around water holes, grazed, and when danger threatened, stampeded.

The weather was sunny and cool, occasionally windy in the mornings, always windy in the afternoons. We hit Mexican restaurants. Julie consulted guidebooks and planned our hikes. We looked at the displays of native artifacts in visitor centers. We walked across and back across the old Navajo Bridge below Glen Canyon Dam, and, further down the road, watched as the winds kicked up great walls of dust that moved across the desert toward our car. When they reached us, they blocked the sun.

We got out two days before the fires started up around Flagstaff.

Our way home took us through the Utah towns of Kanab, Escalante, and Boulder. We walked a trail in Bryce Canyon National Park with a couple of hundred other people, but after that, the crowds thinned out. In Kodachrome Basin State Park, we hiked a six-mile trail and saw six other people, and the landscape—a combination of slot canyons, towering hoodoos, striated hills, all blending into an astonishing, inhuman glory—revealed itself as something other than an artifact of the park system. On the road to Boulder, we got out of the car and hiked off-trail to a lunch spot where we could look down on a two-hundred-foot waterfall as it fell into a slot canyon, and it took us much longer to get there and back than we expected. I began to see that distances could expand as you walked, and that a sometimes-terrifying reality had precedence over all human artifice.

I have no doubt that a trail will soon be built to our lunch spot, to protect the crusted desert soil. It will end at a viewing platform, and from that platform, all you'll be able to see is the human imagination made flesh.

That deep human inscription on the world is an unfortunate side-effect of a tourist economy, but it will become necessary, as the Escalante-Grand Staircase becomes more and more visited. Eventually, I suppose, U.S. Marshals will try to protect everything, and every one of us will be co-opted as deputies.

* * * * *

We left our agoraphobic judge somewhere out in the desert of southern Utah. When we got to the overlook on Galena Summit, the Pleistocene was back in full force. Snow squalls moved up the valley amid quick-moving patches of sunshine. But it was good to arrive at a place where the landscape was the hard straw-colored tundra of early spring, and where the mountains kept the air from escaping.

Arizona and New Mexico were burning. Humans were stampeding, probably in our direction.

We pulled into our snow-covered driveway, built a fire in the woodstove, and began to carry the stuff from our car into a house that was empty, still, and huge. ■

"Capelin" by Graham Blair. Woodcut print 5 x 7.5 inches.

RON McFARLAND

Educated on the Henrys Fork

> "For Angling may be said to be so much like the Mathematicks, that it can ne'er be fully learnt."
>
> "Is it not an Art to deceive a Trout with an artificial Flie?"
>
> —Sir Izaak Walton (1676)

In my last action on the Henrys Fork of the Snake River, I latched onto a sizable brown that my fishing guide Tim pointed out as it fed near the bank a dozen or so feet ahead. Tim is a big guy in his mid-thirties, six-three or six-four, fit, too, as a guide would need to be if he's to spend several hours a day rowing a dory or similar boat, often with two anglers aboard and sometimes against significant currents. That was June 20, 2022, when I'd been scheduled to fish the fabled Madison in southwestern Montana for my first time, but all of Yellowstone had just been closed by catastrophic flooding that ate away several paved roads, a few homes and businesses, and the summer employment dreams of many.

My first guided fishing adventure, a Christmas gift from my wife's daughter and her husband, surprised us. Not being an angler, my wife Georgia was particularly surprised. How would she cope while I spent four eight-hour days drifting and flailing for big rainbows and browns? Quite well, as it happened, and in various ways our angling adventure turned out to be a tribute to her adaptability to unfamiliar surroundings and a shifting array of guests at the 640-acre Ranch in West Yellowstone that dates to the mid-1860s and was celebrating 75 years of its life as dude ranch and first-class fishing resort. Most of the guests, it seemed, represented the better attorneys and physicians of the nation. Throw in a handful of successful entrepreneurs, and you have a social class a goodly cut above hoi polloi, with which Georgia and I tend to identify.

But democracy thrives in the angler's world where social and fiscal aristocrats are subordinate to the blue-collar fishing guide. Or perhaps the guides might better be described as knights errant. They live and work for five or six months in the territory of some of the nation's magical trout streams: the Madison, the Gallatin, the Henrys Fork. When he tabulated scores in a round of crazy rum that came out about even, my father liked to say, "Well, that makes the folks about as good as the people." As kids we had no idea what he was talking about, but we thought it sounded cool. Our arrival happened to coincide with the weekly barbecue, in which staff, guides, and guests mingled easily. In various ways though, the guides were "more equal than others." Certainly, when it came to casting flies, Tim was more than my equal.

As it happens, I fully acknowledge my multitudinous deficiencies when it comes to the art of casting a fly, despite having thrown them around for almost fifty years, so I informed the staff at the Ranch in advance as to my manifold limitations. And I went so far as to send a copy of my 2020 book, *Professor McFarland in Reel Time: Poems and Prose of an Angler,* suggesting they pass it along to whatever poor soul among the guides drew my name in what I supposed would be a lottery, the lucky winners to end up with the most adept fly casters, the losers to be stuck with the likes of me. Over the four days we drifted the Henrys Fork, Tim gave me to understand he has dealt with clients even less proficient than I and therefore in need of even more patient tutelage. I suspect he was just being kind.

Now, college professors do not necessarily acquire socioeconomic status on par with that of corporate lawyers, orthopedists, and entrepreneurs. Setting aside those profs connected with the nation's more elite universities—e.g., the Harvards and Stanfords, the MITs and Johns Hopkinses, the Big Ten and Big Twelve schools—we rank in status closer to the world of the public-school teacher. I recently retired after teaching English (literature and creative writing) for more than fifty years, most of them at the decidedly less prestigious University of Idaho. Georgia retired after teaching English in high schools in Indiana and Spokane. She also taught (still teaches) piano, having received her degree in performance from Indiana University.

As it happened, the staff at the Ranch did not pass along my book to Tim, perhaps in their kindly effort not to prejudice my case. Among the ten essays in the collection, which also includes a pair of short stories, I did hyperbolize here and there "for effect." Case in point, "The Art of Fly Fishing and the Aesthetics of Solitude," which first appeared in *Yale*

Angler's Journal and later in their attractive anthology, *Tight Lines* (2007). That five-pager begins with the facetious assertion that "Fly fishing properly defined is a method of angling which assures the angler that he or she will be granted ample solitude, and therefore one's satisfaction is inversely proportional to one's skill as a caster of flies" (105). The self-image in what follows bears more semblance to the reality of my ineptitude than I then thought to be the case. In fact, my angling on the Henrys Fork revealed that my self-presentation as inept caster of flies was more accurate than I intended. My playful premise: Cast your fly-line wildly, and sensible bait and spinner fishers will give you ample room.

When I edited an anthology on Norman Maclean published by the small, regional Confluence Press in 1988, I fancied myself a decent enough fly fisherman who could boast respectable success with rainbows and cutthroats on the small stream I had then fished for more than two dozen years. On the other hand, after exchanging handwritten letters (pre-email) with Maclean over several years, I found myself more than slightly apprehensive when he visited the Idaho panhandle to give the annual Wallace Stegner Lecture about thirty miles away at Lewis-Clark State College in Lewiston. What if he expected me to take him fly-fishing?

Well, if you've read Maclean's masterful book, *A River Runs through It* (do *not* capitalize the preposition, he would warn), or viewed the film starring Brad Pitt, you'd doubtless recall that passage on the second page when the narrator's brother Paul reminds him that casting a fly "is an art that is performed on a four-count rhythm between ten and two o'clock." It should go without saying that despite my good intentions had *not* mastered that art. Rather, even though I had picked up my fly rod myriad times, my performance would promptly reflect Maclean's Calvinistic/Presbyterian assertion on page three "that man by nature is a damn mess" and that "until man is redeemed he will always take a fly rod too far back." Fortunately for me, Maclean was satisfied with a tour of local streams with my co-editor, Hugh Nichols.

I'd scarcely shaken his hand before inviting Tim to treat me as an unredeemed novice in the art or religion of angling with the fly. And on the first day of my education, I promptly demonstrated nearly every error one might execute, including: 1. Taking the rod too far back

(Maclean's father admonishes him that the rod ought to be brought back closer to noon than to two o'clock); 2. Failing to pause that critical moment before shooting out the line; 3. Exhibiting ignorance of the "reach" or "reach cast," thereby making it more difficult to mend the line in the fast-moving stream; 4. Mending the line ineptly and insufficiently; 5. Stripping the line inefficiently, indeed outright clumsily. And those shortcomings constituted only the beginning. Poor Sir Timothy.

In the days of our drifting and afterwards, I wondered whether someone at the Ranch, perhaps Jess, the Guest Services Administrator, or maybe Josh, the head guide, lined me up with one of the guides known for his teacherly skills. The small river I'd fished successfully for so many years would probably rank as two on a ten-point scale of difficulty. Formerly, it was stocked with planters, but over the past twenty or so years it has reverted to native cutthroat, and while some of these might run to sixteen inches, a good one usually measures thirteen to fourteen. They put up a respectable fight but require little exertion. The trout I imagined bringing to boat on the Henrys Fork would be half again as long, the current much swifter, and the exertion considerably greater. Tim's work was cut out for him, or to cite another cliché, I was a work in progress. Sometimes I felt more like a work in regress.

On our first day, with a heavy hatch of caddisflies at our disposal, I managed to pull in a sizable (by my standards) brown, only the second of my flyfishing experience, which has been limited mostly to rainbows and cutthroats, and a whitefish, which unlike the German brown is native to the region. We bumped fists on both occasions. I also set the hook on a large brown that Tim estimated to be in the twenty-inch range and fought it longer than I'd ever battled any fish on a fly rod. Tim calmly guided me through the ordeal to keep up the tension, let him run, let him work against the reel because the drag is set properly, strip in more line, faster, rod tip up! The big brown won. What did Norman Maclean write? "I shall remember that son of a bitch forever." Maclean was a meticulous writer of the old school, and it is just like him to have opted for "shall" here in preference to "will." With a big fish, Maclean writes, "one moment the world is nuclear and the next it has disappeared." Tim and I did not bump fists. I don't recall exactly what Tim said but could tell he was disappointed for me. Maybe he said, "it happens," or more likely, "there'll be others."

Meanwhile, what of my wife who did not for various reasons feel up to spending five or six hours on a small boat watching me lash the air for trout? Alas, Georgia must fend for herself, but I didn't worry much as she reads, reads, reads and writes, writes, writes and is a wonderful poet. Her first full-length collection, *Body Be Sound*, was released in November 2023. Moreover, she appreciates the values of solitude, and when we married about twenty years ago, we drew on Rilke's words in writing vows to "respect each other's solitude." On the other hand, she's gregarious, and she shines in company. If we had found ourselves amidst what might pass for America's aristocracy, she proved herself more than capable of coping with it. Lady Georgia endeared herself to everyone, both guests and staff. While I was gone for the better part of nine hours every day, as the roundtrip drive to the Henrys Fork came to more than two hours, she spent the time hiking, talking with members of the staff during lunch, and playing the piano to the considerable delight of everyone within earshot. When someone on the staff asked her to play "Happy Birthday" as a surprise for Nathan, the young chef, she obliged with a jazzed-up version of that familiar tune, and it was a hit, just as she was.

If life is a long conversation, Georgia has been one of its monarchs, the very queen of palaver. Breakfasts were delicious but hurried as we anglers needed to catch the boat across Hebgen Lake to connect with our guides by eight o'clock, but she could remain behind unhurried to luxuriate over the chocolate croissants and to share stories with the staff. Then off to the hills where she photographed an array of wildflowers, watched ospreys and eagles soaring, came upon a pair of mountain bluebirds, Idaho's state bird hanging out in Montana. Solitude for her never seems irksome.

We anglers were not deprived when it came to cuisine, and the sumptuous dinners provided us with ideal opportunities for conversation. Chef Nathan offered every evening a choice of seafood (the Chilean seabass memorable), or meat (bison superb one evening, the duck another evening delectable), or desserts (a delightful pavlova). Lyndy, who has owned and managed the resort for more than twenty years, carefully proctored the seating so that over our five dinners, we were never seated with the same couple.

As a result, each evening meal provided a variety of conversation partners, like the couple from Colorado who'd been high school sweethearts and were celebrating their 47th wedding anniversary. It was their fifth fishing vacation at the Ranch. Frank was a retired corporate attorney. They fished in Alaska almost every year. His wife, a tiny woman in her seventies, told of hauling in a 265-pound halibut, refusing to yield her rod to the captain who proposed that one of the men ought to take over. Georgia loved this story, although our stay overlapped theirs by only a couple of days. She also enjoyed talking teacher with Andrea, a poli-sci prof at SUNY-Brockport who used literary texts in some of her courses and who may have enjoyed the best day fishing of anyone during our stay.

The second day of the four proved my best. My casting had improved somewhat, even my roll-casting, and while I remained unable to get the reach-cast under control, I made some progress at mending the line and at recognizing when to haul in and cast anew. With the caddisfly hatch still active, Tim encouraged me to vary between caddis nymphs suspended from a large dry fly such as a golden stonefly and a pair of dry caddis flies. Although I'd heard of anglers tossing two flies, I'd never attempted such a feat myself, but it paid off, especially with the caddis nymphs. Tim could tie clinch knots with remarkable dexterity. As a handwriting sample would demonstrate, small motor skills are not my forte, so not surprisingly, I've preferred #10 or #12 hooks, but the tiny #14 ruled on the Henrys Fork.

Like most fishing guides and the staff at the Ranch, Tim leads a double life. He hails from Wisconsin, and after his five months or so in West Yellowstone, he'll head back home to guide another couple of months (October and November) for bass, pike, and muskie, then join his girlfriend in Santa Fe for a few months. He mentioned fishing and guiding in Mexico and Cuba. A few of the staffers, both men and women, go south for the winter, where they have jobs in Georgia or Florida. Tim graduated from the University of Wisconsin-Whitewater, and although he has chosen not to work as an urban planner, his major, he's the sort of guy who can do things with his hands—build houses, repair decks. I'm the sort of guy who hires men like Tim to repair his deck as any tool in my hand qualifies as a dangerous weapon. My lack of coordination promptly manifests itself when the tool happens to be a fly rod.

That second day I boated five fish, two rainbows and three browns, the best of these running to eighteen inches and the stuff of brag photos. In teaching me how to present the large brown to its best advantage, Tim wisely kept his net suspended under it, or I would be one photo short, which would have been sad, as I consider the German brown the most beautiful of the Salmonidae.

I recalled one notable photo taken of my brother Tom and me in Florida, he displaying a sizable drum, I holding out a bag of donuts. Further comments on my varied experiences with the photography of fishing are recounted in my essay, "Vanishing Perspectives," in the 2022 issue of *The Limberlost Review* where one snapshot features me with surf rod and fourteen-inch hammerhead shark landed on Cocoa Beach. Eat your heart out Hemingway. In *A River Runs through It* Maclean uses such words as "beautiful" and "perfect" when he writes of fly-fishing and particularly of his brother as a master of the art. Although I'd had a good day, such adjectives would not have applied here, and in fact I managed to lose a couple of good fish, probably better than the best I'd coaxed in. But Tim and I did bump fists a few times.

The third day proved disappointing, although one of the three fish I pulled in measured nearly as long as the two best ones of the day before. But once again I lost a big fish, this one escaping just as Tim was about to get it into the net. Confession being good for the soul, I'll confess to having eased up on the rod when I tried to catch a glimpse of the fish at the critical moment. Score one for the rainbow. The most memorable fish of that day, however, neither of us saw, but both of us heard. A hard swish, and as I set the hook, the tippet snapped like a dry twig. The movement of my line reminded me of latching onto an eight-foot nurse shark one afternoon on the Gulf, but when I told the tale later, it came out "torpedo."

Do others who have fished with expert guides find themselves wanting to please the guide as much or even more than they wish to please themselves? It wasn't so much that I was a little embarrassed at my ineptitude as that I felt somehow obliged to impress the guy. At the very least I wanted to cast well enough to avoid the tangles that kept finding their way into my tippets. Tim took my ineptitudes (note the plural) good naturedly, of course. He's a professional, and he would no more express annoyance or frustration with a client than any good professor or teacher would rail at students for *their* ineptitudes. That sort of frustration and annoyance is better reserved for the cocktail hour. And for the record, the Ranch puts on an admirable one.

Return we then to the fourth day, my last on the Henrys Fork. While the weather on the first three days had been admirable, as predicted, it turned against us on the fourth, and Tim made a miscalculation, a bad guess, of his own. Even the best guides and teachers, and Tim surely qualifies, miscalculate from time to time. In the event, Tim anticipated correctly that a green drake hatch would replace the caddis hatch of the previous three days, but he predicted we would be better advised to move lower on the river than we had fished on those days, where we'd observed increasing pressure from other drift boats. I should note here the admirable ease with which the many boats managed to avoid each other—a tribute to the expertise of the guides. On Day 3 we'd noticed at least a dozen such boats plying our stretch of the Henrys along with several anglers who were wading it. Only two other boats appeared on our stretch of the river on this fourth day, at the end of which we would learn that our earlier stretch produced a more notable green drake hatch and better success for other anglers.

Well, that's the way it goes. Our day began propitiously when I boated a handsome brown in the spillway of the diversion dam, but we had few opportunities after that. Again, I tallied one near miss and suspect I could've (should've) done better on a couple of strikes, but the big news of the day was the storm that came down on us only a couple of hours from finishing time, and rain was driving down when I scored my biggest near miss of the day, a sizable brown Tim said. He very nearly managed to net the darned thing.

Let me extol here the Olympic quality of rowing that a good guide must manage day after day. If my shoulder ached some after my myriad casts, far more than I usually attempted while fishing my accustomed, easy stream for two or three hours, I could only imagine how Tim's back must have been suffering when we neared the end of our fourth day as he rowed us to the landing at flank speed as the sky darkened.

And I was surprised to observe how occasionally Tim would leave his seat and push the boat into position for me to cast to a rising trout.

On Day 2, for instance, he anchored the boat near the bank where he'd seen a large brown feeding, and he waited patiently as I worked the spot with many an amateurish toss before we paused to let the fish take a rest and think about it. When we resumed, I managed a couple of respectable casts and caught the thing. We'd spent some forty minutes on that hefty, hard-fighting brown, the one commemorated in the photograph mentioned.

But that was then. Now was thunder and lightning and serious discussion of whether we shouldn't "bug out."

"Don't want you to be the lightning rod," Tim said as I readied my final cast. I thought of a recent PBS special on Benjamin Franklin. Tim noted that the willows and alders along the stream stood higher than we, but neither of us were moved to great optimism by that prospect. I couldn't help reflecting on our possible obituaries: "They died doing what they loved to do." I opined that the Widow Georgia would not be much mollified by that sentiment.

As the seconds between rumble and flash diminished, a steady hailstorm lashed us for several minutes. Watching hail accumulate on one's patio turns out not to be quite the same as sitting it out in the open. Tim turned to with a gusto. While our first day had challenged him because of a steady wind, this day's challenge felt more like survival. We joked about it as we aimed toward the landing, which seemed far more distant than we, or at least I, had thought. When we reached the landing, I sprinted to the Porta Potty, where a more ludicrous obit came to mind: "Retired English Prof Fatally Struck by Lightning in Outhouse."

Back in his truck, I suggested the day had been at least memorable: At least we hadn't been skunked, we'd lost no more than an hour of fish-ing anyway, and besides, we needed to be back at the marina to catch the last ferry of the afternoon that would deliver me across Hebgen Lake to the lodge. But Tim refused to shortchange me. Instead, he took me to another site, just one more—after all, it was my last day here— where we would wade a few feet into the Henrys and fish against the bank. And in this context, he truly proved himself.

How could he have known that big brown would be feeding there, in that exact riffle about five feet from the bank? Right there. Whether by experience, most likely, or by intuition, Tim knew a good one would be waiting for us. I had been relying on green drake nymphs all day, and this would be no exception. But he warned me this would constitute the most "technical" of my tests. The current flowed fast against us, and I would need to make a short but "perfect" (to use Maclean's term) cast of a dozen or so feet without snagging the willow behind me and mending the line very quickly as it ran right back at me.

"When it strikes, set the hook hard and strip the line *fast*. You've gotta be *fast*."

Predictably, no "perfect" cast was to be made by yours truly. There are moments in one's grammatical life when the passive voice seems apposite. How many casts would it take for me to achieve "perfection"? More than five at any rate. At such moments, time suspends itself. You know this will be the last fish of this adventure, of this gift. Several members of the angling aristocracy you have met over the past four days have visited the Ranch multiple times, but you know this will be "it" for you.

"When it strikes, set the hook hard and strip the line fast . . ."

The fish strikes, and you set the hook and begin stripping madly, as advised. But you can't strip line nearly as fast as the fish runs toward you. Unlike the fish you've hooked elsewhere in the Henrys, this one does not surge away but senses its best chance will be to aim itself straight at you.

I'm raising my rod, feeling its arc, and as the trout charges at me, I take a big step back.

"Sploosh!"

What can I do but laugh? I suspect that Tim, who must surely be disappointed in his star pupil, cannot decide whether to laugh or not. With which preposition might I interpret his laughter—"with" or "at" me? Both perhaps. I don't suppose my guide knows me well enough to make a confident call. He asks if I'm okay, and of course I am, although I do feel some slight impairment of my dignity.

Meanwhile, back at the ranch, Georgia, the star of the show, our waitress Kyra's choice for "best guest ever" and per Jess's email "honorary member of the Ranch family," has been receiving fly-casting lessons on the spacious lawn back of the lodge. Steve, her volunteer teacher and staff supervisor, has assured me she has shown herself quite adept. "Impressive," he says. She tells me she feels ready to join me on *our* next angling adventure. ∎

LOIS WELCH

Meeting Jim Welch: Opening Day of Fishing Season Party, May 20, 1967

he late May afternoon was sunny, almost hot. Lilacs were fragrant across the valley. My heels sank into the springy lawn at my colleague Jesse Bier's house up the Rattlesnake Valley, three miles from the U, at the only cocktail party he ever gave for the department. I felt pretty in my yellow wool suit. In those days I sewed a lot and had just completed a perky yellow wool empire-waisted suit whose collar stood up and away from my neck. Annick Smith, the vivacious wife of a colleague, came up to me and asked brightly, "Are you coming to our opening day of fishing season party?"

"What opening day of fishing season party?"

"That David! He probably only invited the guys!"

The only other woman in the English department at that time was a small sixtyish woman who taught teacher education, meaning no one paid any attention to her. Probably neither of us looked to David like fishing types. Annick's husband, David, taught 18th-century British literature, especially Swift. His office was just across the hall from mine. A few years older than I, he was lean, athletic, charming, and had an acerbic wit. He, Annick and the poet Richard Hugo were pals from their Seattle days and came to Missoula at the same time.

"Do you have a sleeping bag?" Annick asked. "Sure! I've camped for years."

"Throw on some jeans, bring your sleeping bag and come on out."

"I've never fished," I reminded her.

"Doesn't matter," she said. "The water's high, we probably won't catch anything anyhow."

Excited, I gathered a few things from home, and drove—top down—in my little blue 1964 Alpine Sunbeam convertible the 25 miles east to Rock Creek and up the dirt road to Valley of the Moon Ranch beside Rock Creek, that fabled trout stream where the Smiths were renting a cabin that year. I felt zippy. Two parties in a single sunny afternoon! Life was good. I turned off Rock Creek Road at a bridge whose logs were thick as garbage cans. I spotted the Smiths' low grey-shingled cabin among the ponderosas, some yards from the creek which was high and loud with spring run-off.

I drew up in front of the little wooden stoop. Richard Hugo was sitting on a wooden bench beside his student Jim Welch. I recognized Jim—tall and skinny, with thick black hair and big glasses. Someone had pointed him out to me that winter in the English seminar room after Hugo had enthused in my office doorway over Jim's first "Indian poem." They were both drinking beer and laughing. I got out, walked up the two wooden steps. Hugo kissed my hand. Jim—not to be outdone—stood and kissed his way up my arm. Hugo and Jim had stopped for a beer at the Milltown Bar before the party, so they were both slightly bolder than usual when I arrived.

After settling in and eating, Jim and I went for a walk under a giant full moon glittering in the racing creek. The mountains rose close by, cliffs like shoulders around us. The meadow was shadowed, the ground uneven. Jim caught me after a stumble and we wandered hand in hand among ponderosas and cottonwoods, avoiding logs and willow bogs in the bright moonlight. Jim was ebullient: "This is the most beautiful place in the world." I was, by contrast, a bit reserved—a little leery of being swept altogether off my feet, by romance or moonlit rippling water. Contrary to the myth that has developed in some quarters about this night, we did not stay out all night, and we did not make wild passionate love on the creek bank.

We did stay out pretty late, and we were pretty passionate, but the creek bank was soggy. At some point we went back to the house, like good guests, and slept in our separate sleeping bags on the floor with the others.

The next day, everyone gathered outside and ate and drank and talked way more than we fished. Eric, the Smith's 10-year-old son, caught several fat trout. Like most of the others, I had no fishing gear. Hugo, fabled fisherman, had brought his rod and washed a generous number of worms. Guests wandered around like a 1923 British film, everyone casually dressed and wearing big sun hats: an unpretentious drama prof and his wife; a philosopher named Allen something who liked Henry James a lot and talked too much. Tall Eric Johnson, an instructor, and his Norwegian wife Kari. Mostly I remember Jim and sunshine, walking the meadow along the creek, chatting in lawn chairs under the ponderosas with friendly folks. Nothing dramatic happened. University demographics were irrelevant. This tall friendly young man slipped into my life.

Late the next afternoon, Jim and I drove back to Missoula—top down, wind in our hair—and decided to go out for dinner. First, we drove back to my little house so I could change. When we came out and I tried to start the car, it didn't.

"The solenoid," I said. having just dealt with that problem in my vexing bagatelle of a vehicle. "I'll put it in gear, and you can just push it back until it clicks."

He pushed. It started. He stood up, aghast, holding a headlight rim in his hand.

"No problem. It always does that."

Later Jim confessed that he feared he'd just jinxed everything at that moment—that rim flew off regularly, as though unwillingly conjoined with the headlight. I retrieved it from the roadside more than once. Off we went to his house where he dropped off his stuff. Having no car, Jim lived within walking distance of the university. Across the river from campus on Madison Street, next to Cippolato's Broadway Market—the only place in Missoula in those days to get Parmesan and good olives and capers—Jim shared a bungalow with two journalism graduate students, John Stromnes and Bob Cushman (son of Dan Cushman the author of *Stay Away Joe*.) "Cush" was perpetually re-assembling his motorcycle in the front room. This afternoon they were sitting on the wide front porch, and teased Jim as he ran in.

At dinner, we told each other about ourselves. We talked family and friends, travel, writing and writers we knew. Jim explained to me that he was from Harlem, Montana, not New York. He was smart, cute, and fun. That he was a graduate student seemed irrelevant; that he was Indian seemed irrelevant; that he was 27 and I was 31 was a bit unsettling. I was swept up by it all, but not quite swept away—I had other irons in the fire still; a leftover romance waned in Portland.

Attentiveness is a kind of intimacy and Jim's quality of listening attentively was surprisingly engaging. You wanted to converse with him. A former colleague, Virginia Carmichael, told me recently how she had met Jim in the '70s when he gave a reading in Houston where she owned a bookstore. Sitting next to him at dinner, she felt wholly present when she talked with him because he listened, she said, "as though you were a valuable, intelligent, even fascinating human being." That was Jim. People always found Jim easy to talk with, though interviewers found him reticent.

That Sunday in May 1967 at Valley of the Moon Ranch, university classes were nearly over. I had exams to give and papers to grade and Jim had papers to write, so we didn't do anything together until the next weekend when we had dinner with novelist colleague Jim Crumley and his first wife Charlie. That year, Crumley and James Lee Burke were both teaching for the first time, having been hired out of the University of Iowa Creative Writing Workshop to teach fiction writing. Crumley was a new, loud, lively, stocky guy, about 5'9" with a great big mustache, from Texas. Charlie was pretty, dark, and animated. She taught high school biology. Both Crumley and Burke were at the very beginning of fine writing careers—at once nervous and confident. Jim and Crumley were already drinking buddies at Missoula's Eddie's Club.

Jim began eating dinner regularly at my house as the summer went along. Cooking for two is always more fun than cooking for one and Jim's food budget was minuscule. While I wasn't a great cook, my repertoire included big salads and numerous dishes made with Campbell's mushroom soup. When Jim liked his first artichoke, I thought, "This is my kind of guy."

As we attended dinner parties and other events together, we began to be known as a couple. I always drove Jim back to his apartment at some point after dinner in those days before we were married because my landlord would have disapproved of my having an overnight boyfriend.

Further, my very Methodist parents would have been horrified. I couldn't face the hassle. These reasons sound prissy now but were very persuasive at the time. After a time, Jim drove home in my car each night and returned the next morning.

Jim worked as a counselor at Upward Bound that summer of 1967. His weeknight curfews meant we only had weekends to play. The Upward Bound Program was a federal college preparatory program for low-income high school students or those from families without college educations. Most of the 50 students were Indian. Jim got the job through his campus Indian connections—there were only six Indian students on campus at that time, in a student body of 7,000 or so. Jim liked working with the kids but felt cooped up in the dorm.

Sometimes we would drive up the Blackfoot River, east of town, convertible top down, open to the glorious afternoons. Once he drove us around the whole 167-mile Rock Creek loop— dirt roads the entire way, from the Interstate at Clinton, east of town, up to Hamilton in the Bitterroot and home—arriving at his dorm well past his 9:00 curfew. They didn't ground him.

My little Hallmark datebook is all the evidence that remains of that spring and summer of 1967 when Jim and I met and decided to marry. All tiny scrawls. No journal. No letters. I have just four photos: David Smith took a prophetic one of us at their Opening Day of Fishing Season party—Jim grinning on the ranch house back steps, me vamping in my tapestry tunic and jeans. Rick and Carole DeMarinis, fellow graduate

Jim and Lois Welch at David and Annick Smith's cabin, 1967.

student friends, took another of us, shortly after this: we were gazing, laughing, into one another's eyes (we later used it for our wedding announcement). Martha Elizabeth (the fifth Mrs. Crumley) recently gave me a copy of a photo Crumley had taken of us at his house the week after we'd met; it's still posted on my fridge.

The fourth photo from that year, a tiny snapshot, was taken the day Jim and I met my siblings. We are standing in front of the fireplace at the family home in Salem, Oregon: my parents, my minister brother Larry and his fiancé Ardyth, my sister Lenore and her minister husband Dick. Everyone looks cheerful, unscathed by the bizarre circuit we'd traveled that day. Just those four photos. Clearly, neither Jim nor I felt the need to document ourselves for posterity. This period was wonderful and decisive. We were falling in love, deciding to make a life together. Documents and chronology barely mattered.

The days slid happily into one another. Neither Jim nor I had expected that a sunny Saturday in May would lead to a major change in our lives. I liked my teaching job, my colleagues, my house—and my life—and wasn't planning anything further. Jim was enjoying graduate school more than he had enjoyed any previous period of his life and

Jim and Lois Welch.

was not making far-ranging plans. He was thrilled with his publications so far, and keeping company with other publishing writers allowed him to think of this as a life. He had no interest in teaching, but—again—the spectacle of improbable Hugo doing it, and doing it so well, kept that as a possibility, just as fog is a possibility some mornings. The days just slid into one another, and we were happy.

Jim was deceptively easy to be with. He was simply fun. He was open, brown-eyed, smiling, attentive, responsive. He was lithe, his clothes clean and crisp. He was ready for whatever came up: fishing, movies, parties, washing the car, walking over the hill. He was eager to go places and see people, just as eager to sit on the terrace and look at the orchard. Though he told me once about an angry episode in his past, he seemed always self-possessed, though shy—out of a deep-seated modesty. You didn't sense invisible barriers in him that so often arise between people. Such barriers prevented openness between me and my family. He had none of those. He just didn't rattle on about himself. Jim seemed centered. Like the sun turned toward you.

Writing seemed Jim's only plan, his sole ambition. He could imagine being a writer like Hemingway or Kerouac or Steinbeck. There were few Indian writers then to serve as models. He was committed, at last, to not failing out of school again. Previous summers he had worked for the Forest Service—in California and Montana. He enjoyed working outdoors with other young men, tromping in the woods, swimming in irrigation canals and going into the nearest town on weekends. At summer's end, they all went back to college.

I always wondered why Jim was attracted to me. I had spent my entire life in school, though I picked strawberries and cherries and beans during summers to earn money right up through high school and graduated to summer cannery jobs in college. American males too often are scared of brainy women. I've frightened quite a number, many possessing advanced degrees themselves. Jim hated school as a child, never excelled, and was only now getting serious about literature. Immune to guilt, he straightforwardly admitted what a mediocre student he had been.

Once, a few years after we married, I asked Jim one evening as I was preparing dinner, "Why me? Why this big-boned Germanic professor?"

"I am Blackfeet and Blackfeet love big women," he replied instantly, cheerfully. I recognized this for the half-teasing evasion of my unanswerable unnecessary question that it was, and never asked again. I suspect I represented to Jim an entrée to a different world, a world he first glimpsed after moving to Missoula—actual writers flourishing in a sizable and respected community. Writers living ordinary Montana lives. Not that I was a writer, but that was my milieu. And he had watched me in the halls of the English department for an entire year before we met. He knew how I interacted with students and faculty, and perhaps even with the empty halls.

The writing life began to seem possible to Jim: if Hugo could be a successful writer, why not Jim? Hugo was the most visibly working-class writer, in his green khaki work pants and blue jeans jacket. We had no elegant Mark Strands nor rich James Merrills around town. Local writers flourished but didn't necessarily get rich. We knew of Bud Guthrie and Dorothy Johnson, but our own friends were enjoying success too. Crumley's first novel *One to Count Cadence* was published with accolades in 1969. (In 2016, there is a Crumley memorial chair in Eddie's Club, now Charley's; there is another at The Depot in Missoula.) Fiction writer Earl Ganz was publishing stories right along, while Hugo and his students published poems everywhere. Carpentry seemed the favored day job for those who didn't teach, so they could work in the summer and spend winters writing.

As a graduate student, Jim was moving inward from the edges of that community. The young writers mostly hung out at Eddie's Club, a working man's bar favored by railroad workers. The walls were covered with local photographer/ bartender Lee Nye's striking black and white portraits of the clients. It was ideal for young (or grizzled) impoverished writers.

Hanging out with other writers was part of the apprenticeship. Jim had brief private bouts of great ambition. A well-hidden corner of his mind was intent on something like the Great American Novel, though he knew Indians weren't eligible. When he took a Milton course, for example, he started writing an epic, stopping only after writing five pages or so of blank verse, realizing how hard it was. That epic impulse resurfaced later, I suspect, when he started writing his novel *Fools Crow*. In 1965, he took his younger brother to San Francisco, where they explored North Beach, hot on the trail of Ferlinghetti, Kerouac and the Beats. Hugo was a poetry magnet and increasingly influential on the national scene. I was part of that swirl.

To me, Jim offered a yes-saying approach to living. I was raised in a world of prohibitions so encircling that possibilities were hard to invent. I loved being around inventive people, particularly verbally inventive people.

My datebook lists a June dinner here, another at Crumley's, a party out at the Potomac Bar, up the Blackfoot River, where we danced to cowboy music on the jukebox. My scrawls refer to Jim with increasing familiarity, changing from "Jim Welch" to JWelch to JW to Jim until they cease—since we did everything together thereafter. We saw each other every few days that June. Events have melted together in my memory. I don't recall the first dinner I fixed him, nor how often he showed me poems. Our first ride up the Blackfoot has fused in my memory with a hundred others.

James Welch and Richard Hugo. Photo by Steve Thompson in The Missoulian, *1969.*

I was too happy, too confused and too busy to write down and sort out my feelings that summer. Juggling boyfriends and tending to my professional life kept me very busy. Summer school was even more intense for me than the regular school year because classes met every day. I put in a couple of hours of preparation after dinner every night. Jim had to be back among his charges as an Upward Bound counselor by 9:00 weeknights, so ours wasn't exactly a whirlwind romance, though our friends considered us a couple almost immediately.
We didn't go out every night or walk around holding hands all day. We didn't have the chance.

It's hard to believe now that we barely even spoke during the week. Cell phones didn't exist. Jim had to use a common phone in the hall of the dorm, since he didn't even have a phone in his dorm room. He called me when he could; there was no calling him.

I went back to Portland for a week in June to see my family, my Portland friends, and the old boyfriend. He was charming still but the magic was gone. When I returned, Jim was waiting anxiously. I picked him up and we made dinner at my house.

"You mustn't go away again," he said, "I can't live without you." That is as close to a proposal scene as we ever got. No bended knee. No little ring box handed across a candlelit table. The Opening Day of Fishing Season Party story always did duty for the Proposal Story.

On August 2, Jim gave his first poetry reading—ever—at Upward Bound, with Vic Charlo, fellow MFA poet and great grandson of the Salish tribal chief. The high school-aged Upward Bounders filled the big meeting room in the dorm, even sitting on the floor. They responded enthusiastically; it was probably everyone's first poetry reading, including the poets! Jim was so nervous as we drove to the reading that he was falling asleep; when I first knew him, that was his default response to anxiety.

Our friends, Bernie and Sharri Knab gave a party for the poets afterwards. Bernie was an instructor I'd known since Portland State. Jim and Vic held a tease fest on the porch: Jim teased Vic about how the Blackfeet always (in the olden days) beat up the Salish in Hellgate Canyon at the east edge of the university because the Salish were such wimps. Vic teased back. I'd never witnessed tribal teasing before—

entirely good-natured and clearly not intended for me or any other white folks to join. I wish I could reconstruct the dialogue.

Once Jim was done with Upward Bound and I with summer school, we'd go driving or walking every day. Driving is serious in Montana. Considerable personal territory can be covered as one covers the physical territory. Because the world flows by, one's mind flows too. Because one is looking ahead, one isn't gazing into the eyes of one's companion. This can allow for conversation of a more meditative or indirect variety. Wildlife, bear stories, trips with family, why foresters are fun, chicken fried steak, basketball, flat tires, dogs.

Jim was writing poems constantly and would bring them for me to read—finished poems on the cheap yellow typing paper we used in those days. I thought they were wonderful. I thought all his poems were wonderful. I was useless to him as an editor because I loved everything he wrote. This is the same paper-grading Lois who was lavish with red ink on student papers in those days.

That Jim was Indian barely registered with me. Being Blackfeet was simply his reality, as mine was being from Oregon.

We compared whose eyes were darker—mine, in fact. We compared what we did as kids. He fished. I didn't. He played basketball, I didn't. I liked school. He didn't. I was raised Methodist, he Catholic. That I was four years older embarrassed me a bit. No one else seemed to notice.

We compared our different experiences all the time, but they never seemed to have much to do with his being Indian and me not. Comparisons usually had more to do with being Methodist or not. His relatives had more fun than mine. He had a whole lot more relatives than I did. Only several years after we were married did I realize one day—filling out the census—that ours was what was called a "bi-racial marriage." Shockingly, that put our relationship on a par with conditions in the South, bringing the civil rights movement into our bedroom. But not really; many Americans seem barely aware that Indians even exist. Jim never wore braids or fringed buckskins and managed to appear thoroughly assimilated into mainstream American culture.

If anyone had any objections to our being together, these seemed to have to do with a young female professor marrying a graduate student. In those days, the prohibition of professor/student relationships had not yet become law. And Jim had never been my student. Hugo, for goodness' sake, had lived an entire year with an undergrad poetry student, and no one fired him. It wasn't condoned but it was overlooked so long as we were discreet. University life was very much an old boys club.

After a cocktail party one evening, one of my senior colleagues asked me, "What will you do if it doesn't work out?"

"I guess I'll do what you did, and what most of the Foreign Language department has been doing all year—get a divorce," I said, never believing for a moment it would happen. It didn't. ∎

James Welch, to the left of Richard Hugo and his wife Ripley. Leonard Robinson, former fiction editor of Esquire magazine is in the back right. Lois Welch is in the front right. Leonard's wife, the poet Patricia Goedicke, took the photo at Ripley Hugo's cabin on the North Fork of the Teton River, about 20 miles west of Choteau Mountain, c. 1979.

PAUL ZARZYSKI

Five Wild Reminiscences of Rick DeMarinis

I
Wylie Street Writers' Party

What an honor in the early '70s for a young aspiring poet to not only be admitted into the Creative Writing Master of Fine Arts degree program at the University of Montana, but also to be welcomed into Missoula's Wylie Street Writers Social Club—Dick and Ripley Hugo, Jim and Lois Welch, Rick and Carole DeMarinis! Little could I have even considered at the time, however, that decades later five of those dear friends, along with my mother and father, and too many others who'd played such seminal roles in my writing life, and otherwise, would be gone. I will forever remember fondly those heyday times on Wylie—even dedicated my 2014 poetry collection, *Steering with My Knees*, "In memory of Ripley and Richard Hugo—With gratitude for all the laughs at 2407 Wylie." My wildest of memories, however, actually occurred at Rick and Carole and daughter Naomi's home, directly across the street at 2408 Wylie. During Rick's celebration-of-life ceremony in Missoula on June 29, 2019, I read the following account of that glorious moment in poetic time and space (excerpted in part from my book *51: 30 Poems, 20 Lyrics, 1 Self-Interview* —Bangtail Press, 2011):

Rick DeMarinis.

Me (Interviewee): . . . Carole and Rick threw The Mother of All First-Book Parties for me after *The Make-up of Ice* was published in 1984. We're talking "back when writers behaved badly," as Jim Harrison put it oh-so-succinctly at Jim Welch's memorial at the Wilma Theater. Back when notorious novelists, to remain anonymous here, were prone to remove cherished heirloom family photographs off the hosts' walls and pull them apart in order to acquire unhindered panes of glass upon which to evenly divide and separate the white, wheel-spoked berms.

Interviewer (Also Me!) Crumley, right? It *had* to be Crumley.
Me, again: I'm not saying. Although, rumors abound that Rick DeMarinis has in his possession a stash of un-retouched snapshots documenting the events of that bash. At one pivotal point during the occasion, Carole snatched a pint of Everclear (she reported the day after is how I know this) away from me and Jim—yes, Crumley, goddamnit—passing it back and forth, tears gushing down all four of our grinning cheeks. What I *do* remember, pretty much solely, is the wild drive to the East Gate liquor store for *re*-supplies at 1:30 a.m., just under the closing time wire—Carole's mother's '71 Monte Carlo, bad shocks and all, roller-coasting down Van Buren Street doing Saint-Christopher-only-knows how many miles-per-minute over the speed limit, Rick slouched low-rider-cool behind the tilted-down wheel, me riding shotgun, and in the back seat, two renowned prose writers nasally inhaling through a straw from one of those amber plastic pharmaceutical vials some non-liquid substance. The Canadian train event, years earlier, documented by the film *Festival Express*, had nothing over a Missoula book party, I tell you. Carole cooked breakfast for me as the sun came up. I strolled out into the brisk fall Rattlesnake Canyon air and wondered if it would all be downhill from then on . . . . Thanks in no small part to Rick's continued major friendship role in my life for another 35 years after that infamous event, it has *not* been.

II
DeMarinOZ Sighting from The Other Side

And then, ten nights after Rick died on June 12, 2019, this dream that I deem metaphorically commensurate with the highest esteem in which I regarded both Rick's writing *and* our Friendship:
I'm pacing in the wings of the stage and getting pumped for a proverbial "really big shoe." Major poetry venue. Might've been the

historic Wilma Theater in Missoula, where years ago, I did, in fact, enjoy an otherworldly interaction with an enthusiastic full house. I peek out from behind the curtain (bad theatrical luck be damned) as I am prone to do, to see if anyone has actually shown up to hear Poetry? There in the middle of a packed auditorium sits Rick. He's sporting his classic "any second now something *really fucking funny* is going to happen" shit-eating grin. I yell loud enough for everyone in the joint to hear, "It's Rick! Rick DeMarinis Is Here!" We're talking a surprise factor akin to Hemingway or Yeats or Dylan Thomas or Richard Hugo Himself being in attendance! I make my way out into the seats—those in the audience sitting in front of Rick turning to witness silly Zarzyski's willingness to blow to itsy-bitsy pieces all protocol. Rick and I throw our arms around each other in a big Italian *"K sue chadda"* ("What's Up!?") *paisano* hug. Rick appeared young and healthy as ever. Oh, and one more note: he was wearing a gun-metal gray, starched and pressed, short-sleeved shirt similar to those worn by auto mechanics or appliance repairmen, sans, of course, his name embroidered in red over the left-hand pocket, because everyone in that auditorium *knew* it was him, the fiction-writer Wizard—out from behind the curtain of mortality, "The Great and Powerful" DeMarinOZ!

III
Rodeo-Poetry Road Trip

Speaking of the "great and powerful," if only I could be granted a magic-lamp-genie wish to transmogrify the dream I just recounted into reality, while turning the following Zarzyski-DeMarinis Oregon Road Trip true story into a dream, albeit somewhat of a nightmare:

It was longtime writer-friend extraordinaire, Gary Gildner, who, during his distinguished writer-in-residence tenure at Reed College (Portland), booked Rick a reading gig in 1983-84. So that Rick wouldn't have to make the drive solo, Gary must've leveraged an appearance for the both of us at Willamette University (Salem). I was still fitting an occasional classic spur-ride to bareback broncs and decided to enter the Eugene Rodeo, hoping to augment the paltry poetry honorarium with an eight-second pay-window trip in the arena. As things turned out, although I'd made a qualified ride, I wound up just out of the money and maybe even in the close-but-no-cigar "crying hole"—5th place when the rodeo paid the top four. It must've been a night show and we must've stayed for the whole shebang because we didn't pull back into Gildner's abode until well after midnight. I remember the driveway between houses being so narrow that I could just barely open the car door enough to slip out. I had never, *ever*, before left my riggin' bag, my precious rodeo gear, out-of-sight overnight, but for some foolish reason—it being only a few hours until daybreak and my bedroom window being mere feet from the car and it feeling like a safe residential neighborhood and our planning an early departure back to Montana—I decided not to bother hauling my "war bag" into the house. I recall feeling exhausted from having to poetically strain to incite the heavily-sedated-zombies-in-tweed Salem audience, as well as from coming down off the buckin' hoss adrenaline high.

    Rick was the first to mosey out with his suitcase come time to leave that morning. I'll never forget his succinct wording: "We've been hit." The back window of the hatchback had been either busted or, more quietly, popped out. Either way, I hadn't heard a peep from my

Eugene Rodeo parking lot: "Rodeo Writers," c.1984.
Left to right, Gary Gildner, Kathryn Terrill, Verlena Orr, Marian Palaia, Rick DeMarinis, and, out of the frame, shutterbug Zarzyski.

bunk "mere feet from the car." My rodeo gear-bag and a stack of CDs gone! I was no-doubt entered in some Montana pitchin' the following weekend, and now minus my most personal—dare I say "intimate?"—tools of the trade, likely destined for some Portland pawn shop. As good-bad-luck would have it, the police found my riggin' and chaps in a neighbor's hedgerow. But my spurs, riding glove, boots, you name it, were history. I had never in my life until then been victimized by theft. Needless to say, for someone who lives as viscerally as do I, both on and off the page, I not only did not take it well, I was out for blood—an artesian geyser of arterial hemoglobin, not one drip less—in return for my torment.

And here's where Rick—heaven bless his pacifist soul for his capacity to assign to his fictional characters every nano-iota of real-life rage—rode to Guido Zarzyski's rescue and saved me, just barely in the nick of incendiary time, from Polish-Mafioso-Rodeo-Poet combustion. I distinctly recall us being somewhere on the snaky Lochsa Highway between Lewiston, Idaho, and Missoula. We'd spoken nary a word since leaving Portland. I had a two-fisted garroted death-grip on the wheel. I mean, we're talking a seething carful of palpable toxic-fog, of venomous silence—a veritable superfund sight on wheels; we're talking skittish Rick feeling as if he'd been buried alive in an economy casket with Hannibal Lecter; we're talking the violent velocity of human atomic matter (*sans* God Particle!) transmogrified into a Homo sapiens Hadron Collider dialed to "HIGH!" "Vengeance is mine, saith the Lord?" Mere child's play next to the surgical nuances of revenge I was envisioning in the smoldering soulless cauldrons of my boiled-oil psyche—Capote's *In Cold Blood*, or, far worse, a Quentin Tarantino script, by comparison, qualifying as appropriate cinematic subject matter for a Disney matinee.

Had our CDs not been filched, who knows, maybe Rick would've endeavored to slip a mood-music disc into the player, although, on second thought, the player may have been excised during the hit, as well. Rick squirmed nervously mile-after-mile in his seat as he visibly strained to think of something, *anything,* he might say to console me, to spill even a shot glass full of chilled perfume into the effluvium of The Dago Volcano's fumarole. Believing, I'm sure, that his imaginary powers had failed him for the first time in his life, he finally oh-so–

pathetically offered-up in the most serious tone he could muster, "You know, Paul, when we get back to Missoula, I'm going to get a gun."

One Mississippi, 2 Mississippi, 3 Mississ... was about how long it took us to burst, in unison, into a raucous laughter that lasted the rest of the way home and for decades thereafter—"Rick? Paul. Have you gotten that gun yet?" prefacing many a phone conversation, which never ceased to trigger the same degree of comical relief we experienced that day while driving back from Portland. Tibetan monk Rick DeMarinis with a gun? About as lethal or menacing, as inconsequential, as a poet with a literary agent. Although the word on the street years later was that Rick did, in fact, take a loaded pistol away from novelist Barry Hannah in the middle of a dark Missoula night. But that's another story—and one nowhere near as funny.

IV
The Burning Women of Far Cry

I was both humbled and scared witless when asked by publisher Aaron Parrett to write a blurb for the Drumlummon Montana Literary Masters Series 2018 Edition of Rick's 1986 novel *The Burning Women of Far Cry*. After tormenting for weeks over what I might say to most emphatically extol Rick's mastery of the language and imagination, I brilliantly decided to just let him do it himself. As the quintessence of my praise for his work, I quoted the inscription he penned into my copy of *Under The Wheat*:

> *for Paul—my partner survivalist: it's the bottom of the ninth, see, two outs. We're trailing 1-0. Gooden is on the mound and he doesn't like Polacks or Dagos. The count is 0 and 2. The bat feels like a railroad tie in your hands. The stands are filed with collection agency thugs. Gooden uncorks a 99-mph fastball. It looks like an albino BB. This is it. You take a big cut, and . . . and . . .*
> *(next page) . . . 590-foot drive into the Hudson River!*
>
> > *Your buddy,*
> > *Rick (The Bambino) D.*
> > *10/21/86*

PAUL ZARZYSKI

V
"Monte Carlo Express—
Post Office Box 258, 15.3 Miles Home"

It must have been sometime in the mid-80s when Rick and Carole offered to sell me her mother's 1971 Chevy Monte Carlo—originally sold by Dee Motor Company in Anaconda, where Carole grew up. I had never owned a vehicle that "new"—had been driving a '69 Ford half-ton pickup and decided I needed something that would get "better mileage?" The car was a wrecking yard dog's dream come real—complete with a caved-in grill and front bumper, and dents a-plenty in its faded burnt-orange exterior—but it ran (with or without brakes) and I was still young enough to military press the 50-ton-sheet steel (or so it seemed) helicopter landing pad hood in order to fill up the oil every time I checked the gas. You bet—the same land barge Rick coxswained down Van Buren in the opening piece to this writing.

When it came to taking a run at and busting through snow drifts to get in and out of the isolated ranch house I lived in south of Augusta, ol' Monte was a D-8 Cat. No matter the weather, we'd make the trip into town once or twice a week to retrieve the mail, which became the triggering subject to a poem speaking to my willpower-less efforts to get back to the ranch before addressing said envelopes beckoning my attention.

I've since had the car mostly restored—painted "viper red," adorned with a new black vinyl top, and outfitted with chrome rally wheels. Although I don't drive it as often (or as hard or far) as I once did, I still punch it up to 80 or 90 out on the wide-open Montana two-lane blue lanes, which seems to suit the full-scale stuffed Looney Tunes Tasmanian Devil strapped into the back seat (same back seat occupied by Bill Kittredge and Jim Crumley during the Van Buren Street liquor quest). Moreover, I never get behind the wheel of Ol' Monte without summoning the passenger spirits of Carole and Rick, to whom this poem is dedicated:

Monte Carlo Express—Post Office Box 258, 15.3 Miles Home

I've checked fence doing 80 in a low-rider
Chevrolet springing the borrow pit
like a pack mule that hates crossing
running water. The torture is too much
when a week's worth of mail—stacked
beside me like a high school majorette
beckoning with her baton
decades back when this car was showroom new—
presses against me. I could never wait and still
can't wait to open what's personal. Steering
with my knees, jackknife gleaming in my lap,
the wheel tilted down full—The Monte, a roulette
ball blur hugging hot asphalt—I shuffle
through the stack and gamble
once again on 8 miles of 2-lane
straightaway. I Frisbee bills and all business
glassine-windowed envelopes,
in which we poets never receive checks,
over the suicide seat headrest, toss
junk mail to the floor-mat collage
on the shotgun side, stick love letters
between my teeth, and maybe I'm better off
not having tasted perfume
for years. *Esquire*, slicker than a hot plastic
sack of slimy grunion, slithers and slides
over, under, and between the seats
leaving its Stetson Cologne scent
like a madam's tomcat mascot marking his turf
on two-for-one night
in a cowboy brothel. Ol' Monte drifts
left across the double yellows on a hill
then right, into the shoulder brome, seed heads
whipping the wheel wells clean, dust swirling
in the side mirror, the Day-Glo

rubber fish in place of plastic Jesus
dashing for the stuntmen grasshoppers
suctioned to the windshield,
their front paws clasped in prayers
that must have saved us from the bridge
abutment already signed
with 4 white crosses for those who did not
quite
      make
            this
                  curve
because of booze, because of snooze, because of
tire or tie rod act-of-God failure
of car or heart, or the piss-poor
penmanship of a good friend
loving me almost to cursive death with this letter.

      For Carole and Rick DeMarinis ■

Richard Hugo

GARY GILDNER

A Late Omelet

> *All day festive tunes*
> *explain your problems are over. You picnic*
> *alone on clean lawn with your legend.*
>
> —Richard Hugo, "In Your Good Dream"

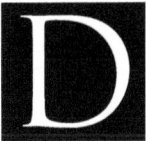ick gave a reading in Des Moines one time when I was teaching at Drake, a solid, generous, relaxed reading, and afterwards lovely Ed Mayo, my colleague, hosted a reception for him at a local hotel. Admirers of Dick's poems and those who'd been smitten at the reading mixed well around this accessible guy. As one of my older students, a new fan, said, "How can you not like people again after a night like tonight?" She was a bad marriage survivor who had promised me, when joining my writing class, that I would be reading only bitterness and sorry I ever saw her. But Dick sent her home with brightness in her eyes. When the reception was over he wanted a quiet nightcap, so we went to my house.

It was about two in the morning then.

We sat at the kitchen table, sipping bourbon, and talked about baseball, jazz, luck, trout fishing in Montana, where he lived then, and Michigan, where I grew up, and Idaho, where we'd both chased the fairest game that lived. Frying rainbows in a pan under the stars beside a stream, how *good* they ate, and how you felt afterwards lying outdoors smelling the night smells.

"Does 'Frying Rainbows in a Pan Under the Stars' work as a title?" one of us said.

"I like it. 'Turning Over Rainbows on a Spit' isn't bad either."

"How about 'On a Skewer'?"

"How about 'On a Truss'?"

"Hold up, I'm aging fast enough!"

We talked about rivers and the names of rivers. Michigan's Au Sable and Manistee. The North Fork Coeur d'Alene and below it the South Fork of the Clearwater in the Idaho panhandle. The Big Hole in Montana. The Big Lost. For those rainbows. Those steelhead, browns, and brookies.

Drinking and talking this way we got hungry.

I stood up and made important steps in the right direction.

Then I stopped and pointed at the refrigerator. "Dick," I said, "I know we have no trout in there. We have nothing worthy of our talk and desires, but I will build us something respectable."

We had had a couple of nightcaps by this time. On top of what we drank at the hotel.

"My friend," he said, "do not worry. I have confidence I've saved up for times like now."

Hearing that, I felt strong.

"I will build us," I said, "an omelet. An omelet with mushrooms and green peppers and onions and pieces of bacon, and I will slice up a fresh tomato on the side. I will toast some seven-grain bread to go with it," I said.

I said all that as if I were running for office. No—mocking running for office. Performing. Sticking up a finger to mark each delicious item I would bring forth to support this grand plan.

"Whoa," he said. "Are we rushing in to this?"

"We might be," I said.

"Let us not rush into anything," he said. "Except possibly our dreams. Come back here and sit down."

I returned to the table and poured another round. We savored being alive. We savored the weather, all kinds of weather. We savored great poems, those written and yet to come. We savored the necks of sweet women. We savored the power of dreams and how canny they are to let us know the proper time to fish. We savored how shaking all the trees in those dreams enlivened the mayflies in them to start a fury of feeding as they fell in the current beside us, and we savored how baseball, nicely underway, is the only game anywhere that allows us to steal home!

Or to try.

We drank to attempting such a steal.

And not forgetting during all this savoring a grand drama waiting for us in the wings. The omelet. Which we would pause now and then in our ranging here and there in order to carefully sharpen its properties and promise, smooth its lines.

By four o'clock or so the idea's time had come.

Again I stood.

I moved with purpose to the refrigerator and found one egg, no mushrooms, no green peppers—not a single, shriveled orphan crouching in the crisper—and no bacon, no tomatoes. The refrigerator possessed that single egg and maybe a finger of milk. The cupboard possessed no onions, the breadbox possessed the heel of a grand loaf of seven-grain bread, a small heel.

I turned to Dick. "Dick," I said, "we have one egg and a heel of bread with which to make our omelet."

He looked at me with an expression of confidence, and said sweetly, "We will enjoy it."

A one-egg no-frills omelet around five o'clock in the morning is not an easy thing to make after the stars have packed up and quit the sky. My omelet turned out to be scrambled egg. And when I searched for plates for some reason I could only put my hands on very large dinnerware. Thus the little vittles, divided in half, arrived at the table as two dandelions (stemless) might have arrived at my daughter Gretchen's play table once upon a time.

Dick, that lovable lug, dug into his egg carefully, like good surgeon, like a man under the close heavens, beside the blessed waters, eating a rainbow . . . murmuring, "Delicious . . . divine . . ."

Or something like that.

*****

The above scene—the getting there—was not easy. To go back almost half a century and raise up, render, give life to an event that to most people was simply a couple of dudes drinking too much one night and turning sloppily sentimental? Come on. Over the years, if I mentioned that evening and was encouraged to write about it, I'd put off even trying. To quote another fellow poet, e. e. cummings, mostpeople are not like you and me. "Mostpeople," he said, making those two words into one clump, "have less in common with ourselves than the square root of minus one." In short, mostpeople were so busy trying to be like everybody else, they ended up amounting to not much in the thinking and feeling areas. By their own choice.

But I digress. I know how difficult it is for some poets to call it a night after giving a good reading. He'd connected. He didn't need Ed Mayo or me to tell him that, though we did anyway, and everybody was happy. Not just my student. And I was happy to have a nightcap or two that evening with someone I greatly admired, over some talk about ordinary things that meant a lot to us—to our ordinary sides. When to take, when to swing away. Follow that good hunch, bet the longshot. Did I worry about how I might describe our nightcaps later? How I might not be able to describe fighting loneliness without saying I was trying to describe fighting loneliness? Without saying, *So anyway, what else is new?*

Here, let me put on some Miles Davis. How about *Kind of Blue*? ■

RE-READINGS

Poems by JIM HARRISON
The THEORY & PRACTICE
of RIVERS

RICK JOHNSON

Stumbling toward Antelope Butte: Reflections on Jim Harrison

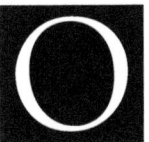On a wilderness walk in July of 2002, I wondered how long I could keep doing such things. Like everything, these trips must end but before my body quits, I could stop carrying so much. This usually occurs to me when the trail is steep. Pulling my gaze from growing amber on the granite peaks, I look down to keep from stumbling on yet another rock and an early evening crumble to the ground.

Eyeing the dirt and plodding along, I inventory my backpack. What would lighten my load? A fool's errand some score miles from the trailhead, but I am no longer thinking about my sore feet. My liquor ration would be lighter if we ever got to a decent spot to cast off the pack and spend the night.

The Theory and Practice of Rivers by Jim Harrison has been in my pack around thirty years. A well-worn wilderness companion. The slim volume of poetry, opened at day's end, expands in my imagination beyond the ounces it weighs. A bit like water to dehydrated food, with this package I just open and add light. Then breathe into the starry night.

> I warned myself all night
> but then halfway between my ears
> I turned toward the heavens
> and reached the top of my head.
> From there I can go just about
> anywhere I want and I've never
> found my way back home.

> —

> As a child, fresh out of the hospital
> with tape covering the left side
> of my face, I began to count birds.
> At age fifty the sum total is precise
> and astonishing, my only secret.

Idaho was there when I needed it. I arrived for the summer in 1979. As the habit of long dusty walks took hold it became clear I wasn't leaving. The Hudson Valley's big river was home. That was where I was raised. That first Idaho summer it became clear I was far from grown. My inside parts were soft, parts I was realizing mattered most. Idaho opened plenty of space for growing, well out of sight from where I came.

I became stronger from hauling sheetrock and drywall mud, pleasing no one, wielding trowels and knives, running up scaffold and ladders. I got good at it. Stumbling often yet staying on my feet were trail-earned skills I found useful to life, too. A couple nimble moves to keep a job led to a small business I owned, pay mostly in an abundance of time for backcountry skiing and near-constant wandering into wild places.

The early winters were lean, when I worked least and read most, books piling up, for the first time with no relation to course work or someone else's curricula or compass. Tucked into the high east-facing corner of a warehouse, my Wood River apartment was a sanctuary of white walls, big windows and high ceilings with a woodstove in the center of the room. I spent a lot of time alone, pre-dawn ears tuned to the nearby highway department garage where I could hear snowplows firing up after a good snow. The giant gape-mouthed snow blower distinctively howled as it headed north to clear Galena Summit, an indicator I'd be finding fresh backcountry powder after the road was cleared.

More often days were clear and wicked cold. When working, I carried fifty-pound buckets of drywall mud back down the outdoor stairs, hauled up to keep from freezing solid in my little pick-up. I started that rattling Courier a couple times by slipping charcoal briquets under the engine on a galvanized garbage-can lid to warm the engine a bit. Other than a bloody gash on my freezing bare hand from a slipped wrench, my first truly successful car repair was installing an electric block heater. I skied often. I read more.

Jim Harrison books started appearing, the first loaned by a friend whose mom encouraged collecting of books. "Keep the good ones, the ones you'll want to read again when you're old. When you are old, they are all new again." Old? I could not imagine it, but I liked the growing piles of books.

Jim Harrison books have Russell Chatham paintings on the cover. You pause over the landscape painting before you read any words. My relationship began with two: a writer and painter. A cover's white frame around the painting are recognizable from across a room or, for me, across many decades. Was that first one *Farmer? A Woman Lit by Fireflies?*

Perhaps it was *Legends of the Fall*. It doesn't matter. I read them all. They were quickly what I wanted to do, feeding something else about what I wanted to be.

It began with the novels, or more accurately the novellas, longer than a short story, shorter than a full book, but good stories to be sure. Wrapped in rough furs in a cave or Patagonia fleece around a white-gas stove, we respond to a good story. Harrison tells tales to be sure.

"There are various stories about this," Harrison once said, "but a true story is in there, if I can ever stop fibbing...

"My mother told me two years before she died, she was an old Swede, her parents were immigrants, so this is a Swedish compliment. She said to me, 'You've made quite a living with your fibs.'"

The novellas and novels attached like scratchy seeds in my socks, embedded and working their way deeper. *Dalva* is in the voice of a strong woman, a woman you want to know, set in the Midwest, the sandhills of Nebraska. Standing at a French farmer's market in Provence it took some doing to get the nose of a woman out of her book, the cover recognizable to me. A translation of *Dalva*. His books are especially popular in France. Limited by our respective languages we spoke of how well Harrison writes in the voice of a woman. "How does he feel that?" she asked.

"Anyone who knows a novelist or poet very well has probably figured out they are not dealing with a true intellectual," Harrison wrote in *The Search for the Genuine*, a nonfiction collection published posthumously in 2022.

> I have often wondered about the peculiar female umbrella I grew up under and what particular effect it had on my work, what drove me to write in a female voice in most of *Dalva*, all of the novella *The Woman Lit by Fireflies*, and a large portion of my most recent novel, *The Road Home*. I could always ask the analyst I've been visiting in New York City for more than twenty years, but I never have. That would be poking needlessly around the sacred veil of art herself. The answer is always in the entire story, not a piece of it.
> And on a wretchedly therapeutic level there's the idea that my capability to write as a woman saved me from a death by drugs and booze, in that manliness in our culture that can paint you into a corner where the only thing left to do is eat roadkill and bite the moon.

Indeed. Sometimes I feel that, too, the near misses I feel as hot wind from train cars flying by inches from my body, deep in the dark, in my bed, my eyes open to the ceiling, thankfully with my wife's sleeping breath beside me. Gratitude comes in funny ways. I grew up among a flock of sisters and female friends. I am comfortable around some women more than many men. Such nurture shaped me, my work, and later my strategy and management, finding myself responsible for not just my own wanderings, but others, too. Harrison's writing hums like low electric current, resonant and just a hair uncomfortable. His poetry and prose is grounded in hunting, fishing, burly eating and drinking, and rich ribald fantasy if not actual adventure, yet beneath every bit of it is empathy and compassion in far greater measure.

The Road Home has an opening roughly embedded in memory from the many times I've repeated it for friends fresh from the loss of a loved canine companion. "It is easy to forget that in the main we die only seven times more slowly than our dogs." The loss of a dog's loving stare strikes deep yet the wound strikes deeper by the measure of a dog year against our own meager string of days.

His novels and novellas provide a good zing to my internal work-ings, yet his nonfiction may have provided more tangible evidence to my approach to the kitchen and dining table and times spent poking around the outdoors. "I never know what to do about my antique obsessions," he said in a 2002 interview. Food. There is a lot of it in those books. Drink. A lot of that, too, moderated foremost by ensuring good quality. Sex. Ditto. Nature comes from where it is, broadly defined, in places pristine and wild, yet no less where well worked over by saw or cow or whatever came by before he took time for a sit and look around. It is all sacred. The literature references run deep, varied and mind-expanding. Mortality is always present, too, just beyond sight, that steady echoing drip you hear when you're looking way back in there.

THE LIMBERLOST REVIEW

Just Before Dark contains the essay "What Have We Done with the Thighs," a serious (well, sorta) alarm to the absence of chicken thighs on restaurant menus and our home-table plates. While more humble a cut, thighs deserve more consideration providing a more tasteful bite than the then-ubiquitous dry and white boneless breast.

> I was strangely silent, sipping or gulping my wine, in hopes I would be asked what was bothering me.
> "What's bothering you?" asked Milliman, who is accustomed to me in full babble about food matters.
> I explained my thigh thoughts, ranging through culinary history down to the socio-political implications of exclusionary food faddism, the penchant for fey minimalism in the upwardly mobile groups. I finished with, "Do you think this all stands for something bigger?

The essay diverts to Gary Snyder's then-new and revelatory book of essays, *The Practice of the Wild*. "Our distance from the source of our food enables us to be superficially more comfortable, and distinctly more ignorant," Snyder says. Harrison ends on a lighter note providing a recipe for chili and reflecting that "The best human thighs are owned by . . ." two women he names from moviesand a *Sports Illustrated* swimsuit calendar. If you're curious, you can look it up. He concludes: "As Pai Chang said a thousand years ago, 'Just melt the inner and outer mind together completely.'"

Not long after reading this I was in Seattle for gatherings with friends around tables, with plates and goblets overfilled and festive. We lived there for a time when my own practice of the wild became a career-long immersion in conservation politics with generous side helpings of big-city education and enrichment of the palate. We returned to see Jim Harrison in a rare public reading at the Fifth Avenue Theater. Getting into the full spirit of things, we gratefully laid a paycheck or so on a long evening's dinner at *Campagne*, a fine French restaurant in Pike Place Market. Needing to visit the little boy's room, right outside the door I ran into, almost literally, Jim Harrison.

"I didn't see you coming," he said, perhaps referring to being blind on the left side, the result of a childhood injury. That we'd nearly clobbered into each other and grinning about it provided some evidence we may have been sipping some red wine. I mentioned being in town for his reading. Somehow this led to chicken thighs and convivial back and forth of sufficient length for the restaurant owner to come looking for his lost tablemate. We laughed about this and continued laughing on into the bathroom to pee.

If the novellas and novels were my early first course, the nonfiction a sustaining slab of protein, then Harrison's poetry is what continues to fill the glass, the favored Bandol I first learned of in his pages.

In 2002, an interviewer referred back to a reviewer's comments after publication of *Locations*, Harrison's second book of poetry from decades before. In 1968, he said, "You are one of the animals. You write from within the natural world not about the natural world." Harrison responded:

> When I was blinded at seven, I sort of retreated into the natural world. Even Shakespeare said, 'We are nature, too.' Sometimes you're outside looking in. But in some times that we value most you are inside looking out . . . and you do feel intensely at home in a way that you don't in a building.

And while nature figures deeply in Harrison's prolific seventeen books of poetry, so does the inevitable end, both as a natural and literary fact. Every trail reaches the end. Every story ends. Jim Harrison died in

2016, a short while after his wife Linda, whom he'd married in 1959. Russell Chatham followed soon after. The book and cover, closed.

I've been going back to the bookshelf these days, and my book piles are still growing. Again, I have much time to read. At times, I stare at the Chathams on my walls.

Harrison once spoke of a friend, a native American, whom he visited when the friend was close to death. The dying man watched as Harrison began to weep, "Oh, calm down. These things happen to people."

"I'll always be walking up Antelope Butte," Harrison wrote in a poem. "I've made this path and nobody else."

My thinned hair has a wilder unkempt look; my drywall tools are cold out in the garage. "Never get rid of your tools," an older worker once warned me. "You never know how this will all go." My life's work used a set of other tools, and on a good day I think it may have done some good, though it was always a bit of an uphill rocky grind, my own wandering climb around Antelope Butte. I kept the tools. I kept the books, and they are new again.

There should be many more trails before I go looking for the windswept ridges of Antelope Butte. I could lighten my step if I lighten my load a bit. Maybe pause to let the Bandol breathe a little longer. Take smaller sips. Perhaps I will. I know I'll keep *The Theory and Practice of Rivers* in the backpack. We will see where the path leads. ∎

* * * * *

Jim Harrison. Photo by Jean-Luc Bertini
from the cover of A Really Big Lunch.

Hard Times

The other boot does not drop from heaven.
I've made this path and nobody else
leading crookedly up through the pasture
where I'll never reach the top of Antelope Butte.
It is here where my mind begins to learn
my heart's language on this endless
wobbly path, veering south and north
informed by my all-too-vivid dreams
which are a compass without a needle.
Today the gods speak in drunk talk
pulling at a heart too old for this walk,
a cold windy day kneeling at the mouth
of a snake den where they killed 800 rattlers.
Moving higher my thumping chest recites the names
of a dozen friends who have died in recent years,
names now incomprehensible as the mountains
across the river far behind me.
I'll always be walking up Antelope Butte.
Perhaps when we die our names are taken
from us by a divine magnet and are free
to flutter here and there with the bodies
of birds. I'll be a simple crow
who can reach the top of Antelope Butte.

—Jim Harrison

WILFRED THESIGER

ARABIAN SANDS

Longmans

KURT CASWELL

Much that Was Noble, Nothing that Was Gracious: Re-reading Wilfred Thesiger's Arabian Sands

Years ago in Keswick, after an old friend and I climbed Scafell Pike in the footsteps of Coleridge and Wordsworth, I walked into a bookstore on Station Street in search of what, I did not know. Coming down from the mountains that day, I felt that I had divested myself of something, that I had dropped what burdens I carried on the scree near the summit peak. The front door of that bookstore called me in, and I went in to find on the display rack inside the door, a book titled *Among the Mountains* (1998) written by a man named Wilfred Thesiger, an assemblage of accounts of the author's travels through the high country in Asia in the 1950s. I bought it and read it and was immediately taken by Thesiger's simplicity, directness, and clarity of language. In Hunza, Thesiger writes, "Despite a very hard frost I slept snugly in my two flea-bags on the snow at some distance from the fire to avoid the sparks, which are bad with juniper wood." In Nuristan, "High up on the snow-covered mountainside I saw a bear." In Chitral, "This wasted a lot of time." The writing is something like haiku, line after line, or it realizes what Buddhists call *suchness*, an evocation of reality untroubled by the distinction between object and meaning. To end the book, Thesiger writes, "Now that the main road is built, the lorries thunder by; the camel caravans are gone, their bells stilled for ever."

I wanted more, certainly, and when I returned home and had a chance to explore Thesiger's work and life, I came to understand that his greatest book is *Arabian Sands* (1959). I read that too, greedily, and recently I reread it, each gloriously clear word of it which rang for me perhaps as the bells of those camel caravans rang for Thesiger. I immediately classed it with a handful of other books that have given my life direction and purpose: Peter Matthiessen's *The Snow Leopard*, Barry Lopez's *Arctic Dreams*, Beryl Markham's *West With the Night*, Bruce Chatwin's *The Songlines*, Antoine de Saint-Exupery's *Wind, Sand and Stars*.

THE LIMBERLOST REVIEW

Sir Wilfred Thesiger, as he would become, was born to privilege in Addis Ababa in 1910 where his father served as British consul general to Ethiopia. His grandfather was second baron Chelmsford, and his uncle, after serving as governor of Queensland and then New South Wales, became viceroy of India. A cousin was a popular film and stage actor of the day. The young Thesiger came to Britain for the first time to be educated at Eton College and the University of Oxford. He was captain of Oxford's boxing team and treasurer of its Exploration Club. Yet something of him remained in Africa, even in those years, and Thesiger returned as soon as he was able, answering a personal invitation in 1930 to attend the coronation of Emperor Haile Selassie of Ethiopia.

For Thesiger, the desert came first and the mountains later. He had heard tales of the great deserts of Arabia and he longed to make a journey across the Rub' al Khali, the Empty Quarter, a vast, waterless region of shifting sands located on the southern Arabian peninsula. Two Europeans had already crossed the Empty Quarter, but there were other routes and much still to explore. *Arabian Sands* is a chronicle of Thesiger's five years of intense travel in the region just after WWII, during which he crossed the Empty Quarter twice.

These journeys would not have been possible without the help and guidance of Thesiger's Bedu companions. He adopts their way of life, a spare and simple way of being stripped of all luxury and comfort, perhaps the well-spring of his spare and simple prose. "They lived in black tents in the desert, or in bare rooms devoid of furnishings in the villages and towns," Thesiger writes. "They had no taste nor inclination for refinements. Most of them demanded only the bare necessities of life, enough food and drink to keep them alive, clothes to cover their nakedness, some form of shelter from the sun and wind, weapons, a few pots, rugs, water skins, and their saddlery. It was a life which produced much that was noble, nothing that was gracious." Here, in the expression of the spareness of Bedu life, is a spareness of expression. The longest sentence in this passage is long only as it is a list, while the others are statements immovably grounded in the physical world. A reader moves from one spare word to another as if following a compass bearing through the sands swept clean by desert winds.

But a man can not live by nobility alone, and so to finance his journeys, Thesiger accepts a job working for the Anti-locust Research Centre based in London to document locust movements and breeding in the Empty Quarter. Locust outbreaks threatened the whole of the Middle East with famine, and it was suspected that the Empty Quarter was at the center of these outbreaks. Thesiger was not much interested in locusts, he tells us, but it was locusts that gave him access to the places he wanted to travel. Locusts gave him the funding he needed, and the political backing to travel in regions closed to foreigners. Locusts, Thesiger writes, were "the golden key to Arabia."

One of the astonishing features of *Arabian Sands* is certainly Thesiger himself, a man born to plenty who favors the hardship and meagerness of desert life. "In the desert I had found a freedom unattainable in civilization; a life unhampered by possessions, since everything that was not a necessity was an encumbrance," Thesiger writes. For an American reader, the use of the word "freedom" is inseparable from a connotation that extends from our Revolutionary War: the right to self government. And now in the 21st century, for many Americans, the word has been stylized to mean that you may say and do anything you want. In America, the word "freedom" is the companion of excess, a complicity with the voracious appetite of

Wilfred Thesiger.

capitalism. But for Thesiger, freedom is a state of un-encumbrance in which one lets go of excess to live as bare and stripped down as possible. He is not driven into the desert by colonial ambition (though he was the first European to travel through much of the region), nor the discovery of new wealth, nor scientific knowledge (despite his work with the Anti-locust Research Centre). He is not even much driven by the hope for a story, which is often a writer's ambition. Thesiger, it seems, endures the hardships of desert travel as the best way to live his life, perhaps the only way he could live it. For Thesiger, life in the desert is freedom from objects and freedom from the kind of culture that forms around the acquisition of them. He finds that letting go of all but the essentials releases him to a life of focus and attention to the physical world and his companions, a state achievable only by ceaseless travel. He is not an ascetic, but rather an explorer, an adventurer, a seeker. He had to go because he needed to know.

  Discovering Thesiger's writing took on a double life for me. I admired and envied the journeys he made, and looked to find a doorway into making such journeys of my own. And I also admired the writing, the easy and seemingly effortless prose that positioned Thesiger as a man who had a story to tell and so turned to writing, as opposed to a writer in search of a story he might tell. I did not know which was better, but I wanted to understand how to live the story first and let the writing come later, if at all. Reading *Arabian Sands*, I concluded that Thesiger was free from any such consideration. Just as I had found in his books an economy of language that I came to regard as an expression of *suchness*, I was struck by the sudden realization that *suchness* was the groundwork of the man who expressed it. Truly, he lived a life in pursuit of "much that was noble," and in living that life he needed "nothing that was gracious."

  While the desert sands offer Thesiger freedom from the trappings of the mechanized world ("All my life I had hated machines," he tells us), he also writes frequently about the goodness of comradeship, about meaning derived from shared experience with one's traveling companions. "The Empty Quarter offered me the chance to win distinction as a traveller; but I believed that it could give me more than this, that in those empty wastes I could find the peace that comes with solitude, and, among the Bedu, comradeship in a hostile world," he writes. Without comradeship, Thesiger asserts, "these journeys would have been a meaningless penance."

When I first read *Arabian Sands*, I was still holding onto the idea that to travel well was to travel alone. I made a few solo journeys into mountains with my backpack, down rivers in my canoe, and all-about western Europe by train. While I quite liked being alone at home, I found that I resisted solo travel even as I tried to endure it. Something was missing from the experience for me when I traveled alone, and I wasn't sure what it was. Re-reading the book has given me a look back into that earlier struggle, a view of the way I slowly transitioned from traveling solo to almost always traveling with a companion. Now I see, as Thesiger may have, that one of the greatest rewards of travel is sharing the experience with a trusted friend.

The Bedu with whom Thesiger travels, and most of the men he meets during his travels, own very little, but they give generously of what little they have. While some take offense to a Christian traveling in a Muslim world, strangers commonly approach him to ask who he is and where he is from, and inevitably invite him to share their tea, coffee, and food, though they might have little. During his first crossing of the Empty Quarter, one of Thesiger's trusted companions gives away his only loincloth to a man in want of one. He then had nothing more to wear than his long shirt to cover himself. When Thesiger scolds his companion and hands him money to recover the loin-cloth—he would need it for the long journey ahead, Thesiger proclaims—the companion says, "'What use will money be to him in the Sands. He wants a loincloth.'"

Another such story from the book: early in his first crossing of the Empty Quarter, a boy appears in the camp and leads Thesiger to his own camp where a few men squat around a fire in the desert. The party has no tent and very little of anything else. They invite Thesiger to join them and hand him what food they have, a bowl of camel's milk dusted with sand. Later, Thesiger reflects on the encounter, "I thought how desperately hard were the lives of the Bedu in this weary land and how gallant and how enduring was their spirit. Now, listening to their talk and watching the little acts of courtesy which they instinctively performed, I knew by comparison how sadly I must fail, how selfish I must prove." Such generosity was a welcomed embarrassment for Thesiger, as he realized that Arabs who might visit England would discover that the English "are as unfriendly to each other as we [the English] must appear to be to them [the Arabs]."

Perhaps a notable sacrifice of living a life of ceaseless travel among a people and in a country not his own, Thesiger makes himself into a man apart. His interests and his experiences set him apart from his British countrymen, and as a Christian among Muslim Bedu, he can never really be one of them. Between his first and second crossing of the Empty Quarter, Thesiger spends some days in an R.A.F camp in southern Arabia. Reflecting on the airmen stationed there, he writes,

> These airmen were my fellow countrymen, and I was proud to be of their race. I knew the essential decency which was the bedrock of their character, their humor, stubbornness, and self-reliance. I knew that if called upon they could adapt themselves to any kind of life, in the desert, in the jungle, in mountains, or on the sea, and that in many respects no race in the world was equal. But the things which interested them bored me. They belonged to an age of machines; they were fascinated by cars and aeroplanes, and found their relaxation in the cinema and the wireless. I knew that I stood apart from them and would never find contentment among them, whereas I could find it among these Bedu, although I should never be one of them.

Perhaps living between worlds this way is simply the way Thesiger preferred to live. For to live so closely to his companions and yet remain an outsider is, to my mind, a further expression of the kind of freedom Thesiger so ardently sought. Thesiger once lamented that if he had known he would write a book about his travels in Arabia, he would have kept better notes. And yet the book is an astonishingly detailed and nuanced account of where he went, what he saw, and who he met. *Arabian Sands* serves as a map of Thesiger and his party's route through the Empty Quarter, just as it is a record of the region's cultural and natural history. For example, he writes eloquently and lovingly of the camels that make the journey possible, and their essentiality to the Bedu way of life. Perhaps no other domesticated animal—with the exception of the dog and horse—is so deeply integrated into an expression of human life. The Bedu claim that the camel cannot survive in the wild deserts of Arabia without them, and the Bedu certainly cannot survive without the camel.

Thesiger is no ethnographer, but even so, *Arabian Sands* is an essential record of the Bedouin people and their way of life. In the final pages of the book, Thesiger realizes that due to political changes in the region and the discovery of oil he "had made [his] last journey in the Empty Quarter," and that "the Bedu with whom [he] had lived and travelled, and in whose company [he] had found contentment, were doomed." Nothing could call back the expropriation of those lands that were once open and free. The Bedu way of life is gone now, and what remains of it is Thesiger's book and a host of photographs he made during his travels, which maintain that same spareness and economy so characteristic of his writing. More than a dozen photographs are collected in *Arabian Sands*, and many more in *The Last Nomad* (1979) and *A Vanished World* (2001). Like *Among the Mountains*, *Arabian Sands* was a book I wandered into as the story of one man's adventure, but in rereading it, I have come to understand that it is also a song sung for a way of life now vanished, and vanishing even then, that it is, as an expression from its author's heart, an epitaph. "As the plane climbed over the town and swung out above the sea," Thesiger writes at the end of his book, "I knew how it felt to go into exile."

And what were the rewards for Thesiger living a life of ceaseless hardship and travel? Nearly nothing, almost everything. After the first crossing of the Empty Quarter, Thesiger writes, "For years the Empty Quarter had represented to me the final, unattainable challenge which the desert offered. . . . Now I had crossed it. To others my journey would have little importance. It would produce nothing except a rather inaccurate map which no one was ever likely to use. It was a personal experience, and the reward had been a drink of clean, nearly tasteless water. I was content with that." An astonishing admittance, that to

travel so far and so hard held little meaning beyond the act itself. What Thesiger admits here in these lines is that while travel offers purpose and meaning to his life, there is no good way to understand why this is so beyond the fact that it is so. After crossing the Empty Quarter for the second time, again comes his admittance that the journey he made in Arabia, in fact the very way he lived his life, has meaning only to itself. "I went there to find peace in the hardship of desert travel and the company of desert peoples," he writes, and then, "it is not the goal but the way there that matters, and the harder the way the more worth while the journey." Here again is an expression of *suchness*.
In rereading *Arabian Sands*, I newly understood that Thesiger's travels were not interludes from which he would one day return home to Britian. Rather, like the Bedu themselves, a daily life of travel was Thesiger's home.

At the time of Thesiger's death in 2003, he was variously described as broad shouldered, lean, standing six feet two inches tall. He had killed both men and lions with his rifle. He was intensely loyal, impossibly generous, hard as nails, fearful of nothing. He had accepted the claim that he was the last explorer. Astonishing circumstances give birth to astonishing people, and *Arabian Sands* is the chronicle of such circumstances and such a man. It is not an exaggeration to say that Thesiger may well be the last explorer, at least until the first women and men journey out from the Earth and establish a base camp on Mars. ■

PAUL LaPRISE

Making the Apple Fall: Re-reading Edward Abbey's The Monkey Wrench Gang

e-reading implies re-researching, re-thinking, and re-assessing, or at least it should for a book that has great meaning in one's life. For me, re-reading Edward Abbey's *The Monkey Wrench Gang* (1975) deserves such attention. At first, the initial critical reaction to the book made me miss what Edward Abbey was trying to say. I always thought the content was glossed over, treated humorously, and missed a deeper message about advocacy and commitment.

First, the book is political. In its magical tale *The Monkey Wrench Gang* involves decisions that clearly have two sides, and, even today, can birth more feeling than intellect, opinion, or "truth." It is a great read, a fun, good story, and deserving of its popularity. However, the message is worth re-exploring after nearly 50 years.

Living in San Francisco in the late-1960s and early-70s was a grand experience for an Idaho country boy who had only left the state once. Not only was I in "The Theatre," I was living in an age of enlightenment and was part of a generation that saw the need for change, fought for change, and made it happen.

Marching, carrying signs, signing petitions, going to jail, going to hear Mario Savio speak on freedom of speech, marching with Cesar Chavez and Dolores Huerta, falling in love with El Teatro Campesino, listening to Angela Davis and the great black leaders of the

decade, protesting the Vietnam war and later Central American corruption engendered by my government, women's rights, gay rights, everyone's rights being denied. I engaged in fights against big oil, the greed of the great timber companies, the pollution of our water, and the annihilation of millions of species. I found my way to Aldo Leopold, Rachel Carson, John McPhee, Bill McKibben, H. D. Thoreau, Annie Dillard, Edward Abbey, and thousands of other voices crying for the wilderness.

And soon Abbey's *Desert Solitaire* and *The Monkey Wrench Gang* found themselves jammed into my backpack. For me, *The Monkey Wrench Gang* exploded like a tornado. It told a great tale of valiant fighters battling the forces of environmental evil and inferring that violence was necessary against this evil.

"Monkey wrenching" became a subversive thing to do, and various groups sprang up and plodded into public lands to fight on a personal level. Although violence was anathema to the peace movement of my generation, we embraced the adventure, the fantasy, and the Quixote-like vision of the novel's four warriors. We loved the vision quest tales and we imagined ourselves following their lead, the implication of violence brushed over as we followed the adventure.

The New York Times gave it a passing nod when the novel appeared in 1975, noting an adventurous tale and not exploring the deeper meaning that I read.

The Monkey Wrench Gang is a fantasia built around four characters who try to stop the environmental destruction of a uniquely beautiful part of the United States. There is the obligatory former Vietnam Green Beret explosives expert, a girl from Brooklyn, a splendid Armenian M.D., and a river guide. They are all plausible and sympathetic in their sometimes-comic torments, and Abbey renders them as convincingly as he does the endangered landscape with all the breathless intensity of a true desolation angel. Abbey trips a bit over the question of violence against people, but an ideological gaff is easily forgivable in light of the heroic adventures of the characters. The reader is soon rooting for them to get away with their "crimes" against environmental exploitation and profiteering.

We loved the tale and ignored the alternative—the alternative being that violence was the key to make the work stick. Though we were against violence against people, "Monkey wrenching" at times seemed justified.

Abbey's memoir *Desert Solitaire* (1968) made the case for an environmental revolution. *The Monkey Wrench Gang* imagined ways to make it happen.

Abbey's path and intentions were clear as early as his student years in New Mexico. In 1956, nearly 20 years before the publication of *The Monkey Wrench Gang,* Abbey completed an M.A. in philosophy at the University of New Mexico. The title and abstract of his M.A. thesis are pretty revealing:

"Anarchism and the Morality of Violence"

> Abstract (in part): . . . If anarchism is to regain the intellectual respectability which it deserves, two preliminary questions must be answered: (1) To what extent is the traditional association of anarchism and violence warranted? And (2) In so far as the association is a valid one, what arguments have the anarchists presented, explicitly or implicitly, to justify the use of violence? It is the purpose of this thesis to investigate the above two questions.

Abbey made the case that violence could make it so painful to destroy the environment that such destruction would eventually cease. He later said in his book *The Journey Home: Some Words in Defense of the American West* (1977) that the damage we are doing to our environment was, in effect, feeding cancer: "Growth for the sake of growth is the ideology of the cancer cell." (pp.78-79)

In the late 1950s and early 1960s Abbey worked seasonally for the National Park Service as a ranger and a fire lookout. He wrote in his journal heavily (and for years), resulting in *Desert Solitaire* (1968), undoubtedly his best work. The book touched on the need for "action" to preserve our sacred places, and *The Monkey Wrench Gang* was Abbey's plan to begin that "action," what he later called "Eco-tage," or sabotage in service to ecology.

To make this more palatable to the public, in an interview Abbey later made a clear moral distinction between sabotage and terrorism, which he defined as violence against people. "The distinction seems quite clear and simple to me," he said. "Sabotage is an act of force or violence against property. Or machinery—in which life is not endangered or should not be."

Abbey believed, as Che Guevera did, that "The revolution is not an apple that falls when it is ripe. You have to make it fall."

And it was clear that eco-tage was not just something the fictional characters of *The Monkey Wrench Gang* practiced themselves. Abbey became a spokesman. In a video interview, Abbey stated:

> I regard defending the wilderness as something like defending your own home. I regard the wilderness as my home, my true ancestral home. And when its being invaded by clear cutters and strip miners, I feel not only the right but the duty, the moral obligation to defend it by any means that I can.

Abbey's words were important in the formation of Earth First!, an organization that first used protest, and then active sabotage, to bring attention to the ecological carnage wrought by government and industry. Though Abbey was never a formal Earth First! member, even today the Earth First! website makes use of his words:

> While there is broad diversity within Earth First! from animal rights vegans to wilderness hunting guides, from monkeywrenchers to careful followers of Gandhi, from whiskey-drinking backwoods riffraff to thoughtful philosophers, from misanthropes to humanists, there is agreement on one thing, the need for action!

Aside from being a popular and noteworthy literary work of an era and a book that inspired and continues to inspire environmental advocacy, *The Monkey Wrench Gang* is a novel often used as a text in university courses in law and politics. The cross-disciplinary use of the novel is a testament to the cultural nerve Abbey touched at the time it was written and the commitment it still inspires.

In an article about the novel for *Law and Politics Book Review* in 2000, Darren Botello-Sampson writes:

> The specificity of the novel should not be ignored. The novel could be particularly pertinent for courses in environmental law and policy, illuminating radical critiques of environmental regulatory policy and confronting the effectiveness and appropriateness of the use of illegal strategies for achieving environmental ends. Even in non-topic-specific courses focusing on law, this story of radical environmental activism supplies ripe and plentiful material for classroom discussions on civil disobedience and other forms of righteous and goal-oriented law breaking.

Hindsight being 20-20, I thought about what might have happened if more of us chose the path of violence in the 1970s instead of the path of compromise in battles for the environment. What values might have been gained had we chosen to disrupt and demolish rather than bargain? Impossible to know. Would it have changed the deforestation of public lands if we had made it too difficult and too expensive for lumber companies to proceed? Would it have saved thousands of acres of land from being poisoned by mining companies? What if we had made it too expensive to use coal and forced the country to invest in renewable technologies in the 1970s? Most importantly, might it have been legal, appropriate, or even applicable?

It does not add to this evaluation to go into chapter and verse about how we have injured ourselves and our world by missing early warnings.

"Wrenching" violence notwithstanding, many of us tried.

In my dotage, I hope I have been one who helped make the apple fall. Abbey's *The Monkey Wrench Gang* continues to invite these questions for future generations. ∎

End Notes

New York Times Book Review, Jim Harrison, Nov 14, 1976.

Edward Abbey, Masters Thesis, University of New Mexico, August 19, 1956. Abstract

Edward Abbey, *The Journey Home: Some Words in Defense of the American West.* The Penguin Publishing Group, 1977.

Edward Abbey, "A Voice in the Wilderness." Transcript of a video. Property of Canyon Productions 1993.

Che Guevera, *Liberation,* Interview, 1965.

Edward Abbey, KAET-TV [Phoenix, Arizona] interview, given in December of 1982.

Earth First! Website, opening abstract, 1980.

Edward Abbey, "Freedom and Wilderness, Wilderness and Freedom," Recordings of Abbey reading excerpts from several of his books on YouTube.

Edward Abbey, *Desert Solitaire.* (Ballantine Books, 1970).

Edward Abbey, *The Monkey Wrench Gang.* (Lippincott 1975).

Edward Abbey, *The Serpents of Paradise, A Reader.* (Henry Holt and Company), 1995.

Darren Botello-Sampson, A Review of *The Monkey Wrench Gang, Law and Politics Book Review,*" Law and Courts Section of the American Political Science Association. Department of Social Sciences, Pittsburg State University, 2000.

BARBARA OLIC-HAMILTON

Only on Earth:
Old Questions Explored in Three New Novels

> "I've visited thirty-one inhabited planets in the universe," the Tralfamadorian told Billy Pilgrim. "And I have studied reports on one hundred more. Only on Earth is there any talk of free will." (86)
> —Kurt Vonnegut, *Slaughterhouse-Five*

Other than the Tralfamadorians' view of time as a mountain range, my 12th grade students thought the most controversial idea in Vonnegut's *Slaughterhouse-Five* (1969) was the idea that Earthlings were the only sentient species in the Universe who believed in free will. That's wrong, they argued. Free will was real. People made their own choices; they weren't controlled by outside forces.

But maybe by inside forces, I asked. What about their inborn nature? Or the nurture they had?

Think back to Shakespeare's *The Tempest*. There's no mention of free will. However, there's talk about nature vs. nurture. Remember that "nurture" doesn't refer to just positive or good events. "Nurture" means what factually happened to the person. *The Tempest* questions which is stronger in the end—the inborn characteristics a person is born with, which make up their nature? Or the environment and childhood upbringing, which makes up their nurture?

In Act IV, Prospero says he has tried to counter Caliban's birthright as the son of the witch Sycorax, but he admits he has failed. He calls Caliban,

> A devil, a born devil, on whose nature
> Nurture can never stick; on whom my pains,
> Humanely taken, all, all lost, quite lost!

Prospero doesn't accuse Caliban of making bad choices. Instead, he concludes that Caliban's nature proved stronger than Prospero's nurturing. Caliban has no free will; he's simply "a devil, a born devil." With all the righteousness of teenagers, my students argued that Caliban did have free will and chose his barbaric behavior. His choices weren't controlled by his inherited nature. They were Caliban's. My students—ready to graduate and leave homes nurtured by their family's rules—adamantly denied that their inborn nature or their family's outward nurture would ever determine their future choices. Instead, their choices would be made using their free will.

It's been years since I've had such literary discussions with teenagers, but I was reminded of them this past year when three excellent new novels delved into this classic, philosophical question of nature vs. nurture.

First, there was Louise Penny's newest mystery, *A World of Curiosities* (2022). Years ago, Chief Inspector Armand Gamache and his second in command, Jean-Guy Beauvoir, rescued 10-year-old Sam and his 13-year-old sister Fiona from an abusive home. Their meth addicted mother had pimped them out to adult men, so both their nature and their destructive nurture formed them. When their biological fathers are revealed, their biological inheritance becomes even darker. Both Gamache and Beauvoir follow the aftermath of the case for years, providing extra support to Sam and Fiona. They try to supply enough positive nurture to mitigate the negative nurture of their childhood. They keep wondering if Sam and Fiona's actions as adults were caused solely by their innate nature. Was the positive nurturing they received after their rescue useless?

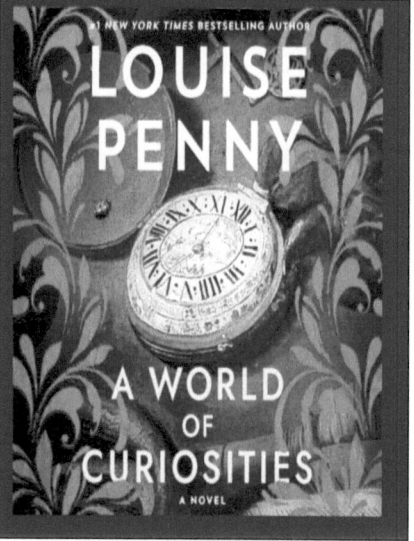

In her "Acknowledgments," Louise Penny says a major theme is forgiveness, and I agree. However, the question of whether nurture can overcome nature, is also a driving force in the novel's plot, resolution, characterization, and the philosophical musings of Chief Inspector Gamache. "Part of [him] railed against the notion of fate, preferring to think they had at least some control over their lives. But another part of him found comfort in the idea of predestination." (377) The Tralfamadorians would see Gamache's comfort in the idea of predestination as proof that free will is an Earthling illusion. The gray areas of this debate enrich Penny's excellent novel, but it provides no easy answer to the question.

Jamie Ford approaches the question through recent discoveries by geneticists. In his "Author's Note" to *The Many Daughters of Afong Moy* (2022), Ford discusses transgenerational epigenetic inheritance, which is the theory that a person's traumas can be passed down to future generations. Experiments show that mice who learn to associate the smell of lemons with mild electrical shocks in their cages can pass down 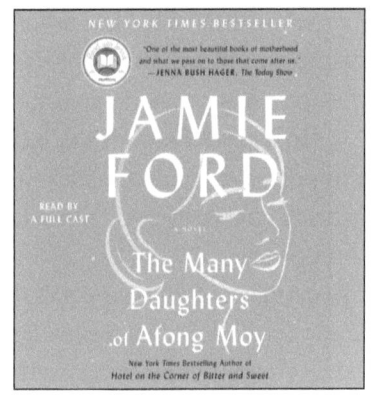 that association. Future generations will fear the scent of lemons even though only the initial generation experienced electrical shocks. Scientists have begun applying this to human behavior, so Ford wonders "if free will is—if not an illusion—a bit of a mirage. That, in addition to the environment we grow up in, the contour and texture of our lives are shaped—in part—by some form of genetic predetermination." (xiv)

With this scientific research as a starting point, Ford stepped into the historical record and plucked out Afong Moy, more commonly known as The Chinese Lady. In 1834 she was brought to America to perform and display her tiny, bound feet. Ford creates a life for her and then imagines six other biologically related women spanning from 1836 to 2086. Each of their voices and their stories is captivating. Each story also contains patterns of behavior—such as the search for a lost lover—that echo other daughters of Afong Moy. The tragedies and joys in their lives are unique and so are their voices. Part of my pleasure while reading this novel was spotting patterns from the other daughters' stories.

Although not a science-fiction novel, the story of Dorothy May, one of the daughters, does describe a futuristic treatment for depression and PTSD where a doctor manipulates memories instead of prescribing drugs or using cognitive-behavioral therapy. After first being overwhelmed by the patterns of past generations she sees, Dorothy chooses to use this new therapy to alter the self-destructive path of her life and the future of her daughter Annabelle's life. Dorothy's life has a "a great third act." It transcends genetic predetermination and shows how Dorothy uses her free will to adapt her inherited traumas and desires instead of being defined by them. The resolution of Ford's novel clearly disagrees with the Tralfamadorian viewpoint.

In *Demon Copperhead*, Barbara Kingsolver expands the idea of transgenerational epigenetic inheritance from one person's family to community traumas caused by outside forces. Jamie Ford identifies this as "generational trauma," and he notes that Native Americans and Black Americans have long talked about living with its effects, as have Holocaust survivors. Studies show that children and grandchildren of Holocaust survivors "appear to show a higher percentage of PTSDs, depression, and anxiety."

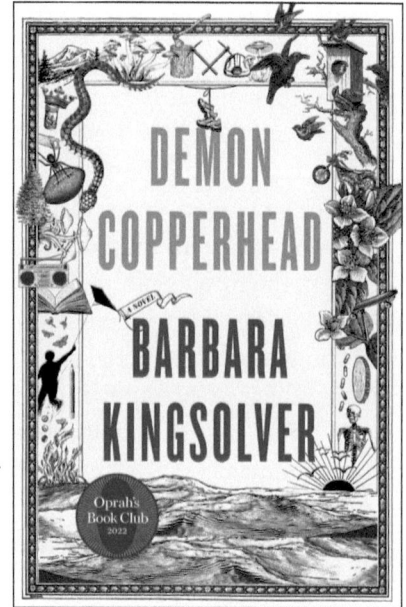

Generational trauma affects everyone in Kingsolver's novel. It is narrated by an adult Damon Fields whose childhood nickname is Demon. "Copperhead" has been added due to his curly red hair. The novel opens with his birth and how it determines his nature, what nurture he'll get, and what the limits will be of his free will,

> Kid born to the junkie is a junkie. He'll grow up
> to be everything you don't want to know . . . This
> kid, if he wanted a shot at the finer things, should
> have got himself delivered to some rich or smart
> or Christian, nonusing type of mother. Anybody,
> will tell you the born of this world are marked
> from the get-out, win or lose.

Before he is twelve, Demon is introduced to drugs, the foster system, slave labor, poverty, and death by overdose or violence. He also learns from the neighboring Peggot family and others that "good people don't give up on the ones they love." (433) He takes care of others even after a football injury leads to his addiction to prescription pain pills.

Kingsolver's title sets the reader up for a comparison to Charles Dickens' *David Copperfield*, and she certainly uses variations of characters' names, the narrative arc, some events, and the first-person point of view of Dickens' novel. However, comparisons of the two novels are superficial and limited because Kingsolver expands the story beyond Demon's traumas to Lee County's past traumas—the ones done to his community. Coal companies prevented other industries from coming into the county so that the only employment choice for men was going down into the coal mines. (279-280) The condescending view in popular media portrayed them as hillbillies, idiots, and rednecks. They were looked down on as people who ignored their terrible economic situation and focused only on the Friday-nights lights of high school football. (323) But most devastating of all, Purdue and other pharmaceutical companies crunched data on the number of pain patients on disability by county and chose to flood Lee County with drug representatives carrying satchels of OxyContin samples. (416) Demon's life and his choices are rimmed in by the generational trauma of his community caused by these outside forces. Demon isn't just doomed by being born to a junkie mother; he is doomed by being born in this community. He inherits his nature and gains his nurture from his mother and the generational trauma of Lee County. He is predestined, marked from the get-go as a loser. A perfect Tralfamadorian example of an Earthling with only the illusion of free will.

However, Kingsolver's novel includes many good people who keep encouraging Demon, providing good choices for him. One person keeps telling him that surviving his childhood made him a better person. She admonishes him to "start trusting the ride, because life is not a total and complete dumpster fire." (507) And in the end, his choices show him that she is right about life. Free will wins here but it leaves Damon Fields with invisible and visible scars. He has a tight regimen that keeps him a non-using drug addict. He has found a way to make a living legally outside of Lee County, and he has someone who loves him. Kingsolver leaves Lee County as a "complete dumpster fire," but she includes individual stories of free will, stories of personal redemption.

After labeling *Demon Copperhead* as a "reimagining" of *David Copperfield*, some reviewers lean into that comparison and describe Kingsolver's novel as a portrait of the self-creation of an artist. True, with help from his friend Tommy, Demon ends up publishing serious comics about social issues. But *Demon Copperhead* feels more like a response to the angry bleakness of J. D. Vance's memoir *Hillbilly Elegy* (2016) than a portrait of a young Appalachian artist. Too much else is going on in the novel. Kingsolver cares too deeply about the people living in the many Lee Counties in the U.S. to narrow *Demon Copperhead* to a narration about the creation of an artist.

Louise Penny, Jamie Ford, and Barbara Kingsolver have created novels that illustrate the limitations of nurture in overcoming a person's inborn nature and their transgenerational epigenetic inheritance. But they also depict characters who make unexpected choices that lead to positive outcomes. It may happen only on Earth, but these Earthlings believe they have free will, and that belief makes all the difference. ∎

TED DYER

The Greater Hugh:
Homage to the Works of Hugh Kenner

In the waning hours of my time as an assistant to the 2003 International Ezra Pound Conference in Sun Valley, Idaho, my supervisor, University of New Mexico English Professor Hugh Witemeyer, who was also the conference director and a top-notch Pound scholar, pulled me aside.

I was already feeling wistful that such a fine conference was coming to a close. Grinning, Hugh broke my melancholy reverie by pointing down the conference-room hallway toward a gangly, professorial man ambling toward us.

Instantly I began searching through my mental Rolodex (we still used those things back then). Could that possibly be the man who we once jokingly referred to as The Greater Hugh, about whom I had often pestered my supervisor—very much a great Hugh in his own right—for information and anecdotes?

Once that signature Einstein haircut came into view, however, there was no doubt: Standing before me was the 6-foot-4 William "Hugh" Kenner, arguably the greatest scholar of literary Modernism, the critic who had placed Ezra Pound at the center of Modernism in his *magnum opus, The Pound Era*. I was speechless; as school kids say nowadays, I was a total fanboy.

On the next night, the final night of the conference, I waited in line after his panel discussion to have Kenner sign two new copies of *The Pound Era*, one for myself and one for the undergraduate professor—Dr. Leonard Oakland, recently retired from Whitworth University—who years earlier had turned me on to Kenner. While he signed, I told Kenner about

Hugh Kenner.

my undergrad teacher and how *The Pound Era* and his many other critical works had completely rearranged my mental furniture.

Next to me as I chattered away that evening was the man who had downed Romanticism with his first shot; who taught us that factual details, not abstractions or poetic diction, defined a literary work and mirrored that work's structure; who forever linked modern art with scientific advancement; who combined close reading with his own brand of historicism and linguistic awareness; and who, thank goodness, had no use whatever for advanced literary theory.

I don't recall my exact words to Kenner that night; doubtless I unleashed a torrent of fanboy gush. Mary Anne Kenner, standing next to her husband, apparently found my comments to be pretentious and lacking in deference.

"So how much of it (*The Pound Era*) did you really understand?" she asked.

"About every seventh word," I replied, sheepishly.

The three of us laughed, and Mrs. Kenner apologized needlessly. A few weeks after that congenial moment, Kenner, 80, died of heart failure at his home in Athens, Georgia,

Ezra Pound.

where he had ended his storied academic career at the University of Georgia. I was stunned. Kenner had often repeated Pound's injunction that each generation should visit its own great men, but I felt that in this case a great man had come to visit me.

Also, Mrs. Kenner's instincts were correct. I was baffled utterly when I left the Whitworth College bookstore in 1975 to peruse my first copy of *The Pound Era*, still the premier study of International Modernism. As a mono-lingual American, I was daunted by *The Pound Era*'s linguistic feast: Latin and Greek in the original, Chinese characters, untranslated snatches of European languages, exotic graphics and photographs, many kinds of history, anecdote, archeology, linguistic analysis, and countless quotes of poetry and prose from sources I never knew existed—all as part of a fragmented and highly intuitive argument presented in what I mistakenly thought was a dense and stylized prose.

I eventually learned that Kenner, in his mature criticism, would contour his style to the subject matter or the author in question, paying homage in the opening pages of *The Pound Era*, for example, to the cadences and syntax of mid-phase Henry James, while simultaneously recreating Ezra Pound's affectionate mimicking of James's speech patterns which Kenner had witnessed personally during visits with "the eminent Confucian" at St. Elizabeth's Hospital in Washington, D.C.: a blending for emphasis of "two" Henry "Jameses"—in effect, pulling off a surprising stylistic double play.

Kenner, moreover, turned this Jamesian gaze in *The Pound Era* to what he called a "patterned energy," the converging and intersecting cultural forces that came together at the inception of the Modernist moment—what Pound had termed a Vortex—and which nearly became, according to Kenner's bold claim, the second European Renaissance. Kenner presents all this on his page as an up-tempo whirl of particulars from a seemingly unlimited and wholly original range of source materials. The overall effect of *The Pound Era* is initially dizzying, like being thrown suddenly into the fabric of an impersonal and seemingly infinite consciousness, a kind of mindscape, that Kenner through his magic presents as an actual historical moment.

In no way conventional, this work brought an entirely new vision to literary criticism: here was a recreation of a specific time from the minds of a few specific artists who were in the act of creating something new. Kenner also successfully projected into the sub-structure of *The Pound Era* a mirror image of the very literary moment he was depicting; he employed, in other words, mimesis to create literary criticism. (The mind boggles at the prospect of other such grand Kennerian syntheses: Imagine reading a book entitled, *The Pope Era,* encompassing Pope, Swift, Gay, Arbuthnot, and Bolingbroke into a single patterned integrity!).

    Several readings, however, elapsed before I realized all this. Initially I would read 25 or 30 pages of *The Pound Era*, lose the thread, start again and lose the thread once more, all the while consoling myself with the notion that if genuine poetry could communicate before it was understood, as ex-patriate American poet T. S. Eliot once claimed, then perhaps the same would be true for great criticism.

    Fittingly, I nearly lost that first copy of *The Pound Era* to a flood in my rented basement residence in Jerome, Idaho, where I was living while working as a reporter for the *Gooding Leader* newspaper in Gooding, Idaho, in 1979. When plucked from the dirty basement water, the book's soggy pages had fused together to form something akin to a giant ravioli noodle. So, I painstakingly separated each page with a butter knife and a hair dryer. The book's spine was hopelessly warped, causing it to splay into a strange fan-like shape, but I managed to save the print on nearly every page, including most of my appallingly naive marginal notes. The rest of my basement-stored books were lost, but not *The Pound Era* That very book still sits proudly on my library shelf and is the copy I just re-read for perhaps the fourth time, not including all those false starts. But I digress.

    What actually buoyed my flagging spirits was stumbling upon gems of *The Pound Era* concision such as this:

> It was the post-Symbolists of the 1890's who brought pictorial images into short poems: theirs was the dead end that we are frequently told Imagism was. Imagism on the other hand made possible the *Cantos* and *Paterson*, long works that with the work of T. S. Eliot are the Symbolist heritage in English.

> The minor poets of [Arthur] Symons's generation
> brought the necessary elements into English verse,
> but lacked the intellectual energy to break, as could
> Imagism, into some realm beyond the mood or the
> impression. For Pound Imagism is energy, is effort.
> It does not appease itself by reproducing what is
> seen, but by setting some other seen thing into
> relation . . . . The "plot" of the poem is that mind's
> activity, fetching some new thing into the field
> of consciousness. The action passing through
> any Imagist poem is the mind's invisible action
> discovering what will come next that may sustain
> the presentation—what image, what rhythm, what
> allusion, what word—to the end that the poem
> shall be 'lord over fact,' not the transcript of the one
> encounter but the Gestalt of many . . . .

Here we have an entire literary movement condensed into a handful of words, gift-wrapped: Imagism defined, defended, elucidated, and historically situated by Pound's innovation and leadership—all in Kenner's allusive yet concise prose.

How did he come to write like this?

The catalyst for his life-long commitment to what Wyndham Lewis called The Men of 1914—Pound, Eliot, James Joyce, Lewis and later Samuel Beckett—occurred, said Kenner, just before his first year of graduate school: the firestorm of controversy that followed Ezra Pound winning the 1948 Bollingen Poetry Prize.

Kenner and Marshall McLuhan—Kenner's mentor and fellow Catholic Canadian—had just visited Pound in St. Elizabeth's on June 4, 1948, enroute to Yale in order to gain Kenner a late admission into the English Ph.D. program. "On the day I met [Pound] I barely knew who he was," Kenner wrote. "It was one of the two or three turning points of my life . . . . My subsequent career stems from those two hours . . . . I knew I was in the presence of the presiding spirit of Modernism."

The Bollingen Prize controversy over Pound's politics peaked right after that visit. His few supporters "were all busy defending the integrity of the awards process, but no one was defending Pound," Kenner wrote.

"Supposing I had nothing to lose, and in fact too naive to realize I was risking my entire future, I decided that if no one would speak up for him I would."

In a mere six weeks that summer before starting at Yale, Kenner tells us that he borrowed a Corona typewriter with a broken right-hand margin stop and began writing on a trestle table under the pines overlooking a lake in Ontario, Canada, putting in six-hour workdays, mid-July through August.

"Using a system I'd picked up from Marshall, I gisted quotations onto little slips, let their affinities prompt the piles they went into, and derived chapters from the piles," he tells us in an introduction to the first full-length study ever written on Ezra Pound: *The Poetry of Ezra Pound* (1951).

Ambitious in scope and thoroughness and enthusiastically reviewed, this book signaled the beginning of Ezra Pound studies. Pound later sent a note of appreciation.

Kenner's *Wyndham Lewis* followed next in 1954.

"When a charlatan like Wyndham Lewis is revived and praised for his wisdom, it is done, predictably, by a Hugh Kenner," snapped reviewing critic Irving Howe. Stung, Kenner soon found an ally in William F. Buckley. Once hired as the new poetry editor of *The National Review*, Kenner exposed Buckley to the brand-new technology of word-processing, while Buckley in turn served as the best man for Kenner's second wedding following the early death of his first wife. The relationship to Buckley and to conservative politics was lifelong (Kenner supported Barry Goldwater in 1964).

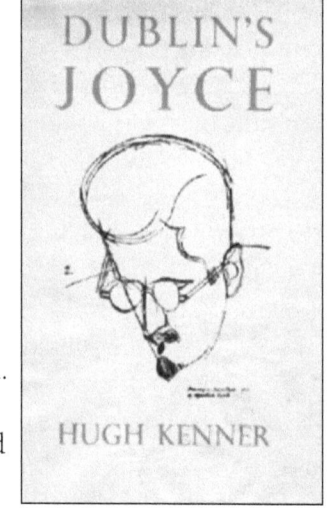

Incredibly, only two years later, in 1956, Kenner fully entered the pantheon of post-WW II Modernist criticism by turning his Yale doctoral dissertation into *Dublin's Joyce*, which quickly became an academic sensation. (In a later introduction to that book, Kenner recalls that as a 1940s undergrad he informed the Chancellor at the University of Toronto of his hope to write a dissertation on Joyce, only to be told that if he wished to "squander" his talents, he had better go elsewhere. The school library did possess a copy of *Ulysses*, Kenner tells us, but to inspect it, a student needed to produce two letters, one from a doctor and one from a clergyman, so Kenner instead had a priest smuggle a personal copy into Canada for him, thus becoming one of the few to read *Finnegans Wake* before *Ulysses*.)

In short order, Kenner's interpretation of James Joyce became almost synonymous with the writer himself. Furthermore, Kenner raised the bar when he presciently claimed—in a decades-early anticipation of Postmodernist linguistic theory—that Joyce's actual "subject was language, the protean empty language of the dead city."

Four years later Kenner triumphed again with his still relevant and compelling study *The Invisible Poet: T. S. Eliot* (1959), jumpstarting new avenues of criticism for Eliot and finalizing the quartet of book-length studies for his top four Modernists, thereby laying claim to his own full-fledged interpretation of International Modernism. By the age of 40, Kenner was a lit-crit celebrity; at his death, he was proclaimed, even by some of his detractors, as the "inventor" of Modernism.

But not everyone cheered this ascent. Early fault-finders saw *Dublin's Joyce* more as a performance than an analysis and deplored what they considered to be its *ex cathedra* tone. Also, in those years Kenner usually dismissed other literary critics, never balancing his views against those of his peers or other schools of criticism.
His was always a school of one.

So when Kenner took sharp issue with acclaimed Joyce biographer Richard Ellmann, whose award-winning biography appeared in 1959, the Joyce community closed ranks against him. Not until the mid-1960s, when he was invited to join the board of the then newly formed *James Joyce Quarterly*, did Kenner fully return to Joyce studies.

This ice thawed further at this time when Kenner rewrote a chapter from *Dublin's Joyce*—the first of his three books on Joyce—into an essay for academic journal publication. Entitled "Joyce's Portrait—A Reconsideration," Kenner updated and reaffirmed his demolition of the quaint notion that Stephen Daedalus, of *A Portrait of the Artist as a Young Man*, was a questing Romantic artistic-hero modeled upon his creator.

Widely anthologized, this piece has become a Joycean touchstone for what was then known as the ironic reading of *Portrait*. His core insight was really quite simple: "Joyce used everything usable from his own experience to create a character not himself."

Concerning Stephen Daedalus, Kenner says that

> Stephen's talk of flying by nets of language, nationality, religion, remains—Stephen's talk. One does not fly by Dublin's nets, though the illusion that one may fly by them may be one of Dublin's sorts of birdlime . . . . Stephen is a young man rather like Joyce who is going to fly like Shelly's skylark; and he is going to fall into cold water, like Icarus or like Oscar Wilde . . . . It is, to put it plainly, possible if not sufficient to regard the *Portrait* as a lower-class Catholic parallel to Wilde's upper-class Protestant career.

Even decades later, the power and originality of "Reconsideration," which offers us a vision of the entire Joyce oeuvre, floods the reader's mind to such an extent that it either overrides all previous interpretations or inspires strong objections and subsequent counter-interpretations.

By the early-1970s, however, Kenner had seemingly calmed these waters by consolidating the initial single-author phase of his publishing career—done mostly in traditional academic prose—into the new collective vision and Vortex prose style of *The Pound Era*. For once, Kenner could now bask in the glow of admiring, if somewhat grudging, reviews. Long live the king.

Next, after his second book on Beckett, Kenner embarked on his second phase as a critic: studies of the three English-speaking nations of International Modernism: *The Homemade World: The American Modernist Writers* (1975), *A Colder Eye: The Modern Irish Writers* (1983) and finally and, most controversially, *A Sinking Island: The Modern English Writers* (1988).

Buoyed by the success of *The Pound Era*, Kenner abandoned all previous diplomatic pretense for this third study. Pulling his heavy artillery down to the skirmish lines, Kenner struck bone with his account of the culture-killing power of English class-consciousness. As a Catholic colonial who steadfastly retained his native Canadian citizenship while teaching for decades in America on a green card, Kenner had always bridled against the stifling exclusiveness of Oxbridge propriety.

To summarize, *Sinking Island* argues that England was poised, at the turn of the 20th Century, to become the center of International Modernism, but instead priggishly rejected its avant-garde native writers, starting with Oscar Wilde (imprisoned for sodomy in 1895), then its avant-garde expatriate writers Joseph Conrad, Ford Madox Ford, James, and Pound, followed, finally, by its exiled Irishmen: Joyce, Beckett, and even William Butler Yeats.

The catastrophe of World War I followed hard upon this rejection, forever destroying in utero—as dramatically depicted in *The Pound Era*—Lewis's and Pound's London Vortex just days before its birth. The "modernism" that emerged after the war, Kenner tells us, was a tepid Victorianism known as Bloomsbury, which broke forever the cultural connection with the avant-garde. The subsequent devastation of World War II and the consequent loss of England's empire sealed the deal. Kenner informs us in *Sinking Island*'s introductory chapter that:

> it has been easy for tight little islanders to dismiss the new literatures as analogous barbarisms. . . . It's fair to say, despite scintillant exceptions, that a half-century's literary goings-on in [England] have given new meaning to the word 'provincial.' How that came about—how the mother-country of 'English' became a headquarters for articulate Philistia—is one of the themes this book addresses.

To batten down the cultural hatches forever, England created, Kenner informs us, a middlebrow publishing industry that eliminated any possible reemergence of a cutting-edge literary insurgency.

This study, to no one's surprise, including Kenner's own publisher, was not a hit in England; few Americans relished it either, since Bloomsbury was ground-zero for the valorization of Virginia

Woolf, the shining star of feminist critics on both sides of the pond. Bruce Bawer's stinging review, "Hugh Kenner: A Sinking Oeuvre" (1988) found a sympathetic audience.

Kenner, however, had already established this sharp tone in *Homemade World*, where he saw fit to give the American Modernist garden a serious weeding. Although he produced powerful and favorable explications of poems by William Carlos Williams and Marianne Moore, and an equally compelling Symbolist/Joycean reading of William Faulkner—plus, as an added bonus, a riveting explication of Scott Fitzgerald—not everyone escaped unscathed.

The poet Wallace Stevens, for example, appears only in the reflected glow of Williams's consummate achievement, and gets tossed into the weed bin as a rhythmically flat and painterly-pretty recycler of Romantic banalities. Hemingway, "the hairy opposite" of Stevens, is then damned with faint praise when held to Joycean standards, whereas Thomas Pynchon, John Barth, and the Russian-born Vladimir Nabokov each earn rebuke as producers of self-consciously empty parodies of *Ulysses*.

Says Kenner of Nabokov: "*Pale Fire* is a mirthless hoax and so is its successor, *Ada or Ardor*: ingenious ships-in-bottles riding plastic seas to the awe of teaching assistants."

But the fireworks really started when Kenner unleashed this same wicked drollery upon Bloomsbury's all-stars in *Sinking Island*, the most prominent being, of course, Virginia Woolf, the "novelist of manners," who gave us the "poor, dim Clarissa Dalloway":

> . . . tending [to her] legacy may be thought of as a Bloomsbury cottage industry . . . . Mrs. Woolf seldom dwells on themes, but alights on them for the duration of a moth's flutter . . . . She is Bloomsbury's sole 'accredited' creator and its proffered emblem of creation's cost: novels each one touchy as an eyeball, achieved between bouts of madness; then the terminal madness of the body in Ouse [River where Woolf drowned herself in 1941]. Save for her, Bloomsbury . . . would be by now a social curio . . . [Her novel] *The Waves*, we know from the start, is a Bloomsbury self-congratulation, unreal from

end to end, voice after voice finely straining for fineness of perception.

And so the demolition continued: into Kenner's dumpster goes the entire Auden group, E.M Forster, Katherine Mansfield, Dylan Thomas, Philip Larkin, George Bernard Shaw, both Leavis's—Q.D. and much of F.R. — and the entire Waugh clan except for Evelyn. Kenner simply ignores many others.

Many Americans in *Homemade* got this same white-out treatment, including E.E. Cummings (no lower-case nonsense allowed in Kenner's index), Robert Lowell, Richard Wilbur, Elizabeth Bishop, James Merrill and Robert Frost—all ignored in favor of the Objectivist Group of poets, Louis Zukofsky and George Oppen, all descendants of Pound. And after Faulkner, supposedly "the last novelist," we have no mention of Saul Bellow, John Updike or Philip Roth.

So, was Kenner just a stodgy old neoclassical Formalist, a get-off-my-lawn scold who yearned wistfully for the 1920s? Undaunted, Kenner simply continued with his advocacy of the distinct lineage that had culminated in Modernism. His preference for comic and satiric forms over what he saw as aspirational and outdated ones (i.e. abstract and "Romantic") was no surprise coming from the Thomas Aquinas of literary criticism.

In his entertaining (many say irritating) fashion in these nation-centered works, Kenner critiques every contemporary writer and cultural player in order to drive home a core tenet of his Modernist vision: the manner in which the individual talent should properly connect with the Western tradition.

Kenner well knew that the era of the Men of 1914 had long since passed but maintained—as a standard of judgment—that their achievements should now be ranked with those of the canonical writers from the classical and renaissance eras. After all, Kenner tells us, a Vortex works across historical boundaries as well as within a given period, thus making all eras, in a sense, contemporaneous.

To build a live tradition, the Modernists, Eliot and Pound especially, gathered loose cultural strands from other eras, languages and cultures —gathering the limbs of Osiris, mythically speaking—to create their own traditions and predecessors, which, as newly reclaimed classics, they subsequently integrated into their own poems. In other words, they reimagined the Old and folded it into their New.

This is also what made International Modernism international. Stay-at-homes like Virginia Woolf simply became connoisseurs of their own insular cultural enclaves, where live dogs always triumph over dead lions.

This Pound/Kenner synthesis for cultural preservation and development is not, however, as many claim, a closed system. By embracing experimentation and the avant-garde, Kenner anticipated today's ongoing experimental tradition in which the breakthrough innovations of Pound and Williams still serve the world as examples of open-form experimentation.

According to Brazil's initial Modernist poetic prophet, Mario de Andrade (1893-1945), for example, International Modernism constituted an immediate "rupture and revolt against the national intelligence" that helped integrate Brazilian literature with Western literature in a way that is still felt to this day, a development which few English speakers know about. Also, Haroldo de Campos (1929-2003), a seminal poet in Brazil since the1950s, revered Pound and translated him into Portuguese.

And finally, we have Kenner's personal story. He was the very gifted and only child born to elderly classics-trained parents in 1923. Both his father, Dr. H.R.H. Kenner, and his mother, Mary Kenner, taught Latin and Greek languages and classical literature, respectively, at the Peterborough Collegiate Institute, the high school of Kenner's birthplace, in the small town of Peterborough, Ontario, Canada.

A bout of influenza robbed the pre-school Kenner of his hearing, a crisis that defined his earliest years. Fortunately, some hearing returned, but Kenner lived his entire life hearing impaired, which thickened his speech and slowed his personal development. Under the tutelage of his devoted parents, Kenner came to terms with a medically troubled childhood by becoming a devoted reader.

Kenner's father, a prominent community leader who earned an honorary law degree, was born in England in 1867, two years after Yeats; his mother, to whom her son dedicated his first book, was born in Ontario in 1882, the same year as Joyce. The International Moderns, were, in effect, part of his parent's generation, and Kenner fully internalized that generation's foundational belief in classical literature and languages.

Thus nurtured, Kenner transformed his troubled childhood beginnings into a stunningly successful academic career, and in the process, developed an unshakable faith in his own critical vision.

What Kenner found in Pound was someone who shared his core beliefs while using them also as a bridge to reach other traditions; discovered in Pound, furthermore, someone whose devotion to Western cultural and aesthetic traditions was so all-consuming that the need to transmit this heritage to future generations became a moral imperative. Pound sacrificed his personal reputation and freedom in an attempt to reform a European-based culture that was careening into economic depression and unending war. Though he failed utterly, Pound heroically established a vision for cultural renewal. Pound's shaky grasp of economics and his appalling anti-Semitic outbursts were not dealbreakers because so much else was at stake. Kenner, in turn, risked his own reputation by linking his vision of Modernism to Pound's.

The daring that Kenner displayed with this gesture has rarely been acknowledged, but current modern-poetry scholar Marjorie Perloff of Stanford University, who endorses Kenner's exceptional achievements (with reservations), concurs. "Far from being the conservative formalist he is now often taken to be, [Kenner] was the great radical among Modernist critics," she writes.

Perloff also tells an anecdote about inviting Hugh and Mary Anne Kenner to join her family at a New York production of Pound's translation of Euripides' *Electra*:

> I had always considered Kenner a cool and collected, even a somewhat forbidding person, a man very much in control of his emotions. Imagine my surprise when I turned around at the end of the performance and saw that Kenner was *weeping*. The tragedy of this *Electra*, so close to the Pound who was confined at St. Elizabeth's at the time when he created her, had brought Kenner to tears. Criticism, after all, is a form of life. And it's the life of Kenner's criticism—its total engagement— that has always made me think of Hugh Kenner as the exemplary critic.

Kenner jokingly referred to himself as an X-ray technician, a fitting epitaph for a critic of penetrating vision who insisted that criticism should always document each era's scientific and technological developments.

Others saw Kenner as a cartographer, a mapmaker who sees, as Pound tells us in *Canto LIX:* ". . . not as land looks on a map/but as sea bord seen by men sailing"—another fitting epitaph to an alert outsider who saw everything fresh with his own eyes.

Or perhaps he will be remembered as the master of what Pound called the "luminous detail," a literary historian who mixed every remembered anecdote and fragment of conversation with previously neglected or unknown information to create several critical narratives that still ring with drama.

His peers remember Kenner as someone who maintained an ox-killing workload throughout his career. On any given day, a friend recalls, Kenner would be "writing a book, doing proofs on another, writing five reviews, four essays, preparing lectures, classes, working out geodesic equations, reading fourteen books, acknowledging nineteen offprints, rewiring the lights, fixing the toilet, [and] being a husband, [and] a father to [seven] children." His daughter Lisa praised her father for showing her how "to raise a top-notch cat."

Kenner's papers, lodged at the University of Texas, fill, at recent count, 106 boxes, three oversized boxes, one card file, one oversized folder, and eleven galley files. These boxes contain 36 books and edited volumes; 439 articles, obituaries and lectures, including some unpublished items; 336 reviews; 23 introductions; and a massive correspondence of approximately 1,500 names.

Kenner also wrote a regular computer column for *Byte* magazine, plus a whole series on contemporary events for *Harper's*, and forty-plus columns for *Art and Antiques* magazine.

In addition, Kenner wrote affectionately about his cherished silent-screen comedians, and is doubtless the only film critic to review the movie, "King Kong," with the aid of *Paradise Lost*. In addition to his major critical works, Kenner also wrote several of what he called "one-evening" books.

Perhaps the best epitaph for the achievement of Hugh Kenner can be found in his most entertaining single-evening book, *Chuck Jones: A Flurry of Drawings* (1994), a tribute to the cartoonist who created many of Kenner's favorites, including the "Road Runner," all the while providing us —of course!—with the entire pre-computer history of cartoon animation.

On an opening page of *Flurry,* he features this quote from a decidedly non-Modernist writer as a dedication to his book:

> We are a people.
> A people do not throw their geniuses away.
> And if they are thrown away, it is our duty
> as artists and as witnesses for the future to
> collect them again for the sake of our children,
> and if necessary, bone by bone.
>
> *—Alice Walker* ■

GROVE KOGER

Staying On:
Paul Bowles' Later Years in Tangier

By 1973, Paul Bowles' readers may have thought that his career was over. And he may well have felt the same way himself. His beloved wife (and fellow writer) Jane Bowles had died on May 4 after an agonizing series of illnesses, and he had found little time or energy for new work. He was 62, and his reputation as an avant-garde existentialist was fading.

However, the next quarter century saw a surprising outpouring of stories and poems and unclassifiable works. They were as good (and usually as dark) as any Bowles had written as a younger man, but their darkness was relieved by prose as limpid as spring water. Bowles also published a steady stream of translations, while editors compiled omnibus collections of his fiction, poetry, letters and even photographs. He was also a composer of note, and concerts of his music were held in Paris and Nice and (at Lincoln Center!) in New York City. Bernardo Bertolucci filmed Bowles' famous novel *The Sheltering Sky*, and even gave the writer a cameo role. It was a busy time for Bowles as well as for his readers, listeners, viewers, and critics, not to mention bibliographers.

* * * * *

Bowles once explained that he preferred working with small presses because he disliked getting rejections. It was an understandable attitude, and one that would shape the later years of his literary career, as a glance at the period illustrates.

The highlight of the booklet *Three Tales*, published by Frank Hallman of New York in 1975, is "Mejdoub," which deals with one of Bowles' favorite themes, the instability of identity. Here a Moroccan pretending to be an insane beggar is taken at his word by the police and locked up. "The months moved by. Through nights and days and nights he lived with the other madmen, and the time came when it scarcely mattered to him anymore, getting to the officials to tell them who he was. Finally he ceased thinking about it."

The title of Bowles' 1977 collection *Things Gone and Things Still Here*, from distinguished California publisher Black Sparrow, suggests a kind of stock-taking, with the title piece considering several Moroccan folk beliefs. One concerns the Haddaoua, a sect whose members are said to be able to exercise their will over animals: "A Haddaoui could go out alone into the countryside and return in a few days with hundreds of goats following him in single-file formation." Bowles describes watching a Haddaoui "become" a goat. "There in front of me was a man's body with a goat inside it, as if the goat had been able to assume the visible form of a man, while at the same time it remained unmistakably a goat." Another belief involves Moroccan *djenoun* (*djinns* or genies), beings whose habitat "is only a few feet below ours." The collection also reprints "Mejdoub" and includes another, more chilling story about transference of personality, "Allal," in which a young Moroccan man switches identities—literally—with a poisonous serpent.

Black Sparrow published another, more substantial collection by Bowles, *Midnight Mass*, in 1981. Most of its stories are set in Morocco, and one of them, "The Eye," begins with this starkly arresting sentence: "Ten or twelve years ago there came to live in Tangier a man who would have done better to stay away." The story was selected by Joyce Carol Oates for inclusion in *Best American Short Stories of 1979*. A gentler story, "Here to Learn," follows a naïve young Moroccan woman who travels halfway round the world on the strength of her beauty, only to discover that she can't go home again.

These three collections are a reminder of the attraction that Morocco had long held for Bowles. He had visited the country for the first time in 1931 at the suggestion of Gertrude Stein, and eventually settled in the city of Tangier in 1947, although he continued to travel periodically. As he explained in his 1972 autobiography *Without Stopping*, he had always been "vaguely certain" that at some point he would "come into a magic place which, in revealing its secrets, would give [him] wisdom and ecstasy—perhaps even death." Living in Tangier, he relished "the idea that in the night . . . sorcery [was] burrowing its invisible tunnels in every direction, from thousands of senders to thousands of unsuspecting recipients." But by the time Bowles wrote "Things

Gone and Things Still Here," the *djenoun* had begun to disappear from the magic place, vanquished by the "proximity of iron and steel."

In 1982, Los Angeles publisher Sylvester & Orphanos published a sumptuous edition—limited and numbered and signed—of "In the Red Room," arguably Bowles' best story. Set in Sri Lanka (Ceylon), where Bowles lived on several occasions in the early 1950s, the story describes an encounter involving an unnamed narrator and his parents with a young man, "Sonny," who urges them to visit his house. Once inside, Sonny seats them in a small bedroom whose walls and ceiling have been painted a "glistening" crimson and whose bed is topped with a "slightly darker red" coverlet. Three portraits—of a young woman, Sonny and another young man—hang on the wall. Sonny sits "stiffly, looking straight ahead, like someone at the theatre." Afterward, the narrator remarks that the brief visit "was like watching television without the sound. You saw everything, but you didn't get what was going on."

A few days later, the narrator encounters an acquaintance who clears up the mystery. It seems that the day after Sonny's wedding, he had found his bride in bed with his best man and proceeded to shoot them both and chop their bodies into pieces. After a few weeks in a mental hospital, he'd been discharged.

The story ends with an ironic exchange between the narrator (who wisely chooses not to tell his parents what he's learned) and his mother, who has been puzzling over the incident. "That room had a particular meaning for him," she remarks. "It was like a sort of shrine." The narrator realizes that "she had got to the core without needing the details," and replies, "I felt that, too . . . Of course, there's no way of knowing." In turn, his mother comments, "Well, what you don't know won't hurt you." The narrator explains that he "had heard her use the expression a hundred times without ever being able to understand what she meant by it, because it seemed so patently untrue. But for once it was apt." He nods his head and replies, "That's right."

Subsequently, Black Sparrow added "In the Red Room" to a second edition of *Midnight Mass* and it was reprinted in *The Best American Short Stories, 1984* and *The Best American Short Stories of the Eighties.*
The year 1982 also saw the publication of Bowles' most original work, *Points in Time*, by London publisher Peter Owen. The short book

consists of eleven sections, one of them all of sixty words long and a few the length (and shape) of short stories, arranged chronologically from Morocco's earliest days through decades of foreign occupation to what was then the present. The collection opens with a glimpse of the country's Atlantic coastline as it must have looked to Hanno, the Carthaginian mariner who sailed down the West African coast about 500 B.C.E. Many of the subsequent episodes explore the relationship between Moslems, Jews, and "Nazarenes," or Christians.

One of the best pieces, which is apparently based on a true incident, concerns one Andrew Layton, an English exporter living in the windy seaside town of Essaouira (Mogador) two centuries ago. Layton becomes involved in a fracas with some farmers and in anger strikes a woman in the face with his whip, dislodging two of her teeth. All parties are called before the Sultan in Marrakech, where Layton straightforwardly admits the crime and the farmers successfully press their demand for "precise retaliation." What follows is pure Bowles: Layton "had the presence of mind to ask that the teeth to be pulled be two molars which recently had been giving him trouble. The complainants agreed to the suggestion. Back teeth being larger and heavier than front teeth, they felt that they were getting the better of the bargain.

The operation went ahead under the intent scrutiny of the villagers. They were waiting to hear the infidel's cries of pain. Layton, however, preserved a stoical silence throughout the ordeal. The molars were washed then presented to the claimants, who went away entirely satisfied.

Impressed with Layton's composure, the Sultan befriends him, hoping that eventually Layton might become British Consul in Marrakech. But no, he will stay in Essaouira. "He had got used to the wind, he said."

Disputes among people of differing religions and nationalities, among the colonizers and the colonized, are usually settled less satisfactorily. "At night in the courtyards of the Rif, grandfathers fashion grenades. Each rock in the ravine shields a man. The Spaniard in the garrison starts from sleep, to find his throat already slashed."

Peter Owen promoted *Points in Time* as "tales from Morocco," while Bowles himself suggested that it was "perhaps lyrical history." Critic Tobias Wolff called it "a nervy, surprising, completely original performance, so original that it can't be referred to any previous category of fiction or non-fiction." I think of it as a suite, but one composed of words rather than notes.

The short 1988 collection *Unwelcome Words*, from Tombouctou Books of Bolinas, California, continues Bowles' string of experiments, and suggests as well that the wind that once blew through Essaouira in *Points in Time* had turned icy. Three of its stories—"New York 1965," "Massachusetts 1932," and "Tangier 1975"—are punctuation-free and unparagraphed monologues dramatizing misunderstanding and madness in locations that, not coincidentally, had personal significance for Bowles. The title story itself consists of six undated letters written to an unidentified recipient. The latter is apparently physically incapacitated and has, according to the former, entered the "final period" of his life. "But as you sink into your self-imposed non-being," we read in the last letter, "I hope you'll remember (you won't) that I made this small and futile attempt to help you remain human."

But those unwelcome words weren't Bowles' final ones. Ecco Press founder Daniel Halpern published a new novella by Bowles, *Too Far from Home*, in a 697-page compilation of "selected writings" under the same

title in 1993. Set in Mali, the novella describes the experiences of an American woman who has fled a disastrous marriage to take refuge with her artist brother in a disconcertingly unfurnished house with no electricity and no running water. Finding herself a "shadow" in a land in which black people are the "real" people (she is, after all, too far from home), the woman unwittingly calls down a fatal curse on two other travelers. Bowles' British publisher, Peter Owen, reprinted the novella the following year, adding sketches by Bowles' friend and longtime Tangier resident Marguerite McBey.

* * * * *

In conclusion, I'd like to mention a surprising connection between Paul Bowles and Idaho. Bowles' short poem "Here I Am" originally appeared in Paris in *This Quarter* in 1929, but you can listen to him read it on a compact disc included in the 1991 edition (edited by Bob Moore) of Boise State University's late lamented *cold-drill*. ■

Paul Bowles.

ALAN MINSKOFF

Time Traveler:
A Re-reading of E. L. Doctorow

The Italian novelist (*My Shadow is Yours*), memoirist (*Story of My People*), translator (*Infinite Jest*), Edoardo Nesi wrote an intriguing series of essays gathered under the title *Sentimental Economy*. Penned during the pandemic, among many fascinating entries—from Italian fabric artistry to a memorable visit to an almost empty Uffizi—the one that stayed with me was a full-throated appreciation of E.L. Doctorow's *World's Fair*. Nesi calls the novel truly great and advises the reader to savor the coming-of-age story/memoir/period piece by reading it deliberately and incrementally.

The same advice can be given for a number of Doctorow's masterworks—*Billy Bathgate* and, of course, *Ragtime*—his eloquent prose, gimlet eye, unerring ear and his remarkable uses of history and time. He needs to be read intentionally to immerse in the eras that give his fiction verisimilitude.

Doctorow's double gift—evoking the past as vivid setting and imaginary launching pad to create characters who embody the moment—is best taken in slow deliberate draughts. The Bronx of the *World's Fair* teams with the city evolving into the motorized modern borough. Edgar, the precocious child narrator, shares the author's first name and elements of his biography.

The author plays with point of view and time. His descriptions of listening to the radio and hearing Hitler are vivid and memorable:

> . . . he shouted in German, which I heard as
> a language full of spitting and gulping and
> galumphing, almost as if the words were
> broken in his teeth; it sounded as if he were
> shattering glass in his mouth, as if he breathed
> fire and made the air explode in front of his face.

This description in the hyper-aware schoolboy voice that Doctorow employs to such good ends flashes to the *Night of Broken Glass* that German Jews experienced on November 9, 1938. While Doctorow is far from Phillip Roth or Saul Bellow in his focus on Jewishness, it does enter this novel in creative ways.

Edgar enters an essay contest that his second-place finish entitles him and his family to a free trip (one they probably wouldn't have taken otherwise) to the Fair. His profile of an American boy includes a telling aside:

> The Typical American Boy [this was
> the essay's theme] is not fearful of Dangers.
> He should be able to go out into the country
> and drink raw milk. Likewise, he should traverse
> the hills and valleys of the city. If he is Jewish,
> he should say so.

Doctorow manipulates point of view and adapts voice with care and cunning. Just as the reader is used to the youthful if wise-beyond-his-years narration from Edgar, his mother, then his older brother take over the story; they act almost as correctives to the child narrator's view of things. The novel's ending chapters return to Edgar's perspective and tone and prepare the reader for the fine set piece of the family's visit to the New York World's Fair in 1939, the ultimate time-traveling moment this visit to the ameliorated American future. Doctorow's detailed unveiling of the feel, tone and texture of the event come through in their initial foray inside.

The General Motors exhibit, everyone's first stop, presented the city of the future where "everything was planned" with 14-lane highways, people living in "streamlined curvilinear buildings," and when you exited wearing the "I HAVE SEEN THE FUTURE" button, he writes, "you were standing precisely on the corner you had just seen." These final chapters as Neri implies encapsulate the purely American optimism about the future that we see today in those folks who firmly believe that tech will solve anything and everything.

* * * * *

Doctorow's most famous and perhaps most lasting work of fiction mines an earlier era in our history and portrays one of the most searing racially charged set of scenes in all our fiction. The novel is, of course, *Ragtime,* and the cause of the carnage is the racist incident when members of the Tarrytown (aptly used) fire brigade decide to waylay the jazz pianist, Coalhouse Walker, Jr., and hold—then wreck—his new car. This act incites the retributive mayhem to follow. This novel teems with reinvented real people. Doctorow uses historical figures to remarkable imagined effects: Houdini, devoted to his mother, daring feats defy every norm; J.P. Morgan, whose beyond-opulent residence provides the setting for the incendiary ending and allows for a scene revealing Henry Ford's virulent antisemitism; and two women Emma Goldman, the fiery socialist and Evelyn Nesbit, the glamour girl whose husband Harry K. Thaw murdered famed architect Stanford White in 1906. Both play significant parts in this historical drama.

His historical cameos animate this fiction. Sigmund Freud comes to the United States and Doctorow has him remark that "America is a mistake, a gigantic mistake." This assertion sets off the author as social commentator on his lifelong empathy for and commitment to the working man and critique of the oppression of capitalism, which he sums up with wicked irony:

> Children suffered no discriminatory treatment. They were valued everywhere they were employed.

Doctorow's turn-of-the-century American world is extraordinary. His characters do remarkable things: an immigrant father, Tateh, who later becomes Hollywood impresario, begins as a street artist, who at one point takes his daughter on a grandly executed six-page public transportation ride from NYC to Boston. This displays Doctorow, the fabulist, armed with exquisite historic details and *hutzpah*. In a novel where a talented but abused black man gets lethal revenge, the glitz of the moment is always balanced by the undertow of the real.

The family at the center of all the goings on, described as Father, in the bunting and fireworks business, longsuffering Mother, Younger Brother, who converts to fellow traveler revolutionary and the all-seeing, unnamed son meet Houdini, entertain, and are entertained by Coalhouse. Their lives (in good novelistic tradition) ultimately intersect with Tateh and his daughter in New Jersey, where Tateh, the emergent filmmaker, hatches the idea of an Our Gang-like film series and his career is set. In a nicely woven conclusion after Coalhouse's violent and tragic end, Doctorow reports the era of ragtime "had run out"; Father dead, Mother marries Tateh; Emma Goldman gets deported. Evelyn Nesbit, looks gone, falls into "obscurity," and Harry K. Thaw, released from the insane asylum, "marched annually at Newport in the Armistice Day parade."

* * * * *

His novel *Billy Bathgate* is again a recreation of a moment this time—here the 1920s and the Great Depression-—realized as a crime-themed parable of a young man who by happenstance is thrown in with Dutch Shultz's mob and lives to tell the tale. It is a barnburner. A tour de force in style—Damon Runyan catapulted into literary fiction—it begins with Billy first recounting how he witnessed a murder on Schultz's boat, then explaining why Schultz took him on:

> I was capable. I knew it before he did,
> although he gave me more than confirmation
> when he said it, he made me his.

He adds on the same page:

> My instructions were simple, when I was not
> doing something I was specifically told to do,
> to pay attention, to miss nothing.

And he ends up virtually in Schultz's inner circle, the teen eventually becomes a made man, and he exists in this crime-filled underworld like a picaro in a 17th century novel—handsome, agile, athletic, yet hyper observant and not risk averse; he even ends up with the boss's girl and survives. But the apprenticeship takes its time and toll on Billy. Schultz gets in trouble with Tom Dewey, then the New York City D.A., and Billy is told to stay put in the Bronx. Doctorow brilliantly contrasts his waiting for instructions with ebullience of street life:

> So that was my situation for those hot Bronx
> days of Indian summer and the Diamond Home
> sprinkler fixing a rainbow every morning like
> a halo over the wet street and the children
> shrieking. I was mournful.

The poetry of daily life in the midst of gangland. Nothing is ever truly predictable for Doctorow, even his mobsters have moments of insight. Schultz first sets eyes on Billy when the boy is wowing the neighborhood with his juggling. The gangster marks him as a boy to watch.

Empathy is a trump suit for the author. Schultz through his bravado and the brutality of his lethal tantrums earns his violent death, gunned down in a john. Yet, the reader can't help but feel for this amoral killer, who dies in a hospital room after the hit—all the while marveling how the swift and lucky Billy slips away from the blood-smeared scene. The novel ends with one of the author's greatest paeans to New York, a page-long, one-sentence paragraph that elevates the sensual cacophony of the street—clatter, vendors, trucks, "gabbling old women"— and Billy pushing a baby carriage:

> . . . and all the life of the city turning out to greet us just as in the old days of happiness, before my father fled, when the family used to go walking to the market, this bazaar of life, Bathgate, in the age of Dutch Schultz.

What writers admire and readers become enamored with is this sense of timeless time, this vitality, intensity of setting, the accuracy of detail and stagecraft. Little wonder so many of Doctorow's works became films. Disparate writers from Michael Chabon, who credits his *Kavalier and Clay* as directly influenced by him, to Jennifer Egan who turned to his novels "as I've wrestled to write a novel set before my lifetime." And Don DeLillo who writes, "In Doctorow, fiction redeems history…."

Much lauded in his own time, especially the 20th century, Doctorow is easily ignored in our present-tense ahistorical moment where many ignore the past in the thrall of the future perfect—the technological fix. Alas, the novel itself takes time. To know how we got to now, read E.L. Doctorow, the great practitioner of this time art, who uses history as context, imaginative springboard and stage set to bring fascinating characters vividly, supremely to life. His works, his imagined worlds, remind us that few endeavors are more rewarding than reading fiction. ∎

ALAN MINSKOFF

E. L. Doctorow.

Ford and Susan Swetnam.

SUSAN H. SWETNAM

On Re-reading Dylan Thomas's "Do Not Go Gentle into That Good Night"

he students in the introduction to literature class I taught in spring of 1987 were cooperative and had become much better readers by midterm. Yet as the poetry unit began, palpable dread filled the classroom. "My friends and I just aren't the kind of people who 'get' poetry," one had apologized in advance during office hours.

Yet during that unit's third session, hands—including his--waved enthusiastically in the air and heads nodded energetically. Somebody even spontaneously commented on the power of technique, a first, though the term "incremental refrain" was not, of course, employed. We were discussing Dylan Thomas's "Do Not Go Gentle into That Good Night," a poetic masterpiece which so fervently, resolutely, musically protests death's end of all earthly possibility. Students confided their anguish over others' deaths; they voiced their dreams of achievement and fears that they might cease to be before they'd really lived. Dylan Thomas had, yet again, enabled what would prove to be the best class session of the semester.

And I was right there with these sentiments, that morning in 1987. Just two years married to my sweetheart, the poet Ford Swetnam, I reached toward the prolonged and full flowering of my own unspooling future—and his—with a visceral yearning. I was so anxious, even phobic about the power of serious illness and death to truncate that future, in fact, that when acquaintances and relatives died in the years that immediately followed, I repeatedly begged off attending funerals, leaving such kindness to a southern boy raised right by his mother, though also bearing his own Thomas-esque tendencies.

* * * * *

"Do Not Go Gentle" is addressed to the poet's father, a man who'd once imagined becoming a writer but settled into a schoolmaster's trade, responsibly providing for his family. Still, it clearly seems written as much for Dylan Thomas himself, composed not at the elder Thomas's deathbed but five years earlier, and echoing themes omnipresent in DT's work. And knowledge of the poet's fate enhances its haunting power, for his own flowering was abbreviated at age 39—ironically in the context of this poem self-abbreviated—by an episode of alcohol poisoning that capped many years of self-destructive excess.

While such romantic flaming-out might have appealed also to my husband in his youthful days, as he matured delight in a world he found so endlessly fascinating, so rich, won out, thank goodness. Before the same cancer that killed his father and grandfather took him at age sixty, he'd assembled a legacy that included four books of poems; he'd infused innumerable students' lives with a love of words and ideas, and modeled for all who knew him kindness, life-affirming humor, contagious curiosity about an encyclopedic range of topics, and deep reverence for the natural world.

I lost myself for a long time after I lost him, though eventually students, friends, words, and that natural world dragged me back to life. Or to a new life, more properly, for as I began to find my feet and realized that I no longer feared my own death, I began to hear an odd but irresistible call to fresh vocation, to a second-act retirement career that would draw something constructive from my husband's passing. I've described that "calling" process elsewhere; in this short space I'll simply invite you to marvel that this former illness/death-phobic now ministers monthly as a hospice massage therapist to twenty or thirty people staggering from a terminal diagnosis, navigating inevitable diminutions of their health and powers, and/or facing oncoming death.

Improbable as that evolution would have seemed back in 1987, frankly now it's hard to imagine doing anything else. For this simple, ancient practice of extending tangible community through kitten's paw kneading, fingertip stretching, energy work, holding and warming is deeply effective—and affecting. Labored breathing eases as gentle touch disrupts the anxiety that triggers a cascade of pain-fueling fight-or-flight hormones; irregular galloping hearts stabilize. Panic attacks yield to essential rest. Cogency—even verbal cogency—appears in
some dementia patients.

Curing patients, it's not. But it's indisputably making their remaining time better, and I often drive home wrapped in the peace I've dedicated myself to conveying to others.

Paradoxically, this seems to me the most life-affirming work I've ever done.

* * * * *

As you've obviously gathered, I've thought a lot about the themes in "Do Not Go Gentle" since taking up hospice massage. And if there's one thing I've learned, it's this: that while on paper anger at inevitable mortality might seem magnificently Byronic, in person its consequences are not something anyone would wish for those they love, or for themselves. Two recent cases come to mind: a man who viciously and continually berated his doctors because they couldn't save him, and a woman who regaled visitors with bitter accounts of her failed aspirations, her "crap, unfair life." While those who tended them did not stint in fulfilling professional responsibilities, as you might expect, none lingered to provide tonic human fellowship, nor to celebrate their "noble" attitudes.

More placid but still implacable denial can prove no less heartbreaking, as with a 95-year-old patient who insisted on chemotherapy after her cancer returned a third time. The treatment blighted her last days, her pain multiplying from tissue damage, her thinking irrevocably blurred. "I'm not going to lose this battle now," she'd proudly told me, evoking the military trope of cancer treatment—an absurd metaphor, of course, given that something is eventually going to make all of us "losers."

Yet I've also witnessed denouements that give me hope, particularly my elderly friend Pat's. Suffering from an untreatable heart condition, she contemplated writers' perspectives on death and dying, entertained Buddhists and Catholic priests in her assisted-living room, lovingly mended old fences, brought gentle frankness to our metaphysical discussions. Though aware her time was short, Pat made friends with the young CNAs who cared for her. She became a trusted grandmother-confidant, listening to their troubles and offering encouragement, building a transitory but beautiful fellowship, demonstrating what it might mean to think of life's final phase as a period with its own particular gifts.

One of the circumstances in my own life for which I'm most grateful is that Ford himself "went gentle" in the end, though he'd once been an iconoclastic rebel, admirer of Thomas, of the Beats, of the Melville who praised Hawthorne for saying "No, in thunder." Like the transformed aged Melville, though, whose last great work is a story of complex and luminous surrender, my husband cultivated acceptance when it became clear that the radiation, the brachytherapy, the chemo weren't halting cancer's progress. The volume of poems he completed in his last year rings with open-ended composure, not fear, as it explores intimations of transcendence in the physical world, celebrates human love in the face of existential uncertainty, reaches toward a peace that entails no compromise.

* * * * *

How different, thus, "Do Not Go Gentle into That Good Night" now appears from the poem that so moved my class and me in 1987. Though admittedly glorious, it now seems like a pose a fervent young man is trying on for heroic size, a grand theoretical manifesto that even its creator ultimately did not heed.

Please understand that I don't mean to denigrate "Do Not Go Gentle" as a poem. Its villanelle form is exquisite, its content pretty much guaranteed to engage the young'uns with big archetypal questions, as they should be engaged. It's still capable of giving me goosebumps, despite all of the above.

I'd respectfully submit, however, that it's perhaps not the best guide for those of us who've reached an age where death is no longer an abstraction.

In my case that age is a healthy, energetic 72, and I admit to harboring still some continued, ungentle jealous yearning for the possibilities ahead—especially the next three books I'm hatching. I don't feel done yet.

Judging what "done" entails, though, is obviously an iffy proposition. After all, barring self-destruction we're all going to go "When Jesus comes to claim us, and says it is enough," as one of Ford's favorite bluegrass gospel songs affirms.

It's a question that bears ongoing attention, anyway, as occurred recently in the unlikely context of a mountain hike, as I heard myself wonder aloud to a younger writer-friend if time would ever seem so short that I'd decline to begin a new writing project.

"Well, that's not going to happen, Susan," she said, grinning. "You just better get used to it. You're going to die in the middle of some book."

I stopped, blinked, regarded her . . . then the meadow rang with the happy laughter.

Of course I'll die in the middle of some book.

Gently, I hope. ■

Forrester Blake, book jacket photo from Johnny Christmas.

BRANT SHORT & NILE SPEARS

Searching for Forrester Blake:
Re-reading a Forgotten Novelist of the American West

lthough his books today are long out of print, Forrester Blake's well-researched novels of the American West were widely widely respected by historians, critics, and other writers of his day for their realism, lively plots regarding conflict and survival, attention to geographical landmarks, and historical accuracy of the time portrayed. A contemporary of novelists Walter Van Tilburg Clark, Vardis Fisher, Dorothy Johnson, and A.B. Guthrie, Blake (1912-1978) is an author whose works deserve academic re-evaluation, critical reassessment, and appreciative new readers.

Aside from publishing a memoir of a wild horse drive, three novels, and an edited collection of folk tales, Blake taught literature at Idaho State University for 30 years before retiring in 1971. He died in Pocatello in 1978 at the age of 66.

For students of Western American literature, he may today be seen as a minor figure, largely overlooked for his humble contribution to the canon of Western literature, his work perhaps overshadowed by that of his more famous contemporaries. Revisiting Blake is an insightful and worthy literary examination of the American West, his books particularly rich in the history and geography of the Southwest and Inter-Rocky Mountain regions.

Little is known of his personal life. Born in 1912, Blake's family moved from Detroit to Oklahoma where, as a boy, he encountered several "frontiersmen" who shared their stories and life experiences. Growing up, his imagination was sparked by the stories of his grandfather, John Y. F. Blake, who commanded a group of Indian scouts in Arizona during the 1880s and engaged in skirmishes with Apache warriors led by Geronimo (Roger Blake). Later, in 1940, Blake met and befriended William Henry Jackson, the famed photographer of the Hayden Survey in the 1870s which mapped the Southwest and also provided the photographs that convinced Congress to create Yellowstone National Park. Brief book jacket blurbs inform us that Blake later served four years in the Eighth Army Air Force during WW II, completed a master's degree at the University of Denver in 1947, and that he traveled extensively throughout the West to learn firsthand about the country he would write about.

But perhaps the experience that fueled Blake's storytelling and love of the West occurred earlier, after completing his sophomore year at the University of Michigan in 1932, when he participated in the last documented long wild horse drive in the United States. Blake's small group of cowboys moved 110 wild mustangs over 400 miles, from the Mescalero Apache Reservation in New Mexico to the Oklahoma Panhandle. This experience is intimately described in his first book *Riding the Mustang Trail*, published by Charles Scribner's Sons in 1935, shepherded to print by legendary Scribner's Editor Maxwell Perkins (Gino Sky).

Blake retold the remarkable experience of his first published book to Idaho writer Gino Sky who took three of Blake's literature classes at Idaho State beginning in 1958 and who later corresponded with Blake as a fellow author. Blake completed his memoir upon returning home and shared it with his grandmother who told him it was good enough to be published. She urged him to go to New York City and find a publisher. She gave him $165 and he hand-carried his manuscript on a train to New York, spending the night at the YMCA. Blake went to Scribner's the morning after he arrived and informed the receptionist that he had a book that he wanted to publish. She then called the editor and told him there is a young man here with a manuscript. At the age of 18, Blake was then sent-up to meet who was to become his first editor, Maxwell Perkins.

Published Novels
Johnny Christmas (NY: William Morrow, 1948)
Wilderness Passage (NY: Random House, 1953)

These two novels examine westward expansion through the eyes of Johnny Christmas and his friend and mentor Tom Gitt. Blake envisioned a trilogy, covering three distinct time periods: 1835 to 1847 (set in Texas, New Mexico, and Colorado); 1857 to 1860 (set in Utah and Idaho); 1877 and beyond (set in Idaho and Oregon, although only the first chapter of the third book was published in 1973 as a short story titled "The Lake"). The final novel in the trilogy, *The Lost Land*, we understand, was drafted but has not been located. Several sources indicate that a draft of this novel, and perhaps other unpublished novels, and papers, including primary resource information, may exist in storage.

Johnny Christmas centers on the human drive to explore and transcend the constraints of community. The novel opens with the Texas War of Independence in April 1836. Johnny has drifted west and joined a band of "Texian" guerilla fighters who support the Texas war for independence. They carry out raids on small villages, fight Mexican soldiers, and evade Comanche warriors. After one such attack in which a priest is killed, a troubled Johnny recalls leaving home and the onset of his journey. Frustrated with his life in the Tennessee hill country, Johnny informs no one other than his grandfather about his plan to leave home. His grandfather had anticipated Johnny's desire to explore the West and reinforces his approval by gifting Johnny two prized possessions that are central to his journey: a Hawken rifle and a roan gelding horse.

> "I been expectin' it," the old man said. "No Christmas
> was ever satisfied with where he was born. I come
> from Virginia to Carolina to here. Your pa could
> have stayed in Carolina, but look where he is.
> West Tennessee. And now you. There's lots of
> country lays west. No tellin', Johnny, where or what
> it'll bet with a young feller like you." (p. 36)

In the aftermath of one violent attack, Johnny refuses to join in looting a local church and forces one of the "Texians" at gunpoint to return stolen sacred items. With this betrayal, Johnny severs ties with the group and makes enemies who will continue to haunt him. He heads further west with an older and seasoned mountain man, Tom Gitt, who also finds the "Texian" raiders to be more a band of mercenaries and less a group of freedom fighters for Texas independence.

The two men spend several years exploring the Southwest, lands that would become New Mexico and Colorado. They live among Native Americans, primarily the Ute Tribe, waiting out the winter and planning their next trapping journey. Both take "wives" and have children with Native women. Although accepted by the tribe, Johnny's frustration builds while living within a community. He leaves alone and explores the region from New Mexico to California, ending in El Pueblo de Los Angeles. Here he takes in the Pacific Ocean and sees the riches California offers and experiences the oppressive presence of Mexican governance. After several years, Johnny returns to Taos and finds that Americans are viewed with hostility by the locals as war is brewing with the United State. The book ends with Johnny inflicting revenge for those who harmed him and innocent Mexican peasants over the years. He leaves Taos, finds his friend Tom Gitt, and the two men retreat to the wilderness once more.

Set in September 1857, the story of Johnny and Tom resumes in *Wilderness Passage*.

In Utah's Uintah Basin, an aging and ill Gitt seeks the warmth and safety of traveling to the Southwest, while Johnny has a much different plan. He intends to travel north to Idaho's Fort Hall trading post, then follow the Snake River, and settle in the Salmon River Country north of Boise.

While descending the Uintas the two mountain men are arrested as U.S. Army spies by the Mormon militia after Brigham Young has declared independence from the United States and announced creation of a sovereign nation christened, "Deseret." It becomes clear that their lives are at risk as the Mormon militia leader grows increasingly paranoid about American military intrusion. Johnny and Tom learn they are being held by some of the radical Mormons who just weeks earlier carried out the Mountain Meadows Massacre where over 120 travelers from Arkansas were murdered without provocation or threat. As the violent nature of these radicalized Mormons becomes evident, Tom and Johnny escape and are joined by the militia leader's wife, Carey Frietag, whose own life has been threatened by militia leaders. The ailing Gitt does not survive the escape. Johnny and Carey journey to the Salmon River Country to start a new life as a couple. Carey is traumatized by the violence she witnessed among the Mormons and the extreme isolation she endures as they wait out winter in a mountain cabin. They meet a group of Missouri settlers camped at Fort Hall and in need of an experienced guide. Carey encourages Johnny to lead the settlers to the Salmon River country to start their new life together. As the settlers stake out their claims and build cabins, the heaviness of living within a community again becomes too much for Johnny. In a poignant ending, Nez Perce tribal travelers, who once accepted Johnny as a friend, take pains to avoid him while he is building a fence for the settlment. Shocked by their indifference and sensing his loss of independence, Johnny takes harsh actions to remove himself from the community and will not promise Carey when or if he will return.

The Franciscan (Garden City NY: Doubleday, 1963)

The Franciscan, Padre Lorenzo de Escalona's character, cascades into a complexity of spiritual conflicts, each connected to a vivid historical character who symbolizes the Spanish Kingdom of New Mexico during 1675. Lorenzo travels to the Capital, Santa Fe, from the Cochiti Pueblo Mission. He witnesses fifty Puebloan medicine chief prisoners flogged and four hangings. At this horrific scene we see his sorrow for the suffering Puebloans and indifferent loyalty to the Spanish administrators as he attempts to console and protect Estrella Guerrero. Estrella, the wife of a Spanish Rancher and a Mestizo of Yaqui and Spanish heritage, experiences her own conflict, passionately desiring to care for Lorenzo and feeling contempt for the Spanish and Christianity.

Upon Lorenzo's return to the Cochití Pueblo he encounters the Pyrenean, a hardened Soldier of Fortune, Sergeant Major Manuelo de Vargas and his two private guards. They also are traveling to Cochití, providing protection to another Franciscan Padre and returning Estreslla and her husband to their ranch. Early in their journey it becomes clear that Vargas' main objective is to locate the Painted Cave and suspected hideout of the Puebloan medicine men and war chiefs, Popé and Cuapá. Vargas believes that Lorenzo is concealing this information which is key to capturing the leaders who conspire to lead a revolt against the Spanish.

The story unfolds with more violence against the Puebloans in reprisal for practicing outlawed pagan rituals. Lorenzo rebukes Vargas in an attempt to protect the Puebloans, which causes the death of one soldier. Padre Lorenzo also experiences a violent encounter with Apache raiders. A distortion of justice occurs when Lorenzo is accused and convicted of sorcery by the Inquisition in Mexico. Lorenzo's punishment results in banishment to the remote Rio Chama in the shadow of the Trushas Peaks. Here there are no missions. Lorenzo serves the isolated Spanish ranchers who are guarded by a few crude and usually abandoned garrisons. In this harsh land of raging mountain streams, deep snows, and hostile tribes, we see the rawness of each character emerging, initially seeking freedom from oppression and now self-imposed prisoners of their environment in a struggle for survival.

Blake chose the climactic year of 1675 leading up to the successful Pueblo Revolt of 1680 and the expulsion of the Spanish from New Mexico for 12 years. The Franciscans had occupied northern New Mexico for 77 years, severely altering the spiritual, economic and cultural lives of the pueblo peoples. The Franciscans' extensive network of missions among the pueblo people fulfilled the Spanish Monarchy's mandate to convert pagan souls to Christianity. Blake's novel contains much more than the events of 1675. Blake's perspective also reveals the establishment of a distinctive Spanish culture after four generations in Northern New Mexico including their enslavement and assimilation attempts with the pueblo peoples who inhabited the lands for centuries.

Blake's scholarly command of historical context is parallel with his dedication in describing the diverse topography, geology, flora, and fauna of the Rio Grande Del Norte and Sangre de Christo mountains. *The Franciscan* is a significant historical novel as it shares Blake's first-hand experience with the regions he explored and the culture he encountered by living among the indigenous peoples of the Southwest and Spanish colonial ancestors.

Literary and Historical Significance

In the 1950s and 1960s Blake's novels were reprinted as paperbacks with pulp fiction cover illustrations and marketed for a wide audience. One report noted 500,000 copies of each of his first two novels were reprinted in 1958 alone (Legris). While the paperbacks allowed his work to have a continuing audience, this marketing format, as well as his lack of published books after 1963, likely contributed to his diminished stature as a serious writer.

Blake's novels, however, deserve renewed attention by students of Western American culture, especially those interested in the region's historical fiction. Three important themes emerge in Blake's writings that prompt this reexamination.

First, Blake's commitment to historical authenticity stands out in the language, behavior and motivations of his characters. His years of research included extensive travels to the geographic locations for each novel's setting. Experiencing the actual terrain was a central part of his writing formula. In 1965 he estimated he had driven over 400,000 miles to survey historic sites as preparation for writing (*ISU Today*, p. 8).

Blake rejected using contemporary boundaries to identify the geography of his novels. Instead, he described landscape features such as mountains and rivers, village and place names, and trails traveled by his characters. In the first two novels, hardback copies included detailed two-page maps on front and back covers that helped readers see the West through the eyes of his characters. Missing from the paperback versions, these maps offered readers an important lens to understand the interaction between the characters and the landscape.

As part of his research, Blake immersed himself in period artifacts and spent years attempting to tell truthful stories about the West. His son Roger recalls being allowed entrance to his father's writing room in the family basement and was amazed by the sight: "The first thing I noticed was a big mound of furs on the floor. There were skins of all types—buffalo, beaver, deer, coyote and the like." Roger then noticed a rifle, "an old Hawken muzzle loader," which, according to his father, was "used by mountain men of the old west" for hunting and protection (Roger Blake 2).

An obsessive researcher, Blake developed an extensive bibliography that examined the history, culture and literature of the region. In the age prior to the internet, bibliographies were essential tools for anyone interested in historical writing. Blake estimated that his Rocky Mountain history bibliography included 50,000 references, including 2,500 chapter references, 10,000 photographic references, and 8,000 references from unindexed references (*ISU Today*, p. 8). Noting the great challenge of time, travel, and expense that research required, Blake published a "Bibliography for Westerners" in the Idaho State

University literary journal *Rendezvous* with a promise to publish more in the future.

Second, his novels offer insight into the cultural clash that emerged when a milieu of peoples were brought together in conflict over land, values, and autonomy. Blake explores the sense of entitlement embraced by many people which sometimes ended in violence. In each novel, the enemy of freedom and individuality is corruption by a larger entity, including the Spanish and Mexican governments, wealthy land barons, greedy American soldiers, radical Mormons, and frontier settlers who traffic in threats and gossip and have little respect for nature. Blake portrayed Native Americans as victims of such corruption and avoided the stereotypes of his era. On a research trip to Montana to examine Native battlefields for a future novel, Blake told his son Roger:

> The soldiers were a band of marauding, blood-thirsty killers. They murdered everybody—men, women, children—and showed no mercy. The Indians did not have a chance. The troops were killing for pleasure—there's no other way to portray it . . . . These were peaceful tribes that had lived on this land for centuries. What right did the white man have to come and take it all? (Roger Blake 11)

Third, Blake's novels explore the central narrative of the American West: the dialectical tension between individual and community (see Rushing). The individual is revered in popular culture, but usually within the larger story of a community. Blake points us to the factual tensions that many see inherent in the 19th century American West. While western pioneers took risks and honored individualism, they did so for the greater good in their view, the establishment of community, safety, and prosperity. Mountain Man culture, represented by Johnny and Tom, rejects life within the boundaries of community, and seeks to live in nature and co-exist with Native allies removed from the constraints of society and government.

Blake envisioned his novels as more than character studies of heroes and villains. In the preface to *Johnny Christmas* he wrote that while historical accuracy is important in creating context, "Of far greater importance to me is the attempt to portray characters and actions and to interpret accurately and subjectively remote American regions." He hoped that Johnny Christmas, an "individualist, free rover of mountains and deserts, symbolizes the frontiersmen who knew the West" and stands as "one American challenge to the defeatist philosophies of today."

Nearly two decades later, Blake continued to argue for the importance of his work.

Declaring that television westerns were "phony" and were "committing a crime against the West," Blake despised how popular culture presented the West. He told his nephew, Michael Blake, that he had refused several Hollywood offers to buy film rights to his novels (John Blake). Ironically, Michael Blake wrote the screenplay for *Dances with Wolves*, based in part on family stories of Forrester's grandfather John Y. F. Blake, who fought in the last "Indian" wars of the 1880s in the Arizona Territory. Hoping to correct the distortions of popular culture, Forrester Blake sought "to paint the real West in words. I want readers to build a picture in their minds of the actual spirit and color of the time and to see the characters and natural settings in a personal way" (*ISU Today*, p. 6)

Concerned about political and cultural changes in United States after World War II, Blake offered a vision of independence and vitality that he saw missing from American culture. Gleaned from years of archival research, first-hand experiences with actual "frontiersmen," and a deep commitment to authenticity, Blake's novels portray individual human struggles that create the "American West" in geographic location and in a cultural mindset linked to values, experiences, and identity. Contemporary readers will find Blake's work worthwhile at many levels and much more than an academic exercise or a repeat of old west mythology. ∎

Forrester and his father Aldrich Blake, late 1940s.

End Notes

Blake, Forrester. 1967. "Bibliography for Westerners." *Rendezvous: Journal of Arts and Letters*. 197 (2): 33-42.

Blake, Forrester. 1948. *Johnny Christmas*. New York: William Morrow.

Blake, Forrester. 1935. *Riding the Mustang Trail*. New York: Scribner's Sons.

Blake, Forrester. 1963. *The Franciscan*. New York: Doubleday.

Blake, Forrester, 1973. "The Lake." *South Dakota Review* 2 (3): 41-60.

Blake, Forrester. 1953. *Wilderness Passage*. New York: Random House.

Blake, John. May 22, 2022. Personal interview.

Blake, Roger 2013. *Ramjet: My Secret Life with PTSD*. Denver: Outskirts Press.

Davidson, J. Levette and Forrester Blake, eds. *Rocky Mountain Tales*. 1947. Norman: University of Oklahoma Press.

Legris, Maurice, 1975. "The Western World of Forrester Blake." *South Dakota Review* 13 (4): 64-77.

Lehman, Claudia Gregory and Anita Nishioka. 1964-65. "He Writes About the 'Real' Old West.' *ISU Today/Idaho State University*, Fall Winter, 5-8.

Rushing, Janice Hocker. 1983. "The Rhetoric of the American Western Myth." *Communication Monographs* 50: 14-32.

Sky, Gino. Spring 2023. Personal interview.

"Untitled" by Jinny DeFoggi. Ink on paper, 2016.

FROM THE ARCHIVE

waltzing with the captain:

Remembering

Richard Brautigan

Greg Keeler

GREG KEELER

Four Thousand Dollars

An excerpt from Waltzing with the Captain: Remembering Richard Brautigan

Editor's Note: *Forty years ago,* Trout Fishing in America *author Richard Brautigan died by his own hand in Bolinas, California. Twenty years later in 2004, Limberlost Press published Greg Keeler's memoir of his friendship with Brautigan when Brautigan moved to Montana from the Bay Area to seclude himself on a 40-acre ranch 35 miles outside Bozeman.*

While teaching writing at Montana State University, Keeler met Brautigan in 1978, invited him to do a week-long residency, and opened a wildly memorable chapter in his own life. Brautigan needed a friend with whom to talk and carouse. Attracted like a moth to the flame, Keeler became that friend and confidant, driver, and clumsy co-conspirator in a number of escapades in the trout streams, bars, and cafés, and along the back roads of Montana. Together they waltzed through many late nights, until Brautigan returned to Bolinas in 1984.

Keeler recalls his times with Brautigan with haunting clarity. The book is illustrated with photographs and the author's cartoon-like drawings at the head of every chapter, Waltzing with the Captain *is darkly funny and poignant in its revealing portrait of an important contemporary American writer, and in its candid story of an often-tested friendship between two poets.*

Forty years after Brautigan's death, we thought it might be worth excerpting a chapter of Keeler's memoir in this edition. "Four Thousand Dollars" is the first chapter of the book.

Copies of Waltzing with the Captain: Remembering Richard Brautigan *are available at* **www.limberlostpress.com**.

*Painting of Greg Keeler and Richard Brautigan by Greg Keeler.
From an original photo by Linda Best, 1982.*

GREG KEELER: REMEMBERING RICHARD BRAUTIGAN

hen I first started teaching at Montana State University in 1975, I had heard rumors about Richard's presence in Paradise Valley, around thirty-five miles from Bozeman, but he was just sort of a larger-than-life fog in my mind, blown in from San Francisco where I used to stand stupidly pensive in front of the public library from which I figured he got a lot of ideas like *The Abortion*. It wasn't until I found out where his house was that I actually began to sense a tangible presence. Once I drove by his big blue mail box then ran back and stuck a note in the outside latch asking if he ever might want to come and read in Bozeman. But no response.

In 1977, Gary Snyder came to Bozeman for a week-long residency. While he was here, Marge, the English Department secretary said that Richard had called and wanted Gary to come out and visit him. Before going, Gary told me a little about Richard. He said they were friends, that Richard used to be a Tokay alcoholic when he was a teenager, that he (like Gary) had married a Japanese woman, and that he (Gary) was going to try to convince Richard to get more involved with the Montana community (since Gary was and still is very much interested in community).

When Gary returned, he said that Richard drank a whole lot of whisky, and at a party, he had passed around a mouse trap and people took turns sticking their fingers in it and trying to pull them back before it snapped. Snyder has a way with understatement. It wasn't until about a year later that I got another note from the secretary. This time, Richard had invited me out to his place along with two students from the M.S.U. Student Programs Board. Community involvement moves in mysterious ways. As I read "bring wine" at the bottom of the note, I didn't know the magnitude of the tradition that I was to enter. The Captain wanted a residency at M.S.U.

So there the three of us were, standing on Richard's porch, holding a bottle of Almaden Chablis and shivering in November snow. Richard welcomed us in, sporting a torn work shirt, blue jeans, and cowboy boots. I glanced down at my blue jeans, cowboy boots and torn work shirt and had a slight premonition. (At one point in our friendship, I called a stray cat on his place a doppleganger and Richard asked me what that meant.) Akiko, his wife was beautiful and appropriately inscrutable. As the evening progressed, the Captain called Flaubert a sack of shit and William Stafford (one of my favorite people and poets) a cunt (because he had told Richard that his children enjoyed Richard's books). And after a while, he picked up his long-haired Siamese cat and threw it at my face. I must have responded with appropriate gullible naivete because he calmed down after a while, probably realizing that I didn't fit his preconception of an English prof.

    He was very gracious to the students and made them both feel a little embarrassed when they tried to start talking business. "Let's not worry about that stuff yet; you're in the country now. Relax." So we all relaxed and ate some very good spaghetti which he had fixed. Aki let us know that she was interested in finding Japanese friends in Bozeman and maybe even in going to school a little. Late that night, when the students were about to drift off, Richard finally said, "Welp, let's have a ball park figure." The students looked at each other and one of them mumbled "Four...." "Four thousand it is," said Richard. The two students gulped, and that was that. Richard would come in April of '79 for a week-long residency.

    When we left, Richard insisted that we take the Trail Creek road home. (We had come via the interstate to Livingston and the two-lane blacktop down Paradise Valley.) Trail Creek is a shortcut that goes up over a dip in the mountains between his house and the Bozeman Pass. Depending on the season, it is gravel, mud, snow, ice, or oiled. Fortunately, the snow hadn't done much and the road was still gravel at that time. Richard and Aki accompanied us to where Trail Creek converged with the two-lane and we bid our first farewell. The Captain liked those back roads. In Paradise Valley, he liked the East River Road which was the old highway on the other side of the Yellowstone River from the newer two-lane. But, as I found out later, the Trail Creek road was Richard's favorite.

    In the following summers, I would see why as I came up over the pass on that road and saw the bluing Absoroka Mountains with vast foothills, the winding Yellowstone, and in the exact middle of the panorama, Richard's bright red barn. It has now been years since he shot himself, and I still have lots of trouble with my emotions when I drive down into Paradise Valley from Trail Creek.

GREG KEELER: REMEMBERING RICHARD BRAUTIGAN

The long view of Richard's house and barn from the Trail Creek road.

A week later, my wife, Judy, and I had the two students, Richard and Aki over for dinner. The Captain leaned back in our cheap wicker K-Mart love seat and fell over backwards. As he drank more and more, he started talking in a small Oriental voice and getting very serious. I would later start calling this late night voice the Imperial Mode. At the time, I thought it was a funny voice, a silly pretentious voice. But I was to find that it was a very sad voice.

Aki laid some toothpicks on our coffee table in the shape of a stick-figure dog with a pointed face. Richard said he wanted to find out how our left brains worked, then put a bottle cap behind the dog and called it the moon. "Make the dog look at the moon," said Aki. Richard nodded puckishly. After several embarrassing minutes of feeling like red-socked, hushpuppied, left-brain scientist nerds, we gave up, and Richard tilted the two toothpicks forming the pointed head perpendicular to the table and said "See, now he can see the moon."

Soon the conversation turned to fishing, and Richard said that the winter fishing was coming soon and did I know about the tiny black nymphs that the cutthroat behind his place on the Yellowstone went crazy over when there was slush in the water? I said I didn't but showed him my favorite wet fly. He said, "That's it...with a minor change," and he took some fingernail scissors and cut the hackles off of it. "There you have it," he said imperially.

Later I found out he had caught so many trout with that nymph, he sent Aki trudging through the snow with armloads of fish to give to their neighbors, Gatz and Marian Hjortsberg.

Around midnight, Richard said, "Any more liquor." I had already rustled up odds and ends of Vodka, Gin, and Canadian whisky (after finishing the wine and bourbon). Now everything was all gone. Time to go," said Richard. Judy wasn't amused, and Akiko didn't seem too thrilled about the exit, but the students were almost asleep and Aki had to drive Richard all the way home over the pass. To my knowledge, Richard never drove. ∎

THE LAST WORD

"George Orwell" by Tom Callos. Linocut, 11 x 14 inches.

CLAY MORGAN

Considerations

The philosopher's job is to clarify.

Some are born lucky. Some can get lucky. Some can't get a break.

The present is already past, and already too late.

Space is not a place. Space is not a thing. Space is what is between things. It is not distance. It is Time.

There are always two sides to a schizophrenic.

Sleeping dogs never lie.

To see inward, look outward.

Life is just a theory, much like evolution.

HOW TO SUCCEED WITHOUT EVEN TRYING
    Be born rich and good looking,
    Tall, athletic and talented,
    Clever and charming and lucky,
    And cunning.

The present is the past, forgetting.

Believing is pretending.

I have nothing against religion, except the religion part.

An afterlife was humanity's greatest invention. Heaven was genius. Hell already existed.

Why does wizened not mean wiser?

THE LIMBERLOST REVIEW

A sound I was. An echo I am.
Am again and again.
Am again.

I can't be crazy if I think I am crazy.

Time is one motion measured against some other motion.

What if the speed of light is actually the speed of time?

Nothing is faster than time. Or slower.

Love is emotion. True love is behavior.

Reality is a two-way street.

Time is no arrow. Time is a boomerang.

Sehewoki'I Newenee'an Katete is the new name for Squaw Butte in Idaho. I hope that clears things up.

For a toddler, happiness is joy; for the young, anticipation; for the old, gratitude.

Happiness has a short memory. Misery never forgets.

Friendship is not earned. And it can't be spent.

Those most curious enjoy their ignorance.

Nothing was never created nor destroyed.

Thinking about thinking is circular reasoning.

Heaven is a dream, dreamed by the dead.

THE LAST WORD: CLAY MORGAN

If there were two of me, we might become friends.

Philosophers can be wrong, and they are.

Most of my life is past, so why live in the present?

All stories are retellings, retold.

People with high IQ scores believe in IQ tests.

The difference between philosophers and physicists is that physicists can measure what they do not know.

The business of America is media.

All politics are personal.

Nothing lasts forever, especially forever.

Reality is not an illusion. Reality is imagination.

Strong memories are often rehearsed and reworked.

Gravity isn't gravity, and never was.

No one has seen nothing, yet.

Distance is only a local concept.

Shooting fish in a barrel isn't as easy as some people think.

Pain is physical consciousness.

Emotion is self-consciousness.

The senses make our emotions feel real.

"Epitaph"
Deeds undid
Thoughts unthought
Words unwrit
Here I rot

Can a dirty mind be brainwashed?

Poetry changes how I misunderstand everything.

The more I know, the more surprised I get.

If I could think as vividly as I dream, and dream as logically as I think, I might never wake up.

Emotion is the body, thinking.

We are born loving. We learn to hate.

If there really were such a thing as evolution, one might expect better outcomes.

Intellectual. Noun. Singular. A word that should always have quotation marks around it.

Space and Time are the same thing, just not in the same space or at the same time.

"Science Is Fiction!" Christian fundamentalist bumper sticker.

Should the study of story be called Fiction Science?

THE LAST WORD: CLAY MORGAN

If a tree falls in the wilderness and there is one there to hear it, there will still be a sound, just no meaning.

The deepest message is always emotion.

Consciousness makes sense of the senses.

Historians pretend to predict the past.

Every gift is an obligation.

People who sleep alone never snore. ∎

"John Steinbeck" by Tom Callos. Linocut, 11 x 14 inches.

CONTRIBUTORS

LIMBERLOST LETTERPRESS

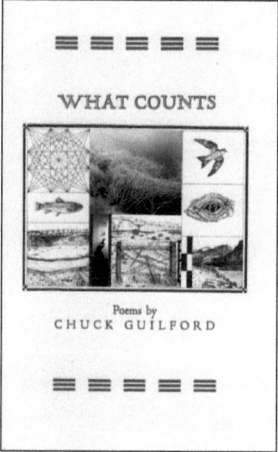

www.limberlostpress.com

CONTRIBUTORS

SHERMAN ALEXIE has published 26 books including his recent memoir *You Don't Have to Say You Love Me* (Little, Brown). He has won the PEN/Faulkner Award for Fiction, the PEN/Malamud Award for Short Fiction, a PEN/Hemingway Citation for Best First Fiction, and the National Book Award for Young People's Literature. Born a Spokane/Coeur d'Alene Indian, Alexie grew up in Wellpinit, Washington, on the Spokane Indian Reservation. He's been an urban Indian since 1994 and lives in Seattle with his family. *A Memory of Elephants,* a letterpress-printed, limited edition chapbook of his poems, was published in the summer of 2020 by Limberlost Press.

KENT ANDERSON is a U.S. Special Forces veteran who served in Vietnam and a former police officer who served in Portland, Oregon, and Oakland, California. He was a protégé of Hollywood director John Milius and wrote screenplays for New Line Cinema for five years. He's the author of several widely praised novels, including *Sympathy for the Devil* (Doubleday, 1987), *Night Dogs* (Dennis McMillian Publications, 1996), as well as a compilation of writings, *Liquor, Guns & Ammo*. His latest novel is *Green Sun* (Mullholland Books, an imprint of Little, Brown, 2018). He lives in New Mexico.

DAN ARMSTRONG is a novelist and publisher of *Mud City Press,* an online magazine focusing on the environment and sustainable agriculture out of Eugene, Oregon. He has published thirteen novels and a collection of short stories through Mud City. His latest, *Quicksand,* published in 2022. He's served as the archivist for the Southern Willamette Valley Bean and Grain Project, on the board of directors for the Lane County Farmers' Market, and as a member of the Lane County Food Policy Council. He won the *Wayne Morris Now Award* for community service in 2010 for his work as a farm advocate.

KEN BABBS, Ohio born and bred, attended graduate school at Stanford University, where in 1958 he met Ken Kesey, Wendell Berry, and other luminary writing fellows in Wallace Stegner's famous writing seminar. He spent five years in the Marine Corps as a helicopter pilot with his last year in Vietnam. In 1964, he "got off the copter and onto the bus" with Kesey and the other Merry Pranksters for their famous cross-country tour to New York, chronicled by Tom Wolfe in *The Electric Kool-Aid Acid Test*

and many other literary and countercultural histories. He shared 43 years of "collaborations and shenanigans" with Kesey, doing shows, co-authoring books, co-editing six issues of *Spit in the Ocean*, and writing a much-praised novel of Vietnam, *Who Shot the Water Buffalo?* He and his wife, a retired English teacher, live on a small farm in the foothills of the Cascade Mountains.

PAUL BEEBE is a retired journalist. He worked for newspapers in Idaho, Pennsylvania, Colorado, and Utah. He lives in Salt Lake City, close to the entrance to Big Cottonwood Canyon, at the interface of the Rocky Mountains and the Great Basin, and a short drive to the Colorado Plateau. He holds degrees in English literature and agriculture, a strange mixture that for him has formed a bridge between the ordinary and the All.

GRAHAM BLAIR is an artist and graphic designer based in St. John's, Newfoundland, specializing in woodcut printmaking for more than 20 years. Holding degrees in cultural anthropology and museum studies from the University of British Columbia, he initially moved from Vancouver to Newfoundland to pursue a doctoral degree but found a place in the St. John's arts community in 2006. He produces his woodcuts by hand using hardwood blocks and a combination of European and Japanese printing techniques with an emphasis on integrating local folklore and history.

ANNE BLEDSOE is a poet and librarian living in the high desert of western Colorado with her husband and son. Her work conveys an interest in the natural world and attention to the everyday.

MARY CLEARMAN BLEW has written or edited 15 books of fiction and nonfiction. The University of Nebraska Press has published four of her novels, *Jackalope Dreams* (2008, winner of the Western Heritage Award), *Ruby Dreams of Janis Joplin* (2018), *Sweep Out the Ashes* (2019), and her latest, *Waltzing Montana* (2021). Her short fiction collection *Runaway* won the Pacific Northwest Booksellers Award, as did her memoir *All But the Waltz: Essays on a Montana Family* (Viking, 1991). She's also the author of a memoir, *This Is Not the Ivy League*. She lives in Moscow, Idaho.

JAN BOLES is an active photographer. Born in Missouri and reared in Texas, he moved to Idaho in 1963 following a year at the Art Center School in Los Angeles. He graduated from The College of Idaho in 1965 and over the years has worked as commercial photographer, publicist, graphic designer, photojournalist, teacher, writer, welder, and artist. Since 1985 jurors have selected his photos for seven Boise Art Museum Biennial and Triennial competitions. In 2016 he received the Idaho Humanities Council award for Outstanding Achievement in the Humanities. In 2018 he retired as director of the Robert E. Smylie Archives at the College of Idaho, a post he held since 1997.

ROD BURKS graduated from the University of Wisconsin-Madison in 1979 with a degree in Art Education. He taught in Kalispell, Montana, for one year, then accepted a position with the Herrett Center at the College of Southern Idaho as an Exhibits Curator. Eventually he joined the family Agriculture and Construction Equipment business in Twin Falls and Caldwell, where he's worked for the past thirty-seven years. After a 40-year lull and encouraged by friendships with numerous artists from the James Castle House Residency Program, he began painting again in 2019.

BOB BUSHNELL was raised in Wilder, Idaho, and attended the University of Idaho, Stanford University, and the University of Washington School of Law. He returned to Boise in 1972 to practice law before becoming a full-time businessman and a single parent, nourished by a membership in the Boise Great Books Club for four decades. He now devotes his time to reading, writing, and cultivating old and new friendships.

TOM CALLOS says he uses relief printmaking "to memorialize authors, poets, scientists, artists, and activists, people who inspire me (and millions of others), as a practice of mindfulness, focus, and meditation." He's spent 50 years learning, practicing, and teaching the martial arts. Making art, he says, requires the same kind of awareness and concentration required in high level martial arts training. He's currently working on making 1,000 portraits to master the printmaking process. See his work at **www.tomcallos.com**.

BONNIE JO CAMPBELL is the bestselling author of *Mothers, Tell Your Daughters, Once Upon a River,* and *American Salvage,* among other works of fiction. She is a National Book Award finalist, a Guggenheim Fellow, and winner of the 2019 Mark Twain Award. W.W. Norton published her new novel, *The Waters,* in January of 2024. She is six foot tall and rides a donkey.

KURT CASWELL was born in Fairbanks, Alaska, and grew up in the Cascade Range in Oregon. He has worked as a teacher in Hokkaido, Japan; on the Navajo Reservation; and at schools in Arizona, California, and Wyoming. Currently, he is professor of creative writing and literature in the Honors College at Texas Tech University in Lubbock, Texas. He's published several nonfiction works, including *Laika's Window: The Legacy of a Soviet Space Dog, Getting to Grey Owl: Journeys on Four Continents, In the Sun's House: My Year Teaching on the Navajo Reservation,* and *Inside Passage,* which won the 2008 River Teeth Literary Nonfiction Book Prize. His latest is *Iceland Summer: Travels along the Ring Road* (Trinity University Press, 2023).

MARK CLEMENS has worked as an editor and designer of college publications, reporter and photographer for newspapers over many years, as well as a creative writing teacher. His stories and poems appear in *Mountain Gazette, The North American Review, Northern Colorado Review, Gray's Sporting Journal, Talking River Review, The Coachella Review* and now *The Limberlost Review.* Born in Missouri and raised in Iowa, he received an MFA from the University of Montana in 1976 and now lives with his wife Karen on the Olympic Peninsula.

JINNY DeFOGGI (1938-2022) was dedicated to her art for more than a half-century, first encouraged by mentor artists and friends Ray and Lorna Obermayr at Idaho State University in the 1960s. With Dennis DeFoggi, her husband of five decades, and her daughter Laurel, she was a great friend and encourager to many writers, artists, readers, thinkers, and creative believers and welcomed them into their home and their fold. Their door was always open. She and Dennis had many shows together, and both exhibited at the Boise Art Museum's juried Idaho Triennial shows of outstanding work by the state's contemporary artists.

CHRIS DeVORE lives in Mountain Home, Idaho, with his wife, Hannah, and their three teenagers. He is the Executive Director of the Mountain Home Arts Council, Grants Manager for Boise's Cabin Center for Readers & Writers, and Editor of *The Whistle Pig* literary journal. He grew up in Polson, Montana, and earned his literature degree from the University of Puget Sound. While writing the story in this edition, he was reading *The Lincoln Highway* by Amor Towles and Louise Glück's *Winter Recipes from the Collective.*

VIRGIL DiBIASE, the son of Italian immigrants, grew up in the woods of rural northeast Ohio. He grew up speaking Italian in his home and speaking English at school. He thought every kid his age spoke Italian at home. His father was a photographer, and when he was 10 years old, he accompanied his father to the dark room and couldn't believe how an image could magically appear on paper before his eyes. He went on to medical school and is a practicing neurologist now living in the woods of rural northwest Indiana.

JIM DODGE is an 80-year-old widower who lives with his dog, dividing his time between an isolated ranch in the wilds of northern California's Gualala River headwaters in coastal Sonoma County and the semi-civilization of the Manila Peninsula between Eureka and Arcata in Humbolt County. His books include the story *Fup* (Simon & Schuster, 1984; Heyday Books, 2014), the novels *Fade Away* (Atlantic Monthly Press, 1987) and *Stone Junction* (Grove/Atlantic, 1990), a collection of poems, *Rain on the River* (Canongate, 2002), and assorted chapbooks, broadsides, essays, and screeds. His most recent letterpress-printed chapbook of poems, *Always Something*, was letterpress printed in a limited edition by Limberlost Press in the fall of 2023.

TED DYER received his MA in English from Washington State University and taught 20 years as a composition instructor for the College of Southern Idaho extension service in Blaine County, Idaho. He also taught literature and jazz history for several years for the Idaho State University Department of Continuing Education. He also worked extensively as a speaker on Ernest Hemingway and Ezra Pound for the Idaho Humanities Council, which has been a moveable feast in its own way.

JACKIE ELO is a Boise-based graphic designer and a wine connoisseur whose passions have merged in her design of wine bottle labels for numerous European wines. She currently co-owns Amphora Wine Company and surrounds herself "with doers, teachers, travelers, artists, drinkers, eaters, and others thirsty for life." Growing up in Bend, Oregon, she is at home in the outdoors, and is an experienced rock climber and marathon runner. In addition to playing guitar and bass in a rock & roll band, her artwork has been part of group and one-woman shows where she's displayed her painting, printmaking, and photography.

REBECCA EVANS is a memoirist, poet, essayist and instructor of frequent writing and empowerment workshops. An adjunct instructor at Boise State University, she teaches teens in the juvenile system. She's also the co-host of *Writer to Writer* on Radio Boise. She is disabled, a Veteran, a Jew, a mother, a worrier, and more. She's earned two MFAs from the University of Nevada, Reno. Her memoir-in-verse, *Tangled by Blood*, is available from Moon Tide Press. Read more at **www.rebeccaevanswriter.com**.

GARY GILDNER's collection of personal essays, *How I Married Michele*, is out from BkMk Press. *Calling from the Scaffold*, his ninth collection of poems, was published by University of Pittsburgh Press in 2022. *The Capital of Kansas City* (BkMk, 2016) is his fifth and most recent book of stories. He has given readings at the Library of Congress, Shakespeare & Company in Paris, the 92nd St. Y and Manhattan Theater Club in New York, and on the ferry crossing Lake Michigan. He lives outside Tucson.

SAMUEL GREEN's most recent collection of poems is *Disturbing the Light* (Carnegie Mellon University Press, 2020). With his wife Sally, he has been co-editor of the award-winning Brooding Heron Press on Waldron Island, Washington, since 1982. He has been a visiting professor at multiple colleges and universities, and he has taught as a visiting Poet-in-the-Schools for nearly 50 years. In 2008 he was selected as the first Poet Laureate of Washington State. Honors include an NEA Fellowship in Poetry, an Artist Trust Fellowship in Literature, a Washington State Book Award in Poetry, and an Honorary Doctorate from Seattle University. From 1966-1970 he was in the U.S. Coast Guard, with service in Vietnam.

SHAUN T. GRIFFIN is the co-founder and development director of the Community Chest, a rural social justice agency serving northwestern Nevada since 1991. Southern Utah University Press released his *Anthem for a Burnished Land*, a memoir, in 2016. *This Is What the Desert Surrenders: New and Selected Poems* came out from Black Rock Press in 2012, and Limberlost Press released his letterpressed chapbook of poems *Driving the Tender Desert Home* in 2014. His most recent books include a collection of essays, *Because the Light Will Not Forgive Me* (University of Nevada Press in 2019), and *The Monastery of Stars* (poems, Kelsay Books 2020). He lives in Virginia City, Nevada, in the shadow of the former home of novelist Walter Van Tilburg Clark.

JIM HEPWORTH's poems, essays, reviews, and interviews have appeared in *Big Sky Journal, Distinctly Montana, Fly Fish Journal, Outside Magazine,* and *The Paris Review.* He has been a recipient of a creative writing fellowship from the Idaho Commission on the Arts and a research fellowship from the Idaho Humanities Council. His books include *Stealing Glances: Three Interviews with Wallace Stegner* (University of New Mexico Press), *Resist Much, Obey Little: Some Notes on Edward Abbey* (Sierra Club, coedited with Greg McNamee), and *The Stories that Shape Us: Nineteen Women Write about the West* (Norton, co-edited with Teresa Jordan). He and his wife, Tanya Gonzales, divide their time between Lewiston, Idaho, and Santa Fe, New Mexico.

GEOF HEWITT lives in Vermont, where he is the state's reigning poetry slam champion. In 1975 Rodale Press commissioned him to travel the country, interviewing self-employed people. Shortly after *Working for Yourself* was published, he took a job with the Vermont Arts Council and later for the Vermont Department of Education. He's the author of a number of books of poetry and still teaches as a visiting writer-in-the-schools and for an undergraduate B.A. program. His latest publications are *The Perfect Heart: Selected & New Poems* (Mayapple Press) and a chapbook, *Affordable Poems, Alternative Facts.*

JIM HEYNEN was born on a farm in northwest Iowa and received his first eight years of education at one of the state's last one-room school houses, Welcome #3. He's the author of several collections of poems, including *A Suitable Church* and *Standing Naked* (poetry), and several collections of stories, including *You Know What Is Right, The One-Room Schoolhouse,* and *The Man Who Kept Cigars in His Cap.* His most recent collection of stories is *The Youngest Boy* (Holy Cow! Press, 2021). He's the former Writer-in-Residence at St. Olaf College in Northfield, Minnesota. A forthcoming collection of poems, *April, Come She Will* is due out in early 2024.

JAY JOHNSON is a lawyer and writer working in Moscow, Idaho. After college, he lived in Oregon, Colorado, Washington, and California before settling in Idaho in 1995. He repaired automobiles and logged for twenty-five years prior to law school. Most of his law practice is criminal defense, generally for indigent clients. His fiction has appeared recently in *The Limberlost Review* and *Talking River Review.*

RICK JOHNSON is a recovering non-profit executive director, running the Idaho Conservation League for twenty-four years. Securing a wilderness designation for the Boulder and White Cloud Mountains in south-central, Idaho, which brought him to a signing ceremony in the Oval Office of the White House with President Barack Obama and receiving the City Club of Boise "Stimpson Award for Civic Engagement." He can now be found on a few stages with guitar in hand, or out roaming with his wife Roberta in the van, or back in Boise working to restore the Snake River to protect Idaho salmon.

WILLIAM JOHNSON is Professor Emeritus of English at Lewis-Clark State College in Lewiston, Idaho, a former Writer-in-Residence for the state of Idaho, author of *A River without Banks*, a collection of essays from Oregon State University Press, and several collections of poetry, including, most recently, *Dogwood* (Limberlost Press). He lives with his wife Cheryl and their cat Manu in a house surrounded by trees, flanked by the Lewiston hills and sky.

DARYL JONES is a former Idaho Writer-in-Residence and recipient of a Creative Writing Fellowship from the National Endowment for the Arts. His book *Someone Going Home Late* won the Natalie Ornish Poetry Award from the Texas Institute for Letters. He strayed from the muse for a score of years while serving as Provost and Vice President for Academic Affairs at Boise State University, but he returned to writing following his retirement. Since then, his poems have appeared in *The American Journal of Poetry*, *The Gettysburg Review*, *New Ohio Review*, *Poet Lore*, *The Southern Review*, and elsewhere.

GREG KEELER is the author of two memoirs, *Waltzing with the Captain: Remembering Richard Brautigan* (Limberlost Press) and *Trash Fish: A Life* (Counterpoint Press), and eight collections of poetry, including, most recently, *The Bluebird Run* (Elk River Books). He writes, paints, fishes, and composes irreverent songs in Bozeman, Montana, where he taught in the English Department of Montana State University for 30 years.

GROVE KOGER is the author of *When the Going Was Good: A Guide to the 99 Best Narratives of Travel, Exploration, and Adventure*; Assistant Editor of *Deus Loci: The Lawrence Durrell Journal*; and former Assistant Editor of *Art Patron* magazine. Recently he's published fiction in *Roi Fainéant* and *Danse Macabre* and nonfiction in *Amsterdam Quarterly* and *History Magazine*. He blogs about travel and related subjects at **worldenoughblog.wordpress.com/author/gkoger/**.

PAUL LaPRISE was born and raised in Sun Valley, Idaho, and spent 28 years in professional and educational theatre before shifting careers and moving into project management in energy reduction. He holds undergraduate and graduate degrees from Idaho State University and University of Maryland. He's taught at Idaho State, University of Maryland, Marietta College, Dana College, the University of Colorado, Zane State University, and Columbus State College. Retired in Columbus, Ohio, he reads, gardens, plays a little guitar on the weekends, attends a dance class for Parkinson's, and stays in the moment.

DAVID LEE is the author of more than two dozen books of poetry. His collection *News from Down to the Café* was nominated for the Pulitzer Prize in 1999, and in 2001 he was a finalist for the position of United States Poet Laureate. He served as Utah's inaugural Poet Laureate from 1997-2002 and later received the Utah Governor's Award for lifetime achievement in the arts. His first book of poems, *The Porcine Legacy*, was published by Copper Canyon Press in 1974, and he is the subject of a PBS documentary *The Pig Poet*. A former seminary student, semi-pro baseball player, and hog farmer, he served for 30 years as Chairman of the Department of Language and Literature at Southern Utah University.

KRISTA LUKAS is the author of a poetry collection, *Fans of My Unconscious*, poems from which were selected for *The Best American Poetry 2006* and *The Writer's Almanac*. Her stories, essays, and interviews have been published in *New Millenium Writings*, *Jewish Women's Literary Annual*, and *Los Angeles Review of Books*. She has read her work and taught workshops in the United States and Europe.

ALBERTA MAYO explores beauty in the ordinary through photography, drawing, and collage. Her early interest in the natural sciences and biology became the foundation for how she sees and engages with the world.

MAUREEN McCOY has been a part-time resident of Taos for many years and has hiked and biked the high country of northern New Mexico. She also has been a professor at Cornell University. She is the author of four novels and, more recently, a slew of personal essays, one of which, "Vickie's Pour House: A Soldier's Peace" was a National Magazine Award finalist. Her work has been included in two volumes of monologues for actors. She is currently writing short stories and looks forward to returning to a stone cottage artist's residency in the west of Ireland.

RON McFARLAND retired from the University of Idaho English department in 2018 after "47 years of blithe self-indulgence." He's the author of 20 books and served as Idaho's first State Writer-in-Residence (1984-1985). Current projects include a collection of poems tentatively titled *A Variable Sense of Things* and a book-length study of the poetry & prose of Chicano writer Gary Soto. His most recent book is a biography of Colonel Edward J. Steptoe (1815-1865), *Edward J. Steptoe and the Indian Wars* (2016).

CHARLOTTE MEARS received her MFA in writing from the University of Arkansas, where she studied with John Clellon Holmes, James Whitehead, and Miller Williams. She has taught writing and literature in eight colleges and universities, received ten awards for her poetry, and published two books of poems, *Sweet Air* (2013) and *Winds of New York* (2014). As often as she can be, Mears is in New Orleans at the Maple Leaf reading series, the longest-running poetry reading series in the South. She currently lives in Madison, Mississippi.

JAN MINICH is the author of two books of poems, *Wild Roses* (Mayapple Press, 2017) and *The Letters of Silver Dollar* (City Art Press, 2002), as well as two chapbooks. His work has been published in several anthologies, including *New Poets of the American West,* and in many poetry journals. He lives in Wellington, Utah, with his wife Nancy Takacs, and cruises Lake Superior in a small boat during the summers. A new book of his poems, *Coming into Grace Harbor* is available from Broadstone Books.

ALAN MINSKOFF moved to Boise, Idaho, from New York in 1972. He lives in Boise and teaches journalism at the College of Idaho. The author of *Idaho Wine Country* and *The Idaho Traveler* (both from Caxton Press), he's also published two chapbooks of poetry from Limberlost Press, *Blue Ink Runs Out on a Partly Cloudy Day* and *Point Blank*. His essays have appeared in *Harper's,* the anthology *Where the Morning Light's Still Blue,* and elsewhere. He reviews audiobooks for *AudioFile Magazine* and can be heard one week a month on its "Behind the Mic" podcast.

CLAY MORGAN is the author of four novels, including *Aura* (Confluence Press, 1983), *Santiago and the Drinking Party* (Viking, 1992, winner of the Pacific Northwest Booksellers Award), and two for young readers, *The Boy Who Spoke Dog* (Dutton, 2003, winner of the VOYA Award), and *The Boy Who Returned from the Sea* (Dutton, 2007). He's also written and co-edited two photo-essay books, *Idaho Unbound* (with Steve Mitchell, 1995), and *Boise: The City and Its People* (with Steve Bly, 1993). He lives with his wife Barbara in Boise, Idaho.

BARBARA OLIC-HAMILTON—originally from a suburb of Chicago where city lights bleached the night sky—moved to the dark skies of rural Idaho in 1976 and then to Boise in 1980. After a long career as a secondary English teacher, she worked as an adjunct instructor at Boise State University and a part-time bookseller. She has spent 17 years in the same book club and 38 years in the same writing group. Recent publications include essays in *BookWomen* and *The Limberlost Review* (2022), and poetry in *Ireland: You Can't Miss It* and *Moon: Writers in the Attic* (2022).

RILEY SOPHIA PENALUNA currently resides in Corvallis, Oregon, though her queer heart belongs to the Salish Sea and the North Cascades. Her bona fides are few, but she has dabbled as a theatre artist and graphic designer, among other creative pursuits. These days she is mainly occupied with making linocut prints of weird little guys at her wobbly kitchen table and posting them to Instagram as **@studio.rsp**.

WILL PETERSON owns Walrus & Carpenter Books in Pocatello, Idaho. An active novelist, poet, and musician throughout his life, he is currently completing the third book —after 20 years—of his only novel trilogy about a man searching for the meaning of his life and justice in the constantly changing environment. He initiated the Rocky Mountain Writers Festival in 1990 and is the lyricist, vocalist, and lead rhythm guitarist for the *Wolverines*, who play every week in Old Town, Pocatello.

MARGARET PETTIS lives in northern Utah. She was a wilderness ranger in Idaho's Sawtooth Wilderness Area before teaching high school English. She is the author of *In the Temple of the Stars* and the nonfiction *Back Roads of Utah*.

JOHN REMBER has lived in Idaho's Sawtooth Valley since 1953. He is the author of three collections of short stories, *Coyote in the Mountains* (Limberlost Press), *Cheerleaders from Gomorrah: Tales from the Lycra Archipelago* (Confluence Press), and *Sudden Death Over Time* (Wordcraft of Oregon); a memoir, *Traplines: On Going Home to Sawtooth Valley* (Alfred Knopf); and a book about writing, *MFA in a Box: A Why to Write Book* (Dream of Things). Another nonfiction work, *A Hundred Little Pieces on the End of the World* was published in 2020 by the University of New Mexico Press, a book that *Population Bomb* author Paul Erlich said was "A brilliantly written, deeply thoughtful, and even humorous book about a very dark topic."

BETTY RODGERS began exploring the world through a lens at a young age, influenced by her father who was a photographer for the Air Force during World War II. She remembers the allure of the red lightbulb in the temporary dark room he would set up in the family bathroom. Betty's images now live in homes, offices, and publications around the country. In 2010, she added documentary filmmaking to her repertoire by partnering with her husband, Ken, to create two award-winning films: *Bravo! Common Men, Uncommon Valor*, and then more recently, *I Married the War*. Both inspiring films have received accolades for bringing to light the individual human cost of war.

KEN RODGERS is a poet, writer and filmmaker who lives in Arizona. Both a Pushcart Prize nominee and a Best American Short Stories nominee, Ken's stories, poems and essays have appeared in a number of fine journals. His published books include a collection of short stories, *The Gods of Angkor Wat* (BK Publications), and two collections of poems, *Trench Dining* (Running Wolf Press) and *Passenger Pigeons* (Jaxon Press.) Along with his wife Betty, Ken co-directed and co-produced *Bravo! Common Men, Uncommon Valor*, a feature-length documentary film about Ken's company of Marines at the Siege of Khe Sanh in 1968. Betty and Ken's latest documentary, *I Married the War*, is about caregivers to combat veterans. Ken blogs fairly regularly at **KennethRodgers.com**.

BRANT SHORT grew up in southern Idaho and studied history and communications at Idaho State University. He later earned a doctorate from Indiana University and taught Communication Studies for 26 years at Northern Arizona University. His scholarship has focused on environmental issues and in recent years he has turned to creative expression, with poems published in *The Limberlost Review, Back Channels, Roanoke Review, New Plains Review*, and several other publications.

GINO SKY is the author of the novels *Appaloosa Rising* (Doubleday, 1980) and *Coyote Silk* (North Atlantic Books, 1987), the story collection *Near the Postcard Beautiful* (Floating Ink Books, 1994), and a dozen collections of poetry, including *Wild Dog Days* (Limberlost Press, 2015). He was an editor of the legendary 1960s literary magazine *Wild Dog* that began in Pocatello, Idaho, and moved on to Salt Lake City, and then to the Haight-Ashbury district of San Francisco prior to the 1967 Summer of Love, publishing many of the great poets of the day. He and his wife Barbara Jensen currently live in Salt Lake City. An interview with Gino appears in the 2020 edition of *The Limberlost Review*.

NILE SPEARS was a native of Southern Idaho but also called the Midwest his home. He attended Idaho State University with an interest in the Liberal Arts. He worked a variety of jobs from trucking to construction to finance, enjoyed oral history, and collected stories of the early American West for more than forty years. He passed away in January of 2024.

KIM STAFFORD is a former Poet Laureate of the State of Oregon (2018-2020). He grew up in Oregon, Iowa, Indiana, California, and Alaska, following his parents as they taught and travelled throughout the West. He is the author of more than a dozen books of poetry and prose, and the director of the Northwest Writing Institute and the William Stafford Center at Lewis & Clark College in Portland, where he has taught since 1979. He has worked as a visiting writer at a host of colleges and schools. His most recent letterpress-printed chapbook of poetry *How to Sleep Cold: Seventeen Poems and Related Writing Prompts from the Outpost Writing Workshop at Billy Meadows* is available from Limberlost Press.

SUSAN SWETNAM retired from Idaho State University's English Department in 2013 to focus on her writing and take up a second-act career as a massage therapist specializing in work with the elderly and hospice patients. She's the author of many articles and essays in national magazines (*Gourmet, Mademoiselle, St. Anthony Messenger*), regional and little magazines, and anthologies. She's published fourteen books, including the 2019 National Catholic Book Award-winning *In the Mystery's Shadow: Reflections on Caring for the Elderly and Dying* (Collegeville MN: Liturgical Press), and the recent *Knitting as a Spiritual Path* (Chicago: ACTA, 2022). The widow of poet and teacher Ford Swetnam, she lives on the edge of the Caribou National Forest south of Pocatello.

NANCY TAKACS's fourth full-length book of poems *Dearest Water* was published by Mayapple Press in 2022. A letterpress-printed chapbook of her poems, *Juniper,* is available from Limberlost Press. She is the inaugural Poet Laureate of Utah's art hub: Helper City, where she directs the Steamboat Mountain reading series. She lives most of the year in Wellington, Utah, and spends time near the Apostle Islands National Lakeshore in Wisconsin, where she enjoys walking the woods and beaches near Lake Superior.

SARAH TRUDEAU is the artist behind Fox and Lune Studio, a small solo printmaking business she started with her husband and young son a few years ago in her home town of Plymouth, Massachusetts. Sarah has been artistic since early childhood, always drawing and painting plants and animals. But it wasn't until less than a decade ago that she discovered the art of printmaking, immediately fell in love, and never looked back. The themes of Sarah's work are predominantly from the natural world, vintage scientific, and folklore. Her work is available for sale through Fox and Lune Studio on Etsy.com.

LOIS WELCH, the widow of novelist James Welch, was born in Salem, Oregon, where Jim was bused daily from Chemawa Indian School past her home to the Catholic grade school where he first learned culture shock. She taught comparative literature at the University of Montana for 35 years. During that time, she published academic articles ranging in subject from Aristotle to Eudora Welty. She directed the Creative Writing program for eight years, and the English department for three, while encouraging and often accompanying Jim on his literary expeditions. She remains in Missoula, Montana, where she is finishing *The Jimoir*, a memoir about their literary life together.

O. ALAN WELTZIEN, longtime English professor at the University of Montana Western (Dillon), retired from teaching in 2020. He has published dozens of articles and nine books, including three poetry collections and a memoir, *A Father and an Island* (2008). He's also the author of a biography of neglected Montana novelist Thomas Savage with the University of Nevada Press.

BARON WORMSER is the author most recently of *Some Months in 1968: A Novel* (Woodhall Press) and *The History Hotel: Poems* (CavanKerry Press). His memoir, *The Road Washes Out in Spring: A Poet's Memoir of Living Off the Grid,* has been reissued by Brandeis University Press. His essays have appeared frequently in *Vox Populi*.

JANET WORMSER is a self-taught painter who has been painting for decades and has exhibited in Maine, Vermont, and elsewhere. She says her painting is "tied up with my spiritual journey, which is about my effort to be present to my life from moment to moment. This applies to my relationship with paint, particularly watercolor because it is not easy to control . . . I encourage the paint to spread, wander, and pool by soaking and/or spraying the paper." More of her work can be seen at **www.janetwormser.com**.

DON ZANCANELLA has won the John S. Simmons/ Iowa Short Fiction Award and an O. Henry Prize. One of his stories was cited as a distinguished story of the year in the 2019 *Best American Short Stories*, and he has published widely in literary magazines. His books include *Western Electric* (University of Iowa Press), a collection of stories set mostly in Wyoming; *Concord* (Serving House Books), a novel about Henry David Thoreau, Sophia Peabody Hawthorne, and Margaret Fuller; and *A Storm in the Stars* (Delphinium/Harper Collins), a novel about the lives of Mary Shelley and Percy Bysshe Shelley and the writing of *Frankenstein*. He was born in Laramie, Wyoming, and has lived in Virginia, Colorado, Missouri, and New Mexico, where he taught at the University of New Mexico. He now lives in Boise, Idaho, with his wife and their rescue dogs.

PAUL ZARZYSKI pulled into Missoula, not knowing a soul, to study in The Creative Writing Program with Richard Hugo and Madeline DeFrees, in September 1973. During the half-century since, he's published a number of books, recorded a six-pack of spoken-word CDs, and, thanks to the cowboy poetry renaissance, has made a living and a life as a performance poet and lyricist at venues that included 34 annual National Cowboy Poetry Gatherings in Elko, Nevada, the National Book, Folk, and Storytelling Festivals, The Kennedy Center Millennium Stage, the Library of Congress, The Australian Stockman's Hall of Fame in Longreach, Festival Hall in London, a Dylan Thomas pub in Swansea, et al. He's appeared, as well, on Garrison Keillor's *A Prairie Home Companion*, aired from The Mother Lode Theater in BUTTE! He is the recipient of the 2005 Montana Governor's Arts Award for Literature.

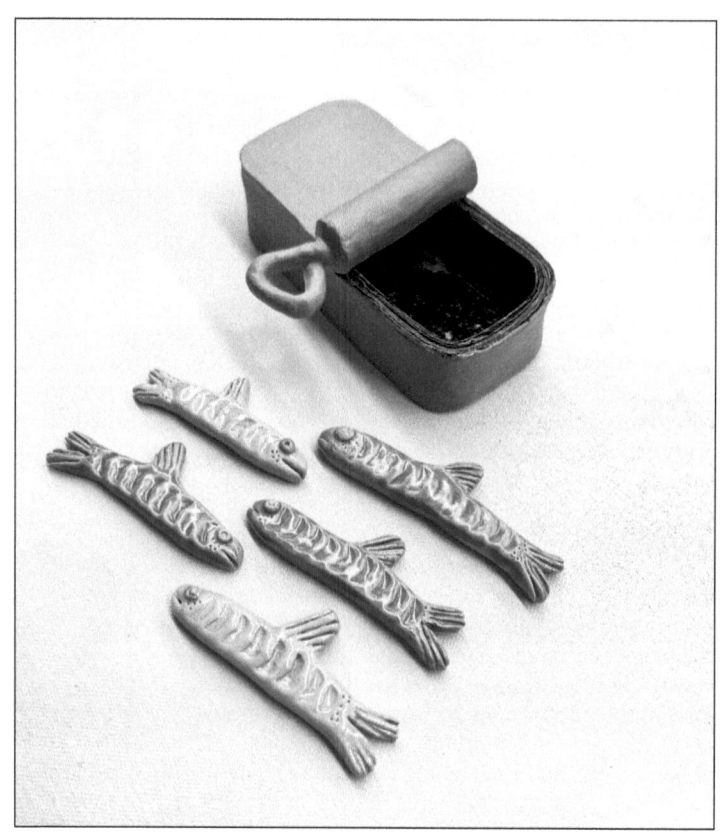

"Tin o' Fish" by Jackie Elo. Clay sculpture.

LIMBERLOST LETTERPRESS

www.limberlostpress.com

FROM LIMBERLOST PRESS

Wild Dog Days
By Gino Sky

In this long poem, published in honor of the poet's 75th year, the indefatigable **Gino Sky**, author of the novel *Appaloosa Rising: The Legend of the Cowboy Buddha* (Doubleday, 1980), reflects on history, memory, and the power of poetry in bringing an end to the Vietnam War.

Publishing a 1960s underground literary magazine called *Wild Dog* that the FBI took notice of, Sky tells a story of all that swirled around the magazine during an eruptive time in America. First published by the poet Ed Dorn in Pocatello in 1963, *Wild Dog* was handed off to Sky who moved it to Salt Lake City and then to San Francisco's Haight-Ashbury District right at the moment of the counter-cultural revolution. Sky exuberantly chronicles the time, the place, and the peace movement with hallucinogenic clarity.

Illustrated with photos of some of the poets who helped hand-crank the small press literary movement, *Wild Dog Days* is dedicated to "every man, every woman, every kid, every dog who marched for peace and stopped the war."

Gino Sky has published two novels, a collection of stories, and a dozen books of poetry (including *Hallelujah 2 Groundhogs & 16 Valentines*, also available from Limberlost Press). *Appaloosa Rising* and his novel *Coyote Silk* (North Atlantic Books, 1987) have been translated and published in Korea. He and his wife Barb Jensen live in Salt Lake City.

Letterpress printed in a limited edition of 400 copies.
$15 (Plus $5 postage) Idaho orders please add 6% state sales tax.
Purchase this and other books at: www.limberlostpress.com

FROM LIMBERLOST PRESS

Gone in October
Last Reflections on Jack Kerouac

By John Clellon Holmes

"He has awed me with his talents, enraged me with his stubbornness, educated me in my craft, hurt me through indifference, dogged my imagination, upset most of my notions, and generally enlarged me as a writer more than anyone else I know."
—*John Clellon Holmes,*
from "The Great Rememberer"

On the July 4th weekend of 1948, John Clellon Holmes (1926-1988) met Jack Kerouac (1922-1969) in New York City for the first time, and the two became lifelong friends. As young, ambitious novelists, Holmes saw Kerouac as a mentor and comrade in a literary movement eventually known as the Beat Generation. They shared New England roots and the same birthday. They were characters in each other's novels, and they fed each other encouragement through letters and get-togethers at Holmes's home in Old Saybrook, Connecticut, until Kerouac's untimely death at 47, on October 21, 1969.

Originally published in a very limited edition by Limberlost Press in 1985, Holmes's essays/memoirs here reflect on Kerouac's burning innovation as a writer, on their New England heritage, on attending his funeral with poets Allen Ginsberg and Gregory Corso, and on the 1982 Naropa Institute celebration of the 25th anniversary of the publication of Kerouac's novel *On the Road,* a gathering which Holmes saw as a last hurrah with other movers and shakers of the Beat movement.

This new edition of *Gone in October,* newly designed and illustrated with more photographs, comprises a deeply heart-felt remembrance of literary friendship and personal loss, reprinted in commemoration of the 2022 Jack Kerouac centennial.

$17.95 (Plus $5 postage) Idaho orders please add 6% state sales tax.
Purchase this and other books at: www.limberlostpress.com

FROM LIMBERLOST PRESS

Waltzing with the Captain: Remembering Richard Brautigan

By Greg Keeler

Teaching English at Montana State University, Greg Keeler met *Trout Fishing in America* author Richard Brautigan in 1978 and opened a wildly memorable chapter in his own life. Having secluded himself on a 40-acre ranch in Paradise Valley, Montana, in the mid-1970s, Brautigan needed a friend with whom to talk and carouse. Attracted like a moth to the flame, Keeler became that friend and confidant, driver and clumsy co-conspirator in a number of escapades on the trout streams and rivers, at bars and cafes, and along the back roads of Montana. Together they waltzed through many late nights, until Brautigan took his own life in Bolinas, California, in 1984.

Two decades after Brautigan's death, Greg Keeler recalls those times with haunting clarity. Illustrated with photographs and the author's cartoon-like drawings at the head of every chapter, *Waltzing with the Captain* is darkly funny and poignant in its revealing portrait of an important contemporary American writer, and in its candid story of an often-tested and bumbling friendship between two poets.

Keeler taught English literature and Creative Writing at Montana State University for 30 years. A prolific painter and musician, he's written several musicals and published a dozen books of poetry, including *American Falls* (Confluence Press, 1987), *Epiphany at Goofy's Gas* (Clark City Press, 1991), and *Almost Happy* (Limberlost Press, 2015). He's recorded more than a dozen CDs of his satiric and flat-out funny collections of songs and poems, including *Live from Nowhere* (Troutball Productions). Winner of a number of awards for teaching and writing, he was awarded the Governor's Award for Outstanding Achievement in the Humanities from the Montana Committee for the Humanities in 2001.

Quality paperback original first edition. 168 pages.
$20 (Plus $5 postage) Idaho orders please add 6% state sales tax.
Purchase this and other books at: www.limberlostpress.com

FROM LIMBERLOST PRESS

A Memory of Elephants

A Chapbook of Poems
By Sherman Alexie

A Memory of Elephants is a deeply reflective, introspective, and confessional collection of poems that explore the mysteries of a mental disorder, regret for things left unsaid to parents before their passing, tribal identity, raising sons in the urban world, the power of love, questions to God.

Printed on Mohawk Superfine paper and folded and sewn by hand into Stonehenge wrappers with illustrations by Erin Ann Jensen.

A Spokane/Coeur d'Alene Indian, Sherman Alexie grew up in Wellpinit, Washington, on the Spokane Indian Reservation. He has been an urban Indian since 1994 and lives in Seattle with his family. He is a poet, short story writer, novelist, and performer, and he has won the PEN/Faulkner Award for Fiction, the PEN/Malamud Award for Short Fiction, a PEN/Hemingway Citation for Best First Fiction, and the National Book Award for Young People's Literature.

He's published 26 books, including his recently released memoir, *You Don't Have to Say You Love Me*, and young adult novel, *The Absolutely True Diary of a Part-Time Indian* (all from Little, Brown Books); *What I've Stolen, What I've Earned*, a book of poetry, from Hanging Loose Press; and *Blasphemy: New and Selected Stories*, from Grove Press. Limberlost Press published letterpress-printed limited editions of his poetry chapbooks *Dangerous Astronomy*, *The Man Who Loves Salmon*, and *Water Flowing Home*. *Smoke Signals*, the movie he wrote and co-produced, won the Audience Award and Filmmakers Trophy at the 1998 Sundance Film Festival.

Letterpress printed in a limited edition of only 500 copies during the COVID-19 summer of 2020 on Mohawk Superfine paper and folded and sewn by hand into Rising Stonehenge wrappers. $55 for signed copies. (Plus $5 postage) Idaho orders please add 6% state sales tax. Purchase this and other books at: www.limberlostpress.com

FROM LIMBERLOST PRESS

John Thomsen & Friends: Songs from Loafer's Glory

AUDIO CD

In commemoration of his 80th year, Limberlost Press has released a CD by longtime Idaho folk musician John Thomsen, of Idaho City, featuring an impressive list of musicians from the region backing up their musical mentor, friend, and collaborator.

John Thomsen & Friends: Songs from Loafer's Glory features an array of favorites by Hank Williams, Hank Snow, Roger Miller, Tex Ritter, Sean McCarthy, and others, as well as a couple of Thomsen originals. Despite decades of making music at folk festivals, weddings, birthdays, political events, plays, dances, funerals, and backyard barbecues, *Songs from Loafer's Glory* is Thomsen's first CD.

Recorded by Sam Aarons of Idaho City Sound over several daylong sessions, the long overdue recording offers a sampling of Thomsen's musical versatility. The CD, which includes a colorful booklet of photos and tributes by admirers, features Thomsen's own "Idaho Spud," a bitingly satirical song-story about nuclear waste, the Atomic Energy Commission, and raising kids on "nuclear taters."

Limberlost Press publisher Rick Ardinger likens the recording to the work of Smithsonian folk music preservationist Alan Lomax, who saved from obscurity so much American folk music during the 20th century.

"Johnny has set the bar for being an authentic folk treasure. I am very fortunate to have had so many great times with 'the Golden Voice of the Boise Basin.'"
  —Dave Daley, fiddle player and longtime More's Creek String Band collaborator

"I have never failed to be impressed by his repertoire and his abilities on guitar, concertina, and Dobro. He was, and is, the complete folklorist and musician. His wit and sense of humor are unmatched."
  —Jake Hoffman, veteran musician, and lap steel guitar artist

"Johnny is a walking library of songs. He knows so many verses and choruses and the stories that go with them that he has to keep his interest by rewriting some with words most clever and slightly scandalous . . . I've been honored to play along, harmonizing on the fly."
  —Beth Wilson, Idaho City folk musician and collaborator

$12 (Plus $5 postage) Idaho orders please add 6% state sales tax. Purchase this and other books at: www.limberlostpress.com

FROM LIMBERLOST PRESS

This Morning's Joy
By Ed Sanders

Here is a collection of anti-war poems that also offers elegies to friends (Allen Ginsberg, Robert Creeley, Harry Smith, Charles Olson), and reflects on memories of revolutionary times and the joys of carrying on despite "war-mongering sleaze" of governments.

Born in 1939, Ed Sanders is a poet, inventive musician, publisher, and founding member of "The Fugs" rock and roll band. Student of Greek, participant exorcisor during the 1967 March on the Pentagon, founder of the Investigative Poetry movement, editor/publisher of *Fuck You* magazine ("published from a secret location on the Lower East Side"), editor of the online *Woodstock Journal*, husband of Miriam R. Sanders for more than a half-century, he carries on poetically and politically, bridging the Beat generation to the Hippie generation, to a contemporary insistence that poetry matters and will change the world.

350 copies letterpress printed and sewn by hand into paper covers. $20 (Plus $5 postage) Idaho orders please add 6% state sales tax. Purchase this and other books at: www.limberlostpress.com

FROM LIMBERLOST PRESS

Complete your collection of *The Limberlost Review* revival
with all five editions!

*Together featuring more than 1,500 pages of poetry, fiction,
essays, memoirs, re-readings, and artwork!*

Interviews with
Clay Morgan, Gino Sky, Mary Clearman Blew, Judith Freeman, and Ken Babbs

Stories by
Sherman Alexie, Kent Anderson, John Rember, Jim Heynen, Gaetha Pace,
Bob Bushnell, Jay Johnson, Jay Parini, Maureen McCoy, Alex Kuo,
Leslie Leek, Don Zancanella, Gary Gildner . . .

Poetry by
Bonnie Jo Campbell, Robert Wrigley, David Lee, Greg Keeler, Ed Sanders,
Ron Padgett, William Johnson, Kim Stafford, Bethany Hurst Schultz, Martin Vest,
Charlotte Mears, Jerry Martien, Nancy Takacs, Robert DeMott,
Ken Rodgers, Sam Green, Jim Dodge . . .

Re-readings by
Ted Dyer, Baron Wormser, Barbara Olic-Hamilton, Alan Minskoff,
Marc Johnson, Rick Johnson, Grove Koger, Brant Short . . .

Artwork by
Rachel Teannalach, Karen Woods, Dennis DeFoggi, Betsie Richardson,
JanyRae Seda, Michael Woods, Alberta Mayo, Glenn Oakley, Royden Card,
Nancy Brossman, Tom Callos, Jackie Elo, Rod Burks, Janet Wormser . . .

And more . . .

Get them all today at: www.limberlostpress.com

CALL FOR SUBMISSIONS 2025

The Limberlost Review
A Literary Journal of the Mountain West

DEADLINE FOR NEXT EDITION
AUGUST 1, 2024

As a literary annual, **The Limberlost Review** is an anthology of work to read and re-read throughout the year. We recommend that new contributors read previous editions to get a sense of what we like and have featured.

We have a special interest in personal essays, stories of memorable moments, experiences, people, mentor writers we've known, and writer/artist friends.

We have a very special interest in **re-readings** of works that have had a personal impact and why certain writers are worth rediscovery, worthy of wider readership.

Old Volkswagen stories . . .
They were reflections of our identity.
They took us across vast landscapes of the West.
They were our homes.

What's in so far . . .
Ted Dyer on Ezra Pound collaborator Wyndham Lewis
David Kuebeck on Beat Generation writer John Clellon Holmes
Alan Minskoff on audiobooks
Vince Hannity on Seamus Heaney
Jonah Andrist on Saul Bellow
Fiction by Barbara Olic-Hamilton

Word documents as attachments accepted:
editors@limberlostpress.com

LIMBERLOST LETTERPRESS

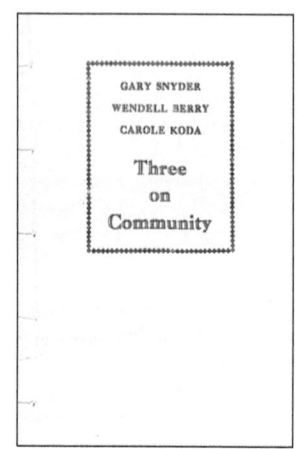

www.limberlostpress.com

COLPOHON

The Limberlost Review body copy is ITC BERKELEY OLD STYLE, based on Frederic W. Goudy's 1938 typeface. It was originally titled "University of California Old Style," which Goudy designed for exclusive use at the University of California Press at Berkeley. After Goudy's death in 1958, the typeface was re-released by Monotype as "Californian." In 1983, ITC redesigned it as "ITC Berkeley Old Style."

The Limberlost Review header font is TRAJAN PRO, designed for Adobe by Carol Twombly in 1989. The design is based on inscribed Roman capital letters such as those on the Trajan Column. Because the Romans didn't use lower-case letters, Twombly designed this as an all-caps typeface.

The Limberlost Review is designed and typeset by Meggan Laxalt Mackey of Studio M Publications & Design in Boise, Idaho, in collaboration with Rick and Rosemary Ardinger of Limberlost Press.

Since its inception, *The Limberlost Review* has celebrated the spirit of excellence in writing, artwork, book design, and typography.

LIMBERLOST PRESS

www.ingramcontent.com/pod-product-compliance
Ingram Content Group UK Ltd.
Pitfield, Milton Keynes, MK11 3LW, UK
UKHW041959230426
12048UKWH00008B/426